PUFFIN CLASSICS

LITTLE MEN

LOUISA MAY ALCOTT (1832–88) was brought up in Pennsylvania in the United States. Her father was not a practical man and Louisa and her three sisters spent their childhood witnessing the failure of a school based on his own radical, idealist educational theories (as in *Little Men*), a farm and a Utopian vegetarian community. By her mid-teens, Louisa had to find a way to supplement the family income.

For some years, she wrote lurid short stories for magazines and newspapers, and for publishers of dime novels – cheap paperback novels with melodramatic plots. Then, in 1862, when the fury of the American Civil War was at its height, Louisa went to Georgetown to work as a nurse. The conditions were frightful and she contracted typhoid fever and pneumonia. Her health was ruined for life, but her reputation was made. From her experience she wrote a series of *Hospital Sketches* which won wide acclaim on publication in 1864. In the same year, an adult novel, *Moods*, based on her love for the famous American philosopher

Henry David Thoreau, was also published.

She was now in demand as a writer, and a forward-thinking publisher persuaded her to write a children's book. At first she was reluctant; but then she realized that in herself and her three sisters, and in their childhood, she had the perfect models (Jo March is modelled on Louisa both in build and character). The result was *Little Women*, first published in book form in 1868 (*Little Men* followed in 1871). This was the earliest American children's novel to become a classic. The tone is moralistic, but not didactic; and though it is called a children's book, the lifelike characters and situations had adults too, eagerly waiting for the next instalment (it was originally published as a magazine serial) and grown men weeping at the tragic episodes. Over a century after the author's death, the book has still just as much power to move its countless readers.

Some other Puffin Classics to enjoy

EIGHT COUSINS
GOOD WIVES
JO'S BOYS
LITTLE MEN
LITTLE WOMEN
Louisa M. Alcott

LOUISA M. ALCOTT

Little Men

Life at Plumfield with Jo's Boys

PUFFIN BOOKS

PUFFIN BOOKS

Published by the Penguin Group
Penguin Books Ltd, 80 Strand, London WC2R 0RL, England
Penguin Putnam Inc., 375 Hudson Street, New York, New York 10014, USA
Penguin Books Australia Ltd, 250 Camberwell Road, Camberwell, Victoria 3124, Australia
Penguin Books Canada Ltd, 10 Alcorn Avenue, Toronto, Ontario, Canada M4V 3B2
Penguin Books India (P) Ltd, 11 Community Centre, Panchsheel Park, New Delhi – 110 017, India
Penguin Books (NZ) Ltd, Cnr Rosedale and Airborne Roads, Albany, Auckland, New Zealand
Penguin Books (South Africa) (Pty) Ltd, 24 Sturdee Avenue, Rosebank 2196, South Africa

Penguin Books Ltd, Registered Offices: 80 Strand, London WC2R 0RL, England

www.penguin.com

First published 1871
Published in Puffin Books 1983
Reissued in this edition 1994

37

Set in 12/15 pt Plantin Monophoto
Filmset by Datix International Limited, Bungay, Suffolk
Printed in England by Clays Ltd, St Ives plc

Contents

NAT

'Please, sir, is this Plumfield?' asked a ragged boy of the man who opened the great gate at which the omnibus left him.

'Yes; who sent you?'

'Mr Laurence. I have got a letter for the lady.'

'All right; go up to the house, and give it to her; she'll see to you, little chap.'

The man spoke pleasantly, and the boy went on, feeling much cheered by the words. Through the soft spring rain that fell on sprouting grass and budding trees, Nat saw a large square house before him – a hospitable-looking house, with an old-fashioned porch, wide steps, and lights shining in many windows. Neither curtains nor shutters hid the cheerful glimmer; and, pausing a moment before he rang, Nat saw many little shadows dancing on the walls, heard the pleasant hum of young voices, and felt that it was hardly possible that the light and warmth and comfort within could be for a homeless 'little chap' like him.

'I hope the lady *will* see to me,' he thought; and gave a timid rap with the great bronze knocker, which was a jovial griffin's head.

A rosy-faced servant-maid opened the door, and smiled as she took the letter which he silently offered.

She seemed used to receiving strange boys, for she pointed to a seat in the hall, and said, with a nod,

'Sit there and drip on the mat a bit, while I take this in to missis.'

Nat found plenty to amuse him while he waited, and stared about him curiously, enjoying the view, yet glad to do so unobserved in the dusky recess by the door.

The house seemed swarming with boys, who were beguiling the rainy twilight with all sorts of amusements. There were boys everywhere, 'upstairs and downstairs and in the lady's chamber', apparently, for various open doors showed pleasant groups of big boys, little boys, and middle-sized boys in all stages of evening relaxation, not to say effervescence. Two large rooms on the right were evidently schoolrooms, for desks, maps, blackboards, and books were scattered about. An open fire burned on the hearth, and several indolent lads lay on their backs before it, discussing a new cricket-ground, with such animation that their boots waved in the air. A tall youth was practising on the flute in one corner, quite undisturbed by the racket all about him. Two or three others were jumping over the desks, pausing, now and then, to get their breath, and laugh at the droll sketches of a little wag who was caricaturing the whole household on a blackboard.

In the room on the left a long supper-table was seen, set forth with great pitchers of new milk, piles of brown and white bread, and perfect stacks of the shiny gingerbread so dear to boyish souls. A flavour of toast was in the air, also suggestions of baked apples, very tantalizing to one hungry little nose and stomach.

The hall, however, presented the most inviting prospect of all, for a brisk game of tag was going on in the upper entry. One landing was devoted to marbles, the other to checkers, while the stairs were occupied by a boy reading, a girl singing lullaby to her doll, two puppies, a kitten, and a constant succession of small boys sliding down the banisters, to the great detriment of their clothes, and danger to their limbs.

So absorbed did Nat become in this exciting race, that he ventured farther and farther out of his corner; and when one very lively boy came down so swiftly that he could not stop himself, but fell off the banisters, with a crash that would have broken any head but one rendered nearly as hard as a cannon-ball by eleven years of constant bumping, Nat forgot himself, and ran up to the fallen rider, expecting to find him half-dead. The boy, however, only winked rapidly for a second, then lay calmly looking up at the new face with a surprised 'Hullo!'

'Hullo!' returned Nat, not knowing what else to say, and thinking that form of reply both brief and easy.

'Are you a new boy?' asked the recumbent youth, without stirring.

'Don't know yet.'

'What's your name?'

'Nat Blake.'

'Mine's Tommy Bangs; come up and have a go, will you?' and Tommy got upon his legs like one suddenly remembering the duties of hospitality.

'Guess I won't, till I see whether I'm going to stay or not,' returned Nat, feeling the desire to stay increase every moment.

'I say, Demi, here's a new one. Come and see to him'; and the lively Thomas returned to his sport with unabated relish.

At his call, the boy reading on the stairs looked up with a pair of big brown eyes, and after an instant's pause, as if a little shy, he put the book under his arm, and came soberly down to greet the newcomer, who found something very attractive in the pleasant face of this slender, mild-eyed boy.

'Have you seen Aunt Jo?' he asked, as if that was some sort of important ceremony.

'I haven't seen anybody yet but you boys; I'm waiting,' answered Nat.

'Did Uncle Laurie send you?' proceeded Demi, politely, but gravely.

'Mr Laurence did.'

'He is Uncle Laurie; and he always sends nice boys.'

Nat looked gratified at the remark, and smiled, in a way that made his thin face very pleasant. He did not know what to say next, so the two stood staring at one another in friendly silence, till the little girl came up with her doll in her arms. She was very like Demi, only not so tall, and had a rounder, rosier face, and blue eyes.

'This is my sister Daisy,' announced Demi, as if presenting a rare and precious creature.

The children nodded to one another; and the little girl's face dimpled with pleasure, as she said, affably,

'I hope you'll stay. We have such good times here; don't we, Demi?'

'Of course, we do; that's what Aunt Jo has Plumfield for.'

'It seems a very nice place indeed,' observed Nat, feeling that he must respond to these amiable young persons.

'It's the nicest place in the world; isn't it, Demi?' said Daisy, who evidently regarded her brother as authority on all subjects.

'No; I think Greenland, where the icebergs and seals are, is more interesting. But I'm fond of Plumfield, and it *is* a very nice place to be in,' returned Demi, who was interested just now in a book on Greenland. He was about to offer to show Nat the pictures and explain them, when the servant returned, saying, with a nod toward the parlour-door,

'All right; you are to stop.'

'I'm glad; now come to Aunt Jo.' And Daisy took him by the hand with a pretty protecting air, which made Nat feel at home at once.

Demi returned to his beloved book, while his sister led the newcomer into a back room, where a stout gentleman was frolicking with two little boys on the sofa, and a thin lady was just finishing the letter which she seemed to have been re-reading.

'Here he is, Aunty!' cried Daisy.

'So this is my new boy? I am glad to see you, my dear, and hope you'll be happy here,' said the lady, drawing him to her, and stroking back the hair from his forehead with a kind hand and a motherly look, which made Nat's lonely little heart yearn toward her.

She was not at all handsome, but she had a merry sort of face, that never seemed to have forgotten certain childish ways and looks, any more than her voice and manner had; and these things, hard to describe but very plain to see and feel, made her a genial, comfortable kind of person, easy to get on with, and generally 'jolly', as boys would say. She saw the little tremble of Nat's lips as she smoothed his hair, and her keen eyes grew softer, but she only drew the shabby figure nearer and said, laughing,

'I am Mother Bhaer, that gentleman is Father Bhaer, and these are the two little Bhaers. Come here, boys, and see Nat.'

The three wrestlers obeyed at once; and the stout man, with a chubby child on each shoulder, came up to welcome the new boy. Rob and Teddy merely grinned at him, but Mr Bhaer shook hands, and pointing to a low chair near the fire, said, in a cordial voice,

'There is a place all ready for thee, my son; sit down and dry thy wet feet at once.'

'Wet? so they are! My dear, off with your shoes this minute, and I'll have some dry things ready for you in a jiffy,' cried Mrs Bhaer, bustling about so energetically, that Nat found himself in the cosy little chair, with dry socks and warm slippers on his feet, before he would have had time to say Jack Robinson, if he had wanted to try. He said 'Thank you, ma'am,' instead; and said it so gratefully, that Mrs Bhaer's eyes grew soft again, and she said something merry, because she felt so tender, which was a way she had.

'These are Tommy Bangs's slippers; but he never will remember to put them on in the house so he shall not have them. They are too big; but that's all the better, you can't run away from us so fast as if they fitted.'

'I don't want to run away, ma'am.' And Nat spread his grimy little hands before the comfortable blaze, with a long sigh of satisfaction.

'That's good! Now I am going to toast you well, and try to get rid of that ugly cough. How long have you had it, dear?' asked Mrs Bhaer, as she rummaged in her big basket for a strip of flannel.

'All winter. I got cold, and it wouldn't get better, somehow.'

'No wonder, living in that damp cellar with hardly a rag to his poor dear back!' said Mrs Bhaer, in a low tone to her husband, who was looking at the boy with a skilful pair of eyes, that marked the thin temples and feverish lips, as well as the hoarse voice and frequent fits of coughing that shook the bent shoulders under the patched jacket.

'Robin, my man, trot up to Nursey, and tell her to give thee the cough-bottle and the liniment,' said Mr Bhaer, after his eyes had exchanged telegrams with his wife's.

Nat looked a little anxious at the preparations, but forgot his fears, in a hearty laugh, when Mrs Bhaer whispered to him, with a droll look,

'Hear my rogue Teddy try to cough. The syrup I'm going to give you has honey in it; and he wants some.'

Little Ted was red in the face with his exertions by the time the bottle came, and was allowed to suck the spoon, after Nat had manfully taken a dose, and had the bit of flannel put about his throat.

These first steps toward a cure were hardly completed, when a great bell rang, and a loud tramping through the hall announced supper. Bashful Nat quaked at the thought of meeting many strange boys, but Mrs Bhaer held out her hand to him, and Rob said, patronizingly, 'Don't be 'fraid; I'll take care of you.'

Twelve boys, six on a side, stood behind their chairs, prancing with impatience to begin, while the tall flute-playing youth was trying to curb their ardour. But no one sat down, till Mrs Bhaer was in her place behind the teapot, with Teddy on her left, and Nat on her right.

'This is our new boy, Nat Blake. After supper you can say, How do you do? Gently, boys, gently.'

As she spoke everyone stared at Nat, and then whisked into their seats, trying to be orderly, and failing utterly. The Bhaers did their best to have the lads behave well at meal times, and generally succeeded pretty well, for their rules were few and sensible, and the boys, knowing that they tried to make things easy and happy, did their best to obey. But there *are* times when hungry boys cannot be repressed without real cruelty, and Saturday evening, after a half-holiday, was one of those times.

'Dear little souls, do let them have one day in which they can howl and racket and frolic, to their hearts' content. A holiday isn't a holiday, without plenty of freedom and fun; and they shall have full swing once a week,' Mrs Bhaer used to say, when prim people wondered why banister-sliding, pillow-fights, and all manner of jovial games were allowed under the once decorous roof of Plumfield.

It did seem at times as if the aforesaid roof was in danger of flying off; but it never did, for a word from Father Bhaer could at any time produce a lull, and the lads had learned that liberty must not be abused. So, in spite of many dark predictions, the school flourished, and manners and morals were insinuated, without the pupils exactly knowing how it was done.

Nat found himself very well off behind the tall

pitchers, with Tommy Bangs just round the corner, and Mrs Bhaer close by, to fill up plate and mug as fast as he could empty them.

'Who is that boy next the girl down at the other end?' whispered Nat to his young neighbour under cover of a general laugh.

'That's Demi Brooke. Mr Bhaer is his uncle.'

'What a queer name!'

'His real name is John, but they call him Demi-John, because his father is John too. That's a joke, don't you see?' said Tommy, kindly explaining. Nat did not see, but politely smiled, and asked, with interest,

'Isn't he a very nice boy?'

'I bet you he is; knows lots and reads like anything.'

'Who is the fat one next him?'

'Oh, that's Stuffy Cole. His name is George, but we call him Stuffy 'cause he eats so much. The little fellow next Father Bhaer is his boy Rob, and then there's big Franz his nephew; he teaches some, and kind of sees to us.'

'He plays the flute, doesn't he?' asked Nat as Tommy rendered himself speechless by putting a whole baked apple into his mouth at one blow.

Tommy nodded, and said, sooner than one would have imagined possible under the circumstances, 'Oh, don't he, though? and we dance sometimes, and do gymnastics to music. I like a drum myself, and mean to learn as soon as ever I can.'

'I like a fiddle best; I can play one too,' said Nat, getting confidential on this attractive subject.

'Can you?' and Tommy stared over the rim of his mug with round eyes, full of interest. 'Mr Bhaer's got an old fiddle, and he'll let you play on it if you want to.'

'Could I? Oh, I would like it ever so much. You see I used to go round fiddling with my father, and another man, till he died.'

'Wasn't that fun?' cried Tommy, much impressed.

'No, it was horrid; so cold in winter, and hot in summer. And I got tired; and they were cross some-times; and I didn't have enough to eat.' Nat paused to take a generous bite of gingerbread, as if to assure himself that the hard times were over and then he added regretfully, 'But I did love my little fiddle, and I miss it. Nicolo took it away when father died, and wouldn't have me any longer, 'cause I was sick.'

'You'll belong to the band if you play good. See if you don't.'

'Do you have a band here?' And Nat's eyes sparkled.

'Guess we do a jolly band, all boys; and they have concerts and things. You just see what happens to-morrow night.'

After this pleasantly exciting remark, Tommy re-turned to his supper, and Nat sank into a blissful reverie over his full plate.

Mrs Bhaer had heard all they said, while apparently absorbed in filling mugs, and overseeing little Ted, who was so sleepy that he put his spoon in his eye, nodded like a rosy poppy, and finally fell fast asleep, with his cheek pillowed on a soft bun. Mrs Bhaer had put Nat next to Tommy, because that roly-poly boy had a frank and social way with him, very attractive to shy persons. Nat felt this, and had made several small confidences during supper, which gave Mrs Bhaer the key to the new boy's character, better than if she had talked to him herself.

In the letter which Mr Laurence had sent with Nat, he had said:

DEAR JO, Here is a case after your own heart. This poor lad is an orphan now, sick and friendless. He had been a street-musician; and I found him in a cellar, mourning for his dead father, and his lost violin. I think there is something in him, and have a fancy that between us we may give this little man a lift. You cure his overtasked body, Fritz help his neglected mind, and when he is ready I'll see if he is a genius or only a boy with a talent which may earn his bread for him. Give him a trial, for the sake of your own boy,   TEDDY

'Of course we will!' cried Mrs Bhaer, as she read the letter; and when she saw Nat, she felt at once that whether he was a genius or not, here was a lonely, sick boy, who needed just what she loved to give, a home, and motherly care. Both she and Mr Bhaer observed him quietly; and in spite of ragged clothes, awkward manners, and a dirty face, they saw much about Nat that pleased them. He was a thin, pale boy, of twelve, with blue eyes, and a good forehead under the rough, neglected hair; an anxious, scared face, at times, as if he expected hard words, or blows; and a sensitive mouth, that trembled when a kind glance fell on him; while a gentle speech called up a look of gratitude, very sweet to see. 'Bless the poor dear, he shall fiddle all day long if he likes,' said Mrs Bhaer to herself as she saw the eager, happy expression on his face, when Tommy talked of the band.

So, after supper, when the lads flocked into the schoolroom for more 'high jinks', Mrs Jo appeared with a violin in her hand, and after a word with her husband, went to Nat, who sat in a corner watching the scene with intense interest.

'Now, my lad, give us a little tune. We want a violin in our band, and I think you will do it nicely.'

She expected that he would hesitate; but he seized the old fiddle at once, and handled it with such loving care, it was plain to see that music was his passion.

'I'll do the best I can, ma'am,' was all he said; and then drew the bow across the strings, as if eager to hear the dear notes again.

There was a great clatter in the room, but as if deaf to any sounds but those he made, Nat played softly to himself, forgetting everything in his delight. It was only a simple negro melody, such as street-musicians play, but it caught the ears of the boys at once, and silenced them, till they stood listening with surprise and pleasure. Gradually they got nearer and nearer, and Mr Bhaer came up to watch the boy; for, as if he was in his element now, Nat played away and never minded anyone, while his eyes shone, his cheeks reddened, and his thin fingers flew, as he hugged the old fiddle and made it speak to all their hearts the language that he loved.

A hearty round of applause rewarded him better than a shower of pennies, when he stopped and glanced about him, as if to say,

'I've done my best; please like it.'

'I say, you do that first rate,' cried Tommy, who considered Nat his *protégé*.

'You shall be first fiddle in my band,' added Franz, with an approving smile.

Mrs Bhaer whispered to her husband,

'Teddy is right: there's something in the child.' And Mr Bhaer nodded his head emphatically, as he clapped Nat on the shoulder, saying, heartily,

'You play well, my son. Come now and play something which we can sing.'

It was the proudest, happiest minute of the poor boy's life when he was led to the place of honour by the piano, and the lads gathered round, never heeding his poor clothes, but eyeing him respectfully, and waiting eagerly to hear him play again.

They chose a song he knew; and after one or two false starts they got going, and violin, flute, and piano led a chorus of boyish voices that made the old roof ring again. It was too much for Nat, more feeble than he knew; and as the final shout died away, his face began to work, he dropped the fiddle, and turning to the wall, sobbed like a little child.

'My dear, what is it?' asked Mrs Bhaer, who had been singing with all her might, and trying to keep little Rob from beating time with his boots.

'You are all so kind – and it's so beautiful – I can't help it,' sobbed Nat, coughing till he was breathless.

'Come with me, dear; you must go to bed and rest; you are worn out, and this is too noisy a place for you,' whispered Mrs Bhaer; and took him away to her own parlour, where she let him cry himself quiet.

Then she won him to tell her all his troubles, and

listened to the little story with tears in her own eyes, though it was not a new one to her.

'My child, you *have* got a father and a mother now, and this is home. Don't think of those sad times any more, but get well and happy; and be sure you shall never suffer again, if we can help it. This place is made for all sorts of boys to have a good time in, and to learn how to help themselves and be useful men, I hope. You shall have as much music as you want, only you must get strong first. Now come up to Nursey and have a bath, and then go to bed, and tomorrow we will lay some nice little plans together.'

Nat held her hand fast in his, but had not a word to say, and let his grateful eyes speak for him, as Mrs Bhaer led him up to a big room, where they found a stout German woman with a face so round and cheery, that it looked like a sort of sun, with the wide frill of her cap for rays.

'This is Nursey Hummel, and she will give you a nice bath, and cut your hair, and make you all "comfy", as Rob says. That's the bathroom in there; and on Saturday nights we scrub all the little lads first, and pack them away in bed before the big ones get through singing. Now then, Rob, in with you.'

As she talked, Mrs Bhaer had whipped off Rob's clothes and popped him into a long bathtub in the little room opening into the nursery.

There were two tubs, besides foot-baths, basins, douche-pipes, and all manner of contrivances for cleanliness. Nat was soon luxuriating in the other bath; and while simmering there, he watched the performances of the two women, who scrubbed, clean night-gowned, and bundled into bed four or five small boys, who, of course, cut up all sorts of capers during the operation, and kept everyone in a gale of merriment till they were extinguished in their beds.

By the time Nat was washed and done up in a blanket by the fire, while Nursey cut his hair, a new detachment of boys arrived and were shut into the bathroom, where they made as much splashing and noise as a school of young whales at play.

'Nat had better sleep here, so that if his cough troubles him in the night you can see that he takes a good draught of flax-seed tea,' said Mrs Bhaer, who was flying about like a distracted hen with a large brood of lively ducklings.

Nursey approved the plan, finished Nat off with a flannel night-gown, a drink of something warm and sweet, and then tucked him into one of the three little beds standing in the room, where he lay looking like a contented mummy, and feeling that nothing more in the way of luxury could be offered him. Cleanliness in itself was a new and delightful sensation; flannel gowns were unknown comforts in his world; sips of 'good stuff' soothed his cough as pleasantly as kind words did his lonely heart; and the feeling that somebody cared for him made that plain room seem a sort of heaven to the homeless child. It was like a cosy dream; and he often shut his eyes to see if it would not vanish when he opened them again. It was too pleasant to let him sleep, and he could not have done so if he had tried, for in a few minutes one of the peculiar institutions of Plumfield was revealed to his astonished but appreciative eyes.

A momentary lull in the aquatic exercises was followed by the sudden appearance of pillows flying in all directions, hurled by white goblins, who came rioting out of their beds. The battle raged in several rooms, all down the upper hall, and even surged at intervals into the nursery, when some hard-pressed warrior took refuge there. No one seemed to mind this explosion in the least; no one forbade it, or even looked surprised. Nursey went on hanging up towels, and Mrs Bhaer looked out clean clothes, as calmly as if the most perfect order reigned. Nay, she even chased one daring boy out of the room, and fired after him the pillow he had slyly thrown at her.

'Won't they hurt 'em?' asked Nat, who lay laughing with all his might.

'Oh dear, no! we always allow one pillow-fight Saturday night. The cases are changed tomorrow; and it gets up a glow after the boys' baths; so I rather like it myself,' said Mrs Bhaer, busy again among her dozen pairs of socks.

'What a very nice school this is!' observed Nat, in a burst of admiration.

'It's an odd one,' laughed Mrs Bhaer; 'but you see we don't believe in making children miserable by too many rules, and too much study. I forbade nightgown parties at first; but, bless you, it was of no use. I could no more keep those boys in their beds, than so many jacks in the box. So I made an agreement with them: I was to allow a fifteen-minute pillow-fight, every Saturday night; and they promised to go properly to bed, every other night. I tried it, and it worked well. If they don't keep their word, no frolic; if they do, I just turn the glasses round, put the lamps in safe places, and let them rampage as much as they like.'

'It's a beautiful plan,' said Nat, feeling that he

should like to join in the fray, but not venturing to propose it the first night. So he lay enjoying the spectacle, which certainly was a lively one.

Tommy Bangs led the assailing party, and Demi defended his own room with a dogged courage, fine to see, collecting pillows behind him as fast as they were thrown, till the besiegers were out of ammunition, when they would charge upon him in a body, and recover their arms. A few slight accidents occurred, but nobody minded, and gave and took sounding thwacks with perfect good humour, while pillows flew like big snowflakes, till Mrs Bhaer looked at her watch, and called out,

'Time is up, boys. Into bed, every man Jack, or pay the forfeit!'

'What is the forfeit?' asked Nat, sitting up in his eagerness to know what happened to those wretches who disobeyed this most peculiar, but public-spirited schoolma'am.

'Lose their fun next time,' answered Mrs Bhaer. 'I give them five minutes to settle down, then put out the lights, and expect order. They are honourable lads, and they keep their word.'

That was evident, for the battle ended as abruptly as it began – a parting shot or two, a final cheer, as Demi fired the seventh pillow at the retiring foe, a few challenges for next time, then order prevailed; and nothing but an occasional giggle, or a suppressed whisper, broke the quiet which followed the Saturday-night frolic, as Mother Bhaer kissed her new boy, and left him to happy dreams of life at Plumfield.

2

THE BOYS

While Nat takes a good long sleep, I will tell my little readers something about the boys, among whom he found himself when he woke up.

To begin with our old friends. Franz was a tall lad, of sixteen now, a regular German, big, blond, and bookish, also very domestic, amiable, and musical. His uncle was fitting him for college, and his aunt for a happy home of his own hereafter, because she carefully fostered in him gentle manners, love of children, respect for women, old and young, and helpful ways about the house. He was her right-hand man on all occasions, steady, kind, and patient; and he loved his merry aunt like a mother, for such she had tried to be to him.

Emil was quite different, being quick-tempered, restless, and enterprising, bent on going to sea, for the blood of the old vikings stirred in his veins, and could not be tamed. His uncle promised that he should go when he was sixteen, and set him to studying navigation, gave him stories of good and famous admirals and heroes to read, and let him lead the life of a frog in river, pond, and brook, when lessons were done. His room looked like the cabin of a man-of-war, for everything was nautical, military, and shipshape. Captain

Kyd was his delight, and his favourite amusement was to rig up like that piratical gentleman, and roar out sanguinary sea-songs at the top of his voice. He would dance nothing but sailors' hornpipes, rolled in his gait, and was as nautical in conversation as his uncle would permit. The boys called him 'Commodore', and took great pride in his fleet, which whitened the pond and suffered disasters that would have daunted any commander but a sea-struck boy.

Demi was one of the children who show plainly the effect of intelligent love and care, for soul and body worked harmoniously together. The natural refinement which nothing but home influence can teach, gave him sweet and simple manners: his mother had cherished an innocent and loving heart in him; his father had watched over the physical growth of his boy, and kept the little body straight and strong on wholesome food and exercise and sleep, while Grandpa March culti-vated the little mind with the tender wisdom of a modern Pythagoras, not tasking it with long, hard lessons, parrot-learned, but helping it to unfold as naturally and beautifully as sun and dew help roses bloom. He was not a perfect child, by any means, but his faults were of the better sort; and being early taught the secret of self-control, he was not left at the mercy of appetites and passions, as some poor little mortals are, and then punished for yielding to the temptations against which they have no armour. A quiet, quaint boy was Demi, serious, yet cheery, quite unconscious that he was unusually bright and beauti-ful, yet quick to see and love intelligence or beauty in other children. Very fond of books, and full of lively fancies, born of a strong imagination and a spiritual nature, these traits made his parents anxious to balance them with useful knowledge and healthful society, lest they should make him one of those pale precocious children who amaze and delight a family sometimes, and fade away like hot-house flowers, because the young soul blooms too soon, and has not a hearty body to root it firmly in the wholesome soil of this world.

So Demi was transplanted to Plumfield, and took so kindly to the life there, that Meg and John and Grandpa felt satisfied that they had done well. Mixing with other boys brought out the practical side of him, roused his spirit, and brushed away the pretty cobwebs he was so fond of spinning in that little brain of his. To be sure, he rather shocked his mother when he came home, by banging doors, saying 'by George' emphatically, and demanding tall thick boots 'that clumped like papa's'. But John rejoiced over him, laughed at his explosive remarks, got the boots, and said contentedly, 'He is doing well; so let him clump. I want my son to be a manly boy, and this temporary roughness won't hurt him. We can polish him up by and by; and as for learning, he will pick that up as pigeons do peas. So don't hurry him.'

Daisy was as sunshiny and charming as ever, with all sorts of little womanlinesses budding in her, for she was like her gentle mother, and delighted in domestic things. She had a family of dolls, whom she brought up in the most exemplary manner; she could not get on without her little work-basket and bits of sewing, which she did so nicely, that Demi frequently pulled out his handkerchief to display her neat stitches, and Baby Josy had a flannel petticoat beautifully made by Sister Daisy. She liked to quiddle about the china-closet, prepare the salt-cellars, put the spoons straight on the table; and every day went round the parlour with her brush, dusting chairs and tables. Demi called her a 'Betty', but was very glad to have her keep his things in order, lend him her nimble fingers in all sorts of work, and help him with his lessons, for they kept abreast there, and had no thought of rivalry.

The love between them was as strong as ever; and no one could laugh Demi out of his affectionate ways with Daisy. He fought her battles valiantly, and never could understand why boys should be ashamed to say 'right out' that they loved their sisters. Daisy adored her twin, thought 'my brother' the most remarkable boy in the world, and every morning, in her little wrapper, trotted to tap at his door with a motherly 'Get up, my dear, it's 'most breakfast time; and here's your clean collar.'

Rob was an energetic morsel of a boy, who seemed to have discovered the secret of perpetual motion, for he never was still. Fortunately, he was not mischievous, nor very brave; so he kept out of trouble pretty well, and vibrated between father and mother like an affectionate little pendulum with a lively tick, for Rob was a chatterbox.

Teddy was too young to play a very important part in the affairs of Plumfield, yet he had his little sphere, and filled it beautifully. Everyone felt the need of a pet at times, and Baby was always ready to accommodate, for kissing and cuddling suited him excellently. Mrs Jo seldom stirred without him; so he had his little finger in all the domestic pies, and everyone found them all the better for it, for they believed in babies at Plumfield.

Dick Brown, and Adolphus or Dolly Pettingill, were two eight-year-olds. Dolly stuttered badly, but was gradually getting over it, for no one was allowed to mock him and Mr Bhaer tried to cure it, by making him talk slowly. Dolly was a good little lad, quite uninteresting and ordinary, but he flourished here, and went through his daily duties and pleasures with placid content and propriety.

Dick Brown's affliction was a crooked back, yet he bore his burden so cheerfully, that Demi once asked in his queer way, 'Do humps make people good-natured? I'd like one if they do.' Dick was always merry, and did his best to be like other boys, for a plucky spirit lived in the feeble little body. When he first came, he was very sensitive about his misfortune, but soon learned to forget it, for no one dared remind him of it, after Mr Bhaer had punished one boy for laughing at him.

'God don't care; for my soul is straight if my back isn't,' sobbed Dick to his tormentor on that occasion; and, by cherishing this idea, the Bhaers soon led him to believe that people also loved his soul, and did not mind his body, except to pity and help him to bear it.

Playing menagerie once with the others, some one said, 'What animal will you be, Dick?'

'Oh, I'm the dromedary; don't you see the hump on my back?' was the laughing answer.

'So you are, my nice little one that don't carry loads, but marches by the elephant first in the procession,' said Demi, who was arranging the spectacle.

'I hope others will be as kind to the poor dear as my boys have learned to be,' said Mrs Jo, quite satisfied with the success of her teaching, as Dick ambled past her, looking like a very happy, but a very feeble little dromedary, beside stout Stuffy, who did the elephant with ponderous propriety.

Jack Ford was a sharp, rather sly lad, who was sent to this school, because it was cheap. Many men would have thought him a smart boy, but Mr Bhaer did not like his way of illustrating that Yankee word, and thought his unboyish keenness and money-loving as much of an affliction as Dolly's stutter, or Dick's hump.

Ned Barker was like a thousand other boys of fourteen, all legs, blunder, and bluster. Indeed the family called him the 'Blunderbuss', and always expected to see him tumble over the chairs, bump against the tables and knock down any small articles near him. He bragged a good deal about what he could do, but seldom did anything to prove it, was not brave, and a little given to tale-telling. He was apt to bully the small boys, and flatter the big ones, and without being at all bad, was just the sort of fellow who could very easily be led astray.

George Cole had been spoilt by an over-indulgent mother, who stuffed him with sweetmeats till he was sick, and then thought him too delicate to study, so that at twelve years old, he was a pale, puffy boy, dull, fretful, and lazy. A friend persuaded her to send him to Plumfield, and there he soon got waked up, for sweet things were seldom allowed, much exercise required, and study made so pleasant, that Stuffy was gently lured along, till he quite amazed his anxious mamma by his improvement, and convinced her that there was really something remarkable in Plumfield air.

Billy Ward was what the Scotch tenderly call an 'innocent', for though thirteen years old, he was like a child of six. He had been an unusually intelligent boy, and his father had hurried him on too fast, giving him all sorts of hard lessons, keeping him at his books six hours a day, and expecting him to absorb knowledge as a Strasburg goose does the food crammed down its throat. He thought he was doing his duty, but he nearly killed the boy, for a fever gave the poor child a sad holiday, and when he recovered, the overtasked brain gave out, and Billy's mind was like a slate over which a sponge has passed, leaving it blank.

It was a terrible lesson to his ambitious father; he could not bear the sight of his promising child, changed to a feeble idiot, and he sent him away to Plumfield, scarcely hoping that he could be helped, but sure that he would be kindly treated. Quite docile and harmless was Billy, and it was pitiful to see how hard he tried to learn, as if groping dimly after the lost knowledge which had cost him so much. Day after day, he pored over the alphabet, proudly said A and B, and thought that he knew them, but on the morrow they were gone, and all the work was to be done over again. Mr Bhaer had infinite patience with him, and kept on in spite of the apparent hopelessness of the task, not caring for book lessons, but trying gently to clear away the mists from the darkened mind, and give it back intelligence enough to make the boy less a burden and an affliction.

Mrs Bhaer strengthened his health by every aid she could invent, and the boys all pitied and were kind to him. He did not like their active plays, but would sit for hours watching the doves, would dig holes for

Teddy till even that ardent grubber was satisfied, or follow Silas, the man, from place to place seeing him work, for honest Si was very good to him, and though he forgot his letters Billy remembered friendly faces.

Tommy Bangs was the scapegrace of the school, and the most trying little scapegrace that ever lived. As full of mischief as a monkey, yet so good-hearted that one could not help forgiving his tricks; so scatter-brained that words went by him like the wind, yet so penitent for every misdeed, that it was impossible to keep sober when he vowed tremendous vows of reformation, or proposed all sorts of queer punishments to be inflicted upon himself. Mr and Mrs Bhaer lived in a state of preparation for any mishap, from the breaking of Tommy's own neck, to the blowing up of the entire family with gunpowder; and Nursey had a particular drawer in which she kept bandages, plasters, and salves for his especial use, for Tommy was always being brought in half-dead; but nothing ever killed him, and he rose from every downfall with redoubled vigour.

The first day he came, he chopped the top off one finger in the hay-cutter, and during the week, fell from the shed roof, was chased by an angry hen who tried to pick his eyes out because he examined her chickens, got run away with, and had his ears boxed violently by Asia, who caught him luxuriously skimming a pan of cream with half a stolen pie. Undaunted, however, by any failures or rebuffs, this indomitable youth went on amusing himself with all sorts of tricks till no one felt safe. If he did not know his lessons, he always had some droll excuse to offer, and as he was usually clever at his books, and as bright as a button in composing answers when he did not know them, he got on pretty well at school. But out of school – Ye gods and little fishes! how Tommy did carouse!

He wound fat Asia up in her own clothes line against the post, and left her there to fume and scold for half an hour one busy Monday morning. He dropped a hot cent down Mary Ann's back as that pretty maid was waiting at table one day when there were gentlemen to dinner, whereat the poor girl upset the soup and rushed out of the room in dismay, leaving the family to think that she had gone mad. He fixed a pail of water up in a tree, with a bit of ribbon fastened to the handle, and when Daisy, attracted by the gay streamer, tried to pull it down, she got a douche bath that spoiled her clean frock and hurt her little feelings very much. He put rough white pebbles in the sugar-bowl when his grandmother came to tea, and the poor old lady wondered why they didn't melt in her cup, but was too polite to say anything. He passed round snuff in church so that five of the boys sneezed with such violence they had to go out. He dug paths in winter time, and then privately watered them so that people should tumble down. He drove poor Silas nearly wild by hanging his big boots in conspicuous places, for his feet were enormous, and he was very much ashamed of them. He persuaded confiding little Dolly to tie a thread to one of his loose teeth, and leave the string hanging from his mouth when he went to sleep, so that Tommy could pull it out without his feeling the dreaded operation. But the tooth wouldn't come at the first tweak, and poor Dolly woke up in great anguish of spirit, and lost all faith in Tommy from that day forth. The last prank had been to give the hens bread soaked in rum, which made them tipsy and scandalized all the other fowls, for the respectable old biddies went staggering about, pecking and clucking in the most maudlin manner, while the family were convulsed with laughter at their antics, till Daisy took pity on them and shut them up in the henhouse to sleep off their intoxication.

These were the boys, and they lived together as happily as twelve lads could, studying and playing, working and squabbling, fighting faults and cultivating virtues in the good old-fashioned way. Boys at other schools probably learned more from books, but less of that better wisdom which makes good men. Latin, Greek, and mathematics were all very well, but in Professor Bhaer's opinion, self-knowledge, self-help, and self-control were more important, and he tried to teach them carefully. People shook their heads sometimes at his ideas, even while they owned that the boys improved wonderfully in manners and morals. But then, as Mrs Jo said to Nat, it was an 'odd school'.

3

SUNDAY

The moment the bell rang next morning Nat flew out of bed, and dressed himself with great satisfaction in the suit of clothes he found on the chair. They were not new, being half-worn garments of one of the well-to-do boys; but Mrs Bhaer kept all such cast-off feathers for the picked robins who strayed into her nest. They were hardly on when Tommy appeared in a high state of clean collar, and escorted Nat down to breakfast.

The sun was shining into the dining-room on the well-spread table, and the flock of hungry, hearty lads who gathered round it. Nat observed that they were much more orderly than they had been the night before, and everyone stood silently behind his chair while little Rob, standing beside his father at the head of the table, folded his hands, reverently bent his curly head, and softly repeated a short grace in the devout German fashion, which Mr Bhaer loved and taught his little son to honour. Then they all sat down to enjoy the Sunday-morning breakfast of coffee, steak, and baked potatoes, instead of the bread and milk fare with which they usually satisfied their young appetites. There was much pleasant talk while the knives and forks rattled briskly, for certain Sunday lessons were to be learned, the Sunday walk settled, and plans for the week discussed. As he listened, Nat thought it seemed as if this day must be a very pleasant one, for he loved quiet, and there was a cheerful sort of ·hush over everything that pleased him very much; because, in spite of his rough life, the boy possessed the sensitive nerves which belong to a music-loving nature.

'Now, my lads, get your morning jobs done, and let me find you ready for church when the bus comes round,' said Father Bhaer, and set the example by going into the schoolroom to get books ready for the morrow.

Everyone scattered to his or her task, for each had some little daily duty, and was expected to perform it faithfully. Some brought wood and water, brushed the steps, or ran errands for Mrs Bhaer. Others fed the pet animals, and did chores about the barn with Franz. Daisy washed the cups, and Demi wiped them, for the twins liked to work together, and Demi had been taught to make himself useful in the little house at home. Even Baby Teddy had his small job to do, and trotted to and fro, putting napkins away, and pushing chairs into their places. For half an hour the lads buzzed about like a hive of bees, then the bus drove round, Father Bhaer and Franz with the eight older boys piled in, and away they went for a three-mile drive to church in town.

Because of the troublesome cough Nat preferred to stay at home with the four small boys, and spent a happy morning in Mrs Bhaer's room, listening to the stories she read them, learning the hymn she taught them, and then quietly employing himself pasting pictures into an old ledger.

'This is my Sunday closet,' she said, showing him shelves filled with picture-books, paint-boxes, architectural blocks, little diaries, and materials for letter-writing. 'I want my boys to love Sunday, to find it a peaceful, pleasant day, when they can rest from common study and play, yet enjoy quiet pleasures, and learn, in simple ways, lessons more important than any taught in school. Do you understand me?' she asked, watching Nat's attentive face.

'You mean to be good?' he said, after hesitating a minute.

'Yes; to be good, and to love to be good. It is hard work sometimes, I know very well; but we all help one another, and so we get on. This is one of the ways in which I try to help my boys,' and she took down a thick book, which seemed half-full of writing, and opened at a page on which there was one word at the top.

'Why, that's my name!' cried Nat, looking both surprised and interested.

'Yes; I have a page for each boy. I keep a little account of how he gets on through the week, and Sunday night I show him the record. If it is bad I am sorry and disappointed, if it is good I am glad and proud; but, whichever it is, the boys know I want to help them, and they try to do their best for love of me and Father Bhaer.'

'I should think they would,' said Nat, catching a glimpse of Tommy's name opposite his own, and wondering what was written under it.

Mrs Bhaer saw his eye on the words, and shook her head, saying as she turned a leaf,

'No, I don't show my records to any but the one to

whom each belongs. I call this my conscience book; and only you and I will ever know what is to be written on the page below your name. Whether you will be pleased or ashamed to read it next Sunday depends on yourself. I think it will be a good report; at any rate, I shall try to make things easy for you in this new place, and shall be quite contented if you keep our few rules, live happily with the boys, and learn something.'

'I'll try, ma'am,' and Nat's thin face flushed up with the earnestness of his desire to make Mrs Bhaer 'glad and proud', not 'sorry and disappointed'. 'It must be a great deal of trouble to write about so many,' he added, as she shut her book with an encouraging pat on the shoulder.

'Not to me, for I really don't know which I like best, writing or boys,' she said, laughing to see Nat stare with astonishment at the last item. 'Yes, I know many people think boys are a nuisance, but that is because they don't understand them. I do; and I never saw the boy yet whom I could not get on capitally with after I had once found the soft spot in his heart. Bless me, I couldn't get on at all without my flock of dear, noisy, naughty, harum-scarum little lads, could I, my Teddy?' and Mrs Bhaer hugged the young rogue, just in time to save the big inkstand from going into his pocket.

Nat, who had never heard anything like this before, really did not know whether Mother Bhaer was a trifle crazy, or the most delightful woman he had ever met. He rather inclined to the latter opinion, in spite of her peculiar tastes, for she had a way of filling up a fellow's plate before he asked, of laughing at his jokes, gently tweaking him by the ear, or clapping him on the shoulder, that Nat found very engaging.

'Now, I think you would like to go into the school-room and practise some of the hymns we are to sing tonight,' she said, rightly guessing the thing of all others that he wanted to do.

Alone with the beloved violin and the music-book propped up before him in the sunny window, while Spring beauty filled the world outside, and Sabbath silence reigned within, Nat enjoyed an hour or two of genuine happiness, learning the sweet old tunes, and forgetting the hard past in the cheerful present.

When the church-goers came back and dinner was over, everyone read, wrote letters home, said their Sunday lessons, or talked quietly to one another, sitting here and there about the house. At three o'clock the entire family turned out to walk, for all the active young bodies must have exercise; and in these walks the active young minds were taught to see and love the providence of God in the beautiful miracles which Nature was working before their eyes. Mr Bhaer always went with them, and in his simple, fatherly way, found for his flock 'Sermons in stones, books in the running brooks, and good in everything'.

Mrs Bhaer with Daisy and her own two boys drove into town, to pay the weekly visit to Grandma, which was busy Mother Bhaer's one holiday and greatest pleasure. Nat was not strong enough for the long walk, and asked to stay at home with Tommy, who kindly offered to do the honours of Plumfield. 'You've seen the house, so come out and have a look at the garden, and the barn, and the menagerie,' said Tommy, when they were left alone with Asia, to see that they didn't get into mischief; for, though Tommy was one of the best-meaning boys who ever adorned knickerbockers, accidents of the most direful nature were always happening to him, no one could exactly tell how.

'What is your menagerie?' asked Nat, as they trotted along the drive that encircled the house.

'We all have pets, you see, and we keep 'em in the corn-barn, and call it the menagerie. Here you are. Isn't my guinea-pig a beauty?' and Tommy proudly presented one of the ugliest specimens of that pleasing animal that Nat ever saw.

'I know a boy with a dozen of 'em, and he said he'd give me one, only I hadn't any place to keep it, so I couldn't have it. It was white, with black spots, a regular rouser, and maybe I could get it for you if you'd like it,' said Nat, feeling it would be a delicate return for Tommy's attentions.

'I'd like it ever so much, and I'll give you this one, and they can live together if they don't fight. Those white mice are Rob's, Franz gave 'em to him. The rabbits are Ned's, and the bantams outside are Stuffy's. That box thing is Demi's turtle-tank, only he hasn't begun to get 'em yet. Last year he had sixty-two, whackers some of 'em. He stamped one of 'em with his name and the year, and let it go; and he says maybe he will find it ever so long after and know it. He read about a turtle being found that had a mark on it that showed it must be hundreds of years old. Demi's such a funny chap.'

'What is in this box?' asked Nat, stopping before a large deep one, half-full of earth.

'Oh, that's Jack Ford's worm-shop. He digs heaps of 'em and keeps 'em here, and when we want any to go a fishing with, we buy some of him. It saves lots of trouble, only he charged too much for 'em. Why, last time we traded I had to pay two cents a dozen, and then got little ones. Jack's mean sometimes, and I told him I'd dig for myself if he didn't lower his prices. Now, I own two hens, those grey ones with top knots, first-rate ones they are too, and I sell Mrs Bhaer the eggs, but I never ask her more than twenty-five cents a dozen, never! I'd be ashamed to do it,' cried Tommy, with a glance of scorn at the worm-shop.

'Who owns the dogs?' asked Nat, much interested in these commercial transactions, and feeling that T. Bangs was a man whom it would be a privilege and a pleasure to patronize.

'The big dog is Emil's. His name is Christopher Columbus. Mrs Bhaer named him because she likes to say Christopher Columbus, and no one minds it if she means the dog,' answered Tommy, in the tone of a showman displaying his menagerie. 'The white pup is Rob's, and the yellow one is Teddy's. A man was going to drown them in our pond, and Pa Bhaer wouldn't let him. They do well enough for the little chaps, I don't think much of 'em myself. Their names are Castor and Pollux.'

'I'd like Toby the donkey best, if I could have anything, it's so nice to ride, and he's so little and good,' said Nat, remembering the weary tramps he had taken on his own tired feet.

'Mr Laurie sent him out to Mrs Bhaer, so she shouldn't carry Teddy on her back when we go to walk. We're all fond of Toby, and he's a first-rate donkey, sir. Those pigeons belong to the whole lot of us, we each have our pet one, and go shares in all the little ones as they come along. Squabs are great fun; there ain't any now, but you can go up and take a look at the old fellows, while I see if Cockletop and Granny have laid any eggs.'

Nat climbed up a ladder, put his head through a trap door and took a long look at the pretty doves billing and cooing in their spacious loft. Some on their nests, some bustling in and out, and some sitting at their doors, while many went flying from the sunny housetop to the straw-strewn farmyard, where six sleek cows were placidly ruminating.

'Everybody has got something but me. I wish I had a dove, or a hen, or even a turtle, all my own,' thought Nat, feeling very poor as he saw the interesting treasures of the other boys. 'How do you get these things?' he asked, when he joined Tommy in the barn.

'We find 'em, or buy 'em, or folks give 'em to us. My father sends me mine; but as soon as I get egg money enough, I'm going to buy a pair of ducks. There's a nice little pond for 'em behind the barn, and people pay well for duck-eggs, and the little duckies are pretty, and it's fun to see 'em swim,' said Tommy, with the air of a millionaire.

Nat sighed, for he had neither father nor money, nothing in the wide world but an old empty pocket-book, and the skill that lay in his ten finger tips. Tommy seemed to understand the question and the sigh which followed his answer, for after a moment of deep thought, he suddenly broke out,

'Look here, I'll tell you what I'll do. If you will hunt eggs for me, I hate it, I'll give you one egg out of every dozen. You keep account, and when you've had twelve, Mother Bhaer will give you twenty-five cents for 'em, and then you can buy what you like, don't you see?'

'I'll do it! What a kind feller you are, Tommy!' cried Nat, quite dazzled by this brilliant offer.

'Pooh! that is not anything. You begin now and rummage the barn, and I'll wait here for you. Granny is cackling, so you're sure to find one somewhere,' and Tommy threw himself down on the hay with a luxurious sense of having made a good bargain, and done a friendly thing.

Nat joyfully began his search, and went rustling from loft to loft till he found two fine eggs, one hidden under a beam, and the other in an old peck measure, which Mrs Cockletop had appropriated.

'You may have one and I'll have the other, that will just make up my last dozen, and tomorrow we'll start fresh. Here, you chalk your accounts up near mine, and then we'll be all straight,' said Tommy, showing a row of mysterious figures on the smooth side of an old winnowing machine.

With a delightful sense of importance, the proud possessor of one egg opened his account with his friend, who laughingly wrote above the figures these imposing words, T. BANGS & CO.

Poor Nat found them so fascinating that he was with difficulty persuaded to go and deposit his first piece of portable property in Asia's store-room. Then they went on again, and having made the acquaintance of the two horses, six cows, three pigs, and one Alderney 'Bossy', as calves are called in New England, Tommy took Nat to a certain old willow-tree that overhung a noisy little brook. From the fence it was an easy scramble into a wide niche between the three big branches, which had been cut off to send out from year to year a crowd of slender twigs, till a green canopy rustled overhead. Here little seats had been fixed, and in a hollow place a closet made big enough to hold a book or two, a dismantled boat and several half-finished whistles.

'This is Demi's and my private place; we made it, and nobody can come up unless we let 'em, except Daisy, we don't mind her,' said Tommy, as Nat looked with delight from the babbling brown water below to the green arch above, where bees were making a musical murmur as they feasted on the long yellow blossoms that filled the air with sweetness.

'Oh, it's just beautiful!' cried Nat. 'I do hope you'll let me up sometimes. I never saw such a nice place in all my life. I'd like to be a bird, and live here always.'

'It is pretty nice. You can come if Demi don't mind, and I guess he won't, because he said last night that he liked you.'

'Did he?' and Nat smiled with pleasure, for Demi's regard seemed to be valued by all the boys, partly because he was Father Bhaer's nephew, and partly because he was such a sober, conscientious little fellow.

'Yes; Demi likes quiet chaps, and I guess he and you will get on if you care about reading as he does.'

Poor Nat's flush of pleasure deepened to a painful scarlet at those last words, and he stammered out,

'I can't read very well; I never had any time; I was always fiddling round, you know.'

'I don't love it myself, but I can do it well enough when I want to,' said Tommy, after a surprised look, which said as plainly as words, 'A boy twelve years old and can't read!'

'I can read music, anyway,' added Nat, rather ruffled at having to confess his ignorance.

'I can't'; and Tommy spoke in a respectful tone, which emboldened Nat to say firmly,

'I mean to study real hard and learn everything I can, for I never had a chance before. Does Mr Bhaer give hard lessons?'

'No, he isn't a bit cross; he sort of explains and gives you a boost over the hard places. Some folks don't; my other master didn't. If we missed a word, didn't we get raps on the head!' and Tommy rubbed his own pate as if it tingled yet with the liberal supply of raps, the memory of which was the only thing he brought away after a year with his 'other master'.

'I think I could read this,' said Nat, who had been examining the books.

'Read a bit, then; I'll help you,' resumed Tommy, with a patronizing air.

So Nat did his best, and floundered through a page with many friendly 'boosts' from Tommy, who told him he would soon 'go it' as well as anybody. Then they sat and talked boy-fashion about all sorts of things, among others, gardening; for Nat, looking down from his perch, asked what was planted in the many little patches lying below them on the other side of the brook.

'These are our farms,' said Tommy. 'We each have our own patch, and raise what we like in it, only we have to choose different things, and can't change till the crop is in, and we must keep it in order all summer.'

'What are you going to raise this year?'

'Wal, I *cattle*ated to hev beans, as they are about the easiest crop a-goin'.'

Nat could not help laughing, for Tommy had pushed back his hat, put his hands in his pockets, and drawled out his words in unconscious imitation of Silas, the man who managed the place for Mr Bhaer.

'Come, you needn't laugh; beans *are* ever so much easier than corn or potatoes. I tried melons last year, but the bugs were a bother, and the old things wouldn't get ripe before the frost, so I didn't have but one good water and two little "mush mellions",' said Tommy, relapsing into a 'Silasism' with the last word.

'Corn looks pretty growing,' said Nat, politely, to atone for his laugh.

'Yes, but you have to hoe it over and over again. Now, six weeks' beans only have to be done once or so, and they get ripe soon. I'm going to try 'em, for I spoke first. Stuffy wanted 'em, but he's got to take peas; they only have to be picked, and he ought to do it, he eats such a lot.'

'I wonder if I shall have a garden?' said Nat, thinking that even corn-hoeing must be pleasant work.

'Of course you will,' said a voice from below, and there was Mr Bhaer returned from his walk, and come to find them, for he managed to have a little talk with every one of the lads sometime during the day, and found that these chats gave them a good start for the coming week.

Sympathy is a sweet thing, and it worked wonders here, for each boy knew that Father Bhaer was interested in him, and some were readier to open their hearts to him than to a woman, especially the older ones, who liked to talk over their hopes and plans man to man. When sick or in trouble they instinctively turned to Mrs Jo, while the little ones made her their mother-confessor on all occasions.

In descending from their nest, Tommy fell into the brook; being used to it, he calmly picked himself out and retired to the house to be dried. This left Nat to Mr Bhaer, which was just what he wished, and, during the stroll they took among the garden plots, he won the lad's heart by giving him a little 'farm', and discussing crops with him as gravely as if the food for the family depended on the harvest. From this pleasant topic they went to others, and Nat had many new and helpful thoughts put into a mind that received them as gratefully as the thirsty earth had received the warm spring rain. All supper time he brooded over them, often fixing his eyes on Mr Bhaer with an inquiring look, that seemed to say, 'I like that, do it again, sir.' I don't know whether the man understood the child's mute language or not, but when the boys were all gathered together in Mrs Bhaer's parlour for the Sunday evening talk, he chose a subject which might have been suggested by the walk in the garden.

As he looked about him Nat thought it seemed more like a great family than a school, for the lads were sitting in a wide half-circle round the fire, some on chairs, some on the rug, Daisy and Demi on the knees of Uncle Fritz, and Rob snugly stowed away in the back of his mother's easy-chair, where he could nod unseen if the talk got beyond his depth. Everyone looked quite comfortable, and listened attentively, for the long walk made rest agreeable, and as every boy there knew that he would be called upon for his views he kept his wits awake to be ready with an answer.

'Once upon a time,' began Mr Bhaer, in the dear old-fashioned way, 'there was a great and wise gardener who had the largest garden ever seen. A wonderful and lovely place it was, and he watched over it with the greatest skill and care, and raised all manner of excellent and useful things. But weeds would grow even in this fine garden; often the ground was bad and the good seeds sown in it would not spring up. He had many under-gardeners to help him. Some did their duty and earned the rich wages he gave them; but others neglected their parts and let them run to waste, which displeased him much. But he was very patient, and for thousands and thousands of years he worked and waited for his great harvest.'

'He must have been pretty old,' said Demi, who was looking straight into Uncle Fritz's face, as if to catch every word.

'Hush, Demi, it's a fairy story,' whispered Daisy.

'No, I think it's a arrygory,' said Demi.

'What is a arrygory?' called out Tommy, who was of an inquiring turn.

'Tell him, Demi, if you can, and don't use words unless you are quite sure you know what they mean,' said Mr Bhaer.

'I do know, Grandpa told me! A fable is a arrygory; it's a story that means something. My "Story without an end" is one, because the child in it means a soul; don't it, Aunty?' cried Demi, eager to prove himself right.

'That's it, dear; and Uncle's story is an allegory, I am quite sure; so listen and see what it means,' returned Mrs Jo, who always took part in whatever was going on, and enjoyed it as much as any boy among them.

Demi composed himself, and Mr Bhaer went on in his best English, for he had improved much in the last five years, and said the boys did it.

'This great gardener gave a dozen or so of little plots to one of his servants, and told him to do his best and see what he could raise. Now this servant was not rich, nor wise, nor very good, but he wanted to help because the gardener had been very kind to him in many ways. So he gladly took the little plots and fell to work. They were all sorts of shapes and sizes, and some were very good soil, some rather stony, and all of them needed much care, for in the rich soil the weeds grew fast, and in the poor soil there were many stones.'

'What was growing in them beside the weeds, and stones?' asked Nat; so interested he forgot his shyness and spoke before them all.

'Flowers,' said Mr Bhaer, with a kind look. 'Even the roughest, most neglected little bed had a bit of heart's-ease or a sprig of mignonette in it. One had roses, sweet peas, and daisies in it' – here he pinched the plump cheek of the little girl leaning on his arm. 'Another had all sorts of curious plants in it, bright pebbles, a vine that went climbing up like Jack's beanstalk, and many good seeds just beginning to sprout; for, you see, *this* bed had been taken fine care of by a wise old man, who had worked in gardens of this sort all his life.'

At this part of the 'arrygory', Demi put his head on one side like an inquisitive bird, and fixed his bright eye on his uncle's face, as if he suspected something and was on the watch. But Mr Bhaer looked perfectly innocent, and went on glancing from one young face to another, with a grave, wistful look, that said much to his wife, who knew how earnestly he desired to do his duty in these little garden plots.

'As I tell you, some of these beds were easy to cultivate – that means to take care of, Daisy – and others were very hard. There was one particularly sunshiny little bed, that might have been full of fruits and vegetables as well as flowers, only it wouldn't take any pains, and when the man sowed, well, we'll say melons in this bed, they came to nothing, because the little bed neglected them. The man was sorry, and kept on trying, though every time the crop failed, all the bed said was, "I forgot."'

Here a general laugh broke out, and everyone looked at Tommy, who had pricked up his ears at the word 'melons', and hung down his head at the sound of his favourite excuse.

'I knew he meant us!' cried Demi, clapping his hands. 'You are the man, and we are the little gardens; aren't we, Uncle Fritz?'

'You have guessed it. Now each of you tell me what crop I shall try to sow in you this spring, so that next autumn I may get a good harvest out of my twelve, no, thirteen, plots,' said Mr Bhaer, nodding at Nat as he corrected himself.

'You can't sow corn and beans and peas in us. Unless you mean we are to eat a great many and get fat,' said Stuffy, with a sudden brightening of his round, dull face as the pleasing idea occurred to him.

'He don't mean that kind of seeds. He means things

to make us good; and the weeds are faults,' cried Demi, who usually took the lead in these talks, because he was used to this sort of thing, and liked it very much.

'Yes, each of you think what you need most, and tell me, and I will help you to grow it; only, you must do your best, or you will turn out like Tommy's melons – all leaves and no fruit. I will begin with the oldest, and ask the mother what she will have in her plot, for we are all parts of the beautiful garden, and may have rich harvests for our Master if we love Him enough,' said Father Bhaer.

'I shall devote the whole of *my* plot to the largest crop of patience I can get, for that is what I need most,' said Mrs Jo, so soberly that the lads fell to thinking in good earnest what they should say when their turns came, and some among them felt a twinge of remorse, that they had helped to use up Mother Bhaer's stock of patience so fast.

Franz wanted perseverance, Tommy steadiness, Ned went in for good temper, Daisy for industry, Demi for 'as much wiseness as Grandpa', and Nat timidly said he wanted so many things he would let Mr Bhaer choose for him. The others chose much the same things, and patience, good temper, and generosity seemed the favourite crops. One boy wished to like to get up early, but did not know what name to give that sort of seed; and poor Stuffy sighed out,

'I wish I loved my lessons as much as I do my dinner, but I can't.'

'We will plant self-denial, and hoe it and water it, and make it grow so well that next Christmas no one will get ill by eating too much dinner. If you exercise your mind, George, it will get hungry just as your body does, and you will love books almost as much as my philosopher here,' said Mr Bhaer; adding, as he stroked the hair off Demi's fine forehead, 'You are greedy also, my son, and you like to stuff your little mind full of fairy tales and fancies, as well as George likes to fill his little stomach with cake and candy. Both are bad, and I want you to try something better. Arithmetic is not half so pleasant as *Arabian Nights*, I know, but it is a very useful thing, and now is the time to learn it, else you will be ashamed and sorry by and by.'

'But, "Harry and Lucy", and "Frank", are not fairy books, and they are all full of barometers, and bricks, and shoeing horses, and useful things, and I'm fond of them; ain't I, Daisy?' said Demi, anxious to defend himself.

'So they are; but I find you reading "Roland and Maybird" a great deal oftener than "Harry and Lucy", and I think you are not half as fond of "Frank" as you are of "Sinbad". Come, I shall make a little bargain with you both – George shall eat but three times a day, and you shall read but one story-book a week, and I will give you the new cricket-ground; only, you must promise to play in it,' said Uncle Fritz in his persuasive way, for Stuffy hated to run about, and Demi was always reading in play hours.

'But we don't like cricket,' said Demi.

'Perhaps not *now*, but you will when you know it. Besides, you do like to be generous, and the other boys want to play, and you can give them the new ground if you choose.'

This was taking them both on the right side, and

they agreed to the bargain, to the great satisfaction of
the rest.

There was a little more talk about the gardens, and
then they all sang together. The band delighted Nat,
for Mrs Bhaer played the piano, Franz the flute, Mr
Bhaer a bass viol, and he himself the violin. A very
simple little concert, but all seemed to enjoy it, and old
Asia, sitting in the corner, joined at times with the
sweetest voice of any, for in this family, master and
servant, old and young, black and white, shared in the
Sunday song, which went up to the Father of them all.
After this they each shook hands with Father Bhaer;
Mother Bhaer kissed them everyone from sixteen-
year-old Franz to little Rob, who kept the tip of her
nose for his own particular kisses, and then they
trooped up to bed.

The light of the shaded lamp that burned in the
nursery shone softly on a picture hanging at the foot
of Nat's bed. There were several others on the walls,
but the boy thought there must be something peculiar about this one, for it had a graceful frame of
moss and cones about it, and on a little bracket underneath stood a vase of wild flowers freshly gathered
from the spring woods. It was the most beautiful
picture of them all, and Nat lay looking at it, dimly
feeling what it meant, and wishing he knew all about
it.

'That's my picture,' said a little voice in the room.
Nat popped up his head, and there was Demi in his
nightgown pausing on his way back from Aunt Jo's
chamber, whither he had gone to get a cot for a cut
finger.

'What is he doing to the children?' asked Nat.

'That is Christ, the Good Man, and He is blessing the children. Don't you know about Him?' said Demi, wondering.

'Not much, but I'd like to, He looks so kind,' answered Nat, whose chief knowledge of the Good Man consisted in hearing His name taken in vain.

'I know all about it, and I like it very much, because it is true,' said Demi.

'Who told you?'

'My Grandpa, he knows everything, and tells the best stories in the world. I used to play with his big books, and make bridges, and railroads, and houses, when I was a little boy,' began Demi.

'How old are you now?' asked Nat, respectfully.

'Most ten.'

'You know a lot of things, don't you?'

'Yes; you see my head is pretty big, and Grandpa says it will take a good deal to fill it, so I keep putting pieces of wisdom into it as fast as I can,' returned Demi, in his quaint way.

Nat laughed, and then said soberly,

'Tell on, please.'

And Demi gladly told on without pause or punctuation. 'I found a very pretty book one day and wanted to play with it, but Grandpa said I mustn't, and showed me the pictures, and told me about them, and I liked the stories very much, all about Joseph and his bad brothers, and the frogs that came up out of the sea, and dear little Moses in the water, and ever so many more lovely ones, but I liked about the Good Man best of all, and Grandpa told it to me so many times that I learned it by heart, and he gave me this picture so I shouldn't forget, and it was put up here once when I was sick, and I left it for other sick boys to see.'

'What makes Him bless the children?' asked Nat, who found something very attractive in the chief figure of the group.

'Because He loved them.'

'Were they poor children?' asked Nat, wistfully.

'Yes, I think so; you see some haven't got hardly any clothes on, and the mothers don't look like rich ladies. He liked poor people, and was very good to them. He made them well, and helped them, and told rich people they must not be cross to them, and they loved Him dearly, dearly,' cried Demi, with enthusiasm.

'Was He rich?'

'Oh no! He was born in a barn, and was so poor. He hadn't any house to live in when He grew up, and nothing to eat sometimes, but what people gave Him, and He went round preaching to everybody, and trying to make them good, till the bad men killed Him.'

'What for?' and Nat sat up in his bed to look and listen, so interested was he in this man who cared for the poor so much.

'I'll tell you all about it; Aunt Jo won't mind;' and Demi settled himself on the opposite bed, glad to tell his favourite story to so good a listener.

Nursey peeped in to see if Nat was asleep, but when she saw what was going on, she slipped away again, and went to Mrs Bhaer, saying with her kind face full of motherly emotion,

'Will the dear lady come and see a pretty sight? It's Nat listening with all his heart to Demi telling the

story of the Christ-child, like a little white angel as he
is.'

Mrs Bhaer had meant to go and talk with Nat a
moment before he slept, for she had found that a
serious word spoken at this time often did much good.
But when she stole to the nursery door, and saw Nat
eagerly drinking in the words of his little friend, while
Demi told the sweet and solemn story as it had been
taught him, speaking softly as he sat with his beautiful
eyes fixed on the tender face above them, her own
filled with tears, and she went silently away, thinking
to herself,

'Demi is unconsciously helping the poor boy better
than I can; I will not spoil it by a single word.'

The murmur of the childish voice went on for a
long time, as one innocent heart preached that great
sermon to another, and no one hushed it. When it
ceased at last, and Mrs Bhaer went to take away the
lamp, Demi was gone and Nat fast asleep, lying with
his face toward the picture, as if he had already learned
to love the Good Man who loved little children, and
was a faithful friend to the poor. The boy's face was
very placid, and as she looked at it she felt that if a
single day of care and kindness had done so much, a
year of patient cultivation would surely bring a grateful
harvest from his neglected garden, which was already
sown with the best of all seed by the little missionary
in the night-gown.

4

STEPPING-STONES

When Nat went into school on Monday morning, he quaked inwardly, for now he thought he should have to display his ignorance before them all. But Mr Bhaer gave him a seat in the deep window, where he could turn his back on the others, and Franz heard him say his lessons there, so no one could hear his blunders or see how he blotted his copy-book. He was truly grateful for this, and toiled away so diligently that Mr Bhaer said, smiling, when he saw his hot face and inky fingers,

'Don't work so hard, my boy; you will tire yourself out, and there is time enough.'

'But I *must* work hard, or I can't catch up with the others. They know heaps, and I don't know anything,' said Nat, who had been reduced to a state of despair by hearing the boys recite their grammar, history, and geography with what he thought amazing ease and accuracy.

'You know a good many things which they don't,' said Mr Bhaer, sitting down beside him, while Franz led a class of small students through the intricacies of the multiplication table.

'Do I?' and Nat looked utterly incredulous.

'Yes; for one thing, you can keep your temper, and

Jack, who is quick at numbers, cannot; that is an excellent lesson, and I think you have learned it well. Then, you can play the violin, and not one of the lads can, though they want to do it very much. But, best of all, Nat, you really care to learn something, and that is half the battle. It seems hard at first, and you will feel discouraged, but plod away, and things will get easier and easier as you go on.'

Nat's face had brightened more and more as he listened, for, small as the list of his learning was, it cheered him immensely to feel that he had anything to fall back upon. 'Yes, I can keep my temper – father's beating taught me that; and I can fiddle, though I don't know where the Bay of Biscay is,' he thought, with a sense of comfort impossible to express. Then he said aloud, and so earnestly that Demi heard him,

'I *do* want to learn, and I *will* try. I never went to school, but I couldn't help it; and if the fellows don't laugh at me, I guess I'll get on first rate – you and the lady are so good to me.'

'They shan't laugh at you; if they do, I'll – I'll – tell them not to,' cried Demi, quite forgetting where he was.

The class stopped in the middle of 7 times 9, and everyone looked up to see what was going on.

Thinking that a lesson in learning to help one another was better than arithmetic just then, Mr Bhaer told them about Nat, making such an interesting and touching little story out of it that the good-hearted lads all promised to lend him a hand, and felt quite honoured to be called upon to impart their stores of wisdom to the chap who fiddled so capitally. This appeal established the right feeling among them, and

Nat had few hindrances to struggle against, for everyone was glad to give him a 'boost' up the ladder of learning.

Till he was stronger, much study was not good for him, however, and Mrs Jo found various amusements in the house for him while others were at their books. But his garden was his best medicine, and he worked away like a beaver, preparing his little farm, sowing his beans, watching eagerly to see them grow, and rejoicing over each green leaf and slender stock that shot up and flourished in the warm spring weather. Never was a garden more faithfully hoed; Mr Bhaer really feared that nothing would find time to grow, Nat kept up such a stirring of the soil; so he gave him easy jobs in the flower garden or among the strawberries, where he worked and hummed as busily as the bees booming all about him.

'This is the crop I like best,' Mrs Bhaer used to say, as she pinched the once thin cheeks now getting plump and ruddy, or stroked the bent shoulders that were slowly straightening up with healthful work, good food, and the absence of that heavy burden, poverty.

Demi was his little friend, Tommy his patron, and Daisy the comforter of all his woes; for, though the children were younger than he, his timid spirit found a pleasure in their innocent society, and rather shrunk from the rough sports of the elder lads. Mr Laurence did not forget him, but sent clothes and books, music and kind messages, and now and then came out to see how his boy was getting on, or took him into town to a concert; on which occasions Nat felt himself translated into the seventh heaven of bliss, for he went to Mr

Laurence's great house, saw his pretty wife and little fairy of a daughter, had a good dinner, and was made so comfortable, that he talked and dreamed of it for days and nights afterward.

It takes so little to make a child happy, that it is a pity in a world full of sunshine and pleasant things, that there should be any wistful faces, empty hands, or lonely little hearts. Feeling this, the Bhaers gathered up all the crumbs they could find to feed their flock of hungry sparrows, for they were not rich, except in charity. Many of Mrs Jo's friends who had nurseries sent her the toys of which their children so soon tired, and in mending these Nat found an employment that just suited him. He was very neat and skilful with those slender fingers of his, and passed many a rainy afternoon with his gum-bottle, paint-box, and knife, repairing furniture, animals, and games, while Daisy was dressmaker to the dilapidated dolls. As fast as the toys were mended, they were put carefully away in a certain drawer which was to furnish forth a Christmas-tree for all the poor children of the neighbourhood, that being the way the Plumfield boys celebrated the birthday of Him who loved the poor and blessed the little ones.

Demi was never tired of reading and explaining his favourite books, and many a pleasant hour did they spend in the old willow, revelling over *Robinson Crusoe*, *Arabian Nights*, *Edgeworth's Tales*, and the other dear immortal stories that will delight children for centuries to come. This opened a new world to Nat, and his eagerness to see what came next in the story helped him on till he could read as well as anybody, and felt so rich and proud with his new accomplishment, that there was danger of his being as much of a bookworm as Demi.

Another helpful thing happened in a most unexpected and agreeable manner. Several of the boys were 'in business', as they called it, for most of them were poor, and knowing that they would have their own way to make by and by, the Bhaers encouraged any efforts at independence. Tommy sold his eggs; Jack speculated in live stock; Franz helped in the teaching, and was paid for it; Ned had a taste for carpentry, and a turning-lathe was set up for him in which he turned all sorts of useful or pretty things, and sold them; while Demi constructed water-mills, whirligigs, and unknown machines of an intricate and useless nature, and disposed of them to the boys.

'Let him be a mechanic if he likes,' said Mr Bhaer. 'Give a boy a trade, and he is independent. Work is wholesome, and whatever talent these lads possess, be it for poetry or ploughing, it shall be cultivated and made useful to them if possible.'

So when Nat came running to him one day to ask with an excited face,

'Can I go and fiddle for some people who are to have a picnic in our woods? They will pay me, and I'd like to earn some money as the other boys do, and fiddling is the only way I know how to do it.'

Mr Bhaer answered readily,

'Go, and welcome. It is an easy and a pleasant way to work, and I am glad it is offered you.'

Nat went, and did so well, that when he came home he had two dollars in his pocket, which he displayed with intense satisfaction, as he told how much he had enjoyed the afternoon, how kind the young people were, and how they had praised his dance-music, and promised to have him again.

'It is so much nicer than fiddling in the street, for then I got none of the money, and now I have it all, and a good time besides. I'm in business now as well as Tommy and Jack, and I like it ever so much,' said Nat, proudly patting the old pocket-book, and feeling like a millionaire already.

He *was* in business truly, for picnics were plenty as summer opened, and Nat's skill was in great demand. He was always at liberty to go if lessons were not neglected, and if the picnics were respectable young people. For Mr Bhaer explained to him that a good plain education is necessary for everyone, and that no amount of money should hire him to go where he might be tempted to do wrong. Nat quite agreed to this, and it was a pleasant sight to see the innocent-hearted lad go driving away in the gay wagons that stopped at the gate for him, or to hear him come fiddling home tired but happy, with his well-earned money in one pocket, and some 'goodies' from the feast for Daisy or little Ted, whom he never forgot.

'I'm going to save up till I get enough to buy a violin for myself, and then I can earn my own living, can't I?' he used to say, as he brought his dollars to Mr Bhaer to keep.

'I hope so, Nat; but we must get you strong and hearty first, and put a little more knowledge into this musical head of yours. Then Mr Laurie will find you a place somewhere, and in a few years we will all come to hear you play in public.'

With much congenial work, encouragement, and hope, Nat found life getting easier and happier every day, and made such progress in his music lessons, that his teacher forgave his slowness in some other things, knowing very well that where the heart is the mind works best. The only punishment the boy ever needed for neglect of more important lessons was to hang up the fiddle and the bow for a day. The fear of losing his bosom friend entirely made him go at his books with a will; and having proved that *he could* master the lessons, what was the use of saying, 'I can't'?

Daisy had a great love of music, and a great reverence for anyone who could make it, and she was often found sitting on the stairs outside Nat's door while he was practising. This pleased him very much, and he played his best for that one quiet little listener; for she never would come in, but preferred to sit sewing her gay patchwork, or tending one of her many dolls, with an expression of dreamy pleasure on her face that made Aunt Jo say, with tears in her eyes,

'So like my Beth,' and go softly by, lest even her familiar presence mar the child's sweet satisfaction.

Nat was very fond of Mrs Bhaer, but found something even more attractive in the good professor, who took fatherly care of the shy feeble boy, who had barely escaped with his life from the rough sea on which his little boat had been tossing rudderless for twelve years. Some good angel must have watched over him, for, though his body had suffered, his soul seemed to have taken little harm, and came ashore as innocent as a shipwrecked baby. Perhaps his love of music kept it sweet in spite of the discord all about him; Mr Laurie said so, and he ought to know. However that might be, Father Bhaer took real pleasure in fostering poor Nat's virtues, and in curing his faults, finding his new pupil as docile and affectionate as a girl. He often called Nat his 'daughter' when speaking of him to Mrs Jo, and she used to laugh at his fancy, for Madame liked manly boys, and thought Nat amiable but weak, though you never would have guessed it, for she petted him as she did Daisy, and he thought her a very delightful woman.

One fault of Nat's gave the Bhaers much anxiety, although they saw how it had been strengthened by fear and ignorance. I regret to say that Nat sometimes told lies. Not very black ones, seldom getting deeper than grey, and often the mildest of white fibs; but that did not matter, a lie is a lie, and though we all tell many polite untruths in this queer world of ours, it is not right, and everybody knows it.

'You cannot be too careful; watch your tongue, and eyes, and hands, for it is easy to tell, and look, and act untruth,' said Mr Bhaer, in one of the talks he had with Nat about his chief temptation.

'I know it, and I don't mean to, but it's so much easier to get along if you ain't very fussy about being exactly true. I used to tell 'em because I was afraid of father and Nicolo, and now I do sometimes because the boys laugh at me. I know it's bad, but I forget,' and Nat looked much depressed by his sins.

'When I was a little lad I used to tell lies! Ach! what fibs they were, and my old grandmother cured me of it – how, do you think? My parents had talked, and cried, and punished, but still did I forget as you. Then said the dear old grandmother, "I shall help you to remember, and put a check on this unruly part," with that she drew out my tongue and snipped the end with her scissors till the blood ran. That was terrible, you may believe, but it did me much good, because it was sore for days, and every word I said came so slowly that I had time to think. After that I was more careful, and got on better, for I feared the big scissors. Yet the dear grandmother was most kind to me in all things, and when she lay dying far away in Nuremberg, she prayed that little Fritz might love God and tell the truth.'

'I never had any grandmothers, but if you think it will cure me, I'll let you snip my tongue,' said Nat, heroically, for he dreaded pain, yet did wish to stop fibbing.

Mr Bhaer smiled, but shook his head.

'I have a better way than that, I tried it once before and it worked well. See now, when you tell a lie I will not punish you, but you shall punish me.'

'How?' asked Nat, startled at the idea.

'You shall ferrule me in the good old-fashioned way, I seldom do it myself, but it may make you remember better to give me pain than to feel it yourself.'

'Strike you? Oh, I couldn't!' cried Nat.

'Then mind that tripping tongue of thine. I have no wish to be hurt, but I would gladly bear much pain to cure this fault.'

This suggestion made such an impression on Nat, that for a long time he set a watch upon his lips and was desperately accurate, for Mr Bhaer judged rightly, that love of him would be more powerful with Nat than fear for himself. But alas! one sad day Nat was off his guard, and when peppery Emil threatened to thrash him, if it was he who had run over his garden and broken down his best hills of corn, Nat declared he didn't, and then was ashamed to own up that he did do it, when Jack was chasing him the night before.

He thought no one would find it out, but Tommy happened to see him, and when Emil spoke of it a day or two later, Tommy gave his evidence, and Mr Bhaer heard it. School was over, and they were all standing about in the hall, and Mr Bhaer had just sat down on the straw settee, to enjoy his frolic with Teddy; but when he heard Tommy, and saw Nat turn scarlet, and look at him with a frightened face, he put the little boy down, saying, 'Go to thy mother, bübchen, I will come soon,' and taking Nat by the hand led him into the school, and shut the door.

The boys looked at one another in silence for a minute, then Tommy slipped out and peeping in at the half-closed blinds, beheld a sight that quite bewildered him. Mr Bhaer had just taken down the long rule that hung over his desk, so seldom used that it was covered with dust.

'My eye! he's going to come down heavy on Nat this time. Wish I hadn't told,' thought good-natured Tommy, for to be ferruled was the deepest disgrace at this school.

'You remember what I told you last time?' said Mr Bhaer, sorrowfully, not angrily.

'Yes; but please don't make me, I can't bear it,' cried Nat, backing up against the door with both hands behind him, and a face full of distress.

'Why don't he up and take it like a man? I would,' thought Tommy, though his heart beat fast at the sight.

'I shall keep my word, and you must remember to

tell the truth. Obey me, Nat, take this and give me six good strokes.'

Tommy was so staggered by this last speech that he nearly tumbled down the bank, but saved himself, and hung on to the window ledge, staring in with eyes as round as the stuffed owl's on the chimney-piece.

Nat took the rule, for when Mr Bhaer spoke in that tone everyone obeyed him, and, looking as scared and guilty as if about to stab his master, he gave two feeble blows on the broad hand held out to him. Then he stopped and looked up half-blind with tears, but Mr Bhaer said steadily.

'Go on, and strike harder.'

As if seeing that it must be done, and eager to have the hard task soon over, Nat drew his sleeve across his eyes and gave two more quick hard strokes that reddened the hand, yet hurt the giver more.

'Isn't that enough?' he asked in a breathless sort of tone.

'Two more,' was all the answer, and he gave them, hardly seeing where they fell, then threw the rule all across the room, and hugging the kind hand in both his own, laid his face down on it sobbing out in a passion of love, and shame, and penitence,

'I will remember! Oh! I will!'

Then Mr Bhaer put an arm about him, and said in a tone as compassionate as it had just now been firm,

'I think you will. Ask the dear God to help you, and try to spare us both another scene like this.'

Tommy saw no more, for he crept back to the hall, looking so excited and sober that the boys crowded round him to ask what was being done to Nat.

In a most impressive whisper Tommy told them,

and they looked as if the sky was about to fall, for this reversing the order of things almost took their breath away.

'He made me do the same thing once,' said Emil, as if confessing a crime of the deepest dye.

'And you hit him? dear old Father Bhaer? By thunder, I'd just like to see you do it now!' said Ned, collaring Emil in a fit of righteous wrath.

'It was ever so long ago. I'd rather have my head cut off than do it now,' and Emil mildly laid Ned on his back instead of cuffing him, as he would have felt it his duty to do on any less solemn occasion.

'How could you?' said Demi, appalled at the idea.

'I was hopping mad at the time, and thought I shouldn't mind a bit, rather like it perhaps. But when I'd hit Uncle one good crack, everything he had ever done for me came into my head all at once somehow, and I couldn't go on. No, sir! if he'd laid me down and walked on me, I wouldn't have minded, I felt so mean'; and Emil gave himself a good thump in the chest to express his sense of remorse for the past.

'Nat's crying like anything, and feels no end sorry, so don't let's say a word about it; will we?' said tender-hearted Tommy.

'Of course we won't, but it's awful to tell lies,' and Demi looked as if he found the awfulness much increased when the punishment fell not upon the sinner, but his best Uncle Fritz.

'Suppose we all clear out, so Nat can cut upstairs if he wants to,' proposed Franz, and led the way to the barn, their refuge in troublous times.

Nat did not come to dinner, but Mrs Jo took some up to him, and said a tender word, which did him

good, though he could not look at her. By and by the
lads playing outside heard the violin, and said among
themselves: 'He's all right now.' He was all right, but
felt shy about going down, till, opening his door to slip
away into the woods, he found Daisy sitting on the
stairs with neither work nor doll, only her little handkerchief in her hand, as if she had been mourning for
her captive friend.

'I'm going to walk; want to come?' asked Nat, trying
to look as if nothing was the matter, yet feeling very
grateful for her silent sympathy, because he fancied
everyone must look upon him as a wretch.

'Oh, yes!' and Daisy ran for her hat, proud to be
chosen as a companion by one of the big boys.

The others saw them go, but no one followed, for
boys have a great deal more delicacy than they get
credit for, and the lads instinctively felt that, when in
disgrace, gentle little Daisy was their most congenial
friend.

The walk did Nat good, and he came home quieter
than usual, but looking cheerful again, and hung all
over with daisy-chains, made by his little playmate
while he lay on the grass and told her stories.

No one said a word about the scene of the morning,
but its effect was all the more lasting for that reason,
perhaps. Nat tried his very best, and found much help,
not only from the earnest little prayers he prayed to
his Friend in heaven, but also in the patient care of the
earthly friend, whose kind hand he never touched
without remembering that it had willingly borne pain
for his sake.

5

PATTY PANS

'What's the matter, Daisy?'

'The boys won't let me play with them.'

'Why not?'

'They say girls can't play football.'

'They can, for I've done it!' and Mrs Bhaer laughed at the remembrance of certain youthful frolics.

'I know I can play; Demi and I used to, and have nice times, but he won't let me now because the other boys laugh at him,' and Daisy looked deeply grieved at her brother's hardness of heart.

'On the whole, I think he is right, deary. It's all very well when you two are alone, but it is too rough a game for you with a dozen boys; so I'd find some nice little play for myself.'

'I'm tired of playing alone!' and Daisy's tone was very mournful.

'I'll play with you by and by, but just now I must fly about and get things ready for a trip into town. You shall go with me and see mamma, and if you like you can stay with her.'

'I should like to go and see her and Baby Josy, but I'd rather come back, please. Demi would miss me, and I love to be here, Aunty.'

'You can't get on without your Demi, can you?' and

Aunt Jo looked as if she quite understood the love of the little girl for her only brother.

''Course I can't; we're twins, and so we love each other more than other people,' answered Daisy, with a brightening face, for she considered being a twin one of the highest honours she could ever receive.

'Now, what will you do with your little self while I fly round?' asked Mrs Bhaer, who was whisking piles of linen into a wardrobe with great rapidity.

'I don't know, I'm tired of dolls and things; I wish you'd make up a new play for me, Aunty Jo,' said Daisy, swinging listlessly on the door.

'I shall have to think of a brand new one, and it will take me some time; so suppose you go down and see what Asia has got for your lunch,' suggested Mrs Bhaer, thinking that would be a good way in which to dispose of the little hindrance for a time.

'Yes, I think I'd like that, if she isn't cross,' and Daisy slowly departed to the kitchen, where Asia, the black cook, reigned undisturbed.

In five minutes Daisy was back again, with a wide-awake face, a bit of dough in her hand and a dab of flour on her little nose.

'O Aunty! please could I go and make gingersnaps and things? Asia isn't cross, and she says I may, and it would be such fun, please do,' cried Daisy, all in one breath.

'Just the thing, go and welcome, make what you like, and stay as long as you please,' answered Mrs Bhaer, much relieved, for sometimes the one little girl was harder to amuse than the dozen boys.

Daisy ran off, and while she worked, Aunt Jo racked her brain for a new play. All of a sudden she seemed to have an idea, for she smiled to herself, slammed the doors of the wardrobe, and walked briskly away, saying, 'I'll do it, if it's a possible thing!'

What it was no one found out that day, but Aunt Jo's eyes twinkled so when she told Daisy she had thought of a new play, and was going to buy it, that Daisy was much excited and asked questions all the way into town, without getting answers that told her anything. She was left at home to play with the new baby and delight her mother's eyes, while Aunt Jo went off shopping. When she came back with all sorts of queer parcels in corners of the carry-all, Daisy was so full of curiosity that she wanted to go back to Plumfield at once. But her aunt would not be hurried, and made a long call in mamma's room, sitting on the floor with baby in her lap, making Mrs Brooke laugh at the pranks of the boys, and all sorts of droll nonsense.

How her aunt told the secret Daisy could not imagine, but her mother evidently knew it, for she said, as she tied on the little bonnet and kissed the rosy little face inside, 'Be a good child, my Daisy, and learn the nice new play Aunty has got for you. It's a most useful and interesting one, and it is very kind of her to play it with you, because she does not like it very well herself.'

This last speech made the two ladies laugh heartily, and increased Daisy's bewilderment. As they drove away something rattled in the back of the carriage.

'What's that?' asked Daisy, pricking up her ears.

'The new play,' answered Mrs Jo, solemnly.

'What is it made of?' cried Daisy.

'Iron, tin, wood, brass, sugar, salt, coal, and a hundred other things.'

'How strange! what colour is it?'

'All sorts of colours.'

'Is it large?'

'Part of it is, and a part isn't.'

'Did I ever see one?'

'Ever so many, but never one so nice as this.'

'Oh! what can it be? I can't wait. When *shall* I see it?' and Daisy bounced up and down with impatience.

'Tomorrow morning, after lessons.'

'Is it for the boys too?'

'No, all for you and Bess. The boys will like to see it, and want to play one part of it. But you can do as you like about letting them.'

'I'll let Demi, if he wants to.'

'No fear that they won't all want to, especially Stuffy,' and Mrs Bhaer's eyes twinkled more than ever, as she patted a queer knobby bundle in her lap.

'Let me feel just once,' prayed Daisy.

'Not a feel; you'd guess in a minute and spoil the fun.'

Daisy groaned and then smiled all over her face, for through a little hole in the paper she caught a glimpse of something bright.

'How *can* I wait so long? Couldn't I see it today?'

'Oh dear, no! it has got to be arranged, and ever so many parts fixed in their places. I promised Uncle Teddy that you shouldn't see it till it was all in apple-pie order.'

'If Uncle knows about it then it *must* be splendid!' cried Daisy, clapping her hands; for this kind, rich, jolly uncle of hers was as good as a fairy godmother to the children, and was always planning merry surprises, pretty gifts, and droll amusements for them.

'Yes; Teddy went and bought it with me, and we had such fun in the shop choosing the different parts. He would have everything fine and large, and my little plan got regularly splendid when he took hold. You must give him your very best kiss when he comes, for he is the kindest uncle that ever went and bought a charming little coo – Bless me! I nearly told you what it was!' and Mrs Bhaer cut that most interesting word short off in the middle, and began to look over her bills as if afraid she would let the cat out of the bag if she talked any more. Daisy folded her hands with an air of resignation, and sat quite still trying to think what play had a 'coo' in it.

When they got home she eyed every bundle that was taken out, and one large heavy one, which Franz took straight upstairs and hid in the nursery, filled her with amazement and curiosity. Something very mysterious went on up there that afternoon, for Franz was hammering, and Asia trotting up and down, and Aunt Jo flying around like a will-o'-the-wisp, with all sorts of things under her apron, while little Ted, who was the only child admitted, because he couldn't talk plain, babbled and laughed, and tried to tell what the 'sumpin pitty' was.

All this made Daisy half wild, and her excitement spread among the boys, who quite overwhelmed Mother Bhaer with offers of assistance, which she declined by quoting their own words to Daisy,

'Girls can't play with boys. This is for Daisy, and Bess, and me, so we don't want you.' Whereupon the young gentlemen meekly retired, and invited Daisy to a game of marbles, horse, football, anything she liked, with a sudden warmth and politeness which astonished her innocent little soul.

Thanks to these attentions, she got through the afternoon, went early to bed, and next morning did her lessons with an energy which made Uncle Fritz wish that a new game could be invented every day. Quite a thrill pervaded the schoolroom when Daisy was dismissed at eleven o'clock, for everyone knew that *now* she was going to have the new and mysterious play.

Many eyes followed her as she ran away, and Demi's mind was so distracted by this event that when Franz asked him where the desert of Sahara was, he mournfully replied, 'In the nursery,' and the whole school laughed at him.

'Aunt Jo, I've done all my lessons, and I can't wait one single minute more!' cried Daisy, flying into Mrs Bhaer's room.

'It's all ready, come on;' and tucking Ted under one arm, and her work-basket under the other, Aunt Jo promptly led the way upstairs.

'I don't see anything,' said Daisy, staring about her as she got inside the nursery door.

'Do you hear anything?' asked Aunt Jo, catching Ted back by his little frock as he was making straight for one side of the room.

Daisy did hear an odd crackling, and then a purry little sound as of a kettle singing. These noises came from behind a curtain drawn before a deep bay window. Daisy snatched it back, gave one joyful 'Oh!' and then stood gazing with delight at – what do you think?

A wide seat ran round the three sides of the window; on one side hung and stood all sorts of little pots and pans, gridirons and skillets; on the other side a small dinner and tea set; and on the middle part a cooking-stove. Not a tin one, that was of no use, but a real iron stove, big enough to cook for a large family of very hungry dolls. But the best of it was that a real fire burned in it, real steam came out of the nose of the little tea-kettle, and the lid of the little boiler actually danced a jig, the water inside bubbled so hard. A pane of glass had been taken out and replaced by a sheet of tin, with a hole for the small funnel, and real smoke went sailing away outside so naturally, that it did one's heart good to see it. The box of wood with a hod of charcoal stood near by; just above hung dustpan, brush and broom; a little market basket was on the low table at which Daisy used to play, and over the back of her little chair hung a white apron with a bib and a droll mob cap. The sun shone in as if he enjoyed the fun, the little stove roared beautifully, the kettle steamed, the new tins sparkled on the walls, the pretty china stood in tempting rows, and it was altogether as cheery and complete a kitchen as any child could desire.

Daisy stood quite still after the first glad 'Oh!' but her eyes went quickly from one charming object to another, brightening as they looked, till they came to Aunt Jo's merry face; there they stopped as the happy little girl hugged her, saying gratefully,

'O Aunty, it's a splendid new play! can I really cook at the dear stove, and have parties and mess, and sweep, and make fires that truly burn? I like it so much! What made you think of it?'

'Your liking to make gingersnaps with Asia made

me think of it,' said Mrs Bhaer, holding Daisy, who frisked as if she would fly. 'I knew Asia wouldn't let you mess in her kitchen very often, and it wouldn't be safe at this fire up here, so I thought I'd see if I could find a little stove for you, and teach you to cook; that would be fun, and useful too. So I travelled round among the toy shops, but everything large cost too much and I was thinking I should have to give it up, when I met Uncle Teddy. As soon as he knew what I was about, he said he wanted to help, and insisted on buying the biggest toy stove we could find. I scolded, but he only laughed, and teased me about my cooking when we were young, and said I must teach Bess as well as you, and went on buying all sorts of nice little things for my "cooking class", as he called it.'

'I'm so glad you met him!' said Daisy, as Mrs Jo stopped to laugh at the memory of the funny time she had with Uncle Teddy.

'You must study hard and learn to make all kinds of things, for he says he shall come out to tea very often, and expects something uncommonly nice.'

'It's the sweetest, dearest kitchen in the world, and I'd rather study with it than do anything else. Can't I learn pies, and cake, and macaroni, and everything?' cried Daisy, dancing round the room with a new saucepan in one hand and the tiny poker in the other.

'All in good time. This is to be a useful play, I am to help you, and you are to be my cook, so I shall tell you what to do, and show you how. Then we shall have things fit to eat, and you will be really learning how to cook on a small scale. I'll call you Sally, and say you are a new girl just come,' added Mrs Jo, settling down to work, while Teddy sat on the floor sucking his thumb, and staring at the stove as if it was a live thing, whose appearance deeply interested him.

'That will be so lovely! What shall I do first?' asked Sally, with such a happy face and willing air that Aunt Jo wished all new cooks were half as pretty and pleasant.

'First of all, put on this clean cap and apron. I am rather old-fashioned, and I like my cook to be very tidy.'

Sally tucked her curly hair into the round cap, and put on the apron without a murmur, though usually she rebelled against bibs.

'Now, you can put things in order, and wash up the new china. The old set needs washing also, for my last girl was apt to leave it in a sad state after a party.'

Aunt Jo spoke quite soberly, but Sally laughed, for she knew who the untidy girl was who had left the cups sticky. Then she turned up her cuffs, and with a sigh of satisfaction began to stir about her kitchen, having little raptures now and then over the 'sweet rolling pin', the 'darling dish-tub', or the 'cunning pepper-pot'.

'Now, Sally, take your basket and go to market; here is the list of things I want for dinner,' said Mrs Jo, giving her a bit of paper when the dishes were all in order.

'Where is the market?' asked Daisy, thinking that the new play got more and more interesting every minute.

'Asia is the market.'

Away went Sally, causing another stir in the school-room as she passed the door in her new costume, and whispered to Demi, with a face full of delight, 'It's a perfectly splendid play!'

Old Asia enjoyed the joke as much as Daisy, and laughed jollily as the little girl came flying into the room with her cap all on one side, the lids of her basket rattling like castanets, and looking like a very crazy little cook.

'Mrs Aunt Jo wants these things, and I must have them right away,' said Daisy, importantly.

'Let's see, honey; here's two pounds of steak, potatoes, squash, apples, bread, and butter. The meat ain't come yet; when it does I'll send it up. The other things are all handy.'

Then Asia packed one potato, one apple, a bit of squash, a little pat of butter, and a roll, into the basket, telling Sally to be on the watch for the butcher's boy, because he sometimes played tricks.

'Who is he?' and Daisy hoped it would be Demi.

'You'll see,' was all Asia would say; and Sally went off in great spirits, singing a verse from dear Mary Howitt's sweet story in rhyme,

> *'Away went little Mabel,*
> *With the wheaten cake so fine,*
> *The new-made pot of butter,*
> *And the little flask of wine.'*

'Put everything but the apple into the store-closet for the present,' said Mrs Jo, when the cook got home.

There was a cupboard under the middle shelf, and on opening the door fresh delights appeared. One half was evidently the cellar, for wood, coal, and kindlings were piled there. The other half was full of little jars, boxes, and all sorts of droll contrivances for holding small quantities of flour, meal, sugar, salt, and other household stores. A pot of jam was there, a little tin box of gingerbread, a cologne bottle full of currant wine, and a tiny canister of tea. But the crowning charm was two doll's pans of new milk with cream actually rising on it, and a wee skimmer all ready to skim it with. Daisy clasped her hands at this delicious spectacle, and wanted to skim immediately. But Aunt Jo said,

'Not yet; you will want the cream to eat on your apple-pie at dinner, and must not disturb it till then.'

'Am I going to have pie?' cried Daisy, hardly believing that such bliss could be in store for her.

'Yes; if your oven does well we will have two pies, one apple and one strawberry,' said Mrs Jo, who was nearly as much interested in the new play as Daisy herself.

'Oh, what next?' asked Sally, all impatience to begin.

'Shut the lower draught of the stove, so that the oven may heat. Then wash your hands and get out the flour, sugar, salt, butter and cinnamon. See if the pie-board is clean, and pare your apple ready to put in.'

Daisy got things together with as little noise and spilling as could be expected, from so young a cook.

'I really don't know how to measure for such tiny pies; I must guess at it, and if these don't succeed, we must try again,' said Mrs Jo, looking rather perplexed, and very much amused with the small concern before her. 'Take that little pan full of flour, put in a pinch of salt, and then rub in as much butter as will go on that plate. Always remember to put your dry things together first, and then the wet. It mixes better so.'

'I know how; I saw Asia do it. Don't I butter the pie plates too? She did, the first thing,' said Daisy, whisking the flour about at a great rate.

'Quite right! I do believe you have a gift for cooking, you take to it so cleverly,' said Aunt Jo, approvingly. 'Now a dash of cold water, just enough to wet it; then scatter some flour on the board, work in a little, and roll the paste out; yes, that's the way. Now put dabs of butter all over it, and roll it out again. We won't have our pastry very rich, or the dolls will get dyspeptic.'

Daisy laughed at the idea, and scattered the dabs with a liberal hand. Then she rolled and rolled with her delightful little pin, and having got her paste ready, proceeded to cover the plates with it. Next the apple was sliced in, sugar and cinnamon lavishly sprinkled over it, and then the top crust put on with breathless care.

'I always wanted to cut them round, and Asia never would let me. How nice it is to do it all my ownty donty self!' said Daisy, as the little knife went clipping round the doll's plate poised on her hand.

All cooks, even the best, meet with mishaps sometimes, and Sally's first one occurred then, for the knife went so fast that the plate slipped, turned a somersault in the air, and landed the dear little pie upside down on the floor. Sally screamed, Mrs Jo laughed, Teddy scrambled to get it, and for a moment confusion reigned in the new kitchen.

'It didn't spill or break, because I pinched the edges together so hard; it isn't hurt a bit, so I'll prick holes in it, and then it will be ready,' said Sally, picking up the capsized treasure and putting it into shape with a childlike disregard of the dust it had gathered in its fall.

'My new cook has a good temper, I see, and that is such a comfort,' said Mrs Jo. 'Now open the jar of strawberry jam, fill the uncovered pie, and put some strips of paste over the top as Asia does.'

'I'll make a D in the middle, and have zigzags all round; that will be so interesting when I come to eat it,' said Sally, loading her pie with quirls and flourishes that would have driven a real pastry cook wild. '*Now* I put them in!' she exclaimed, when the last grimy knob had been carefully planted in the red field of jam, and with an air of triumph she shut them into the little oven.

'Clear up your things; a good cook never lets her utensils collect. Then pare your squash and potatoes.'

'There is only one potato,' giggled Sally.

'Cut it in four pieces, so it will go into the little kettle, and put the bits into cold water till it is time to cook them.'

'Do I soak the squash too?'

'No, indeed! just pare it and cut it up, and put it into the steamer over the pot. It is drier so, though it takes longer to cook.'

Here a scratching at the door caused Sally to run and open it, when Kit appeared with a covered basket in his mouth.

'Here's the butcher's boy!' cried Daisy, much tickled at the idea, as she relieved him of his load, whereat he licked his lips and began to beg, evidently thinking that it was his own dinner, for he often carried it to his master in that way. Being undeceived, he departed in great wrath and barked all the way downstairs, to ease his wounded feelings.

In the basket were two bits of steak (doll's pounds), a baked pear, a small cake, and paper with them on which Asia had scrawled, 'For Missy's lunch, if her cookin' don't turn out well.'

'I don't want any of her old pears and things; my cooking *will* turn out well, and I'll have a splendid dinner; see if I don't!' cried Daisy, indignantly.

'We may like them if company should come. It is always well to have something in the store-room,' said Aunt Jo, who had been taught this valuable fact by a series of domestic panics.

'Me is hundry,' announced Teddy, who began to think what with so much cooking going on it was about time for somebody to eat something. His mother gave him her work-basket to rummage, hoping to keep him quiet till dinner was ready, and returned to her housekeeping.

'Put on your vegetables, set the table, and then have some coals kindling ready for the steak.'

What a thing it was to see the potatoes bobbing about in the little pot; to peep at the squash getting soft so fast in the tiny steamer; to whisk open the oven door every five minutes to see how the pies got on, and at last when the coals were red and glowing, to put two real steaks on a finger-long gridiron and proudly turn them with a fork. The potatoes were done first, and no wonder, for they had boiled frantically all the while. They were pounded up with a little pestle, had much butter and no salt put in (cook forgot it in the excitement of the moment), then it was made into a mound in a gay red dish, smoothed over with a knife dipped in milk, and put in the oven to brown.

So absorbed in these last performances had Sally been, that she forgot her pastry till she opened the door to put in the potato, then a wail arose, for, alas! alas! the little pies were burnt black!

'Oh, my pies! my darling pies! they are all spoilt!' cried poor Sally, wringing her dirty little hands as she surveyed the ruin of her work. The tart was especially pathetic, for the quirls and zigzags stuck up in all directions from the blackened jelly, like the walls and chimney of a house after a fire.

'Dear, dear, I forgot to remind you to take them out; it's just my luck,' said Aunt Jo, remorsefully. 'Don't cry, darling, it was my fault; we'll try again after dinner,' she added, as a great tear dropped from Sally's eyes and sizzled on the hot ruins of the tart.

More would have followed, if the steak had not blazed up just then, and so occupied the attention of cook, that she quickly forgot the lost pastry.

'Put the meat-dish and your own plates down to warm, while you mash the squash with butter, salt, and a little pepper on the top,' said Mrs Jo, devoutly hoping that the dinner would meet with no further disasters.

The 'cunning pepper-pot' soothed Sally's feelings, and she dished up her squash in fine style. The dinner was safely put upon the table; the six dolls were seated three on a side; Teddy took the bottom, and Sally the top. When all were settled, it was a most imposing spectacle, for one doll was in full ball costume, another in her night-gown; Jerry, the worsted boy, wore his red winter suit, while Annabella, the noseless darling,

was airily attired in nothing but her own kid skin.
Teddy, as father of the family, behaved with great
propriety, for he smilingly devoured everything offered
him, and did not find a single fault. Daisy beamed
upon her company like the weary, warm, but hospit-
able hostess, so often to be seen at larger tables than
this, and did the honours with an air of innocent
satisfaction, which we do *not* often see elsewhere.

The steak was so tough, that the little carving-knife
would not cut it; the potato did not go round, and
the squash was very lumpy; but the guests appeared
politely unconscious of these trifles; and the master and
mistress of the house cleared the table with appetites
that anyone might envy them. The joy of skimming a
jug-full of cream mitigated the anguish felt for the loss
of the pies, and Asia's despised cake proved a treasure
in the way of dessert.

'That is the nicest lunch I ever had; can't I do it
every day?' asked Daisy as she scraped up and ate the
leavings all round.

'You can cook things every day after lessons, but I
prefer that you should eat your dishes at your regular
meals, and only have a bit of gingerbread for lunch.
Today, being the first time, I don't mind, but we must
keep our rules. This afternoon you can make something for tea if you like,' said Mrs Jo, who had enjoyed
the dinner-party very much, though no one had invited
her to partake.

'Do let me make flapjacks for Demi, he loves them
so, and it's such fun to turn them and put sugar in
between,' cried Daisy, tenderly wiping a yellow stain
off Annabella's broken nose, for Bella had refused to
eat squash when it was pressed upon her as good for

'lumatism', a complaint which it is no wonder she suffered from, considering the lightness of her attire.

'But if you give Demi goodies, all the others will expect some also, and then you will have your hands full.'

'Couldn't I have Demi come up to tea alone just this one time, and after that I could cook things for the others if they were good,' proposed Daisy, with sudden inspiration.

'That is a capital idea, Posy! We will make your little messes rewards for the good boys, and I don't know one among them who would not like something nice to eat more than almost anything else. If little men are like big ones, good cooking will touch their hearts and soothe their tempers delightfully,' added Aunt Jo, with a merry nod toward the door, where stood Papa Bhaer, surveying the scene with a face full of amusement.

'That last hit was for me, sharp woman. I accept it, for it is true; but if I had married thee for thy cooking, heart's dearest, I should have fared badly all these years,' answered the professor, laughing, as he tossed Teddy, who became quite apoplectic in his endeavours to describe the feast he had just enjoyed.

Daisy proudly showed her kitchen, and rashly promised Uncle Fritz as many flapjacks as he could eat. She was just telling about the new rewards when the boys, headed by Demi, burst into the room snuffing the air like a pack of hungry hounds, for school was out, dinner was not ready, and the fragrance of Daisy's steak led them straight to the spot.

A prouder little damsel was never seen than Sally as she displayed her treasures and told the lads what was in store for them. Several rather scoffed at the idea of her cooking anything fit to eat, but Stuffy's heart was won at once, Nat and Demi had firm faith in her skill, and the others said they would wait and see. All admired the kitchen, however, and examined the stove with deep interest. Demi offered to buy the boiler on the spot, to be used in a steam-engine which he was constructing; and Ned declared that the best and biggest saucepan was just the thing to melt his lead in when he ran bullets, hatchets and such trifles.

Daisy looked so alarmed at these proposals, that Mrs Jo then and there made and proclaimed a law that no boy should touch, use, or even approach the sacred stove without a special permit from the owner thereof. This increased its value immensely in the eyes of the gentlemen, especially as any infringement of the law would be punished by the forfeiture of all right to partake of the delicacies promised to the virtuous.

At this point the bell rang, and the entire population went down to dinner, which meal was enlivened by each of the boys giving Daisy a list of things he would like to have cooked for him as fast as he earned them. Daisy, whose faith in her stove was unlimited, promised everything, if Aunt Jo would tell her how to make them. This suggestion rather alarmed Mrs Jo, for some of the dishes were quite beyond her skill – wedding-cake, for instance, bull's eye candy, and cabbage soup with herrings and cherries in it, which Mr Bhaer proposed as his favourite, and immediately reduced his wife to despair, for German cookery was beyond her.

Daisy wanted to begin again the minute dinner was done, but she was only allowed to clear up, fill the kettle ready for tea, and wash out her apron, which looked as if she had cooked a Christmas feast. She was then sent out to play till five o'clock, for Uncle Fritz said that too much study, even at cooking stoves, was bad for little minds and bodies, and Aunt Jo knew by long experience how soon new toys lose their charm if they are not prudently used.

Everyone was very kind to Daisy that afternoon. Tommy promised her the first fruits of his garden, though the only visible crop just then was pigweed; Nat offered to supply her with wood, free of charge; Stuffy quite worshipped her; Ned immediately fell to work on a little refrigerator for her kitchen; and Demi, with a punctuality beautiful to see in one so young, escorted her to the nursery just as the clock struck five. It was not time for the party to begin, but he begged so hard to come in and help that he was allowed privileges few visitors enjoy, for he kindled the fire, ran errands, and watched the progress of his supper with intense interest. Mrs Jo directed the affair as she came and went, being very busy putting up clean curtains all over the house.

'Ask Asia for a cup of sour cream, then your cakes will be light without much soda, which I don't like,' was the first order.

Demi tore downstairs, and returned with the cream, also a puckered-up face, for he had tasted it on his way, and found it so sour that he predicted the cakes would be uneatable. Mrs Jo took this occasion to deliver a short lecture from the step-ladder on the chemical properties of soda, to which Daisy did not listen, but Demi did, and understood it, as he proved by the brief but comprehensive reply,

'Yes, I see, soda turns sour things sweet, and the fizzling up makes them light. Let's see you do it, Daisy.'

'Fill that bowl nearly full of flour and add a little salt to it,' continued Mrs Jo.

'Oh dear, everything has to have salt in it, seems to me,' said Sally, who was tired of opening the pill-box in which it was kept.

'Salt is like good humour, and nearly everything is better for a pinch of it, Posy,' and Uncle Fritz stopped as he passed, hammer in hand, to drive up two or three nails for Sally's little pans to hang on.

'You are not invited to tea, but I'll give you some cakes, and I won't be cross,' said Daisy, putting up her floury little face to thank him with a kiss.

'Fritz, you must not interrupt my cooking class, or I'll come in and moralize when you are teaching Latin. How would you like that?' said Mrs Jo, throwing a great chintz curtain on his head.

'Very much, try it and see,' and the amiable Father Bhaer went singing and tapping about the house like a mammoth woodpecker.

'Put the soda into the cream, and when it "fizzles", as Demi says, stir it into the flour, and beat it up as hard as ever you can. Have your griddle hot, butter it well, and then fry away till I come back,' and Aunt Jo vanished also.

Such a clatter as the little spoon made, and such a beating as the batter got, it quite foamed, I assure you; and when Daisy poured some on to the griddle, it rose like magic into a puffy flapjack, that made Demi's mouth water. To be sure, the first one stuck and scorched, because she forgot the butter, but after that first failure all went well, and six capital little cakes were safely landed in a dish.

'I think I'd like maple-syrup better than sugar,' said Demi from his armchair, where he had settled himself after setting the table in a new and peculiar manner.

'Then go and ask Asia for some,' answered Daisy, going into the bathroom to wash her hands.

While the nursery was empty something dreadful happened. You see, Kit had been feeling hurt all day because he had carried meat safely and yet got none to pay him. He was not a bad dog, but he had his little faults like the rest of us, and could not always resist temptation. Happening to stroll into the nursery at that moment, he smelt the cakes, saw them unguarded on the low table, and never stopping to think of consequences, swallowed all six at one mouthful. I am glad to say that they were very hot, and burned him so badly that he could not repress a surprised yelp. Daisy heard it, ran in, saw the empty dish, also the end of a yellow tail disappearing under the bed. Without a word she seized that tail, pulled out the thief, and shook him till his ears flapped wildly, then bundled him downstairs to the shed, where he spent a lonely evening in the coal-bin.

Cheered by the sympathy which Demi gave her, Daisy made another bowlful of batter, and fried a dozen cakes, which were even better than the others. Indeed, Uncle Fritz after eating two sent up word that he had never tasted any so nice, and every boy at the table below envied Demi at the flapjack party above.

It was a truly delightful supper, for the little teapot lid only fell off three times, and the milk just upset but once; the cakes floated in syrup, and the toast had a delicious beef-steak flavour, owing to cook's using the gridiron to make it on. Demi forgot philosophy, and stuffed like any carnal boy, while Daisy planned sumptuous banquets, and the dolls looked on smiling affably.

'Well, dearies, have you had a good time?' asked Mrs Jo, coming up with Teddy on her shoulder.

'A *very* good time. I shall come again *soon*,' answered Demi, with emphasis.

'I'm afraid you have eaten too much, by the look of the table.'

'No, I haven't; I only ate fifteen cakes, and they were very little ones,' protested Demi, who had kept his sister busy supplying his plate.

'They won't hurt him, they are so nice,' said Daisy, with such a funny mixture of maternal fondness and housewifely pride that Aunt Jo could only smile and say,

'Well, on the whole, the new game is a success, then?'

'*I* like it,' said Demi, as if his approval was all that was necessary.

'It is the dearest play ever made!' cried Daisy, hugging her little dish-tub as she proposed to wash up the cups. 'I just wish everybody had a sweet cooking stove like mine,' she added, regarding it with affection.

'This play ought to have a name,' said Demi, gravely removing the syrup from his countenance with his tongue.

'It has.'

'Oh, what?' asked both children, eagerly.

'Well, I think we will call it Patty pans,' and Aunt Jo retired, satisfied with the success of her last trap to catch a sunbeam.

6

A FIREBRAND

'Please, ma'am, could I speak to you? It is something very important,' said Nat, popping his head in at the door of Mrs Bhaer's room.

It was the fifth head which had popped in during the last half-hour; but Mrs Jo was used to it, so she looked up, and said briskly,

'What is it, my lad?'

Nat came in, shut the door carefully behind him, and said in an eager, anxious tone,

'Dan has come.'

'Who is Dan?'

'He's a boy I used to know when I fiddled round the streets. He sold papers, and he was kind to me, and I saw him the other day in town, and told him how nice it was here, and he's come.'

'But, my dear, that is rather a sudden way to pay a visit.'

'Oh, it isn't a visit; he wants to stay if you will let him!' said Nat, innocently.

'Well, but I don't know about that,' began Mrs Bhaer, rather startled by the coolness of the proposition.

'Why, I thought you liked to have poor boys come and live with you, and be kind to 'em as you were to me,' said Nat, looking surprised and alarmed.

'So I do, but I like to know something about them first. I have to choose them, because there are so many. I have not room for all. I wish I had.'

'I told him to come because I thought you'd like it, but if there isn't room he can go away again,' said Nat, sorrowfully.

The boy's confidence in her hospitality touched Mrs Bhaer, and she could not find the heart to disappoint his hope, and spoil his kind little plan, so she said,

'Tell me about this Dan.'

'I don't know anything, only he hasn't got any folks, and he's poor, and he was good to me, so I'd like to be good to him if I could.'

'Excellent reasons every one; but really, Nat, the house is full, and I don't know where I could put him,' said Mrs Bhaer, more and more inclined to prove herself the haven of refuge he seemed to think her.

'He could have my bed, and I could sleep in the barn. It isn't cold now, and I don't mind, I used to sleep anywhere with father,' said Nat, eagerly.

Something in his speech and face made Mrs Jo put her hand on his shoulder, and say in her kindest tone:

'Bring in your friend, Nat; I think we must find room for him without giving him your place.'

Nat joyfully ran off, and soon returned followed by a most unprepossessing boy, who slouched in and stood looking about him, with a half bold, half sullen look, which made Mrs Bhaer say to herself, after one glance,

'A bad specimen, I am afraid.'

'This is Dan,' said Nat, presenting him as if sure of his welcome.

'Nat tells me you would like to come and stay with us,' began Mrs Jo, in a friendly tone.

'Yes,' was the gruff reply

'Have you no friends to take care of you?'

'No.'

'Say, "No, ma'am,"' whispered Nat.

'Shan't neither,' muttered Dan.

'How old are you?'

'About fourteen.'

'You look older. What can you do?'

'Most anything.'

'If you stay here we shall want you to do as the others do, work and study as well as play. Are you willing to agree to that?'

'Don't mind trying.'

'Well, you can stay a few days, and we will see how we get on together. Take him out, Nat, and amuse him till Mr Bhaer comes home, when we will settle about the matter,' said Mrs Jo, finding it rather difficult to get on with this cool young person, who fixed his big black eyes on her with a hard, suspicious expression, sorrowfully unboyish.

'Come on, Nat,' he said, and slouched out again.

'Thank you, ma'am,' added Nat, as he followed him, feeling without quite understanding the difference in the welcome given to him and to his ungracious friend.

'The fellows are having a circus out in the barn; don't you want to come and see it?' he asked, as they came down the wide steps on to the lawn.

'Are they big fellows?' said Dan.

'No; the big ones are gone fishing.'

'Fire away, then,' said Dan.

Nat led him to the great barn and introduced him to his set, who were disporting themselves among the half-empty lofts. A large circle was marked out with hay on the wide floor, and in the middle stood Demi with a long whip, while Tommy, mounted on the much-enduring Toby, pranced about the circle playing being a monkey.

'You must pay a pin apiece, or you can't see the show,' said Stuffy, who stood by the wheelbarrow in which sat the band, consisting of a pocket-comb blown upon by Ned, and a toy drum beaten spasmodically by Rob.

'He's company, so I'll pay for both,' said Nat, handsomely, as he stuck two crooked pins in the dried mushrooms which served as money-box.

With a nod to the company they seated themselves on a couple of boards, and the performance went on. After the monkey act, Ned gave them a fine specimen of his agility by jumping over an old chair, and running up and down ladders, sailor fashion. Then Demi danced a jig with a gravity beautiful to behold. Nat was called upon to wrestle with Stuffy, and speedily laid that stout youth upon the ground. After this, Tommy proudly advanced to turn a somersault, an accomplishment which he had acquired by painful perseverance, practising in private till every joint of his little frame was black and blue. His feats were received with great applause, and he was about to retire, flushed with pride and a rush of blood to the head, when a scornful voice in the audience was heard to say,

'Ho! that ain't anything!'

'Say that again, will you?' and Tommy bristled up like an angry turkey-cock.

'Do you want to fight?' said Dan, promptly descending from the barrel and doubling up his fists in a businesslike manner.

'No, I don't'; and the candid Thomas retired a step, rather taken aback by the proposition.

'Fighting isn't allowed!' cried the others, much excited.

'You're a nice lot,' sneered Dan.

'Come, if you don't behave, you shan't stay,' said Nat, firing up at that insult to his friends.

'I'd like to see him do better than I did, that's all,' observed Tommy, with a swagger.

'Clear the way, then,' and without the slightest preparation Dan turned three somersaults one after the other and came up on his feet.

'You can't beat that, Tom; you always hit your head and tumble flat,' said Nat, pleased at his friend's success.

Before he could say any more the audience were electrified by three more somersaults backwards, and a short promenade on the hands, head down, feet up. This brought down the house, and Tommy joined in the admiring cries which greeted the accomplished gymnast as he righted himself, and looked at them with an air of calm superiority.

'Do you think I could learn to do it without its hurting me very much?' Tom meekly asked, as he rubbed the elbows which still smarted after the last attempt.

'What will you give me if I'll teach you?' said Dan.

'My new jack-knife; it's got five blades, and only one is broken.'

'Give it here, then.'

Tommy handed it over with an affectionate look at its smooth handle. Dan examined it carefully, then putting it into his pocket, walked off, saying with a wink,

'Keep it up till you learn, that's all.'

A howl of wrath from Tommy was followed by a general uproar, which did not subside till Dan, finding himself in a minority, proposed that they should play stick-knife, and whichever won should have the treasure. Tommy agreed, and the game was played in a circle of excited faces, which all wore an expression of satisfaction, when Tommy won and secured the knife in the depth of his safest pocket.

'You come off with me, and I'll show you round,' said Nat, feeling that he must have a little serious conversation with his friend in private.

What passed between them no one knew, but when they appeared again, Dan was more respectful to everyone, though still gruff in his speech, and rough in his manner; and what else could be expected of the poor lad who had been knocking about the world all his short life with no one to teach him any better?

The boys had decided that they did not like him, and so they left him to Nat, who soon felt rather oppressed by the responsibility, but was too kind-hearted to desert him.

Tommy, however, felt that in spite of the jack-knife transaction, there was a bond of sympathy between them, and longed to return to the interesting subject of somersaults. He soon found an opportunity, for Dan, seeing how much he admired him, grew more amiable, and by the end of the first week was quite intimate with the lively Tom.

Mr Bhaer, when he heard the story and saw Dan, shook his head, but only said quietly,

'The experiment may cost us something, but we will try it.'

If Dan felt any gratitude for his protection, he did not show it, and took without thanks all that was given him. He was ignorant, but very quick to learn when he chose; had sharp eyes to watch what went on about him; a saucy tongue, rough manners, and a temper that was fierce and sullen by turns. He played with all his might, and played well at almost all the games. He was silent and gruff before grown people, and only now and then was thoroughly social among the lads. Few of them really liked him, but few could help admiring his courage and strength, for nothing daunted him, and he knocked tall Franz flat on one occasion with an ease that caused all the others to keep at a respectful distance from his fists. Mr Bhaer watched him silently, and did his best to tame the 'Wild Boy', as they called him, but in private the worthy man shook his head, and said soberly, 'I *hope* the experiment will turn out well, but I am a little afraid it may cost too much.'

Mrs Bhaer lost her patience with him half a dozen times a day, yet never gave him up, and always insisted that there was something good in the lad, after all; for he was kinder to animals than to people, he liked to rove about in the woods, and, best of all, little Ted was fond of him. What the secret was no one could discover, but Baby took to him at once – gabbled and crowed whenever he saw him – preferred his strong back to ride on to any of the others – and called him 'My Danny' out of his own little head. Teddy was the only creature to whom Dan showed any affection, and this was only manifested when he thought no one else could see it; but mothers' eyes are quick, and motherly hearts instinctively divine who love their babies. So Mrs Jo soon saw and felt that there *was* a soft spot in rough Dan, and bided her time to touch and win him.

But an unexpected and decidedly alarming event upset all their plans, and banished Dan from Plumfield.

Tommy, Nat, and Demi began by patronizing Dan, because the other lads rather slighted him; but soon they each felt there was a certain fascination about the bad boy, and from looking down upon him they came to looking up, each for a different reason. Tommy admired his skill and courage; Nat was grateful for past kindness; and Demi regarded him as a sort of animated story book, for when he chose Dan could tell his adventures in a most interesting way. It pleased Dan to have the three favourites like him, and he exerted himself to be agreeable, which was the secret of his success.

The Bhaers were surprised, but hoped the lads would have a good influence over Dan, and waited with some anxiety, trusting that no harm would come of it.

Dan felt they did not quite trust him, and never showed them his best side, but took a wilful pleasure in trying their patience and thwarting their hopes as far as he dared.

Mr Bhaer did not approve of fighting, and did not think it a proof of either manliness or courage for two lads to pommel one another for the amusement of the rest. All sorts of hardy games and exercises were encouraged, and the boys were expected to take hard knocks and tumbles without whining; but black eyes and bloody noses given for the fun of it were forbidden as a foolish and a brutal play.

Dan laughed at this rule, and told such exciting tales of his own valour, and the many frays that he had been in, that some of the lads were fired with a desire to have a regular good 'mill'.

'Don't tell, and I'll show you how,' said Dan; and, getting half a dozen of the lads together behind the barn, he gave them a lesson in boxing, which quite satisfied the ardour of most of them. Emil, however, could not submit to be beaten by a fellow younger than himself – for Emil was past fourteen, and a plucky fellow – so he challenged Dan to a fight. Dan accepted at once, and the others looked on with intense interest.

What little bird carried the news to headquarters no one ever knew, but, in the very hottest of the fray, when Dan and Emil were fighting like a pair of young bulldogs, and the others with fierce, excited faces were cheering them on, Mr Bhaer walked into the ring, plucked the combatants apart with a strong hand, and said, in the voice they seldom heard,

'I can't allow this, boys! Stop it at once; and never let me see it again. I keep a school for boys, not for wild beasts. Look at each other and be ashamed of yourselves.'

'You let me go, and I'll knock him down again,'

shouted Dan, sparring away in spite of the grip on his collar.

'Come on, come on, I ain't thrashed yet!' cried Emil, who had been down five times, but did not know when he was beaten.

'They are playing be gladdy – what-you-call-'ems, like the Romans, Uncle Fritz,' called out Demi, whose eyes were bigger than ever with the excitement of this new pastime.

'They were a fine set of brutes; but we have learned something since then, I hope, and I cannot have you make my barn a Colosseum. Who proposed this?' asked Mr Bhaer.

'Dan,' answered several voices.

'Don't you know that it is forbidden?'

'Yes,' growled Dan, sullenly.

'Then why break the rule?'

'They'll all be molly-coddles, if they don't know how to fight.'

'Have you found Emil a molly-coddle? He doesn't look much like one,' and Mr Bhaer brought the two face to face. Dan had a black eye, and his jacket was torn to rags; but Emil's face was covered with blood from a cut lip and a bruised nose, while a bump on his forehead was already as purple as a plum. In spite of his wounds, however, he still glared upon his foe, and evidently panted to renew the fight.

'He'd make a first-rater if he was taught,' said Dan, unable to withhold the praise from the boy who made it necessary for him to do his best.

'He'll be taught to fence and box by and by, and till then I think he will do very well without any lessons in mauling. Go and wash your faces; and remember,

Dan, if you break any more of the rules again, you will be sent away. That was the bargain; do your part and we will do ours.'

The lads went off, and after a few more words to the spectators, Mr Bhaer followed to bind up the wounds of the young gladiators. Emil went to bed sick, and Dan was an unpleasant spectacle for a week.

But the lawless lad had no thought of obeying, and soon transgressed again.

One Saturday afternoon as a party of the boys went out to play, Tommy said,

'Let's go down to the river, and cut a lot of new fish-poles.'

'Take Toby to drag them back, and one of us can ride him down,' proposed Stuffy, who hated to walk.

'That means *you*, I suppose; well, hurry up, lazy-bones,' said Dan.

Away they went, and having got the poles were about to go home, when Demi unluckily said to Tommy, who was on Toby with a long rod in his hand,

'You look like the picture of the man in the bullfight, only you haven't got a red cloth, or pretty clothes on.'

'I'd like to see one; wouldn't you?' said Tommy, shaking his lance.

'Let's have one; there's old Buttercup in the big meadow, ride at her, Tom, and see her run,' proposed Dan, bent on mischief.

'No, you mustn't,' began Demi, who was learning to distrust Dan's propositions.

'Why not, little fuss-button?' demanded Dan.

'I don't think Uncle Fritz would like it.'

'Did he ever say we must not have a bullfight?'

'No, I don't think he ever did,' admitted Demi.

'Then hold your tongue. Drive on, Tom, and here's a red rag to flap at the old thing. I'll help you to stir her up,' and over the wall went Dan, full of the new game, and the rest followed like a flock of sheep; even Demi, who sat upon the bars, and watched the fun with interest.

Poor Buttercup was not in a very good mood, for she had been lately bereft of her calf, and mourned for the little thing most dismally. Just now she regarded all mankind as her enemies (and I do not blame her), so when the matadore came prancing toward her with the red handkerchief flying at the end of his long lance, she threw up her head, and gave a most appropriate 'Moo!' Tommy rode gallantly at her, and Toby, recognizing an old friend, was quite willing to approach; but when the lance came down on her back with a loud whack, both cow and donkey were surprised and disgusted. Toby backed with a bray of remonstrance, and Buttercup lowered her horns angrily.

'At her again, Tom; she's jolly cross, and will do it capitally!' called Dan, coming up behind with another rod, while Jack and Ned followed his example.

Seeing herself thus beset, and treated with such disrespect, Buttercup trotted round the field, getting more and more bewildered and excited every moment, for whichever way she turned, there was a dreadful boy, yelling and brandishing a new and very disagreeable sort of whip. It was great fun for them, but real misery for her, till she lost patience and turned the tables in the most unexpected manner. All at once she wheeled short round, and charged full at her old friend

Toby, whose conduct cut her to the heart. Poor slow Toby backed so precipitately that he tripped over a stone, and down went horse, matadore, and all, in one ignominious heap, while distracted Buttercup took a surprising leap over the wall, and galloped wildly out of sight down the road.

'Catch her, stop her, head her off! run, boys, run!' shouted Dan, tearing after her at his best pace, for she was Mr Bhaer's pet Alderney, and if anything happened to her, Dan feared it would be all over with him. Such a running and racing and bawling and puffing as there was before she was caught! The fish-poles were left behind; Toby was trotted nearly off his legs in the chase; and every boy was red, breathless, and scared. They found poor Buttercup at last in a flower garden, where she had taken refuge, worn out with the long run. Borrowing a rope for a halter, Dan led her home, followed by a party of very sober young gentlemen, for the cow was in a sad state, having strained her shoulder in jumping, so that she limped, her eyes looked wild, and her glossy coat was wet and muddy.

'You'll catch it this time, Dan,' said Tommy, as he led the wheezing donkey beside the maltreated cow.

'So will you, for you helped.'

'We all did, but Demi,' added Jack.

'He put it into our heads,' said Ned.

'I told you not to do it,' cried Demi, who was most broken-hearted at poor Buttercup's state.

'Old Bhaer will send me off, I guess. Don't care if he does,' muttered Dan, looking worried in spite of his words.

'We'll ask him not to, all of us,' said Demi, and the

others assented with the exception of Stuffy, who cherished the hope that all the punishment might fall on one guilty head. Dan only said, 'Don't bother about me'; but he never forgot it, even though he led the lads astray again, as soon as the temptation came.

When Mr Bhaer saw the animal, and heard the story, he said very little, evidently fearing that he should say too much in the first moments of impatience. Buttercup was made comfortable in her stall, and the boys sent to their rooms till supper-time. This brief respite gave them time to think the matter over, to wonder what the penalty would be, and to try to imagine where Dan would be sent. He whistled briskly in his room, so that no one should think he cared a bit; but while he waited to know his fate, the longing to stay grew stronger and stronger, the more he recalled the comfort and kindness he had known here, the hardship and neglect he had felt elsewhere. He knew they tried to help him, and at the bottom of his heart he was grateful, but his rough life had made him hard and careless, suspicious and wilful. He hated restraint of any sort, and fought against it like an untamed creature, even while he knew it was kindly meant, and dimly felt that he would be the better for it. He made up his mind to be turned adrift again, to knock about the city as he had done nearly all his life; a prospect that made him knit his black brows, and look about the cosy little room with a wistful expression that would have touched a much harder heart than Mr Bhaer's if he had seen it. It vanished instantly, however, when the good man came in, and said in his accustomed grave way,

'I have heard all about it, Dan, and though you have

broken the rules again, I am going to give you one more trial, to please Mother Bhaer.'

Dan flushed up to his forehead at this unexpected reprieve, but he only said in his gruff way,

'I didn't know there was any rule about bull-fighting.'

'As I never expected to have any at Plumfield, I never did make such a rule,' answered Mr Bhaer, smiling in spite of himself at the boy's excuse. Then he added gravely, 'But one of the first and most important of our few laws is the law of kindness to every dumb creature on the place. I want everybody and everything to be happy here, to love, and trust, and serve us, as we try to love and trust and serve them faithfully and willingly. I have often said that you were kinder to the animals than any of the other boys, and Mrs Bhaer liked that trait in you very much, because she thought it showed a good heart. But you have disappointed us in that, and we are sorry, for we hoped to make you quite one of us. Shall we try again?'

Dan's eyes had been on the floor, and his hands nervously picking at the bit of wood he had been whittling as Mr Bhaer came in, but when he heard the kind voice ask that question, he looked up quickly, and said in a more respectful tone than he had ever used before,

'Yes, please.'

'Very well, then, we will say no more, only you will stay at home from the walk tomorrow, as the other boys will and all of you must wait on poor Buttercup till she is well again.'

'I will.'

'Now, go down to supper, and do your best, my boy, more for your own sake than for ours.' Then Mr Bhaer shook hands with him, and Dan went down more tamed by kindness than he would have been by the good whipping which Asia had strongly recommended.

Dan did try for a day or two, but not being used to it, he soon tired and relapsed into his old wilful ways. Mr Bhaer was called from home on business one day, and the boys had no lessons. They liked this, and played hard till bedtime, when most of them turned in and slept like dormice. Dan, however, had a plan in his head, and when he and Nat were alone, he unfolded it.

'Look here!' he said, taking from under his bed a bottle, a cigar, and a pack of cards, 'I'm going to have some fun, and do as I used to with the fellows in town. Here's some beer, I got it off the old man at the station, and this cigar; you can pay for 'em, or Tommy will, he's got heaps of money, and I haven't a cent. I'm going to ask him in; no, you go, they won't mind you.'

'The folks won't like it,' began Nat.

'They won't know. Daddy Bhaer is away, and Mrs Bhaer's busy with Ted; he's got croup or something, and she can't leave him. We shan't sit up late or make any noise, so where's the harm?'

'Asia will know if we burn the lamp long, she always does.'

'No, she won't, I've got the dark lantern on purpose; it don't give much light, and we can shut it quick if we hear anyone coming,' said Dan.

This idea struck Nat as a fine one, and lent an air of

romance to the thing. He started off to tell Tommy, but put his head in again to say,

'You want Demi, too, don't you?'

'No, I don't; the Deacon will roll up eyes and preach if you tell him. He will be asleep, so just tip the wink to Tom and cut back again.'

Nat obeyed, and returned in a minute with Tommy half dressed, rather tousled about the head and very sleepy, but quite ready for fun as usual.

'Now, keep quiet, and I'll show you how to play a first-rate game called "Poker",' said Dan, as the three revellers gathered round the table, on which were set forth the bottle, the cigar, and the cards. 'First we'll all have a drink, then we'll take a go at the "weed", and then we'll play. That's the way men do, and it's jolly fun.'

The beer circulated in a mug, and all three smacked their lips over it, though Nat and Tommy did not like the bitter stuff. The cigar was worse still, but they dared not say so, and each puffed away till he was dizzy or choked when he passed the 'weed' on to his neighbour. Dan liked it, for it seemed like old times when he now and then had a chance to imitate the low men who surrounded him. He drank, and smoked, and swaggered as much like them as he could, and, getting into the spirit of the part he assumed, he soon began to swear under his breath for fear someone should hear him. 'You mustn't; it's wicked to say "Damn"!' cried Tommy, who had followed his leader so far.

'Oh, hang! don't you preach, but play away; it's part of the fun to swear.'

'I'd rather say "thunder-turtles",' said Tommy, who

had composed this interesting exclamation and was very proud of it.

'And I'll say "The devil"; that sounds well,' added Nat, much impressed by Dan's manly ways.

Dan scoffed at their 'nonsense', and swore stoutly as he tried to teach them the new game.

But Tommy was very sleepy, and Nat's head began to ache with the beer and the smoke, so neither of them was very quick to learn, and the game dragged. The room was nearly dark, for the lantern burned badly; they could not laugh loud nor move about much, for Silas slept next door in the shed-chamber, and altogether the party was dull. In the middle of a deal Dan stopped suddenly, called out, 'Who's that?' in a startled tone, and at the same moment drew the slide over the light. A voice in the darkness said tremulously, 'I can't find Tommy,' and then there was the quick patter of bare feet running away down the entry that led from the wing to the main house.

'It's Demi! he's gone to call someone; cut into bed, Tom, and don't tell!' cried Dan, whisking all signs of the revel out of sight, and beginning to tear off his clothes, while Nat did the same.

Tommy flew to his room and dived into bed, where he lay laughing till something burned his hand, when he discovered that he was still clutching the stump of the festive cigar, which he happened to be smoking when the revel broke up.

It was nearly out, and he was about to extinguish it carefully when Nursey's voice was heard, and fearing it would betray him if he hid it in the bed, he threw it underneath, after a final pinch which he thought finished it.

Nursey came in with Demi, who looked much amazed to see the red face of Tommy reposing peacefully upon his pillow.

'He wasn't there just now, because I woke up and could not find him anywhere,' said Demi, pouncing on him.

'What mischief are you at now, bad child?' asked Nursey, with a good-natured shake, which made the sleeper open his eyes to say meekly,

'I only ran into Nat's room to see him about something. Go away, and let me alone; I'm awful sleepy.'

Nursey tucked Demi in, and went off to reconnoitre, but only found two boys slumbering peacefully in Dan's room. 'Some little frolic,' she thought, and as there was no harm done she said nothing to Mrs Bhaer who was busy and worried over little Teddy.

Tommy was sleepy, and telling Demi to mind his own business and not ask questions, he was snoring in ten minutes, little dreaming what was going on under his bed. The cigar did not go out, but smouldered away on the straw carpet till it was nicely on fire, and a hungry little flame went creeping along till the dimity bedcover caught, then the sheets, and then the bed itself. The beer made Tommy sleep heavily, and the smoke stupefied Demi, so they slept on till the fire began to scorch them, and they were in danger of being burned to death.

Franz was sitting up to study, and as he left the schoolroom he smelt the smoke, dashed upstairs and saw it coming in a cloud from the left wing of the house.

Without stopping to call anyone, he ran into the room, dragged the boys from the blazing bed, and splashed all the water he could find at hand on to the flames. It checked but did not quench the fire, and the children, wakened on being tumbled topsy-turvy into a cold hall, began to roar at the top of their voices. Mrs Bhaer instantly appeared, and a minute after Silas burst out of his room shouting 'Fire!' in a tone that raised the whole house. A flock of white goblins with scared faces crowded into the hall, and for a minute everyone was panic-stricken.

Then Mrs Bhaer found her wits, bade Nursey see to the burnt boys, and sent Franz and Silas downstairs for some tubs of wet clothes which she flung on to the bed, over the carpet, and up against the curtains, now burning finely, and threatening to kindle the walls.

Most of the boys stood dumbly looking on, but Dan and Emil worked bravely, running to and fro with water from the bathroom, and helping to pull down the dangerous curtains.

The peril was soon over, and ordering the boys all back to bed, and leaving Silas to watch lest the fire broke out again, Mrs Bhaer and Franz went to see how the poor boys got on. Demi had escaped with one burn and a grand scare, but Tommy had not only most of his hair scorched off his head, but a great burn on his arm, that made him half crazy with the pain. Demi was soon made cosy, and Franz took him away to his own bed, where the kind lad soothed his fright and hummed him to sleep as cosily as a woman. Nursey watched over poor Tommy all night, trying to ease his misery, and Mrs Bhaer vibrated between him and little Teddy with oil and cotton, paregoric and squills, saying to herself from time to time, as if she found great amusement in the thought, 'I always *knew*

Tommy would set the house on fire, and now he has done it!'

When Mr Bhaer got home next morning he found a nice state of things. Tommy in bed, Teddy wheezing like a little grampus, Mrs Jo quite used up and the whole flock of boys so excited that they all talked at once, and almost dragged him by main force to view the ruins. Under his quiet management things soon fell into order, for everyone felt that he was equal to a dozen conflagrations, and worked with a will at whatever task he gave them.

There was no school that morning, but by afternoon the damaged room was put to rights, the invalids were better, and there was time to hear and judge the little culprits quietly. Nat and Tommy told their parts in the mischief, and were honestly sorry for the danger they had brought to the dear old house and all in it. But Dan put on his devil-may-care look, and would not own that there was much harm done.

Now, of all things, Mr Bhaer hated drinking, gambling, and swearing; smoking he had given up that the lads might not be tempted to try it, and it grieved and angered him deeply to find that the boy, with whom he had tried to be most forbearing, should take advantage of his absence to introduce these forbidden vices, and teach his innocent little lads to think it manly and pleasant to indulge in them. He talked long and earnestly to the assembled boys, and ended by saying, with an air of mingled firmness and regret,

'I think Tommy is punished enough, and that scar on his arm will remind him for a long time to let these things alone. Nat's fright will do for him, for he is really sorry, and does try to obey me. But you, Dan, have been many times forgiven, and yet it does no good. I cannot have my boys hurt by your bad example, nor my time wasted in talking to deaf ears, so you can say good-bye to them all, and tell Nursey to put up your things in my little black bag.'

'Oh! sir, where is he going?' cried Nat.

'To a pleasant place up in the country, where I sometimes send boys when they don't do well here. Mr Page is a kind man, and Dan will be happy there if he chooses to do his best.'

'Will he ever come back?' asked Demi.

'That will depend on himself; I hope so.'

As he spoke, Mr Bhaer left the room to write his letter to Mr Page, and the boys crowded round Dan very much as people do about a man who is going on a long and perilous journey to unknown regions.

'I wonder if you'll like it,' began Jack.

'Shan't stay if I don't,' said Dan, coolly.

'Where will you go?' asked Nat.

'I may go to sea, or out west, or take a look at California,' answered Dan, with a reckless air that quite took away the breath of the little boys.

'Oh, don't! stay with Mr Page awhile and then come back here; do, Dan,' pleaded Nat, much affected at the whole affair.

'I don't care where I go, or how long I stay, and I'll be hanged if I ever come back here,' with which wrathful speech Dan went away to put up his things, every one of which Mr Bhaer had given him.

That was the only good-bye he gave the boys, for they were all talking the matter over in the barn when he came down, and he told Nat not to call them. The wagon stood at the door, and Mrs Bhaer came out to speak to Dan, looking so sad that his heart smote him, and he said in a low tone,

'May I say good-bye to Teddy?'

'Yes, dear; go in and kiss him, he will miss his Danny very much.'

No one saw the look in Dan's eyes as he stooped over the crib, and saw the little face light up at first sight of him, but he heard Mrs Bhaer say pleadingly,

'Can't we give the poor lad *one* more trial, Fritz?' and Mr Bhaer answer in his steady way,

'My dear, it is not best, so let him go where he can do no harm to others, while they do good to him, and by and by he shall come back, I promise you.'

'He's the only boy we ever failed with, and I am so grieved, for I thought there was the making of a fine man in him, spite of his faults.'

Dan heard Mrs Bhaer sigh, and he wanted to ask for *one more* trial himself, but his pride would not let him, and he came out with the hard look on his face, shook hands without a word, and drove away with Mr Bhaer, leaving Nat and Mrs Jo to look after him with tears in their eyes.

A few days afterwards they received a letter from Mr Page, saying that Dan was doing well, whereat they all rejoiced. But three weeks later came another letter, saying that Dan had run away, and nothing had been heard of him, whereat they all looked sober, and Mr Bhaer said,

'Perhaps I ought to have given him another chance.'

Mrs Bhaer, however, nodded wisely and answered, 'Don't be troubled, Fritz; the boy will come back to us, I'm sure of it.'

But time went on and no Dan came.

7

NAUGHTY NAN

'Fritz, I've got a new idea,' cried Mrs Bhaer, as she met her husband one day after school.

'Well, my dear, what is it?' and he waited willingly to hear the new plan, for some of Mrs Jo's ideas were so droll, it was impossible to help laughing at them, though usually they were quite sensible, and he was glad to carry them out.

'Daisy needs a companion, and the boys would be all the better for another girl among them; you know we believe in bringing up little men and women together, and it is high time we acted up to our belief. They pet and tyrannize over Daisy by turns, and she is getting spoilt. Then they must learn gentle ways, and improve their manners, and having girls about will do it better than anything else.'

'You are right, as usual. Now, who shall we have?' asked Mr Bhaer, seeing by the look in her eye that Mrs Jo had someone all ready to propose.

'Little Annie Harding.'

'What! Naughty Nan, as the lads call her?' cried Mr Bhaer, looking very much amused.

'Yes, she is running wild at home since her mother died, and is too bright a child to be spoilt by servants. I have had my eye on her for some time, and when I

met her father in town the other day I asked him why
he did not send her to school. He said he would gladly
if he could find as good a school for girls as ours was
for boys. I know he would rejoice to have her come; so
suppose we drive over this afternoon and see about it.'

'Have not you cares enough now, my Jo, without
this little gypsy to torment you?' asked Mr Bhaer,
patting the hand that lay on his arm.

'Oh dear, no,' said Mother Bhaer, briskly. 'I like
it, and never was happier than since I had my wilder-
ness of boys. You see, Fritz, I feel a great sympathy
for Nan, because I was such a naughty child myself
that I know all about it. She is full of spirits, and
only needs to be taught what to do with them to be
as nice a little girl as Daisy. Those quick wits of hers
would enjoy lessons if they were rightly directed, and
what is now a tricksy midget would soon become a
busy, happy child. I know how to manage her, for I
remember how my blessed mother managed me,
and –'

'And if you succeed half as well as she did, you will
have done a magnificent work,' interrupted Mr Bhaer,
who laboured under the delusion that Mrs B. was the
best and most charming woman alive.

'Now, if you make fun of my plan, I'll give you bad
coffee for a week, and then where are you, sir?' cried
Mrs Jo, tweaking him by the ear just as if he was one
of the boys.

'Won't Daisy's hair stand erect with horror at Nan's
wild ways?' asked Mr Bhaer, presently, when Teddy
had swarmed up his waistcoat, and Rob up his back,
for they always flew at their father the minute school
was done.

'At first, perhaps, but it will do Posy good. She is getting prim and Bettyish, and needs stirring up a bit. She always has a good time when Nan comes over to play, and the two will help each other without knowing it. Dear me, half the science of teaching is knowing how much children do for one another, and when to mix them.'

'I only hope she won't turn out another firebrand.'

'My poor Dan! I never can quite forgive myself for letting him go,' sighed Mrs Bhaer.

At the sound of the name, little Teddy, who had never forgotten his friend, struggled down from his father's arms, and trotted to the door, looked out over the sunny lawn with a wistful face, and then trotted back again, saying, as he always did when disappointed of the longed-for sight,

'My Danny's tummin' soon.'

'I really think we ought to have kept him, if only for Teddy's sake, he was so fond of him, and perhaps baby's love would have done for him what we failed to do.'

'I've sometimes felt that myself; but after keeping the boys in a ferment, and nearly burning up the whole family, I thought it safer to remove the firebrand, for a time at least,' said Mr Bhaer.

'Dinner's ready, let me ring the bell,' and Rob began a solo upon that instrument which made it impossible to hear one's self speak.

'Then I may have Nan, may I?' asked Mrs Jo.

'A dozen Nans if you want them, my dear,' answered Mr Bhaer, who had room in his fatherly heart for all the naughty neglected children in the world.

When Mrs Bhaer returned from her drive that

afternoon, before she could unpack the load of little boys, without whom she seldom moved, a small girl of ten skipped out at the back of the carry-all, and ran into the house, shouting,

'Hi, Daisy! where are you?'

Daisy came, and looked pleased to see her guest, but also a trifle alarmed, when Nan said, still prancing, as if it was impossible to keep still,

'I'm going to stay here always, papa says I may, and my box is coming tomorrow, all my things had to be washed and mended, and your aunt came and carried me off. Isn't it great fun?'

'Why, yes. Did you bring your big doll?' asked Daisy, hoping she had, for on the last visit Nan had ravaged the baby house, and insisted on washing Blanche Matilda's plaster face, which spoilt the poor dear's complexion for ever.

'Yes, she's somewhere round,' returned Nan, with unmaternal carelessness. 'I made you a ring coming along, and pulled the hairs out of Dobbin's tail. Don't you want it?' and Nan presented a horse-hair ring in token of friendship, as they had both vowed they would never speak to one another again when they last parted.

Won by the beauty of the offering, Daisy grew more cordial, and proposed retiring to the nursery, but Nan said, 'No, I want to see the boys, and the barn,' and ran off, swinging her hat by one string till it broke, when she left it to its fate on the grass.

'Hullo! Nan!' cried the boys as she bounced in among them with the announcement,

'I'm going to stay.'

'Hooray!' bawled Tommy from the wall on which

he was perched, for Nan was a kindred spirit, and he foresaw 'larks' in the future.

'I can bat; let me play,' said Nan, who could turn her hand to anything, and did not mind hard knocks.

'We ain't playing now, and our side beat without you.'

'I can beat you in running, anyway,' returned Nan, falling back on her strong point.

'Can she?' asked Nat of Jack.

'She runs very well for a girl,' answered Jack, who looked down upon Nan with condescending approval.

'Will you try?' said Nan, longing to display her powers.

'It's too hot,' and Tommy languished against the wall as if quite exhausted.

'What's the matter with Stuffy?' asked Nan, whose quick eyes were roving from face to face.

'Ball hurt his hand; he howls at everything,' answered Jack, scornfully.

'I don't, I never cry, no matter how much I'm hurt; it's babyish,' said Nan, loftily.

'Pooh! I could make you cry in two minutes,' returned Stuffy, rousing up.

'See if you can.'

'Go and pick that bunch of nettles, then,' and Stuffy pointed to a sturdy specimen of that prickly plant growing by the wall.

Nan instantly 'grasped the nettle', pulled it up, and held it with a defiant gesture, in spite of the almost unbearable sting.

'Good for you,' cried the boys, quick to acknowledge courage even in one of the weaker sex.

More nettled than she was, Stuffy determined to get

a cry out of her somehow, and he said tauntingly, 'You are used to poking your hands into everything, so that isn't fair. Now go and bump your head real hard against the barn, and see if you don't howl then.'

'Don't do it,' said Nat, who hated cruelty.

But Nan was off, and running straight at the barn, she gave her head a blow that knocked her flat, and sounded like a battering-ram. Dizzy, but undaunted, she staggered up, saying stoutly, though her face was drawn with pain,

'That hurt, but I don't cry.'

'Do it again,' said Stuffy, angrily; and Nan *would* have done it, but Nat held her; and Tommy, forgetting the heat, flew at Stuffy like a little game-cock, roaring out,

'Stop it, or I'll throw you over the barn!' and so shook and hustled poor Stuffy that for a minute he did not know whether he was on his head or his heels.

'She told me to,' was all he could say, when Tommy let him alone.

'Never mind if she did; it is awfully mean to hurt a little girl,' said Demi, reproachfully.

'Ho! I don't mind; I ain't a little girl, I'm older than you and Daisy; so now,' cried Nan, ungratefully.

'Don't preach, Deacon, you bully Posy every day of your life,' called out the Commodore, who just then hove in sight.

'I don't hurt her; do I, Daisy?' and Demi turned to his sister, who was 'pooring' Nan's tingling hands, and recommending water for the purple lump rapidly developing itself on her forehead.

'You are the best boy in the world,' promptly answered Daisy; adding, as truth compelled her to do,
'You do hurt me sometimes, but you don't mean to.'

'Put away the bats and things, and mind what you
are about, my hearties. No fighting allowed aboard
this ship,' said Emil, who rather lorded it over the
others.

'How do you do, Madge Wildfire?' said Mr Bhaer,
as Nan came in with the rest to supper. 'Give the right
hand, little daughter, and mind thy manners,' he
added, as Nan offered him her left.

'The other hurts me.'

'The poor little hand! what has it been doing to get
those blisters?' he asked, drawing it from behind her
back, where she had put it with a look which made
him think she had been in mischief.

Before Nan could think of any excuse, Daisy burst
out with the whole story, during which Stuffy tried to
hide his face in a bowl of bread and milk. When the
tale was finished, Mr Bhaer looked down the long
table towards his wife, and said with a laugh in his
eyes,

'This rather belongs to your side of the house, so I
won't meddle with it, my dear.'

Mrs Jo knew what he meant, but she liked her little
black sheep all the better for her pluck, though she
only said in her soberest way,

'Do you know why I asked Nan to come here?'

'To plague me,' muttered Stuffy, with his mouth
full.

'To help me make little gentlemen of you, and I
think you have shown that some of you need it.'

Here Stuffy retired into his bowl again, and did not

emerge till Demi made them all laugh by saying, in his slow wondering way,

'How can she, when she's such a tomboy!'

'That's just it, she needs help as much as you, and I expect you to set her an example of good manners.'

'Is she going to be a little gentleman too?' asked Rob.

'She'd like it; wouldn't you, Nan?' added Tommy.

'No, I shouldn't; I hate boys!' said Nan, fiercely, for her hand still smarted, and she began to think that she might have shown her courage in some wiser way.

'I am sorry you hate my boys, because they *can* be well-mannered, and most agreeable when they choose. Kindness in looks and words and ways is true politeness, and anyone can have it if they only try to treat other people as they like to be treated themselves.'

Mrs Bhaer had addressed herself to Nan, but the boys nudged one another, and appeared to take the hint for that time at least, and passed the butter; said 'please', and 'thank you', 'yes, sir', and 'no, ma'am', with unusual elegance and respect. Nan said nothing, but kept herself quiet and refrained from tickling Demi, though strongly tempted to do so, because of the dignified airs he put on. She also appeared to have forgotten her hatred of boys, and played 'I spy' with them till dark. Stuffy was observed to offer her frequent sucks of his candy-ball during the game, which evidently sweetened her temper, for the last thing she said on going to bed was,

'When my battledore and shuttle-cock comes, I'll let you all play with 'em.'

Her first remark in the morning was 'Has my box come?' and when told that it would arrive sometime during the day, she fretted and fumed, and whipped her doll, till Daisy was shocked. She managed to exist, however, till five o'clock, when she disappeared, and was not missed till supper-time, because those at home thought she had gone to the hill with Tommy and Demi.

'I saw her going down the avenue alone as hard as she could pelt,' said Mary Ann, coming in with the hasty-pudding, and finding everyone asking, 'Where is Nan?'

'She has run home, little gypsy!' cried Mrs Bhaer, looking anxious.

'Perhaps she has gone to the station to look after her luggage,' suggested Franz.

'That is impossible, she does not know the way, and if she found it she could never carry the box a mile,' said Mrs Bhaer, beginning to think that her new idea might be rather a hard one to carry out.

'It would be like her,' and Mr Bhaer caught up his hat to go and find the child, when a shout from Jack, who was at the window, made everyone hurry to the door.

There was Miss Nan, to be sure, tugging along a large band-box tied up in a linen bag. Very hot and dusty and tired did she look, but marched stoutly along, and came puffing up to the steps, where she dropped her load with a sigh of relief, and sat down upon it, observing as she crossed her tired arms,

'I couldn't wait any longer, so I went and got it.'

'But you did not know the way,' said Tommy, while the rest stood round enjoying the joke.

'Oh, I found it, I never get lost.'

'It's a mile, how could you go so far?'

'Well, it was pretty far, but I rested a good deal.'

'Wasn't that thing very heavy?'

'It's so round, I couldn't get hold of it good, and I thought my arms would break right off.'

'I don't see how the station-master let you have it,' said Tommy.

'I didn't say anything to him. He was in the little ticket place, and didn't see me, so I just took it off the platform.'

'Run down and tell him it is all right, Franz, or old Dodd will think it is stolen,' said Mr Bhaer, joining in the shout of laughter at Nan's coolness.

'I told you we would send for it if it did not come. Another time you must wait, for you will get into trouble if you run away. Promise me this, or I shall not dare to trust you out of my sight,' said Mrs Bhaer, wiping the dust off Nan's little hot face.

'Well, I won't, only papa tells me not to put off doing things, so I don't.'

'That is rather a poser; I think you had better give her some supper now, and a private lecture by and by,' said Mr Bhaer, too much amused to be angry at the young lady's exploit.

The boys thought it 'great fun', and Nan entertained them all supper-time with an account of her adventures; for a big dog had barked at her, a man had laughed at her, a woman had given her a doughnut, and her hat had fallen into the brook when she stopped to drink, exhausted with her exertion.

'I fancy you will have your hands full now, my dear; Tommy and Nan are quite enough for one woman,' said Mr Bhaer, half an hour later.

'I know it will take some time to tame the child, but

she is such a generous, warm-hearted little thing, I should love her even if she were twice as naughty,' answered Mrs Jo, pointing to the merry group, in the middle of which stood Nan, giving away her things right and left, as lavishly as if the big band-box had no bottom.

It was those good traits that soon made little 'Giddy-gaddy', as they called her, a favourite with everyone. Daisy never complained of being dull again, for Nan invented the most delightful plays, and her pranks rivalled Tommy's, to the amusement of the whole school. She buried her big doll and forgot it for a week, and found it well mildewed when she dug it up. Daisy was in despair, but Nan took it to the painter who was at work about the house, got him to paint it brick red, with staring black eyes, then she dressed it up with feathers, and scarlet flannel, and one of Ned's leaden hatchets; and in the character of an Indian chief, the late Poppydilla tomahawked all the other dolls, and caused the nursery to run red with imaginary gore. She gave away her new shoes to a beggar child, hoping to be allowed to go barefoot, but found it impossible to combine charity and comfort, and was ordered to ask leave before disposing of her clothes. She delighted the boys by making a fire-ship out of a shingle with two large sails wet with turpentine, which she lighted, and then sent the little vessel floating down the brook at dusk. She harnessed the old turkey-cock to a straw wagon, and made him trot round the house at a tremendous pace. She gave her coral necklace for four unhappy kittens, which had been tormented by some heartless lads, and tended them for days as gently as a mother, dressing their wounds with cold cream, feeding them with a doll's spoon, and mourning over them when they died, till she was consoled by one of Demi's best turtles. She made Silas tattoo an anchor on her arm like his, and begged hard to have a blue star on each cheek, but he dared not do it, though she coaxed and scolded till the soft-hearted fellow longed to give in. She rode every animal on the place, from the big horse Andy to the cross pig, from whom she was rescued with difficulty. Whatever the boys dared her to do she instantly attempted, no matter how dangerous it might be, and they were never tired of testing her courage.

Mr Bhaer suggested that they should see who would study best, and Nan found as much pleasure in using her quick wits and fine memory as her active feet and merry tongue, while the lads had to do their best to keep their places, for Nan showed them that girls could do most things as well as boys, and some things better. There were no rewards in school, but Mr Bhaer's 'Well done!' and Mrs Bhaer's good report in the conscience book, taught them to love duty for its own sake, and try to do it faithfully, sure that sooner or later the recompense would come. Little Nan was quick to feel the new atmosphere, to enjoy it, to show that it was what she needed; for this little garden was full of sweet flowers, half hidden by the weeds; and when kind hands gently began to cultivate it, all sorts of green shoots sprung up, promising to blossom beautifully in the warmth of love and care, the best climate for young hearts and souls all the world over.

8

PRANKS AND PLAYS

As there is no particular plan to this story, except to describe a few scenes in the life of Plumfield for the amusement of certain little persons, we will gently ramble along in this chapter and tell some of the pastimes of Mrs Jo's boys. I beg leave to assure my honoured readers that most of the incidents are taken from real life, and that the oddest are the truest; for no person, no matter how vivid an imagination he may have, can invent anything half so droll as the freaks and fancies that originate in the lively brains of little people.

Daisy and Demi were full of these whims, and lived in a world of their own, peopled with lovely or grotesque creatures, to whom they gave the queerest names, and with whom they played the queerest games. One of these nursery inventions was an invisible sprite called 'The Naughty Kitty-mouse', whom the children had believed in, feared, and served for a long time. They seldom spoke of it to anyone else, kept their rites as private as possible; and, as they never tried to describe it even to themselves, this being had a vague mysterious charm very agreeable to Demi, who delighted in elves and goblins. A most whimsical and tyrannical imp was the Naughty Kitty-mouse, and

Daisy found a fearful pleasure in its service, blindly obeying its most absurd demands, which were usually proclaimed from the lips of Demi, whose powers of invention were great. Rob and Teddy sometimes joined in these ceremonies, and considered them excellent fun, although they did not understand half that went on.

One day after school Demi whispered to his sister, with an ominous wag of the head,

'The Kitty-mouse wants us this afternoon.'

'What for?' asked Daisy anxiously.

'A *sackerryfice*,' answered Demi, solemnly. 'There must be a fire behind the big rock at two o'clock, and we must all bring the things we like best, and burn them!' he added, with an awful emphasis on the last words.

'Oh, dear! I love the new paper dollies Aunt Amy painted for me best of anything; must I burn them up?' cried Daisy, who never thought of denying the unseen tyrant anything it demanded.

'Every one. I shall burn my boat, my best scrapbook, and *all* my soldiers,' said Demi, firmly.

'Well, I will; but it's too bad of Kitty-mouse to want our very nicest things,' sighed Daisy.

'A *sackerryfice* means to give up what you are fond of, so we *must*,' explained Demi, to whom the new idea had been suggested by hearing Uncle Fritz describe the customs of the Greeks to the big boys who were reading about them in school.

'Is Rob coming too?' asked Daisy.

'Yes, and he is going to bring his toy village; it is all made of wood, you know, and will burn nicely. We'll have a grand bonfire, and see them blaze up, won't we?'

This brilliant prospect consoled Daisy, and she ate her dinner with a row of paper dolls before her, as a sort of farewell banquet.

At the appointed hour the sacrificial train set forth, each child bearing the treasures demanded by the insatiable Kitty-mouse. Teddy insisted on going also, and seeing that all the others had toys, he tucked a squeaking lamb under one arm, and old Annabella under the other, little dreaming what anguish the latter idol was to give him.

'Where are you going, my chickens?' asked Mrs Jo, as the flock passed her door.

'To play by the big rock; can't we?'

'Yes, only don't go near the pond, and take good care of baby.'

'I always do,' said Daisy, leading forth her charge with a capable air.

'Now, you must all sit round, and not move till I tell you. This flat stone is an altar, and I am going to make a fire on it.'

Demi then proceeded to kindle up a small blaze, as he had seen the boys do at picnics. When the flame burned well, he ordered the company to march round it three times and then stand in a circle.

'I shall begin, and as fast as my things are burnt, you must bring yours.'

With that he solemnly laid on a little paper book full of pictures, pasted in by himself; this was followed by a dilapidated boat, and then one by one the unhappy leaden soldiers marched to death. Not one faltered or hung back, from the splendid red and yellow captain to the small drummer who had lost his legs; all vanished in the flames and mingled in one common pool of melted lead.

'Now, Daisy!' called the high priest of Kitty-mouse, when his rich offerings had been consumed, to the great satisfaction of the children.

'My dear dollies, how *can* I let them go?' moaned Daisy, hugging the entire dozen with a face full of maternal woe.

'You must,' commanded Demi; and with a farewell kiss to each, Daisy laid her blooming dolls upon the coals.

'Let me keep one, the dear blue thing, she is so sweet,' besought the poor little mamma, clutching her last in despair.

'More! more!' growled an awful voice, and Demi cried, 'That's the Kitty-mouse! she must have every one, quick, or she will scratch us.'

In went the precious blue belle, flounces, rosy hat, and all, and nothing but a few black flakes remained of that bright band.

'Stand the houses and trees round, and let them catch themselves; it will be like a real fire then,' said Demi, who liked variety in his 'sackerryfices'.

Charmed by this suggestion, the children arranged the doomed village, laid a line of coals along the main street, and then sat down to watch the conflagration. It was somewhat slow to kindle owing to the paint, but at last one ambitious little cottage blazed up, fired a tree of the palm species, which fell on to the roof of a large family mansion, and in a few minutes the entire town was burning merrily. The wooden population stood and stared at the destruction like blockheads, as they were, till they also caught and blazed away without a cry. It took some time to reduce the town to ashes, and the lookers-on enjoyed the spectacle immensely, cheering as each house fell, dancing like wild Indians when the steeple flamed aloft, and actually casting one wretched little churn-shaped lady, who had escaped to the suburbs, into the very heart of the fire.

The superb success of this last offering excited Teddy to such a degree, that he first threw his lamb into the conflagration, and before it had time even to roast, he planted poor dear Annabella on the funeral pyre. Of course she did not like it, and expressed her anguish and resentment in a way that terrified her infant destroyer. Being covered with kid, she did not blaze, but did what was worse, she *squirmed*. First one leg curled up, then the other, in a very awful and lifelike manner; next she flung her arms over her head as if in great agony; her head itself turned on her shoulders, her glass eyes fell out, and with one final writhe of her whole body, she sank down, a blackened mass, on the ruins of the town. This unexpected demonstration startled everyone and frightened Teddy half out of his little wits. He looked, then screamed and fled toward the house, roaring 'Marmar' at the top of his voice.

Mrs Bhaer heard the outcry and ran to the rescue, but Teddy could only cling to her and pour out in his broken way something about, 'poor Bella hurted', 'a dreat fire', and 'all the dollies dorn'. Fearing some dire mishap, his mother caught him up and hurried to the scene of action, where she found the blind worshippers of Kitty-mouse mourning over the charred remains of the lost darling.

'What have you been at? Tell me all about it,' said Mrs Jo, composing herself to listen patiently, for the culprits looked so penitent, she forgave them beforehand.

With some reluctance Demi explained their play, and Aunt Jo laughed till the tears ran down her cheeks, the children were so solemn, and the play was so absurd.

'I thought you were too sensible to play such a silly game as this. If I had any Kitty-mouse I'd have a good one who liked to play in safe pleasant ways, and not destroy and frighten. Just see what a ruin you have made; all Daisy's pretty dolls, Demi's soliders, and Rob's new village, beside poor Tedd's pet lamb, and dear old Annabella. I shall have to write up in the nursery the verse that used to come in the boxes of toys,

The children of Holland take pleasure in making,
What the children of Boston take pleasure in breaking.

Only I shall put Plumfield instead of Boston.'

'We never will again, truly, truly!' cried the repentant little sinners, much abashed at this reproof.

'Demi told us to,' said Rob.

'Well, I heard Uncle tell about the Greece people, who had altars and things, and so I wanted to be like them, only I hadn't any live creatures to sackerryfice, so we burnt up our toys.'

'Dear me, that is something like the bean story,' said Aunt Jo, laughing again.

'Tell about it,' suggested Daisy, to change the subject.

'Once there was a poor woman who had three or four little children, and she used to lock them up in her room when she went out to work, to keep them safe. One day when she was going away she said,

"Now, my dears, don't let the baby fall out of the window, don't play with the matches, and don't put beans up your noses." Now the children had never dreamed of doing the last thing, but she put it into their heads, and the minute she was gone, they ran and stuffed their naughty little noses full of beans, just to see how it felt, and she found them all crying when she came home.'

'Did it hurt?' asked Rob, with such intense interest that his mother hastily added a warning sequel, lest a new edition of the bean story should appear in her own family.

'Very much, as I know, for when *my* mother told me this story, I was so silly that I went and tried it myself. I had no beans, so I took some little pebbles, and poked several into my nose. I did not like that at all, and wanted to take them out very soon, but one would not come, and I was so ashamed to tell what a goose I had been that I went for hours with the stone still hurting me very much. At last the pain got so bad I had to tell, and when my mother could not get it out the doctor came. Then I was put in a chair and held tight, Rob, while he used his ugly little pinchers till the stone hopped out. Dear me! how my wretched little nose did ache, and how people laughed at me!' and Mrs Jo shook her head in a dismal way, as if the memory of her sufferings was too much for her.

Rob looked deeply impressed and I am glad to say took the warning to heart. Demi proposed that they should bury poor Annabella, and in the interest of the funeral Teddy forgot his fright. Daisy was soon consoled by another batch of dolls from Aunt Amy, and the Naughty Kitty-mouse seemed to be appeased by the last offerings, for she tormented them no more.

'Brops' was the name of a new and absorbing play, invented by Bangs. As the interesting animal is not to be found in any Zoological Garden, unless Du Chaillu has recently brought one from the wilds of Africa, I will mention a few of its peculiar habits and traits, for the benefit of inquiring minds. The Brop is a winged quadruped, with a human face of a youthful and merry aspect. When it walks the earth it grunts, when it soars it gives a shrill hoot, occasionally it goes erect, and talks good English. Its body is usually covered with a substance much resembling a shawl, sometimes red, sometimes blue, often plaid, and, strange to say, they frequently change skins with one another. On their heads they have a horn very like a stiff brown paper lamplighter. Wings of the same substance flap upon their shoulders when they fly; this is never very far from the ground, as they usually fall with violence if they attempt any lofty flights. They browse over the earth, but can sit up and eat like the squirrel. Their favourite nourishment is the seed-cake; apples also are freely taken, and sometimes raw carrots are nibbled when food is scarce. They live in dens, where they have a sort of nest, much like a clothes-basket, in which the little Brops play till their wings are grown. These singular animals quarrel at times, and it is on these occasions that they burst into human speech, call each other names, cry, scold, and sometimes tear off horns and skin, declaring fiercely that they 'won't play'. The few privileged persons who have studied them are inclined to think them a remarkable mixture of the monkey, the sphinx, the roc, and the queer creatures seen by the famous Peter Wilkins.

This game was a great favourite, and the younger children beguiled many a rainy afternoon flapping or creeping about the nursery, acting like little bedlamites and being as merry as little grigs. To be sure, it was rather hard upon clothes, particularly trouser-knees and jacket elbows; but Mrs Bhaer only said, as she patched and darned,

'We do things just as foolish, and not half so harmless. If I could get as much happiness out of it as the little dears do, I'd be a Brop myself.'

Nat's favourite amusements were working in his garden, and sitting in the willow-tree with his violin, for that green nest was a fairy world to him, and there he loved to perch, making music like a happy bird. The lads called him 'Old Chirper', because he was always humming, whistling, or fiddling, and they often stopped a minute in their work or play to listen to the soft tones of the violin, which seemed to lead a little orchestra of summer sounds. The birds appeared to regard him as one of themselves, and fearlessly sat on the fence or lit among the boughs to watch him with their quick bright eyes. The robins in the apple-tree near by evidently considered him a friend, for the father bird hunted insects close beside him, and the little mother brooded as confidingly over her blue eggs as if the boy was only a new sort of blackbird, who cheered her patient watch with his song. The brown brook babbled and sparkled below him, the bees haunted the clover fields on either side, friendly faces peeped at him as they passed, the old house stretched its wide wings hospitably toward him, and with a blessed sense of rest and love and happiness, Nat dreamed for hours in this nook, unconscious what healthful miracles were being wrought upon him.

One listener he had who never tired, and to whom he was more than a mere schoolmate. Poor Billy's chief delight was to lie beside the brook, watching leaves and bits of foam dance by, listening dreamily to the music in the willow-tree. He seemed to think Nat a sort of angel who sat aloft and sang, for a few baby memories still lingered in his mind and seemed to grow brighter at these times. Seeing the interest he took in Nat, Mr Bhaer begged him to help them lift the cloud from the feeble brain by this gentle spell. Glad to do anything to show his gratitude, Nat always smiled on Billy when he followed him about, and let him listen undisturbed to the music which seemed to speak a language he could understand. 'Help one another' was a favourite Plumfield motto, and Nat learned how much sweetness is added to life by trying to live up to it.

Jack Ford's peculiar pastime was buying and selling; and he bid fair to follow in the footsteps of his uncle, a country merchant, who sold a little of everything and made money fast. Jack had seen the sugar sanded, the molasses watered, the butter mixed with lard, and things of that kind, and laboured under the delusion that it was all a proper part of the business. His stock in trade was of a different sort but he made as much as he could out of every worm he sold, and always got the best of the bargain when he traded with the boys for string, knives, fish-hooks, or whatever the article might be. The boys, who all had nicknames, called him 'Skinflint', but Jack did not care as long as the old tobacco-pouch in which he kept his money grew heavier and heavier.

He established a sort of auction-room, and now and

then sold off all the odds and ends he had collected, or helped the lads exchange things with one another. He got bats, balls, hockey-sticks, etc., cheap, from one set of mates, furbished them up, and let them for a few cents a time to another set, often extending his business beyond the gates of Plumfield in spite of the rules. Mr Bhaer put a stop to some of his speculations, and tried to give him a better idea of business talent than mere sharpness in overreaching his neighbours. Now and then Jack made a bad bargain, and felt worse about it than about any failure in lessons or conduct, and took his revenge on the next innocent customer who came along. His account-book was a curiosity; and his quickness at figures quite remarkable. Mr Bhaer praised him for this, and tried to make his sense of honesty and honour as quick; and, by and by, when Jack found that he could not get on without these virtues, he owned that his teacher was right.

Cricket and football the boys had of course; but, after the stirring accounts of those games in the immortal *Tom Brown at Rugby*, no feeble female pen may venture to do more than respectfully allude to them.

Emil spent his holidays on the river or the pond, and drilled the elder lads for a race with certain town boys, who now and then invaded their territory. The race duly came off, but as it ended in a general shipwreck, it was not mentioned in public; and the Commodore had serious thoughts of retiring to a desert island, so disgusted was he with his kind for a time. No desert island being convenient, he was forced to remain among his friends, and found consolation in building a boat-house.

The little girls indulged in the usual plays of their

age improving upon them somewhat as their lively fancies suggested. The chief and most absorbing play was called *Mrs Shakespeare Smith*; the name was provided by Aunt Jo, but the trials of the poor lady were quite original. Daisy was Mrs S. S., and Nan by turns her daughter or a neighbour, Mrs Giddygaddy.

No pen can describe the adventures of these ladies, for in one short afternoon their family was the scene of births, marriages, deaths, floods, earthquakes, tea parties, and balloon ascensions. Millions of miles did these energetic women travel, dressed in hats and habits never seen before by mortal eye, perched on the bed, driving the posts like mettlesome steeds, and bouncing up and down till their heads spun. Fits and fires were the pet afflictions, with a general massacre now and then by way of change. Nan was never tired of inventing fresh combinations, and Daisy followed her leader with blind admiration. Poor Teddy was a frequent victim, and was often rescued from real danger, for the excited ladies were apt to forget that he was not of the same stuff as their long-suffering dolls. Once he was shut into a closet for a dungeon, and forgotten by the girls, who ran off to some out-of-door game. Another time he was half drowned in the bathtub, playing be a 'cunning little whale'. And, worst of all, he was cut down just in time after being hung up for a robber.

But the institution most patronized by all was the Club. It had no other name, and it needed none, being the only one in the neighbourhood. The elder lads got it up, and the younger were occasionally admitted if they behaved well. Tommy and Demi were honorary members, but were always obliged to retire unpleasantly early, owing to circumstances over which they had no control. The proceedings of this club were somewhat peculiar, for it met at all sorts of places and hours, had all manner of queer ceremonies and amusements, and now and then was broken up tempestuously, only to be re-established, however, on a firmer basis.

Rainy evenings the members met in the schoolroom, and passed the time in games; chess, morris, backgammon, fencing matches, recitations, debates, or dramatic performances of a darkly tragical nature. In summer the barn was the rendezvous, and what went on there no uninitiated mortal knows. On sultry evenings the Club adjourned to the brook for aquatic exercises, and the members sat about in airy attire, frog-like and cool. On such occasions the speeches were unusually eloquent, quite flowing, as one might say; and if any orator's remarks displeased the audience, cold water was thrown upon him till his ardour was effectually quenched. Franz was president, and maintained order admirably, considering the unruly nature of the members. Mr Bhaer never interfered with their affairs, and was rewarded for this wise forbearance by being invited now and then to behold the mysteries unveiled, which he appeared to enjoy much.

When Nan came she wished to join the Club, and caused great excitement and division among the gentlemen by presenting endless petitions, both written and spoken, disturbing their solemnities by insulting them through the key-hole, performing vigorous solos on the door, and writing up derisive remarks on walls and fences, for she belonged to the 'Irrepressibles'. Finding these appeals vain, the girls, by the advice of Mrs Jo, got up an institution of their own, which they called the Cosy Club. To this they magnanimously invited the gentlemen whose youth excluded them from the other one, and entertained these favoured beings so well with little suppers, new games devised by Nan, and other pleasing festivities, that, one by one, the elder boys confessed a desire to partake of these more elegant enjoyments, and, after much consultation, finally decided to propose an interchange of civilities.

The members of the Cosy Club were invited to adorn the rival establishment on certain evenings, and to the surprise of the gentlemen their presence was not found to be a restraint upon the conversation or amuse-ment of the regular frequenters which could not be said of all Clubs, I fancy. The ladies responded hand-somely and hospitably to these overtures of peace, and both institutions flourished long and happily.

9

DAISY'S BALL

MRS SHAKESPEARE SMITH would like to have
Mr John Brooke, Mr Thomas Bangs, and Mr
Nathaniel Blake to come to her ball at three
o'clock today.

P.S. Nat must bring his fiddle, so we can dance,
and all the boys must be good, or they cannot
have any of the nice things we have cooked.

This elegant invitation would, I fear, have been
declined, but for the hint given in the last line of the
postscript.

'They *have* been cooking lots of goodies, I smelt
'em. Let's go,' said Tommy.

'We needn't stay after the feast, you know,' added
Demi.

'I never went to a ball. What do you have to do?'
asked Nat.

'Oh, we just play be men, and sit round stiff and
stupid like grown-up folks, and dance to please the
girls. Then we eat up everything, and come away as
soon as we can.'

'I think I could do that,' said Nat, after considering
Tommy's description for a minute.

'I'll write and say we'll come'; and Demi despatched

the following gentlemanly reply,

We will come. Please have lots to eat.

J. B. Esquire

Great was the anxiety of the ladies about their first ball, because if everything went well they intended to give a dinner-party to the chosen few.

'Aunt Jo likes to have the boys play with us, if they are not rough; so we must make them like our balls, then they will do them good,' said Daisy, with her maternal air, as she set the table and surveyed the store of refreshments with an anxious eye.

'Demi and Nat will be good, but Tommy will do something bad, I know he will,' replied Nan, shaking her head over the little cake-basket which she was arranging.

'Then I shall send him right home,' said Daisy, with decision.

'People don't do so at parties, it isn't proper.'

'I shall never ask him any more.'

'That would do. He'd be sorry not to come to the dinner-ball, wouldn't he?'

'I guess he would! we'll have the splendidest things ever seen, won't we? Real soup with a ladle and a tureem (she meant *tureen*), and a little bird for turkey, and gravy, and all kinds of nice vegytubbles.' Daisy never *could* say vegetables properly, and had given up trying.

'It is 'most three, and we ought to dress,' said Nan, who had arranged a fine costume for the occasion, and was anxious to wear it.

'I am the mother, so I shan't dress up much,' said

Daisy, putting on a night-cap ornamented with a red bow, one of her aunt's long skirts, and a shawl; a pair of spectacles and a large pocket handkerchief completed her toilette, making a plump, rosy little matron of her.

Nan had a wreath of artificial flowers, a pair of old pink slippers, a yellow scarf, a green muslin skirt, and a fan made of feathers from the duster; also, as a last touch of elegance, a smelling-bottle without any smell in it.

'I am the daughter, so I rig up a good deal, and I must sing and dance, and talk more than you do. The mothers only get the tea and be proper, you know.'

A sudden very loud knock caused Miss Smith to fly into a chair, and fan herself violently, while her mamma sat bolt upright on the sofa, and tried to look quite calm and 'proper'. Little Bess, who was on a visit, acted the part of maid, and opened the door, saying with a smile, 'Wart in, gemplemun; it's all weady.'

In honour of the occasion, the boys wore high paper collars, tall black hats, and gloves of every colour and material, for they were an afterthought, and not a boy among them had a perfect pair.

'Good day, mum,' said Demi, in a deep voice, which was so hard to keep up that his remarks had to be extremely brief.

Everyone shook hands and then sat down, looking so funny, yet so sober, that the gentlemen forgot their manners, and rolled in their chairs with laughter.

'Oh, don't!' cried Mrs Smith, much distressed.

'You can't ever come again if you act so,' added

Miss Smith, rapping Mr Bangs with her bottle because
he laughed loudest.

'I can't help it, you look so like fury,' gasped Mr
Bangs, with most uncourteous candour.

'So do you, but I shouldn't be so rude as to say so.
He shan't come to the dinner-ball, shall he, Daisy?'
cried Nan, indignantly.

'I think we had better dance now. Did you bring
your fiddle, sir?' asked Mrs Smith, trying to preserve
her polite composure.

'It is outside the door,' and Nat went to get it.

'Better have tea first,' proposed the unabashed
Tommy, winking openly at Demi to remind him that
the sooner the refreshments were secured, the sooner
they could escape.

'No, we never have supper first; and if you don't
dance well you won't have any supper at all, *not one
bit, sir*,' said Mrs Smith, so sternly that her wild
guests saw she was not to be trifled with, and grew
overwhelmingly civil all at once.

'I will take Mr Bangs and teach him the polka, for
he does not know it fit to be seen,' added the hostess,
with a reproachful look that sobered Tommy at once.

Nat struck up, and the ball opened with two couples,
who went conscientiously through a somewhat varied
dance. The ladies did well, because they liked it, but
the gentlemen exerted themselves from more selfish
motives, for each felt that he must earn his supper,
and laboured manfully toward that end. When everyone was out of breath they were allowed to rest; and,
indeed, poor Mrs Smith needed it, for her long dress
had tripped her up many times. The little maid passed
round molasses and water in such small cups that one

guest actually emptied nine. I refrain from mentioning his name, because this mild beverage affected him so much that he put cup and all into his mouth at the ninth round, and choked himself publicly.

'You must ask Nan to play and sing now,' said Daisy to her brother, who sat looking very much like an owl, as he gravely regarded the festive scene between his high collars.

'Give us a song, mum,' said the obedient guest, secretly wondering where the piano was.

Miss Smith sailed up to an old secretary which stood in the room, threw back the lid of the writing-desk, and sitting down before it, accompanied herself with a vigour which made the old desk rattle as she sang that new and lovely song, beginning

> *'Gaily the troubadour*
> *Touched his guitar,*
> *As he was hastening*
> *Home from the war.'*

The gentlemen applauded so enthusiastically that she gave them 'Bounding Billows', 'Little Bo-Peep', and other gems of song, till they were obliged to hint that they had had enough. Grateful for the praises bestowed upon her daughter, Mrs Smith graciously announced,

'*Now* we will have tea. Sit down carefully, and don't grab.'

It was beautiful to see the air of pride with which the good lady did the honours of her table, and the calmness with which she bore the little mishaps that occurred. The best pie flew wildly on the floor when she tried to cut it with a very dull knife; the bread and butter vanished with a rapidity calculated to dismay a housekeeper's soul; and, worst of all, the custards were so soft that they had to be drunk up, instead of being eaten elegantly with the new tin spoons.

I grieve to state that Miss Smith squabbled with the maid for the best jumble, which caused Bess to toss the whole dish into the air, and burst out crying amid a rain of falling cakes. She was comforted by a seat at the table, and the sugar-bowl to empty; but during this flurry a large plate of patties was mysteriously lost, and could not be found. They were the chief ornament of the feast, and Mrs Smith was indignant at the loss, for she had made them herself, and they were beautiful to behold. I put it to any lady if it was not hard to have one dozen delicious patties (made of flour, salt, and water, with a large raisin in the middle of each, and much sugar over the whole) swept away at one fell swoop?

'You hid them, Tommy; I know you did!' cried the outraged hostess, threatening her suspected guest with the milk-pot.

'I didn't!'

'You did!'

'It isn't proper to contradict,' said Nan, who was hastily eating up the jelly during the fray.

'Give them back, Demi,' said Tommy.

'That's a fib, you've got them in your own pocket,' bawled Demi, roused by the false accusation.

'Let's take 'em away from him. It's too bad to make Daisy cry,' suggested Nat, who found his first ball more exciting than he expected.

Daisy was already weeping, Bess like a devoted

servant mingled her tears with those of her mistress, and Nan denounced the entire race of boys as 'plaguey things'. Meanwhile the battle raged among the gentlemen, for, when the two defenders of innocence fell upon the foe, that hardened youth intrenched himself behind a table and pelted them with the stolen tarts, which were very effective missiles, being nearly as hard as bullets. While his ammunition held out the besieged prospered, but the moment the last patty flew over the parapet, the villain was seized, dragged howling from the room, and cast upon the hall floor in an ignominious heap. The conquerors then returned flushed with victory, and while Demi consoled poor Mrs Smith, Nat and Nan collected the scattered tarts, replaced each raisin in its proper bed, and rearranged the dish so that it really looked almost as well as ever. But their glory had departed, for the sugar was gone, and no one cared to eat them after the insult offered to them.

'I guess we had better go,' said Demi, suddenly, as Aunt Jo's voice was heard on the stairs.

'P'r'aps we had,' and Nat hastily dropped a stray jumble that he had just picked up.

But Mrs Jo was among them before the retreat was accomplished, and into her sympathetic ear the young ladies poured the story of their woes.

'No more balls for these boys till they have atoned for this bad behaviour by doing something kind to you,' said Mrs Jo, shaking her head at the three culprits.

'We were only in fun,' began Demi.

'I don't like fun that makes other people unhappy. I am disappointed in you, Demi, for I hoped you would never learn to tease Daisy. Such a kind little sister as she is to you.'

'Boys always tease their sisters; Tom says so,' muttered Demi.

'I don't intend that *my* boys shall, and I must send Daisy home if you cannot play happily together,' said Aunt Jo, soberly.

At this awful threat, Demi sidled up to his sister, and Daisy hastily dried her tears, for to be separated was the worst misfortune that could happen to the twins.

'Nat was bad too, and Tommy was baddest of all,' observed Nan, fearing that two of the sinners would not get their fair share of punishment.

'I am sorry,' said Nat, much ashamed.

'I ain't!' bawled Tommy through the keyhole, where he was listening, with all his might.

Mrs Jo wanted very much to laugh, but kept her countenance, and said impressively, as she pointed to the door,

'You can go, boys, but remember, you are not to speak to or play with the little girls till I give you leave. You don't deserve the pleasure, so I forbid it.'

The ill-mannered young gentlemen hastily retired, to be received outside with derision and scorn by the unrepentant Bangs, who would not associate with them for at least fifteen minutes. Daisy was soon consoled for the failure of her ball, but lamented the edict that parted her from her brother, and mourned over his shortcomings in her tender little heart. Nan rather enjoyed the trouble, and went about turning up her pug nose at the three, especially Tommy, who pretended not to care, and loudly proclaimed his satisfaction at being rid of those 'stupid girls'. But in his secret soul he soon repented of the rash act that caused this banishment from the society he loved, and every hour of separation taught him the value of the 'stupid girls'.

The others gave in very soon, and longed to be friends, for now there was no Daisy to pet and cook for them; no Nan to amuse and doctor them; and, worst of all, no Mrs Jo to make home pleasant and life easy for them. To their great affliction, Mrs Jo seemed to consider herself one of the offended girls, for she hardly spoke to the outcasts, looked as if she did not see them when she passed, and was always too busy now to attend to their requests. This sudden and entire exile from favour cast a gloom over their souls, for when Mother Bhaer deserted them, their sun had set at noon-day, as it were, and they had no refuge left.

This unnatural state of things actually lasted for three days, then they could bear it no longer, and fearing that the eclipse might become total, went to Mr Bhaer for help and counsel.

It is my private opinion that he had received instructions how to behave if the case should be laid before him. But no one suspected it, and he gave the afflicted boys some advice, which they gratefully accepted and carried out in the following manner:

Secluding themselves in the garret, they devoted several play-hours to the manufacture of some mysterious machine, which took so much paste that Asia grumbled, and the little girls wondered mightily. Nan nearly got her inquisitive nose pinched in the door, trying to see what was going on, and Daisy sat about, openly lamenting that they could not all play nicely together, and not have any dreadful secrets. Wednesday afternoon was fine, and after a good deal of consultation about wind and weather, Nat and Tommy went off, bearing an immense flat parcel hidden under many newspapers. Nan nearly died with suppressed curiosity, Daisy nearly cried with vexation, and both quite trembled with interest when Demi marched into Mrs Bhaer's room, hat in hand, and said, in the politest tone possible to a mortal boy of his years,

'Please, Aunt Jo, would you and the girls come out to a surprise party we have made for you? Do, it's a *very* nice one.'

'Thank you, we will come with pleasure; only, I must take Teddy with me,' replied Mrs Bhaer, with a smile that cheered Demi like sunshine after rain.

'We'd like to have him. The little wagon is all ready for the girls; and you won't mind walking just up to Pennyroyal Hill, will you, Aunty?'

'I should like it exceedingly; but are you quite sure I shall not be in the way?'

'Oh, no, indeed! we want you very much; and the party will be spoilt if you don't come,' cried Demi, with great earnestness.

'Thank you kindly, sir'; and Aunt Jo made him a grand curtsey, for she liked frolics as well as any of them.

'Now, young ladies, we must not keep them waiting; on with the hats, and let us be off at once. I'm all impatience to know what the surprise is.'

As Mrs Bhaer spoke everyone bustled about, and in five minutes the three little girls and Teddy were packed into the 'clothes-basket', as they called the wicker wagon which Toby drew. Demi walked at the head of the procession, and Mrs Jo brought up the rear, escorted by Kit. It was a most imposing party, I assure you, for Toby had a red feather-duster on his head, two remarkable flags waved over the carriage, Kit had a blue bow on his neck, which nearly drove him wild, Demi wore a nosegay of dandelions in his buttonhole, and Mrs Jo carried the queer Japanese umbrella in honour of the occasion.

The girls had little flutters of excitement all the way; and Teddy was so charmed with the drive that he kept dropping his hat overboard, and when it was taken from him he prepared to tumble out himself, evidently feeling that it behoved him to do something for the amusement of the party.

When they came to the hill 'nothing was to be seen but the grass blowing in the wind', as the fairy books say, and the children looked disappointed. But Demi said, in his most impressive manner,

'Now, you all get out and stand still and the surprise party will come in'; with which remark he retired behind a rock, over which heads had been bobbing at intervals for the last half-hour.

A short pause of intense suspense, and then Nat, Demi, and Tommy marched forth, each bearing a new kite, which they presented to the three young ladies. Shrieks of delight arose, but were silenced by the boys, who said, with faces brimful of merriment, 'That isn't all the surprise'; and, running behind the rock, again emerged bearing a fourth kite of superb size, on which was printed, in bright yellow letters, 'For Mother Bhaer'.

'We thought you'd like one, too, because you were angry with us, and took the girls' part,' cried all three, shaking with laughter, for this part of the affair evidently *was* a surprise to Mrs Jo.

She clapped her hands, and joined in the laugh, looking thoroughly tickled at the joke.

'Now, boys, that is regularly splendid! Who did think of it?' she asked, receiving the monster kite with as much pleasure as the little girls did theirs.

'Uncle Fritz proposed it when we planned to make the others; he said you'd like it, so we made a bouncer,' answered Demi, beaming with satisfaction at the success of the plot.

'Uncle Fritz knows what I like. Yes, these are magnificent kites, and we were wishing we had some the other day when you were flying yours, weren't we, girls?'

'That's why we made them for you,' cried Tommy, standing on his head as the most appropriate way of expressing his emotions.

'Let us fly them,' said energetic Nan.

'I don't know how,' began Daisy.

'We'll show you, we want to!' cried all the boys in a burst of devotion, as Demi took Daisy's, Tommy Nan's, and Nat, with difficulty, persuaded Bess to let go her little blue one.

'Aunty, if you will wait a minute, we'll pitch yours for you,' said Demi, feeling that Mrs Bhaer's favour must not be lost again by any neglect of theirs.

'Bless your buttons, dear, I know all about it; and here is a boy who will toss up for me,' added Mrs Jo, as the professor peeped over the rock with a face full of fun.

He came out at once, tossed up the big kite, and Mrs Jo ran off with it in fine style, while the children stood and enjoyed the spectacle. One by one all the kites went up, and floated far overhead like gay birds, balancing themselves on the fresh breeze that blew steadily over the hill. Such a merry time as they had! running and shouting, sending up the kites or pulling them down, watching their antics in the air, and feeling them tug at the string like live creatures trying to escape. Nan was quite wild with the fun, Daisy thought the new play nearly as interesting as dolls, and little Bess was so fond of her 'boo tite', that she would only let it go on very short flights, preferring to hold it in her lap and look at the remarkable pictures painted on it by Tommy's dashing brush. Mrs Jo enjoyed hers immensely, and it acted as if it knew who owned it, for it came tumbling down head first when least expected, caught on trees, nearly pitched into the river, and finally darted away to such a height that it looked a mere speck among the clouds.

By and by everyone got tired, and fastening the kite-strings to trees and fences, all sat down to rest, except Mr Bhaer, who went off to look at the cows, with Teddy on his shoulder.

'Did you ever have such a good time as this before?' asked Nat, as they lay about on the grass, nibbling pennyroyal like a flock of sheep.

'Not since I last flew a kite, years ago, when I was a girl,' answered Mrs Jo.

'I'd like to have known you when you were a girl, you must have been so jolly,' said Nat.

'I was a naughty little girl, I am sorry to say.'

'I like naughty little girls,' observed Tommy, looking at Nan, who made a frightful grimace at him in return for the compliment.

'Why don't I remember you then, Aunty? Was I too young?' asked Demi.

'Rather, dear.'

'I suppose my memory hadn't come then. Grandpa says that different parts of the mind unfold as we grow up, and the memory part of my mind hadn't unfolded when you were little, so I can't remember how you looked,' explained Demi.

'Now, little Socrates, you had better keep that question for grandpa, it is beyond me,' said Aunt Jo, putting on the extinguisher.

'Well, I will, *he* knows about those things, and *you* don't,' returned Demi, feeling that on the whole kites were better adapted to the comprehension of the present company.

'Tell about the last time you flew a kite,' said Nat, for Mrs Jo had laughed as she spoke of it, and he thought it might be interesting.

'Oh, it was only rather funny, for I was a great girl of fifteen, and was ashamed to be seen at such a play. So Uncle Teddy and I privately made our kites, and stole away to fly them. We had a capital time, and were resting as we are now, when suddenly we heard voices, and saw a party of young ladies and gentlemen coming back from a picnic. Teddy did not mind, though he was rather a large boy to be playing with a kite, but I was in a great flurry, for I knew I should be sadly laughed at, and never hear the last of it, because my wild ways amused the neighbours as much as Nan's do us.

'"What shall I do?" I whispered to Teddy, as the voices drew nearer and nearer.

'"I'll show you," he said, and whipping out his knife he cut the strings. Away flew the kites, and when the people came up we were picking flowers as properly as you please. They never suspected us, and we had a grand laugh over our narrow escape.'

'Were the kites lost, Aunty?' asked Daisy.

'Quite lost, but I did not care, for I made up my mind that it would be best to wait till I was an old lady before I played with kites again; and you see I have waited,' said Mrs Jo, beginning to pull in the big kite, for it was getting late.

'Must we go now?'

'I must, or you won't have any supper; and that sort of surprise party would not suit you, I think, my chickens.'

'Hasn't our party been a nice one?' asked Tommy, complacently.

'Splendid!' answered everyone.

'Do you know why? It is because *your* guests have behaved themselves, and tried to make everything go well. You understand what I mean, don't you?'

'Yes'm,' was all the boys said, but they stole a shamefaced look at one another, as they meekly shouldered their kites and walked home, thinking of another party where the guests had *not* behaved themselves, and things had gone badly on account of it.

10

HOME AGAIN

July had come, and haying begun; the little gardens were doing finely, and the long summer days were full of pleasant hours. The house stood open from morning till night, and the lads lived out of doors, except at school time. The lessons were short, and there were many holidays, for the Bhaers believed in cultivating healthy bodies by much exercise, and our short summers are best used in out-of-door work. Such a rosy, sunburnt, hearty set as the boys became; such appetites as they had; such sturdy arms and legs, as outgrew jackets and trousers; such laughing and racing all over the place; such antics in house and barn; such adventures in the tramps over hill and dale; and such satisfaction in the hearts of the worthy Bhaers, as they saw their flock prospering in mind and body, I cannot begin to describe. Only one thing was needed to make them quite happy, and it came when they least expected it.

One balmy night when the little lads were in bed, the elder ones bathing down at the brook, and Mrs Bhaer undressing Teddy in her parlour, he suddenly cried out, 'Oh, my Danny!' and pointed to the window, where the moon shone brightly.

'No, lovey, he is not there, it was the pretty moon,' said his mother.

'No, no, Danny at a window; Teddy saw him,' persisted baby, much excited.

'It might have been,' and Mrs Bhaer hurried to the window, hoping it would prove true. But the face was gone, and nowhere appeared any signs of a mortal boy; she called his name, ran to the front door with Teddy in his little shirt, and made him call too, thinking the baby voice might have more effect than her own. No one answered, nothing appeared, and they went back much disappointed. Teddy would not be satisfied with the moon, and after he was in his crib kept popping up his head to ask if Danny was not 'tummin' soon'.

By and by he fell asleep, the lads trooped up to bed, the house grew still, and nothing but the chirp of the crickets broke the soft silence of the summer night. Mrs Bhaer sat sewing, for the big basket was always piled with socks, full of portentous holes, and thinking of the lost boy. She had decided that baby had been mistaken, and did not even disturb Mr Bhaer by telling him of the child's fancy, for the poor man got little time to himself till the boys were abed, and he was busy writing letters. It was past ten when she rose to shut up the house. As she paused a minute to enjoy the lovely scene from the steps, something white caught her eye on one of the haycocks scattered over the lawn. The children had been playing there all the afternoon, and, fancying that Nan had left her hat as usual, Mrs Bhaer went out to get it. But as she approached, she saw that it was neither hat nor handkerchief, but a shirt sleeve with a brown hand sticking out of it. She hurried round the haycock, and there lay Dan, fast asleep.

Ragged, dirty, thin, and worn-out he looked; one foot was bare, the other tied up in the old gingham jacket which he had taken from his own back to use as a clumsy bandage for some hurt. He seemed to have hidden himself behind the haycock, but in his sleep had thrown out the arm that had betrayed him. He sighed and muttered as if his dreams disturbed him, and once when he moved, he groaned as if in pain, but still slept on quite spent with weariness.

'He must not lie here,' said Mrs Bhaer, and stooping over him she gently called his name. He opened his eyes and looked at her, as if she was a part of his dream, for he smiled and said drowsily, 'Mother Bhaer, I've come home.'

The look, the words, touched her very much, and she put her hand under his head to lift him up, saying in her cordial way,

'I thought you would, and I'm so glad to see you, Dan.' He seemed to wake thoroughly then, and started up looking about him as if he suddenly remembered where he was, and doubted even that kind welcome. His face changed, and he said in his old rough way,

'I was going off in the morning. I only stopped to peek in, as I went by.'

'But why not come in, Dan? Didn't you hear us call you? Teddy saw, and cried for you.'

'Didn't suppose you'd let me in,' he said, fumbling with a little bundle which he had taken up as if going immediately.

'Try and see,' was all Mrs Bhaer answered, holding out her hand and pointing to the door, where the light shone hospitably.

With a long breath, as if a load was off his mind,

Dan took up a stout stick, and began to limp toward the house, but stopped suddenly, to say inquiringly,

'Mr Bhaer won't like it. I ran away from Page.'

'He knows it, and was sorry, but it will make no difference. Are you lame?' asked Mrs Jo, as he limped on again.

'Getting over a wall a stone fell on my foot and smashed it. I don't mind,' and he did his best to hide the pain each step cost him.

Mrs Bhaer helped him into her own room, and, once there, he dropped into a chair, and laid his head back, white and faint with weariness and suffering.

'My poor Dan! drink this, and then eat a little; you are at home now, and Mother Bhaer will take good care of you.'

He only looked up at her with eyes full of gratitude, as he drank the wine she held to his lips, and then began slowly to eat the food she brought him. Each mouthful seemed to put heart into him, and presently he began to talk as if anxious to have her know all about him.

'Where have you been, Dan?' she asked, beginning to get out some bandages.

'I ran off more'n a month ago. Page was good enough, but too strict. I didn't like it, so I cut away down the river with a man who was going in his boat. That's why they couldn't tell where I'd gone. When I left the man, I worked for a couple of weeks with a farmer, but I thrashed his boy, and then the old man thrashed me, and I ran off again and walked here.'

'All the way?'

'Yes, the man didn't pay me, and I wouldn't ask for it. Took it out in beating the boy,' and Dan laughed, yet looked ashamed, as he glanced at his ragged clothes and dirty hands.

'How did you live? It was a long, long tramp for a boy like you.'

'Oh, I got on well enough, till I hurt my foot. Folks gave me things to eat, and I slept in barns and tramped by day. I got lost trying to make a short cut, or I'd have been here sooner.'

'But if you did not mean to come in and stay with us, what were you going to do?'

'I thought I'd like to see Teddy again, and you; and then I was going back to my old work in the city, only I was so tired I went to sleep on the hay. I'd have been gone in the morning, if you hadn't found me.'

'Are you sorry I did?' and Mrs Jo looked at him with a half merry, half reproachful look, as she knelt down to look at his wounded foot.

The colour came up into Dan's face, and he kept his eyes fixed on his plate, as he said very low, 'No, ma'am, I'm glad, I wanted to stay, but I was afraid you –'

He did not finish, for Mrs Bhaer interrupted him by an exclamation of pity, as she saw his foot, for it was seriously hurt.

'When did you do it?'

'Three days ago.'

'And you have walked on it in this state?'

'I had a stick, and I washed it at every brook I came to, and one woman gave me a rag to put on it.'

'Mr Bhaer must see and dress it at once,' and Mrs Jo hastened into the next room, leaving the door ajar behind her, so that Dan heard all that passed.

'Fritz, that boy has come back.'

'Who? Dan?'

'Yes, Teddy saw him at the window, and we called to him, but he went away and hid behind the haycocks on the lawn. I found him there just now fast asleep, and half dead with weariness and pain. He ran away from Page a month ago, and has been making his way to us ever since. He pretends that he did not mean to let us see him, but go on to the city and his old work, after a look at us. It is evident, however, that the hope of being taken in has led him here through everything, and there he is waiting to know if you will forgive and take him back.'

'Did he say so?'

'His eyes did, and when I waked him, he said, like a lost child, "Mother Bhaer, I've come home." I hadn't the heart to scold him, and just took him in like a poor little black sheep back to the fold. I may keep him, Fritz?'

'Of course you may! This proves to me that we have a hold on the boy's heart, and I would no more send him away now than I would my own Rob.'

Dan heard a soft little sound, as if Mrs Jo thanked her husband without words, and, in the instant's silence that followed, two great tears that had slowly gathered in the boy's eyes brimmed over and rolled down his dusty cheeks. No one saw them, for he brushed them hastily away; but in that little pause I think Dan's old distrust for these good people vanished for ever, the soft spot in his heart was touched, and he felt an impetuous desire to prove himself worthy of the love and pity that was so patient and forgiving. He said nothing, he only wished the wish with all his might, resolved to try in his blind boyish way, and sealed his resolution with the tears which neither pain, fatigue, nor loneliness could wring from him.

'Come and see his foot. I am afraid it is badly hurt, for he has kept on three days through heat and dust, with nothing but water and an old jacket to bind it up with. I tell you, Fritz, that boy is a brave lad, and will make a fine man yet.'

'I hope so, for your sake, enthusiastic woman, your faith deserves success. Now, I will go and see your little Spartan. Where is he?'

'In my room; but, dear, you'll be very kind to him, no matter how gruff he seems. I am sure that is the way to conquer him. He won't bear sternness nor much restraint, but a soft word and infinite patience will lead him as it used to lead me.'

'As if you ever were like this little rascal!' cried Mr Bhaer, laughing, yet half angry at the idea.

'I was in spirit, though I showed it in a different way. I seem to know by instinct how he feels, to understand what will win and touch him, and to sympathize with his temptations and faults. I am glad I do, for it will help me to help him; and if I can make a good man of this wild boy, it will be the best work of my life.'

'God bless the work, and help the worker!'

Mr Bhaer spoke now as earnestly as she had done, and both came in together to find Dan's head down upon his arm, as if he was quite overcome by sleep. But he looked up quickly, and tried to rise as Mr Bhaer said pleasantly,

'So you like Plumfield better than Page's farm. Well, let us see if we can get on more comfortably this time than we did before.'

'Thanky, sir,' said Dan, trying not to be gruff, and finding it easier than he expected.

'Now the foot! Ach! – this is not well. We must have Dr Firth tomorrow. Warm water, Jo, and old linen.'

Mr Bhaer bathed and bound up the wounded foot, while Mrs Jo prepared the only empty bed in the house. It was in the little guest-chamber leading from the parlour, and often used when the lads were poorly, for it saved Mrs Jo from running up and down, and the invalids could see what was going on. When it was ready, Mr Bhaer took the boy in his arms, carried him in, and helped him undress, laid him on the little white bed, and left him with another hand-shake, and a fatherly 'Good night, my son.'

Dan dropped asleep at once, and slept heavily for several hours; then his foot began to throb and ache, and he awoke to toss about uneasily, trying not to groan lest anyone should hear him, for he *was* a brave lad, and did bear pain like 'a little Spartan', as Mr Bhaer called him.

Mrs Jo had a way of flitting about the house at night, to shut the windows if the wind grew chilly, to draw mosquito curtains over Teddy, or look after Tommy, who occasionally walked in his sleep. The least noise waked her, and as she often heard imaginary robbers, cats, and conflagrations, the doors stood open all about, so her quick ear caught the sound of Dan's little moans, and she was up in a minute. He was just giving his hot pillow a despairing thump when a light came glimmering through the hall, and Mrs Jo crept in, looking like a droll ghost, with her hair in a great knob on the top of her head, and a long grey dressing-gown trailing behind her.

'Are you in pain, Dan?'

'It's pretty bad; but I didn't mean to wake you.'

'I'm a sort of owl, always flying about at night. Yes, your foot is like fire; the bandages must be wet again,' and away flapped the maternal owl for more cooling stuff, and a great mug of ice water.

'Oh, that's *so* nice!' sighed Dan, as the wet bandages went on again, and a long draught of water cooled his thirsty throat.

'There, now, sleep your best, and don't be frightened if you see me again, for I'll slip down by and by, and give you another sprinkle.'

As she spoke, Mrs Jo stooped to turn the pillow and smooth the bed-clothes, when, to her great surprise, Dan put his arm round her neck, drew her face down to his, and kissed her, with a broken 'Thank you, ma'am,' which said more than the most eloquent speech could have done; for the hasty kiss, the muttered words, meant, 'I'm sorry, I will try.' She understood it, accepted the unspoken confession, and did not spoil it by any token of surprise. She only remembered that he had no mother, kissed the brown cheek half hidden on the pillow, as if ashamed of that little touch of tenderness, and left him, saying, what he long remembered, 'You are my boy now, and if you choose you can make me proud and glad to say so.'

Once again, just at dawn, she stole down to find him so fast asleep that he did not wake, and showed no sign of consciousness as she wet his foot, except that the lines of pain smoothed themselves away, and left his face quite peaceful.

The day was Sunday, and the house so still that he never waked till near noon, and, looking round him,

saw an eager little face peering in at the door. He held
out his arms, and Teddy tore across the room to cast
himself bodily upon the bed, shouting, 'My Danny's
tum!' as he hugged and wriggled with delight. Mrs
Bhaer appeared next, bringing breakfast, and never
seeming to see how shamefaced Dan looked at the
memory of the little scene last night. Teddy insisted
on giving him his 'betfus', and fed him like a baby,
which, as he was not very hungry, Dan enjoyed very
much.

Then came the doctor, and the poor Spartan had a
bad time of it, for some of the little bones of his foot
were injured, and putting them to rights was such a
painful job that Dan's lips were white, and great drops
stood on his forehead, though he never cried out, and
only held Mrs Jo's hand so tight that it was red long
afterwards.

'You must keep this boy quiet, for a week at least,
and not let him put his foot to the ground. By that
time, I shall know whether he may hop a little with a
crutch, or stick to his bed for a while longer,' said Dr
Firth, putting up the shining instruments that Dan did
not like to see.

'It will get well sometime, won't it?' he asked,
looking alarmed at the word 'crutches'.

'I hope so'; and with that the doctor departed,
leaving Dan much depressed; for the loss of a foot is a
dreadful calamity to an active boy.

'Don't be troubled, I am a famous nurse, and we
will have you tramping about as well as ever in a
month,' said Mrs Jo, taking a hopeful view of the case.

But the fear of being lame haunted Dan, and
even Teddy's caresses did not cheer him; so Mrs Jo

proposed that one or two of the boys should come in and pay him a little visit, and asked whom he would like to see.

'Nat and Demi; I'd like my hat, too, there's something in it I guess they'd like to see. I suppose you threw away my bundle of plunder?' said Dan, looking rather anxious as he put the question.

'No, I kept it, for I thought they must be treasures of some kind, you took such care of them'; and Mrs Jo brought him his old straw hat stuck full of butterflies and beetles, and a handkerchief containing a collection of odd things picked up on his way: birds' eggs, carefully done up in moss, curious shells and stones, bits of fungus, and several little crabs, in a state of great indignation at their imprisonment.

'Could I have something to put these fellers in? Mr Hyde and I found 'em, and they are first-rate ones, so I'd like to keep and watch 'em; can I?' asked Dan, forgetting his foot, and laughing to see the crabs so sidling and backing over the bed.

'Of course you can; Polly's old cage will be just the thing. Don't let them nip Teddy's toes while I get it,' and away went Mrs Jo, leaving Dan overjoyed to find that his treasures were not considered rubbish, and thrown away.

Nat, Demi, and the cage arrived together, and the crabs were settled in their new house, to the great delight of the boys, who, in the excitement of the performance, forgot any awkwardness they might otherwise have felt in greeting the runaway. To these admiring listeners Dan related his adventures much more fully than he had done to the Bhaers. Then he displayed his 'plunder', and described each article so well, that Mrs Jo, who had retired to the next room to leave them free, was surprised and interested, as well as amused, at their boyish chatter.

'How much the lad knows of these things! how absorbed he is in them! and what a mercy it is just now, for he cares so little for books, it would be hard to amuse him while he is laid up; but the boys can supply him with beetles and stones to any extent, and I am glad to find out this taste of his; it is a good one, and may perhaps prove the making of him. If he should turn out a great naturalist, and Nat a musician, I should have cause to be proud of this year's work'; and Mrs Jo sat smiling over her book as she built castles in the air, just as she used to do when a girl, only then they were for herself, and now they were for other people, which is the reason perhaps that some of them came to pass in reality – for charity is an excellent foundation to build anything upon.

Nat was most interested in the adventures, but Demi enjoyed the beetles and butterflies immensely, drinking in the history of their changeful little lives as if it were a new and lovely sort of fairy tale – for, even in his plain way, Dan told it well, and found great satisfaction in the thought that here at least the small philosopher could learn of him. So interested were they in the account of catching a musk rat, whose skin was among the treasures, that Mr Bhaer had to come himself to tell Nat and Demi it was time for the walk. Dan looked so wistfully after them as they ran off, that Father Bhaer proposed carrying him to the sofa in the parlour for a little change of air and scene.

When he was established, and the house quiet, Mrs Jo, who sat near by showing Teddy pictures, said, in an interested tone, as she nodded towards the treasures still in Dan's hands,

'Where did you learn so much about these things?'

'I always liked 'em, but didn't know much till Mr Hyde told me.'

'Who was Mr Hyde?'

'Oh, he was a man who lived round in the woods studying these things – I don't know what you call him – and wrote about frogs, and fishes, and so on. He stayed at Page's, and used to want me to go and help him, and it was great fun, 'cause he told me ever so much, and was uncommon jolly and wise. Hope I'll see him again sometime.'

'I hope you will,' said Mrs Jo, for Dan's face had brightened up, and he was so interested in the matter that he forgot his usual taciturnity.

'Why, he could make birds come to him, and rabbits and squirrels didn't mind him any more than if he was a tree. He never hurt 'em, and they seemed to know him. Did you ever tickle a lizard with a straw?' asked Dan, eagerly.

'No, but I should like to try it.'

'Well, I've done it, and it's so funny to see 'em turn over and stretch out, they like it so much. Mr Hyde used to do it; and he'd make snakes listen to him while he whistled and he knew just when certain flowers would blow, and bees wouldn't sting him, and he'd tell the wonderfullest things about fish and flies, and the Indians and the rocks.'

'I think you were so fond of going with Mr Hyde, you rather neglected Mr Page,' said Mrs Jo, slyly.

'Yes, I did; I hated to have to weed and hoe when I might be tramping round with Mr Hyde. Page thought

such things silly, and called Mr Hyde crazy because
he'd lay hours watching a trout or a bird.'

'Suppose you say lie instead of lay, it is better
grammar,' said Mrs Jo, very gently; and then added,
'Yes, Page is a thorough farmer, and would not understand that a naturalist's work was just as interesting,
and perhaps just as important as his own. Now, Dan,
if you really love these things, as I think you do, and I
am glad to see it, you shall have time to study them
and books to help you; but I want you to do something
besides, and to do it faithfully, else you will be sorry
by and by, and find that you have got to begin again.'

'Yes, ma'am,' said Dan, meekly, and looked a little
scared by the serious tone of the last remarks, for he
hated books, yet had evidently made up his mind to
study anything she proposed.

'Do you see that cabinet with twelve drawers in it?'
was the next very unexpected question.

Dan did see two tall old-fashioned ones standing on
either side of the piano; he knew them well, and had
often seen nice bits of string, nails, brown paper, and
such useful matters come out of the various drawers.
He nodded and smiled. Mrs Jo went on,

'Well, don't you think those drawers would be good
places to put your eggs, and stones, and shells, and
lichens?'

'Oh, splendid, but you wouldn't like my things
"cluttering round", as Mr Page used to say, would
you?' cried Dan, sitting up to survey the old piece of
furniture with sparkling eyes.

'I like litter of that sort; and if I didn't, I should
give you the drawers, because I have a regard for
children's little treasures, and think they should be

treated respectfully. Now, I am going to make a bargain with you, Dan, and I hope you will keep it
honourably. Here are twelve good-sized drawers, one
for each month of the year, and they shall be yours as
fast as you earn them, by doing the little duties that
belong to you. I believe in rewards of a certain kind,
especially for young folks; they help us along, and
though we may begin by being good for the sake of the
reward, if it is rightly used, we shall soon learn to love
goodness for itself.'

'Do you have 'em?' asked Dan, looking as if this was
new talk for him.

'Yes, indeed! I haven't learnt to get on without them
yet. My rewards are not drawers, or presents, or holidays, but they are things which I like as much as you
do the others. The good behaviour and success of my
boys is one of the rewards I love best, and I work for it
as I want you to work for your cabinet. Do what you
dislike, and do it well, and you get two rewards – one,
the prize you see and hold; the other, the satisfaction
of a duty cheerfully performed. Do you understand
that?'

'Yes, ma'am.'

'We all need these little helps; so you shall try to do
your lessons and your work, play kindly with all the
boys, and use your holidays well; and if you bring me
a good report, or if I see and know it without words –
for I'm quick to spy out the good little efforts of my
boys – you shall have a compartment in the drawer for
your treasures. See, some are already divided into four
parts, and I will have the others made in the same
way, a place for each week; and when the drawer is
filled with curious and pretty things, I shall be as

proud of it as you are; prouder, I think – for in the pebbles, mosses, and gay butterflies, I shall see good resolutions carried out, conquered faults, and a promise well kept. Shall we do this, Dan?'

The boy answered with one of the looks which said much, for it showed that he felt and understood her wish and words, although he did not know how to express his interest and gratitude for such care and kindness. She understood the look, and seeing by the colour that flushed up to his forehead that he was touched, as she wished him to be, she said no more about that side of the new plan, but pulled out the upper drawer, dusted it, and set it on two chairs before the sofa, saying briskly,

'Now, let us begin at once by putting those nice beetles in a safe place. These compartments will hold a good deal, you see. I'd pin the butterflies and bugs round the sides; they will be quite safe there, and leave room for the heavy things below. I'll give you some cotton wool, and clean paper and pins, and you can get ready for the week's work.'

'But I can't go out to find any new things,' said Dan, looking piteously at his foot.

'That's true; never mind, we'll let these treasures do for this week, and I dare say the boys will bring you loads of things if you ask them.'

'They don't know the right sort; besides, if I lay, no, *lie* here all the time, I can't work and study, and earn my drawers.'

'There are plenty of lessons you can learn lying there, and several little jobs of work you can do for me.'

'Can I?' and Dan looked both surprised and pleased.

'You can learn to be patient and cheerful in spite of pain and no play. You can amuse Teddy for me, wind cotton, read to me when I sew, and do many things without hurting your foot, which will make the days pass quickly, and not be wasted ones.'

Here Demi ran in with a great butterfly in one hand, and a very ugly little toad in the other.

'See, Dan, I found them, and ran back to give them to you; aren't they beautiful ones?' panted Demi, all out of breath.

Dan laughed at the toad, and said he had no place to put him, but the butterfly was a beauty, and if Mrs Jo would give him a big pin, he would stick it right up in the drawer.

'I don't like to see the poor thing struggle on a pin; if it must be killed, let us put it out of pain at once with a drop of camphor,' said Mrs Jo, getting out the bottle.

'I know how to do it – Mr Hyde always killed 'em that way – but I didn't have any camphor, so I use a pin,' and Dan gently poured a drop on the insect's head, when the pale green wings fluttered an instant, and then grew still.

This dainty little execution was hardly over when Teddy shouted from the bedroom, 'Oh, the little trabs are out, and the big one's eaten 'em all up.' Demi and his aunt ran to the rescue, and found Teddy dancing excitedly in a chair, while two little crabs were scuttling about the floor, having got through the wires of the cage. A third was clinging to the top of the cage, evidently in terror of his life, for below appeared a sad yet funny sight. The big crab had wedged himself into the little recess where Polly's cup used to stand, and there he sat eating one of his relations in the coolest way. All the claws of the poor victim were pulled off, and he was turned upside down, his upper shell held in one claw close under the mouth of the big crab like a dish, while he leisurely ate out of it with the other claw, pausing now and then to turn his queer bulging eyes from side to side, and to put out a slender tongue and lick them in a way that made the children scream with laughter. Mrs Jo carried the cage in for Dan to see the sight, while Demi caught and confined the wanderers under an inverted wash-bowl.

'I'll have to let these fellers go, for I can't keep 'em in the house,' said Dan, with evident regret.

'I'll take care of them for you, if you will tell me how, and they can live in my turtle-tank just as well as not,' said Demi, who found them more interesting even than his beloved slow turtles. So Dan gave him directions about the wants and habits of the crabs, and Demi bore them away to introduce them to their new home and neighbours. 'What a good boy he is!' said Dan, carefully settling the first butterfly, and remembering that Demi had given up his walk to bring it to him.

'He ought to be, for a great deal has been done to make him so.'

'He's had folks to tell him things, and to help him; I haven't,' said Dan, with a sigh, thinking of his neglected childhood, a thing he seldom did, and feeling as if he had not had fair play somehow.

'I know it, dear, and for that reason I don't expect as much from you as from Demi, though he is younger; you shall have all the help that we can give you now, and I hope to teach you how to help yourself in the best way. Have you forgotten what Father Bhaer told you when you were here before, about wanting to be good, and asking God to help you?'

'No, ma'am,' very low.

'Do you try that way still?'

'No, ma'am,' lower still.

'Will you do it every night to please me?'

'Yes, ma'am,' very soberly.

'I shall depend on it, and I think I shall know if you are faithful to your promise, for these things always show to people who believe in them, though not a word is said. Now here is a pleasant story about a boy who hurt his foot worse than you did yours; read it, and see how bravely he bore his troubles.'

She put that charming little book, *The Crofton Boys,* into his hands, and left him for an hour, passing in and out from time to time that he might not feel lonely. Dan did not love to read, but soon got so interested that he was surprised when the boys came home. Daisy brought him a nosegay of wild flowers, and Nan insisted on helping bring him his supper, as he lay on the sofa with the door open into the dining-room, so that he could see the lads at table, and they could nod socially to him over their bread and butter.

Mr Bhaer carried him away to his bed early, and Teddy came in his night-gown to say good night, for he went to his little nest with the birds.

'I want to say my prayers to Danny; may I?' he asked, and when his mother said, 'Yes,' the little fellow knelt down by Dan's bed, and folding his chubby hands, said softly,

'Pease Dod bess everybody, and hep me to be dood.'

Then he went away smiling with sleepy sweetness over his mother's shoulder.

But after the evening talk was done, the evening song sung, and the house grew still with beautiful Sunday silence, Dan lay in his pleasant room wide awake, thinking new thoughts, feeling new hopes and desires stirring in his boyish heart, for two good angels had entered in: love and gratitude began the work which time and effort were to finish; and with an earnest wish to keep his first promise, Dan folded his hands together in the darkness, and softly whispered Teddy's little prayer,

'Please God bless everyone, and help me to be good.'

11

UNCLE TEDDY

For a week Dan only moved from bed to sofa; a long week and a hard one, for the hurt foot was very painful at times, the quiet days very wearisome to the active lad, longing to be out enjoying the summer weather, and especially difficult was it to be patient. But Dan did his best, and everyone helped him in their various ways; so the time passed, and he was rewarded at last by hearing the doctor say, on Saturday morning,

'This foot is doing better than I expected. Give the lad the crutch this afternoon, and let him stump about the house a little.'

'Hooray!' shouted Nat, and raced away to tell the other boys the good news.

Everybody was very glad, and after dinner the whole flock assembled to behold Dan crutch himself up and down the hall a few times before he settled in the porch to hold a sort of *levée*. He was much pleased at the interest and good will shown him, and brightened up more and more every minute; for the boys came to pay their respects, the little girls fussed about him with stools and cushions, and Teddy watched over him as if he was a frail creature unable to do anything for himself. They were still sitting and standing about the steps, when a carriage stopped at the gate, a hat was waved from it, and with a shout of 'Uncle Teddy! Uncle Teddy!' Rob scampered down the avenue as fast as his short legs would carry him. All the boys but Dan ran after him to see who should be first to open the gate, and in a moment the carriage drove up with boys swarming all over it, while Uncle Teddy sat laughing in the midst, with his little daughter on his knee.

'Stop the triumphal car and let Jupiter descend,' he said, and jumping out ran up the steps to meet Mrs Bhaer, who stood smiling and clapping her hands like a girl.

'How goes it, Teddy?'

'All right, Jo.'

Then they shook hands, and Mr Laurie put Bess into her aunt's arms, saying, as the child hugged her tight, 'Goldilocks wanted to see you so much that I ran away with her, for I was quite pining for a sight of you myself. We want to play with your boys for an hour or so, and to see how "the old woman who lived in a shoe, and had so many children she did not know what to do", is getting on.'

'I'm so glad! Play away, and don't get into mischief,' answered Mrs Jo, as the lads crowded round the pretty child, admiring her long golden hair, dainty dress, and lofty ways, for the little 'Princess', as they called her, allowed no one to kiss her, but sat smiling down upon them, and graciously patting their heads with her little, white hands. They all adored her, especially Rob, who considered her a sort of doll, and dared not touch her lest she should break, but worshipped her at a respectful distance, made happy by an occasional mark of favour from her little highness. As she immediately

demanded to see Daisy's kitchen, she was borne off by
Mrs Jo, with a train of small boys following. The
others, all but Nat and Demi, ran away to the menagerie and gardens to have all in order; for Mr Laurie
always took a general survey, and looked disappointed
if things were not flourishing.

Standing on the steps, he turned to Dan, saying like
an old acquaintance, though he had only seen him
once or twice before,

'How is the foot?'

'Better, sir.'

'Rather tired of the house, aren't you?'

'Guess I am!' and Dan's eyes roved away to the
green hills and woods where he longed to be.

'Suppose we take a little turn before the others come
back? That big, easy carriage will be quite safe and
comfortable, and a breath of fresh air will do you
good. Get a cushion and a shawl, Demi, and let's carry
Dan off.'

The boys thought it a capital joke, and Dan looked
delighted, but asked, with an unexpected burst of
virtue,

'Will Mrs Bhaer like it?'

'Oh, yes; we settled all that a minute ago.'

'You didn't say anything about it, so I don't see how
you could,' said Demi, inquisitively.

'We have a way of sending messages to one another,
without any words. It is a great improvement on the
telegraph.'

'I know – it's eyes; I saw you lift your eyebrows,
and nod toward the carriage, and Mrs Bhaer laughed
and nodded back again,' cried Nat, who was quite at
his ease with kind Mr Laurie by this time.

'Right. Now then, come on,' and in a minute Dan found himself settled in the carriage, his foot on a cushion on the seat opposite, nicely covered with a shawl, which fell down from the upper regions in a most mysterious manner, just when they wanted it. Demi climbed up to the box beside Peter, the black coachman. Nat sat next Dan in the place of honour, while Uncle Teddy would sit opposite – to take care of the foot, he said, but really that he might study the faces before him – both so happy, yet so different, for Dan's was square, and brown, and strong, while Nat's was long, and fair, and rather weak, but very amiable with its mild eyes and good forehead.

'By the way, I've got a book somewhere here that you may like to see,' said the oldest boy of the party, diving under the seat and producing a book which made Dan exclaim,

'Oh! by George, isn't that a stunner?' as he turned the leaves, and saw fine plates of butterflies, and birds, and every sort of interesting insect, coloured like life. He was so charmed that he forgot his thanks, but Mr Laurie did not mind, and was quite satisfied to see the boy's eager delight, and to hear his exclamations over certain old friends as he came to them. Nat leaned on his shoulder to look, and Demi turned his back to the horses, and let his feet dangle inside the carriage, so that he might join in the conversation.

When they got among the beetles, Mr Laurie took a curious little object out of his vest-pocket, and laying it in the palm of his hand, said,

'There's a beetle that is thousands of years old'; and then, while the lads examined the queer stone-bug, that looked so old and grey, he told them how it came

out of the wrappings of a mummy, after lying for ages
in a famous tomb. Finding them interested, he went
on to tell about the Egyptians, and the strange and
splendid ruins they have left behind them – the Nile,
and how he sailed up the mighty river, with the handsome dark men to work his boat; how he shot alligators,
saw wonderful beasts and birds; and afterwards crossed
the desert on a camel, who pitched him about like a
ship in a storm.

'Uncle Teddy tells stories 'most as well as Grandpa,'
said Demi, approvingly, when the tale was done, and
the boys' eyes asked for more.

'Thank you,' said Mr Laurie, quite soberly, for he
considered Demi's praise worth having, for children
are good critics in such cases, and to suit them is an
accomplishment that anyone may be proud of.

'Here's another trifle or two that I tucked into my
pocket as I was turning over my traps to see if I had
anything that would amuse Dan,' and Uncle Teddy
produced a fine arrow-head and a string of wampum.

'Oh! tell about the Indians,' cried Demi, who was
fond of playing wigwam.

'Dan knows lots about them,' added Nat.

'More than I do, I dare say. Tell us something,' and
Mr Laurie looked as interested as the other two.

'Mr Hyde told me; he's been among 'em, and can
talk their talk, and likes 'em,' began Dan, flattered by
their attention, but rather embarrassed by having a
grown-up listener.

'What is wampum for?' asked curious Demi, from
his perch.

The others asked questions likewise, and, before he
knew it, Dan was reeling off all Mr Hyde had told

him, as they sailed down the river a few weeks before. Mr Laurie listened well, but found the boy more interesting than the Indians, for Mrs Jo had told him about Dan, and he rather took a fancy to the wild lad, who ran away as he himself had often longed to do, and who was slowly getting tamed by pain and patience.

'I've been thinking that it would be a good plan for you fellows to have a museum of your own; a place in which to collect all the curious and interesting things that you find, and make, and have given you. Mrs Jo is too kind to complain, but it is rather hard for her to have the house littered up with all sorts of rattletraps – half-a-pint of dor-bugs in one of her best vases, for instance, a couple of dead bats nailed up in the back entry, wasps' nests tumbling down on people's heads, and stones lying round everywhere, enough to pave the avenue. There are not many women who would stand that sort of thing, are there, now?'

As Mr Laurie spoke with a merry look in his eyes, the boys laughed and nudged one another, for it was evident that someone told tales out of school, else how could he know of the existence of these inconvenient treasures.

'Where can we put them, then?' said Demi, crossing his legs and leaning down to argue the question.

'In the old carriage-house.'

'But it leaks, and there isn't any window, nor any place to put things, and it's all dust and cobwebs.'

'Wait till Gibbs and I have touched it up a bit, and then see how you like it. He is to come over on Monday to get it ready; then next Saturday I shall come out, and we will fix it up, and make the beginning, at least, of a fine little museum. Everyone can bring his things, and have a place for them; and Dan is to be the head man, because he knows most about such matters, and it will be quiet, pleasant work for him now that he can't knock about much.'

'Won't that be jolly?' cried Nat, while Dan smiled all over his face and had not a word to say, but hugged his book, and looked at Mr Laurie as if he thought him one of the greatest public benefactors that ever blessed the world.

'Shall I go round again, sir?' asked Peter, as they came to the gate, after two slow turns about the half-mile triangle.

'No, we must be prudent, else we can't come again. I must go over the premises, take a look at the carriage-house, and have a little talk with Mrs Jo before I go'; and, having deposited Dan on his sofa to rest and enjoy his book, Uncle Teddy went off to have a frolic with the lads who were raging about the place in search of him. Leaving the little girls to mess upstairs, Mrs Bhaer sat down by Dan, and listened to his eager account of the drive till the flock returned, dusty, warm, and much excited about the new museum, which everyone considered the most brilliant idea of the age.

'I always wanted to endow some sort of an institution, and I am going to begin with this,' said Mr Laurie, sitting down on a stool at Mrs Jo's feet.

'You have endowed one already. What do you call this?' and Mrs Jo pointed to the happy-faced lads, who had camped upon the floor about them.

'I call it a very promising Bhaer-garden, and I'm proud to be a member of it. Did you know I was the head boy in this school?' he asked, turning to Dan, and changing the subject skilfully, for he hated to be thanked for the generous things he did.

'I thought Franz was!' answered Dan, wondering what the man meant.

'Oh, dear no! I'm the first boy Mrs Jo ever had to take care of, and I was such a bad one that she isn't done with me yet, though she has been working at me for years and years.'

'How old she must be!' said Nat, innocently.

'She began early, you see. Poor thing! she was only fifteen when she took me, and I led her such a life, it's a wonder she isn't wrinkled and grey, and quite worn out,' and Mr Laurie looked up at her laughing.

'Don't, Teddy; I won't have you abuse yourself so'; and Mrs Jo stroked the curly black head at her knee as affectionately as ever, for, in spite of everything, Teddy was her boy still.

'If it hadn't been for you, there never would have been a Plumfield. It was my success with you, sir, that gave me courage to try my pet plan. So the boys may thank you for it, and name the new institution "The Laurence Museum", in honour of its founder – won't we, boys?' she added, looking very like the lively Jo of old times.

'We will! we will!' shouted the boys, throwing up their hats, for though they had taken them off on entering the house, according to rule, they had been in too much of a hurry to hang them up.

'I'm as hungry as a bear, can't I have a cookie?' asked Mr Laurie, when the shout subsided and he had expressed his thanks by a splendid bow.

'Trot out and ask Asia for the gingerbread-box,

Demi. It isn't in order to eat between meals, but, on this joyful occasion, we won't mind, and have a cookie all round,' said Mrs Jo; and when the box came she dealt them out with a liberal hands everyone munching away in a social circle.

Suddenly, in the midst of a bite, Mr Laurie cried out, 'Bless my heart, I forgot grandma's bundle!' and running out to the carriage, returned with an interesting white parcel, which, being opened, disclosed a choice collection of beasts, birds, and pretty things cut out of crisp sugary cake, and baked a lovely brown.

'There's one for each, and a letter to tell which is whose. Grandma and Hannah made them, and I tremble to think what would have happened to me if I had forgotten to leave them.'

Then, amid much laughing and fun, the cakes were distributed. A fish for Dan, a fiddle for Nat, a book for Demi, a monkey for Tommy, a flower for Daisy, a hoop for Nan, who had driven twice round the triangle without stopping, a star for Emil, who put on airs because he studied astronomy, and, best of all, an omnibus for Franz, whose great delight was to drive the family bus. Stuffy got a fat pig, and the little folks had birds, and cats, and rabbits, with black currant eyes.

'Now I must go. Where is my Goldilocks? Mamma will come flying out to get her if I'm not back early,' said Uncle Teddy, when the last crumb had vanished, which it speedily did, you may be sure.

The young ladies had gone into the garden, and while they waited till Franz looked them up, Jo and Laurie stood at the door talking together.

'How does little Giddy-gaddy come on?' he asked,

for Nan's pranks amused him very much, and he was never tired of teasing Jo about her.

'Nicely; she is getting quite mannerly, and begins to see the error of her wild ways.'

'Don't the boys encourage her in them?'

'Yes; but I keep talking, and lately she has improved much. You saw how prettily she shook hands with you, and how gentle she was with Bess. Daisy's example has its effect upon her, and I'm quite sure that a few months will work wonders.'

Here Mrs Jo's remarks were cut short by the appearance of Nan tearing round the corner at a breakneck pace, driving a mettlesome team of four boys, and followed by Daisy trundling Bess in a wheelbarrow. Hats off, hair flying, whip cracking, and barrow bumping, up they came in a cloud of dust, looking as wild a set of little hoydens as one would wish to see.

'So these are the model children, are they? It's lucky I didn't bring Mrs Curtis out to see your school for the cultivation of morals and manners; she would never have recovered from the shock of this spectacle,' said Mr Laurie, laughing at Mrs Jo's premature rejoicing over Nan's improvement.

'Laugh away; I'll succeed yet. As you used to say at College, quoting some professor, "Though the experiment has failed, the principle remains the same",' said Mrs Bhaer, joining in the merriment.

'I'm afraid Nan's example is taking effect upon Daisy, instead of the other way. Look at my little princess! she has utterly forgotten her dignity, and is screaming like the rest. Young ladies, what does this mean?' and Mr Laurie rescued his small daughter from impending destruction, for the four horses were champing their bits and curvetting madly all about her, as she sat brandishing a great whip in both hands.

'We're having a race, and I beat,' shouted Nan.

'I could have run faster, only I was afraid of spilling Bess,' screamed Daisy.

'Hi! go long!' cried the princess, giving such a flourish with her whip that the horses ran away, and were seen no more.

'My precious child! come away from this ill-mannered crew before you are quite spoilt. Good-bye, Jo! Next time I come, I shall expect to find the boys making patchwork.'

'It wouldn't hurt them a bit. I don't give in, mind you; for my experiments always fail a few times before they succeed. Love to Amy and my blessed Marmee,' called Mrs Jo, as the carriage drove away; and the last Mr Laurie saw of her, she was consoling Daisy for her failure by a ride in the wheelbarrow, and looking as if she liked it.

Great was the excitement all the week about the repairs in the carriage-house, which went briskly on in spite of the incessant questions, advice, and meddling of the boys. Old Gibbs was nearly driven wild with it all, but managed to do his work nevertheless; and by Friday night the place was all in order – roof mended, shelves up, walls white-washed, a great window cut at the back, which let in a flood of sunshine, and gave them a fine view of the brook, the meadows, and the distant hills; and over the great door, painted in red letters, was 'The Laurence Museum'.

All Saturday morning the boys were planning how it should be furnished with their spoils, and when Mr

Laurie arrived, bringing an aquarium which Mrs Amy said she was tired of, their rapture was great.

The afternoon was spent in arranging things, and when the running and lugging and hammering was over, the ladies were invited to behold the institution.

It certainly was a pleasant place, airy, clean, and bright. A hop-vine shook its green bells round the open window, the pretty aquarium stood in the middle of the room, with some delicate water plants rising above the water, and gold-fish showing their brightness as they floated to and fro below. On either side of the window were rows of shelves ready to receive the curiosities yet to be found. Dan's tall cabinet stood before the great door which was fastened up, while the small door was to be used. On the cabinet stood a queer Indian idol, very ugly, but very interesting; old Mr Laurence sent it, as well as a fine Chinese junk in full sail, which had a conspicuous place on the long table in the middle of the room. Above, swinging in a loop, and looking as if she was alive, hung Polly, who died at an advanced age, had been carefully stuffed, and was now presented by Mrs Jo. The walls were decorated with all sorts of things. A snake's skin, a big wasps' nest, a birch-bark canoe, a string of birds' eggs, wreaths of grey moss from the South, and a bunch of cotton-pods. The dead bats had a place, also a large turtle-shell, and an ostrich-egg proudly presented by Demi, who volunteered to explain these rare curiosities to guests whenever they liked. There were so many stones that it was impossible to accept them all, so only a few of the best were arranged among the shells on the shelves, the rest were piled up in corners, to be examined by Dan at his leisure.

Everyone was eager to give something, even Silas, who sent home for a stuffed wild-cat killed in his youth. It was rather moth-eaten and shabby, but on a high bracket and best side foremost the effect was fine, for the yellow glass eyes glared, and the mouth snarled so naturally, that Teddy shook in his little shoes at sight of it, when he came bringing his most cherished treasure, one cocoon, to lay upon the shrine of science.

'Isn't it beautiful? I'd no idea we had so many curious things. I gave that; don't it look well? We might make a lot by charging something for letting folks see it.'

Jack added that last suggestion to the general chatter that went on as the family viewed the room.

'This is a free museum and if there is any speculating on it I'll paint out the name over the door,' said Mr Laurie, turning so quickly that Jack wished he had held his tongue.

'Hear! hear!' cried Mr Bhaer.

'Speech! speech!' added Mrs Jo.

'Can't, I'm too bashful. You give them a lecture yourself – you are used to it,' Mr Laurie answered, retreating towards the window, meaning to escape. But she held him fast, and said, laughing as she looked at the dozen pairs of dirty hands about her,

'If I did lecture, it would be on the chemical and cleansing properties of soap. Come now, as the founder of the institution, you really ought to give us a few moral remarks, and we will applaud tremendously.'

Seeing that there was no way of escaping, Mr Laurie looked up at Polly hanging overhead, seemed to find inspiration in the brilliant old bird, and sitting down upon the table, said, in his pleasant way,

'There *is* one thing I'd like to suggest, boys, and that is, I want you to get some good as well as much pleasure out of this. Just putting curious or pretty things here won't do it; so suppose you read up about them, so that when anybody asks questions you can answer them, and understand the matter. I used to like these things myself, and should enjoy hearing about them now, for I've forgotten all I once knew. It wasn't much, was it, Jo? Here's Dan now, full of stories about birds and bugs, and so on; let him take care of the museum, and once a week the rest of you take turns to read a composition, or tell about some animal, mineral, or vegetable. We should all like that, and I think it would put considerable useful knowledge into our heads. What do you say, Professor?'

'I'd like it much, and will give the lads all the help I can. But they will need books to read up these new subjects, and we have not many, I fear,' began Mr Bhaer, looking much pleased, and planning many fine lectures on geology, which he liked. 'We should have a library for the special purpose.'

'Is that a useful sort of book, Dan?' asked Mr Laurie, pointing to the volume that lay open by the cabinet.

'Oh, yes! it tells all I want to know about insects. I had it here to see how to fix the butterflies right. I covered it, so it is not hurt'; and Dan caught it up, fearing the lender might think him careless.

'Give it here a minute'; and, pulling out his pencil, Mr Laurie wrote Dan's name in it, saying, as he set the book up on one of the corner shelves, where nothing stood but a stuffed bird without a tail, 'There, that is the beginning of the museum library. I'll hunt up some more books, and Demi shall keep them in order. Where are those jolly little books we used to read, Jo? *Insect Architecture* or some such name – all about ants having battles, and bees having queens, and crickets eating holes in our clothes and stealing milk, and larks of that sort.'

'In the garret at home. I'll have them sent out, and we will plunge into Natural History with a will,' said Mrs Jo, ready for anything.

'Won't it be hard to write about such things?' asked Nat, who hated compositions.

'At first, perhaps; but you will soon like it. If you think that hard, how would you like to have this subject given to you, as it was to a girl of thirteen: A conversation between Themistocles, Aristides, and Pericles on the proposed appropriation of the funds of the confederacy of Delos for the ornamentation of Athens?' said Mrs Jo.

The boys groaned at the mere sound of the long names, and the gentlemen laughed at the absurdity of the lesson.

'Did she write it?' asked Demi, in an awe-stricken tone.

'Yes, but you can imagine what a piece of work she made of it, though she was rather a bright child.'

'I'd like to have seen it,' said Mr Bhaer.

'Perhaps I can find it for you; I went to school with her,' and Mrs Jo looked so wicked that everyone knew who the little girl was.

Hearing of this fearful subject for a composition quite reconciled the boys to the thought of writing about familiar things. Wednesday afternoon was appointed for the lectures, as they preferred to call them, for some chose to talk instead of write. Mr Bhaer promised a portfolio in which the written productions should be kept, and Mrs Bhaer said she would attend the course with great pleasure.

Then the dirty-handed society went off to wash, followed by the Professor, trying to calm the anxiety of Rob, who had been told by Tommy that all water was full of invisible pollywogs.

'I like your plan very much, only don't be too generous, Teddy,' said Mrs Bhaer, when they were left alone. 'You know most of the boys have got to paddle their own canoes when they leave us, and too much sitting in the lap of luxury will unfit them for it.'

'I'll be moderate, but do let me amuse myself. I get desperately tired of business sometimes, and nothing freshens me up like a good frolic with your boys. I like that Dan very much, Jo. He isn't demonstrative; but he has the eye of a hawk, and when you have tamed him a little he will do you credit.'

'I'm so glad you think so. Thank you very much for your kindness to him, especially for this museum affair; it will keep him happy while he is lame, give me a chance to soften and smooth this poor, rough lad, and make him love us. What did inspire you with such a beautiful, helpful idea, Teddy?' asked Mrs Bhaer, glancing back at the pleasant room, as she turned to leave it.

Laurie took both her hands in his, and answered, with a look that made her eyes fill with happy tears,

'Dear Jo! I have known what it is to be a motherless boy, and I never can forget how much you and yours have done for me all these years.'

12

HUCKLEBERRIES

There was a great clashing of tin pails, much running to and fro, and frequent demands for something to eat, one August afternoon, for the boys were going huckle-berrying, and made as much stir about it as if they were setting out to find the North-West Passage.

'Now, my lads, get off as quietly as you can, for Rob is safely out of the way, and won't see you,' said Mrs Bhaer, as she tied Daisy's broad-brimmed hat, and settled the great blue pinafore in which she had enveloped Nan.

But the plan did not succeed, for Rob had heard the bustle, decided to go, and prepared himself, without a thought of disappointment. The troop was just getting under way when the little man came marching down-stairs with his best hat on, a bright tin pail in his hand, and a face beaming with satisfaction.

'Oh, dear! now we shall have a scene,' sighed Mrs Bhaer, who found her eldest son very hard to manage at times.

'I'm all ready,' said Rob, and took his place in the ranks with such perfect unconsciousness of his mistake, that it really was very hard to undeceive him.

'It's too far for you, my love; stay and take care of me, for I shall be alone,' began his mother.

'You've got Teddy. I'm a big boy, so I can go; you said I might when I was bigger, and I am now,' persisted Rob, with a cloud beginning to dim the brightness of his happy face.

'We are going up to the great pasture, and it's ever so far; we don't want you tagging on,' cried Jack, who did not admire the little boys.

'I won't tag, I'll run and keep up. O Mamma! let me go! I want to fill my new pail, and I'll bring 'em all to you. Please, please, I will be good!' prayed Robby, looking up at his mother, so grieved and disappointed that her heart began to fail her.

'But, my deary, you'll get so tired and hot you won't have a good time. Wait till I go, and then we will stay all day, and pick as many berries as you want.'

'You never do go, you are so busy, and I'm tired of waiting. I'd rather go and get the berries for you all myself. I love to pick 'em, and I want to fill my new pail dreffly,' sobbed Rob.

The pathetic sight of great tears tinkling into the dear new pail, and threatening to fill it with salt water instead of huckleberries, touched all the ladies present. His mother patted the weeper on his back; Daisy offered to stay at home with him; and Nan said, in her decided way,

'Let him come; I'll take care of him.'

'If Franz was going I wouldn't mind, for he is very careful; but he is haying with the father, and I'm not sure about the rest of you,' began Mrs Bhaer.

'It's so far,' put in Jack.

'I'd carry him if I was going – wish I was,' said Dan, with a sigh.

'Thank you, dear, but you must take care of your

foot. I wish I could go. Stop a minute, I think I can
manage it after all'; and Mrs Bhaer ran out to the
steps, waving her apron wildly.

Silas was just driving away in the hay-cart, but
turned back, and agreed at once, when Mrs Jo proposed that he should take the whole party to the
pasture, and go for them at five o'clock.

'It will delay your work a little, but never mind; we
will pay you in huckleberry pies,' said Mrs Jo, knowing
Silas's weak point.

His rough, brown face brightened up, and he said,
with a cheery 'Haw! haw!' – 'Wal now, Mis' Bhaer, if
you go to bribin' of me, I shall give in right away.'

'Now, boys, I have arranged it so that you can all
go,' said Mrs Bhaer, running back again, much relieved, for she loved to make them happy, and always
felt miserable when she had disturbed the serenity of
her little sons; for she believed that the small hopes
and plans and pleasures of children should be tenderly
respected by grown-up people, and never rudely
thwarted or ridiculed.

'Can I go?' said Dan, delighted.

'I thought especially of you. Be careful, and never
mind the berries, but sit about and enjoy the lovely
things which you know how to find all about you,'
answered Mrs Bhaer, who remembered his kind offer
to her boy.

'Me too! me too!' sung Rob, dancing with joy, and
clapping his precious pail and cover like castanets.

'Yes, and Daisy and Nan must take good care of
you. Be at the bars at five o'clock, and Silas will come
for you all.'

Robby cast himself upon his mother in a burst of

gratitude, promising to bring her every berry he picked, and not eat one. Then they were all packed into the hay-cart, and went rattling away, the brightest face among the dozen being that of Rob, as he sat between his two temporary little mothers, beaming upon the whole world, and waving his best hat; for his indulgent mamma had not the heart to bereave him of it, since this was a gala-day to him.

Such a happy afternoon as they had, in spite of the mishaps which usually occur on such expeditions! Of course Tommy came to grief, tumbled upon a hornets' nest and got stung; but being used to woe, he bore the smart manfully, till Dan suggested the application of damp earth, which much assuaged the pain. Daisy saw a snake, and in flying from it lost half her berries; but Demi helped her to fill up again, and discussed reptiles most learnedly the while. Ned fell out of a tree, and split his jacket down the back, but suffered no other fracture. Emil and Jack established rival claims to a certain thick patch, and while they were squabbling about it, Stuffy quickly and quietly stripped the bushes and fled to the protection of Dan, who was enjoying himself immensely. The crutch was no longer necessary, and he was delighted to see how strong his foot felt as he roamed about the great pasture, full of interesting rocks and stumps, with familiar little creatures in the grass, and well-known insects dancing in the air.

But of all the adventures that happened on this afternoon that which befell Nan and Rob was the most exciting, and it long remained one of the favourite histories of the household. Having explored the country pretty generally, torn three rents in her frock, and scratched her face in a barberry-bush, Nan began to pick the berries that shone like big, black beads on the low, green bushes. Her nimble fingers flew, but still her basket did not fill up as rapidly as she desired, so she kept wandering here and there to search for better places, instead of picking contentedly and steadily as Daisy did. Rob followed Nan, for her energy suited him better than his cousin's patience, and he too was anxious to have the biggest and best berries for Marmar.

'I keep putting 'em in, but it don't fill up, and I'm so tired,' said Rob, pausing a moment to rest his short legs, and beginning to think huckleberrying was not all his fancy painted it; for the sun blazed, Nan skipped hither and thither like a grasshopper, and the berries fell out of his pail almost as fast as he put them in, because, in his struggles with the bushes, it was often upside-down.

'Last time we came they were ever so much thicker over that wall – great bouncers; and there is a cave there, where the boys made a fire. Let's go and fill our things quick, and then hide in the cave and let the others find us,' proposed Nan, thirsting for adventures.

Rob consented, and away they went, scrambling over the wall and running down the sloping fields on the other side, till they were hidden among the rocks and underbrush. The berries were thick, and at last the pails were actually full. It was shady and cool down there, and a little spring gave the thirsty children a refreshing drink out of its mossy cup.

'Now we will go and rest in the cave, and eat our lunch,' said Nan, well satisfied with her success so far.

'Do you know the way?' asked Rob.

''Course I do; I've been once, and I always remember. Didn't I go and get my box all right?'

That convinced Rob, and he followed blindly as Nan led him over stock and stone, and brought him, after much meandering, to a small recess in the rock, where the blackened stones showed that fires had been made.

'Now, isn't it nice?' asked Nan, as she took out a bit of bread-and-butter, rather damaged by being mixed up with nails, fishhooks, stones and other foreign substances, in the young lady's pocket.

'Yes; do you think they will find us soon?' asked Rob, who found the shadowy glen rather dull, and began to long for more society.

'No, I don't; because if I hear them, I shall hide, and have fun making them find me.'

'P'raps they won't come.'

'Don't care; I can get home myself.'

'Is it a great way?' asked Rob, looking at his little, stubby boots, scratched and wet with his long wandering.

'It's six miles, I guess.' Nan's ideas of distance were vague, and her faith in her own powers great.

'I think we better go now,' suggested Rob, presently.

'I shan't go till I have picked over my berries'; and Nan began what seemed to Rob an endless task.

'Oh, dear! you said you'd take good care of me,' he sighed, as the sun seemed to drop behind the hill all of a sudden.

'Well, I *am* taking care of you as hard as I can. Don't be cross, child; I'll go in a minute,' said Nan, who considered five-year-old Robby a mere infant compared to herself.

So little Rob sat looking anxiously about him, and waiting patiently, for, spite of some misgivings, he felt great confidence in Nan.

'I guess it's going to be night pretty soon,' he observed, as if to himself, as a mosquito bit him, and the frogs in a neighbouring marsh began to pipe up for the evening concert.

'My goodness me! so it is. Come right away this minute, or they will be gone,' cried Nan, looking up from her work, and suddenly perceiving that the sun was down.

'I heard a horn about an hour ago; maybe they were blowing for us,' said Rob, trudging after his guide as she scrambled up the steep hill.

'Where was it?' asked Nan, stopping short.

'Over that way'; he pointed with a dirty little finger in an entirely wrong direction.

'Let's go that way and meet them'; and Nan wheeled about, and began to trot through the bushes, feeling a trifle anxious, for there were so many cowpaths all about she could not remember which way they came.

On they went over stock and stone again, pausing now and then to listen for the horn, which did not blow any more, for it was only the moo of a cow on her way home.

'I don't remember seeing that pile of stones – do you?' asked Nan, as she sat on a wall to rest a moment and take an observation.

'I don't remember anything, but I want to go home,' and Rob's voice had a little tremble in it that made

Nan put her arms round him and lift him gently down, saying, in her most capable way,

'I'm going just as fast as I can, dear. Don't cry, and when we come to the road, I'll carry you.'

'Where is the road?' and Robby wiped his eyes to look for it.

'Over by that big tree. Don't you know that's the one Ned tumbled out of?'

'So it is. Maybe they waited for us; I'd like to ride home – wouldn't you?' and Robby brightened up as he plodded along toward the end of the great pasture.

'No, I'd rather walk,' answered Nan, feeling quite sure that she would be obliged to do so, and preparing her mind for it.

Another long trudge through the fast-deepening twilight and another disappointment, for when they reached the tree, they found to their dismay that it was not the one Ned climbed, and no road anywhere appeared.

'Are we lost?' quavered Rob, clasping his pail in despair.

'Not much. I don't just see which way to go, and I guess we'd better call.'

So they both shouted till they were hoarse, yet nothing answered but the frogs in full chorus.

'There is another tall tree over there, perhaps that's the one,' said Nan, whose heart sunk within her, though she still spoke bravely.

'I don't think I can go any more; my boots are so heavy I can't pull 'em'; and Robby sat down on a stone quite worn out.

'Then we must stay here all night. *I* don't care much, if snakes don't come.'

'I'm frightened of snakes. I can't stay all night. Oh, dear! I don't like to be lost,' and Rob puckered up his face to cry, when suddenly a thought occurred to him, and he said, in a tone of perfect confidence,

'Marmar will come and find me – she always does; I ain't afraid now.'

'She won't know where we are.'

'She didn't know I was shut up in the ice-house, but she found me. I know she'll come,' returned Robby, so trustfully, that Nan felt relieved, and sat down by him, saying, with a remorseful sigh,

'I wish we hadn't run away.'

'You made me; but I don't mind much – Marmar will love me just the same,' answered Rob, clinging to his sheet-anchor when all other hope was gone.

'I'm so hungry. Let's eat our berries,' proposed Nan after a pause, during which Rob began to nod.

'So am I, but I can't eat mine, 'cause I told Marmar I'd keep them all for her.'

'You'll have to eat them if no one comes for us,' said Nan, who felt like contradicting everything just then. 'If we stay here a great many days, we shall eat up all the berries in the field, and then we shall starve,' she added, grimly.

'I shall eat sassafras. I know a big tree of it, and Dan told me how squirrels dig up the roots and eat them, and I love to dig,' returned Rob, undaunted by the prospect of starvation.

'Yes; and we can catch frogs, and cook them. My father ate some once, and he said they were nice,' put in Nan, beginning to find a spice of romance even in being lost in a huckleberry pasture.

'How could we cook frogs? we haven't got any fire.'

'I don't know; next time I'll have matches in my pocket,' said Nan, rather depressed by this obstacle to the experiment in frog-cookery.

'Couldn't we light a fire with a fire-fly?' asked Rob, hopefully, as he watched them flitting to and fro like winged sparks.

'Let's try'; and several minutes were pleasantly spent in catching the flies, and trying to make them kindle a green twig or two. 'It's a lie to call them fire-flies when there isn't a fire in them,' Nan said, throwing one unhappy insect away with scorn, though it shone its best, and obligingly walked up and down the twigs to please the innocent little experimenters.

'Marmar's a good while coming,' said Rob, after another pause, during which they watched the stars overhead, smelt the sweet fern crushed under foot, and listened to the crickets' serenade.

'I don't see why God made any night; day is so much pleasanter,' said Nan, thoughtfully.

'It's to sleep in,' answered Rob, with a yawn.

'Then do go to sleep,' said Nan, pettishly.

'I want my own bed. Oh, I wish I could see Teddy!' cried Rob, painfully reminded of home by the soft chirp of birds safe in their little nests.

'I don't believe your mother will ever find us,' said Nan, who was becoming desperate, for she hated patient waiting of any sort. 'It's so dark she won't see us.'

'It was all black in the ice-house, and I was so scared I didn't call her, but she saw me; and she will see me now, no matter how dark it is,' returned confiding Rob, standing up to peer into the gloom for the help which never failed him.

'I see her! I see her!' he cried, and ran as fast as his tired legs would take him toward a dark figure slowly approaching. Suddenly he stopped, then turned about, and came stumbling back, screaming in a great panic,

'No, it's a bear, a big, black one!' and hid his face in Nan's skirts.

For a moment Nan quailed; even her courage gave out at thought of a real bear, and she was about to turn and flee in great disorder, when a mild, 'Moo!' changed her fear to merriment, as she said laughing,

'It's a cow, Robby! the nice, black cow we saw this afternoon.'

The cow seemed to feel that it was not just the thing to meet two little people in her pasture after dark, and the amiable beast paused to inquire into the case. She let them stroke her, and stood regarding them with her soft eyes so mildly, that Nan, who feared no animal but a bear, was fired with a desire to milk her.

'Silas taught me how; and berries and milk would be so nice,' she said, emptying the contents of her pail into her hat, and boldly beginning her new task, while Rob stood by and repeated, at her command, the poem from Mother Goose:

> 'Cushy cow, bonny, let down your milk,
>   Let down your milk to me,
> And I will give you a gown of silk,
>   A gown of silk and a silver tee.'

But the immortal rhyme had little effect, for the benevolent cow had already been milked, and had only half a gill to give the thirsty children.

'Shoo! get away! you are an old cross patch,' cried

Nan, ungratefully, as she gave up the attempt in despair; and poor Mooly walked on with a gentle gurgle of surprise and reproof.

'Each can have a sip, and then we must take a walk. We shall go to sleep if we don't; and lost people mustn't sleep. Don't you know how Hannah Lee in the pretty story slept under the snow and died?'

'But there isn't any snow now, and it's nice and warm,' said Rob, who was not blessed with as lively a fancy as Nan.

'No matter, we will poke about a little, and call some more; and then, if nobody comes, we will hide under the bushes, like Hop-o'-my-thumb and his brothers.'

It was a very short walk, however, for Rob was so sleepy he could not get on, and tumbled down so often that Nan entirely lost patience, being half distracted by the responsibility she had taken upon herself.

'If you tumble down again, I'll shake you,' she said, lifting the poor little man up very kindly as she spoke, for Nan's bark was much worse than her bite.

'Please don't. It's my boots – they keep slipping so'; and Rob manfully checked the sob just ready to break out, adding, with a plaintive patience that touched Nan's heart, 'If the skeeters didn't bite me so, I could go to sleep till Marmar comes.'

'Put your head on my lap, and I'll cover you up with my apron; I'm not afraid of the night,' said Nan, sitting down and trying to persuade herself that she did not mind the shadow nor the mysterious rustlings all about her.

'Wake me up when she comes,' said Rob, and was fast asleep in five minutes with his head in Nan's lap under the pinafore.

The little girl sat for some fifteen minutes, staring about her with anxious eyes, and feeling as if each second was an hour. Then a pale light began to glimmer over the hill-top, and she said to herself,

'I guess the night is over and morning is coming. I'd like to see the sun rise, so I'll watch, and when it comes up we can find our way right home.'

But before the moon's round face peeped above the hill to destroy her hope, Nan had fallen asleep, leaning back in a little bower of tall ferns, and was deep in a midsummer night's dream of fire-flies and blue aprons, mountains of huckleberries, and Robby wiping away the tears of a black cow, who sobbed, 'I want to go home! I want to go home!'

While the children were sleeping, peacefully lulled by the drowsy hum of many neighbourly mosquitoes, the family at home were in a great state of agitation. The hay-cart came at five, and all but Jack, Emil, Nan, and Rob were at the bars ready for it. Franz drove instead of Silas, and when the boys told him that the others were going home through the wood, he said, looking ill-pleased, 'They ought to have left Rob to ride, he will be tired out by the long walk.'

'It's shorter that way, and they will carry him,' said Stuffy, who was in a hurry for his supper.

'You are sure Nan and Rob went with them?'

'Of course they did; I saw them getting over the wall, and sung out that it was 'most five, and Jack called back that they were going the other way,' explained Tommy.

'Very well, pile in then,' and away rattled the hay-cart with the tired children and the full pails.

Mrs Jo looked sober when she heard of the division of the party, and sent Franz back with Toby to find and bring the little ones home. Supper was over, and the family sitting about in the cool hall as usual, when Franz came trotting back, hot, dusty, and anxious.

'Have they come?' he called out when half-way up the avenue.

'No!' and Mrs Jo flew out of her chair looking so alarmed that everyone jumped up and gathered round Franz.

'I can't find them anywhere,' he began; but the words were hardly spoken when a loud 'Hullo!' startled them all, and the next minute Jack and Emil came round the house.

'Where are Nan and Rob?' cried Mrs Jo, clutching Emil in a way that caused him to think his aunt had suddenly lost her wits.

'I don't know. They came home with the others, didn't they?' he answered, quickly.

'No; George and Tommy said they went with you.'

'Well, they didn't. Haven't seen them? We took a swim in the pond, and came by the wood,' said Jack, looking alarmed, as well he might.

'Call Mr Bhaer, get the lanterns, and tell Silas I want him.'

That was all Mrs Jo said, but they knew what she meant, and flew to obey orders. In ten minutes, Mr Bhaer and Silas were off to the wood, and Franz tearing down the road on Old Andy to search the great pasture. Mrs Jo caught up some food from the table, a little bottle of brandy from the medicine-closet, took a lantern, and bidding Jack and Emil come with her, and the rest not stir, she trotted away on Toby, never stopping for hat or shawl. She heard someone running after her, but said not a word till, as she paused to call and listen, the light of her lantern shone on Dan's face.

'You here! I told Jack to come,' she said, half-inclined to send him back, much as she needed help.

'I wouldn't let him; he and Emil hadn't had any supper, and I wanted to come more than they did,' he said, taking the lantern from her and smiling up in her face with the steady look in his eyes that made her feel as if, boy though he was, she had someone to depend on.

Off she jumped, and ordered him on to Toby, in spite of his pleading to walk; then they went on again along the dusty, solitary road, stopping every now and then to call and hearken breathlessly for little voices to reply.

When they came to the great pasture, other lights were already flitting to and fro like will-o'-the-wisps, and Mr Bhaer's voice was heard shouting, 'Nan! Rob! Rob! Nan!' in every part of the field. Silas whistled and roared, Dan plunged here and there on Toby, who seemed to understand the case, and went over the roughest places with unusual docility. Often Mrs Jo hushed them all, saying, with a sob in her throat, 'The noise may frighten them, let me call; Robby will know *my* voice'; and then she would cry out the beloved little name in every tone of tenderness, till the very echoes whispered it softly, and the winds seemed to waft it willingly; but still no answer came.

The sky was overcast now, and only brief glimpses of the moon were seen, heat-lightning darted out of the dark clouds now and then, and a faint far-off rumble as of thunder told that a summer storm was brewing.

'O my Robby! my Robby!' mourned poor Mrs Jo, wandering up and down like a pale ghost, while Dan kept beside her like a faithful fire-fly. 'What shall I say to Nan's father if she comes to harm? Why did I ever trust my darling so far away? Fritz, do you hear anything?' And when a mournful 'No' came back, she wrung her hands so despairingly, that Dan sprung down from Toby's back, tied the bridle to the bars, and said, in his decided way,

'They may have gone down to the spring – I'm going to look.'

He was over the wall and away so fast that she could hardly follow him; but when she reached the spot, he lowered the lantern and showed her with joy the marks of little feet in the soft ground about the spring. She fell down on her knees to examine the tracks, and then sprung up, saying eagerly,

'Yes; that is the mark of my Robby's little boots! Come this way, they must have gone on.'

Such a weary search! But now some inexplicable instinct seemed to lead the anxious mother, for presently Dan uttered a cry, and caught up a little shining object lying in the path. It was the cover of the new tin pail, dropped in the first alarm of being lost. Mrs Jo hugged and kissed it as if it were a living thing; and when Dan was about to utter a glad shout to bring the others to the spot, she stopped him, saying, as she hurried on, 'No, let *me* find them; I let Rob go, and I want to give him back to his father all myself.'

A little farther on Nan's hat appeared, and after

passing the place more than once, they came at last upon the babes in the wood, both sound asleep. Dan never forgot the little picture on which the light of his lantern shone that night. He thought Mrs Jo would cry out, but she only whispered 'Hush!' as she softly lifted away the apron, and saw the little ruddy face below. The berry-stained lips were half-open as the breath came and went, the yellow hair lay damp on the hot forehead, and both the chubby hands held fast the little pail still full.

The sight of the childish harvest, treasured through all the troubles of that night for her, seemed to touch Mrs Jo to the heart, for suddenly she gathered up her boy, and began to cry over him, so tenderly, yet so heartily, that he woke up, and at first seemed bewildered. Then he remembered, and hugged her close, saying with a laugh of triumph,

'I knew you'd come! O Marmar! I did want you so!' For a moment they kissed and clung to one another, quite forgetting all the world; for no matter how lost and soiled and worn-out wandering sons may be, mothers can forgive and forget everything as they fold them in their fostering arms. Happy the son whose faith in his mother remains unchanged, and who, through all his wanderings, has kept some filial token to repay her brave and tender love.

Dan meantime picked Nan out of her bush, and, with a gentleness none but Teddy ever saw in him before, he soothed her first alarm at the sudden waking, and wiped away her tears; for Nan also began to cry for joy, it was so good to see a kind face and feel a strong arm round her after what seemed to her ages of loneliness and fear.

'My poor little girl, don't cry! You are all safe now, and no one shall say a word of blame tonight,' said Mrs Jo, taking Nan into her capacious embrace, and cuddling both children as a hen might gather her lost chickens under her motherly wings.

'It was my fault; but I *am* sorry. I tried to take care of him, and I covered him up and let him sleep, and didn't touch his berries, though I was *so* hungry; and I never will do it again – truly never, never,' sobbed Nan, quite lost in a sea of penitence and thankfulness.

'Call them now, and let us get home,' said Mrs Jo; and Dan, getting upon the wall, sent the joyful word 'Found!' ringing over the field:

How the wandering lights came dancing from all sides, and gathered round the little group among the sweet fern bushes! Such a hugging, and kissing, and talking, and crying, as went on must have amazed the glow-worms, and evidently delighted the mosquitoes, for they hummed frantically, while the little moths came in flocks to the party, and the frogs croaked as if they could not express their satisfaction loudly enough.

Then they set out for home – a queer party, for Franz rode on to tell the news; Dan and Toby led the way; then came Nan in the strong arms of Silas, who considered her 'the smartest little baggage he ever saw', and teased her all the way home about her pranks. Mr Bhaer would let no one carry Rob but himself, and the little fellow, refreshed by sleep, sat up, and chattered gaily, feeling himself a hero, while his mother went beside him holding on to any part of his precious little body that came handy, and never tired of hearing him say, 'I *knew* Marmar would come,' or seeing him lean down to kiss her, and put a plump berry into her mouth, ''Cause he picked 'em all for her'.

The moon shone out just as they reached the avenue, and all the boys came shouting to meet them, so the lost lambs were borne in triumph and safety, and landed in the dining-room, where the unromantic little things demanded supper instead of preferring kisses and caresses. They were set down to bread and milk, while the entire household stood round to gaze upon them. Nan soon recovered her spirits, and recounted her perils with a relish now that they were all over. Rob seemed absorbed in his food, but put down his spoon all of a sudden, and set up a doleful roar.

'My precious, why do you cry?' asked his mother, who still hung over him.

'I'm crying 'cause I was lost,' bawled Rob, trying to squeeze out a tear, and failing entirely.

'But you are found now. Nan says you didn't cry out in the field, and I was glad you were such a brave boy.'

'I was so busy being frightened I didn't have any time then. But I want to cry now, 'cause I don't like to be lost,' explained Rob, struggling with sleep, emotion, and a mouthful of bread and milk.

The boys set up such a laugh at this funny way of making up for lost time, that Rob stopped to look at them, and the merriment was so infectious, that after a surprised stare he burst out into a merry 'Ha, ha!' and beat his spoon upon the table as if he enjoyed the joke immensely.

'It is ten o'clock; into bed, every man of you,' said Mr Bhaer, looking at his watch.

'And, thank Heaven! there will be no empty ones tonight,' added Mrs Bhaer, watching, with full eyes, Robby going up in his father's arms, and Nan escorted by Daisy and Demi, who considered her the most interesting heroine of their collection.

'Poor Aunt Jo is so tired she ought to be carried up herself,' said gentle Franz, putting his arm round her as she paused at the stair-foot, looking quite exhausted by her fright and long walk.

'Let's make an armchair,' proposed Tommy.

'No, thank you, my lads; but somebody may lend me a shoulder to lean on,' answered Mrs Jo.

'Me! me!' and half a dozen jostled one another, all eager to be chosen, for there was something in the pale motherly face that touched the warm hearts under the round jackets.

Seeing that they considered it an honour, Mrs Jo gave it to the one who had earned it, and nobody grumbled when she put her arm on Dan's broad shoulder, saying, with a look that made him colour up with pride and pleasure,

'He found the children; so I think he must help me up.'

Dan felt richly rewarded for his evening's work, not only that he was chosen from all the rest to go proudly up bearing the lamp, but because Mrs Jo said, heartily, 'Good night, my boy! God bless you!' as he left her at her door.

'I wish I *was* your boy,' said Dan, who felt as if danger and trouble had somehow brought him nearer than ever to her.

'You shall be my oldest son,' and she sealed her promise with a kiss that made Dan hers entirely.

Little Rob was all right next day, but Nan had a headache, and lay on Mother Bhaer's sofa with cold-cream upon her scratched face. Her remorse was quite gone, and she evidently thought being lost rather a fine amusement. Mrs Jo was not pleased with this state of things, and had no desire to have her children led from the paths of virtue, or her pupils lying round loose in huckleberry fields. So she talked soberly to Nan, and tried to impress upon her mind the difference between liberty and licence, telling several tales to enforce her lecture. She had not decided how to punish Nan, but one of these stories suggested a way, and as Mrs Jo liked odd penalties she tried it.

'All children run away,' pleaded Nan, as if it was as natural and necessary a thing as measles or whooping cough.

'Not all, and some who do run away don't get found again,' answered Mrs Jo.

'Didn't you do it yourself?' asked Nan, whose keen little eyes saw some traces of a kindred spirit in the serious lady who was sewing so morally before her.

Mrs Jo laughed, and owned that she did.

'Tell about it,' demanded Nan, feeling that she was getting the upper hand in the discussion.

Mrs Jo saw that, and sobered down at once, saying, with a remorseful shake of the head,

'I did it a good many times, and led my poor mother rather a hard life with my pranks, till she cured me.'

'How?' and Nan sat up with a face full of interest.

'I had a new pair of shoes once, and wanted to show them; so, though I was told not to leave the garden, I ran away and was wandering about all day. It was in the city, and why I wasn't killed I don't know. Such a time as I had. I frolicked in the park with dogs, sailed boats in the Back Bay with strange boys, dined with a little Irish beggar-girl on salt fish and potatoes, and was found at last fast asleep on a door-step with my arms round a great dog. It was late in the evening, and I was as dirty as a little pig, and the new shoes were worn out – I had travelled so far.'

'How nice!' cried Nan, looking all ready to go and do it herself.

'It was *not* nice next day'; and Mrs Jo tried to keep her eyes from betraying how much she enjoyed the memory of her early capers.

'Did your mother whip you?' asked Nan, curiously.

'She never whipped me but once, and then she begged my pardon, or I don't think I ever should have forgiven her, it hurt my feelings so much.'

'Why did she beg your pardon? – my father don't.'

'Because, when she had done it, I turned round and said, "Well, you are mad yourself, and ought to be whipped as much as me." She looked at me a minute, then her anger all died out, and she said, as if ashamed, "You are right, Jo, *I am* angry; and why should I punish you for being in a passion when I set you such a bad example? Forgive me, dear, and let us try to help one another in a better way." I never forgot it, and it did me more good than a dozen rods.'

Nan sat thoughtfully turning the little cold-cream jar for a minute, and Mrs Jo said nothing, but let that idea get well into the busy little mind that was so quick to see and feel what went on about her.

'I like that,' said Nan, presently, and her face looked less elfish, with its sharp eyes, inquisitive nose, and mischievous mouth. 'What did your mother do to you when you ran away that time?'

'She tied me up to the bed-post with a long string, so that I could not go out of the room, and there I stayed all day with the little worn-out shoes hanging up before me to remind me of my fault.'

'I should think that *would* cure anybody,' cried Nan, who loved her liberty above all things.

'It did cure me, and I think it will you, so I am going to try it,' said Mrs Jo, suddenly taking a ball of strong twine out of a drawer in her work-table.

Nan looked as if she was decidedly getting the worst of the argument now, and sat feeling much crestfallen while Mrs Jo tied one end round her waist and the other to the arm of the sofa, saying, as she finished,

'I don't like to tie you up like a naughty little dog, but if you don't remember any better than a dog, I must treat you like one.'

'I'd just as lief be tied up as not – I like to play dog'; and Nan put on a don't-care face, and began to growl and grovel on the floor.

Mrs Jo took no notice, but leaving a book or two and a handkerchief to her, she went away, and left Miss Nan to her own devices. This was not agreeable, and after sitting a moment she tried to untie the cord. But it was fastened in the belt of her apron behind, so she began on the knot at the other end. It soon came loose, and, gathering it up, Nan was about to get out of the window, when she heard Mrs Jo say to somebody as she passed through the hall,

'No, I don't think she will run away now; she is an honourable little girl, and knows that I do it to help her.'

In a minute Nan whisked back, tied herself up, and
began to sew violently. Rob came in a moment after,
and was so charmed with the new punishment, that he
got a jump-rope and tethered himself to the other arm
of the sofa in the most social manner.

'I got lost too, so I ought to be tied up as much as
Nan,' he explained to his mother when she saw the
new captive.

'I'm not so sure that you don't deserve a little
punishment, for you knew it was wrong to go far away
from the rest.'

'Nan took me,' began Rob, willing to enjoy the
novel penalty, but not willing to take the blame.

'You needn't have gone. You have got a conscience,
though you are a little boy, and you must learn to
mind it.'

'Well, my conscience didn't prick me a bit when she
said "Let's get over the wall,"' answered Rob, quoting
one of Demi's expressions.

'Didn't you stop to see if it did?'

'No.'

'Then you cannot tell.'

'I guess it's such a little conscience that it don't
prick hard enough for me to feel it,' added Rob, after
thinking over the matter for a minute.

'We must sharpen it up. It's bad to have a dull
conscience; so you may stay here till dinner-time, and
talk about it with Nan. I trust you both not to untie
yourselves till I say the word.'

'No, we won't,' said both, feeling a certain sense of
virtue in helping to punish themselves.

For an hour they were very good, then they grew
tired of one room, and longed to get out. Never had

the hall seemed so inviting; even the little bedroom acquired a sudden interest, and they would gladly have gone in and played tent with the curtains of the best bed. The open windows drove them wild because they could not reach them; and the outer world seemed so beautiful, they wondered how they ever found the heart to say it was dull. Nan pined for a race round the lawn, and Rob remembered with dismay that he had not fed his dog that morning, and wondered what poor Pollux would do. They watched the clock, and Nan did some nice calculations in minutes and seconds, while Rob learned to tell all the hours between eight and one so well that he never forgot them. It was maddening to smell the dinner, to know that there was to be succotash and huckleberry pudding, and to feel that they would not be on the spot to secure good helps of both. When Mary Ann began to set the table, they nearly cut themselves in two trying to see what meat there was to be; and Nan offered to help her make the beds, if she would only see that she had 'lots of sauce on her pudding'.

When the boys came bursting out of school, they found the children tugging at their halters like a pair of restive little colts, and were much edified, as well as amused, by the sequel to the exciting adventures of the night.

'Untie me now, Marmar my conscience will prick like a pin next time, I know it will,' said Rob, as the bell rang, and Teddy came to look at him with sorrowful surprise.

'We shall see,' answered his mother, setting him free. He took a good run down the hall, back through the dining-room, and brought up beside Nan, quite beaming with virtuous satisfaction.

'I'll bring her dinner to her, may I?' he asked, pitying his fellow-captive.

'That's my kind little son! Yes, pull out the table, and get a chair'; and Mrs Jo hurried away to quell the ardour of the others, who were always in a raging state of hunger at noon.

Nan ate alone, and spent a long afternoon attached to the sofa. Mrs Bhaer lengthened her bonds so that she could look out of the window; and there she stood watching the boys play, and all the little summer creatures enjoying their liberty. Daisy had a picnic for the dolls on the lawn, so that Nan might see the fun if she could not join in it. Tommy turned his best somer-saults to console her; Demi sat on the steps reading aloud to himself, which amused Nan a good deal; and Dan brought a little tree-toad to show her as the most delicate attention in his power.

But nothing atoned for the loss of freedom; and a few hours of confinement taught Nan how precious it was. A good many thoughts went through the little head that lay on the window-sill during the last quiet hour when all the children went to the brook to see Emil's new ship launched. She was to have christened it, and had depended on smashing a tiny bottle of currant-wine over the prow as it was named *Josephine* in honour of Mrs Bhaer. Now she had lost her chance, and Daisy wouldn't do it half so well. Tears rose to her eyes as she remembered that it was all her own fault; and she said aloud, addressing a fat bee who was rolling about in the yellow heart of a rose just under the window,

'If you have run away, you'd better go right home, and tell your mother you are sorry, and never do so any more.'

'I am glad to hear you give him such good advice, and I think he has taken it,' said Mrs Jo, smiling, as the bee spread his dusty wings and flew away.

Nan brushed off a bright drop or two that shone on the window-sill, and nestled against her friend as she took her on her knee, adding kindly – for she had seen the little drops, and knew what they meant,

'Do you think my mother's cure for running away a good one?'

'Yes, ma'am,' answered Nan, quite subdued by her quiet day.

'I hope I shall not have to try it again.'

'I guess not;' and Nan looked up with such an earnest little face that Mrs Jo felt satisfied, and said no more, for she liked to have her penalties do their own work, and did not spoil the effect by too much moralizing.

Here Rob appeared, bearing with infinite care what Asia called a 'sarcer pie', meaning one baked in a saucer.

'It's made out of some of my berries, and I'm going to give you half at supper-time,' he announced with a flourish.

'What makes you, when I'm so naughty?' asked Nan, meekly.

'Because we got lost together. You ain't going to be naughty again, are you?'

'Never,' said Nan, with great decision.

'Oh, goody! now let's go and get Mary Ann to cut this for us all ready to eat; it's 'most tea-time'; and Rob beckoned with the delicious little pie.

Nan started to follow, then stopped, and said,
'I forgot, I can't go.'

'Try and see,' said Mrs Bhaer, who had quietly
untied the cord sash while she had been talking.

Nan saw that she was free, and with one tempestuous
kiss to Mrs Jo, she was off like a humming-bird,
followed by Robby, dribbling huckleberry juice as he
ran.

13

GOLDILOCKS

After the last excitement peace descended upon Plumfield and reigned unbroken for several weeks, for the elder boys felt that the loss of Nan and Rob lay at their door, and all became so paternal in their care that they were rather wearying while the little ones listened to Nan's recital of her perils so many times, that they regarded being lost as the greatest ill humanity was heir to, and hardly dared to put their little noses outside the great gate lest night should suddenly descend upon them, and ghostly black cows come looming through the dusk.

'It is too good to last,' said Mrs Jo; for years of boy-culture had taught her that such lulls were usually followed by outbreaks of some sort, and when less wise women would have thought that the boys had become confirmed saints, she prepared herself for a sudden eruption of the domestic volcano.

One cause of this welcome calm was a visit from little Bess, whose parents lent her for a week while they were away with Grandpa Laurence, who was poorly. The boys regarded Goldilocks as a mixture of child, angel, and fairy, for she was a lovely little creature, and the golden hair which she inherited from her blonde mamma enveloped her like a shining veil, behind which she smiled upon her worshippers when gracious, and hid herself when offended. Her father would not have it cut and it hung below her waist, so soft and fine and bright, that Demi insisted that it was silk spun from a cocoon. Everyone praised the little Princess, but it did not seem to do her harm, only to teach her that her presence brought sunshine, her smiles made answering smiles on other faces, and her baby griefs filled every heart with tenderest sympathy.

Unconsciously, she did her young subjects more good than many a real sovereign, for her rule was very gentle and her power was felt rather than seen. Her natural refinement made her dainty in all things, and had a good effect upon the careless lads about her. She would let no one touch her roughly or with unclean hands, and more soap was used during her visits than at any other time, because the boys considered it the highest honour to be allowed to carry her highness, and the deepest disgrace to be repulsed with the disdainful command, 'Do away, dirty boy!'

Loud voices displeased her and quarrelling frightened her; so gentler tones came into the boyish voices as they addressed her, and squabbles were promptly suppressed in her presence by lookers-on if the principals could not restrain themselves. She liked to be waited on, and the biggest boys did her little errands without a murmur, while the small lads were her devoted slaves in all things. They begged to be allowed to draw her carriage, bear her berry-basket, or pass her plate at table. No service was too humble, and Tommy and Ned came to blows before they could decide which should have the honour of blacking her little boots.

Nan was especially benefited by a week in the society of a well-bred lady, though such a very small one; for Bess would look at her with a mixture of wonder and alarm in her great blue eyes when the hoyden screamed and romped; and she shrunk from her as if she thought her a sort of wild animal. Warm-hearted Nan felt this very much. She said at first, 'Pooh! I don't care!' But she did care, and was so hurt when Bess said, 'I love my tuzzin best, tause she is twiet,' that she shook poor Daisy till her teeth chattered in her head, and then fled to the barn to cry dismally. In that general refuge for perturbed spirits she found comfort and good counsel from some source or other. Perhaps the swallows from their mud-built nests overhead twittered her a little lecture on the beauty of gentleness. However that might have been, she came out quite subdued, and carefully searched the orchard for a certain kind of early apple that Bess liked because it was sweet and small and rosy. Armed with this peace-offering, she approached the Princess, and humbly presented it. To her great joy it was graciously accepted, and when Daisy gave Nan a forgiving kiss, Bess did likewise, as if she felt that she had been too severe, and desired to apologize. After this they played pleasantly together, and Nan enjoyed the royal favour for days. To be sure she felt a little like a wild bird in a pretty cage at first, and occasionally had to slip out to stretch her wings in a long flight, or to sing at the top of her voice, where neither would disturb the plump turtledove Daisy, nor the dainty golden canary Bess. But it did her good; for, seeing how everyone loved the little Princess for her small graces and virtues, she began to imitate her, because Nan wanted much love, and tried hard to win it.

Not a boy in the house but felt the pretty child's influence, and was improved by it without exactly knowing how or why, for babies can work miracles in the hearts that love them. Poor Billy found infinite satisfaction in staring at her, and though she did not like it she permitted it without a frown, after she had been made to understand that he was not quite like the others, and on that account must be more kindly treated. Dick and Dolly overwhelmed her with willow whistles, the only thing they knew how to make, and she accepted but never used them. Rob served her like a little lover, and Teddy followed her like a pet dog. Jack she did not like, because he was afflicted with warts and had a harsh voice. Stuffy displeased her because he did not eat tidily, and George tried hard not to gobble, that he might not disgust the dainty little lady opposite. Ned was banished from court in utter disgrace when he was discovered tormenting some unhappy field-mice. Goldilocks never could forget the sad spectacle, and retired behind her veil when he approached, waving him away with an imperious little hand, and crying, in a tone of mingled grief and anger,

'No, I tarn't love him; he tut the poor mouses' little tails off, and they queeked!'

Daisy promptly abdicated when Bess came, and took the humble post of chief cook, while Nan was first maid of honour; Emil was chancellor of the exchequer, and spent the public moneys lavishly in getting up spectacles that cost whole ninepences. Franz was prime minister, and directed her affairs of state, planned royal progresses through the kingdom, and kept foreign powers in order. Demi was her philosopher, and fared much better than such gentlemen usually do among crowned heads. Dan was her standing army, and defended her territories gallantly; Tommy was court fool, and Nat a tuneful Rizzio to this innocent little Mary.

Uncle Fritz and Aunt Jo enjoyed this peaceful episode, and looked on at the pretty play in which the young folk unconsciously imitated their elders, without adding the tragedy that is so apt to spoil the dramas acted on the larger stage.

'They teach us quite as much as we teach them,' said Mr Bhaer.

'Bless the dears! they never guess how many hints they give us as to the best way of managing them,' answered Mrs Jo.

'I think you were right about the good effect of having girls among the boys. Nan has stirred up Daisy, and Bess is teaching the little bears how to behave better than we can. If this reformation goes on as it has begun, I shall soon feel like Dr Blimber with his model young gentlemen,' said the Professor, laughing, as he saw Tommy not only remove his own hat, but knock off Ned's also, as they entered the hall where the Princess was taking a ride on the rocking-horse, attended by Rob and Teddy astride of chairs, and playing gallant knights to the best of their ability.

'You will never be a Blimber, Fritz, you couldn't do it if you tried; and our boys will never submit to the forcing process of that famous hot-bed. No fear that they will be too elegant: American boys like liberty too well. But good manners they cannot fail to have, if we give them the kindly spirit that shines through the simplest demeanour, making it courteous and cordial, like yours, my dear old boy.'

'Tut! tut! we will not compliment; for if I begin you will run away, and I have a wish to enjoy this happy half hour to the end'; yet Mr Bhaer looked pleased with the compliment, for it was true, and Mrs Jo felt that she had received the best her husband could give her, by saying that he found his truest rest and happiness in her society.

'To return to the children: I have just had another proof of Goldilocks' good influence,' said Mrs Jo, drawing her chair nearer the sofa, where the Professor lay resting after a long day's work in his various gardens. 'Nan hates sewing, but for love of Bess has been toiling half the afternoon over a remarkable bag in which to present a dozen of our love-apples to her idol when she goes. I praised her for it, and she said, in her quick way, "I like to sew for other people; it is stupid sewing for myself." I took the hint, and shall give her some little shirts and aprons for Mrs Carney's children. She is so generous, she will sew her fingers sore for them, and I shall not have to make a task of it.'

'But needlework is not a fashionable accomplishment, my dear.'

'Sorry for it. My girls shall learn all I can teach them about it, even if they give up the Latin, Algebra, and half a dozen ologies it is considered necessary for girls to muddle their poor brains over now-a-days. Amy means to make Bess an accomplished woman; but the dear's mite of a forefinger has little pricks on it already, and her mother has several specimens of needlework which she values more than the clay bird without a bill, that filled Laurie with such pride when Bess made it.'

'I also have a proof of the Princess's power,' said Mr Bhaer, after he had watched Mrs Jo sew on a button with an air of scorn for the whole system of fashionable education. 'Jack is so unwilling to be classed with Stuffy and Ned, as distasteful to Bess, that he came to me a little while ago, and asked me to touch his warts with caustic. I have often proposed it, and he never would consent; but now he bore the smart manfully, and consoles his present discomfort by hopes of future favour, when he can show her fastidious ladyship a smooth hand.'

Mrs Bhaer laughed at the story, and just then Stuffy came in to ask if he might give Goldilocks some of the bonbons his mother had sent him.

'She is not allowed to eat sweeties; but if you like to give her the pretty box with the pink sugar-rose in it, she would like it very much,' said Mrs Jo, unwilling to spoil this unusual piece of self-denial, for the 'fat boy' seldom offered to share his sugar-plums.

'Won't she eat it? I shouldn't like to make her sick,' said Stuffy eyeing the delicate sweetmeat lovingly, yet putting it into the box.

'Oh, no, she won't touch it, if I tell her it is to look at, not to eat. She will keep it for weeks, and never think of tasting it. Can you do as much?'

'I should hope so! I'm ever so much older than she is,' cried Stuffy, indignantly.

'Well, suppose we try. Here, put your bonbons in this bag, and see how long you can keep them. Let me count – two hearts, four red fishes, three barley-sugar horses, nine almonds, and a dozen chocolate drops. Do you agree to that?' asked sly Mrs Jo, popping the sweeties into her little spool-bag.

'Yes,' said Stuffy with a sigh; and pocketing the forbidden fruit, he went away to give Bess the present, that won a smile from her, and permission to escort her round the garden.

'Poor Stuffy's heart has really got the better of his stomach at last, and his efforts will be much encouraged by the rewards Bess gives him,' said Mrs Jo.

'Happy the man who can put temptation in his pocket and learn self-denial from so sweet a little teacher!' added Mr Bhaer, as the children passed the window, Stuffy's fat face full of placid satisfaction, and Goldilocks surveying her sugar-rose with polite interest, though she would have preferred a real flower with a 'pitty smell'.

When her father came to take her home, a universal wail arose, and the parting gifts showered upon her increased her luggage to such an extent that Mr Laurie proposed having out the big wagon to take it into town. Everyone had given her something; and it was found difficult to pack white mice, cake, a parcel of shells, apples, a rabbit kicking violently in a bag, a large cabbage for his refreshment, a bottle of minnows, and a mammoth bouquet. The farewell scene was moving, for the Princess sat upon the hall-table, surrounded by her subjects. She kissed her cousins, and held out her hand to the other boys, who shook it gently with various soft speeches, for they were taught not to be ashamed of showing their emotions.

'Come again soon, little dear,' whispered Dan fastening his best green-and-gold beetle in her hat.

'Don't forget me, Princess, whatever you do,' said

the engaging Tommy, taking a last stroke of the pretty
hair.

'I am coming to your house next week, and then I
shall see you, Bess,' added Nat, as if he found consolation in the thought.

'Do shake hands now,' cried Jack, offering a smooth
paw.

'Here are two nice new ones to remember us by,'
said Dick and Dolly, presenting fresh whistles, quite
unconscious that seven old ones had been privately
deposited in the kitchen-stove.

'My little precious! I shall work you a book-mark
right away, and you must keep it *always*,' said Nan,
with a warm embrace.

But of all the farewells, poor Billy's was the most
pathetic, for the thought that she was really going
became so unbearable that he cast himself down before
her, hugging her little blue boots and blubbering despairingly, 'Don't go away! oh, don't!' Goldilocks was
so touched by this burst of feeling, that she leaned
over and lifting the poor lad's head, said, in her soft,
little voice,

'Don't cry, poor Billy! I will tiss you and tum adain
soon.'

This promise consoled Billy, and he fell back beaming with pride at the unusual honour conferred upon
him.

'Me too! me too!' clamoured Dick and Dolly, feeling
that their devotion deserved some return. The others
looked as if they would like to join in the cry; and
something in the kind, merry faces about her moved
the Princess to stretch out her arms and say, with
reckless condescension,

'I will tiss evvybody!'

Like a swarm of bees about a very sweet flower, the affectionate lads surrounded their pretty playmate, and kissed her till she looked like a little rose, not roughly, but so enthusiastically, that nothing but the crown of her hat was visible for a moment. Then her father rescued her, and she drove away still smiling and waving her hands, while the boys sat on the fence screaming like a flock of guinea-fowls, 'Come back! come back!' till she was out of sight.

They all missed her, and each dimly felt that he was better for having known a creature so lovely, delicate, and sweet; for little Bess appealed to the chivalrous instinct in them as something to love, admire, and protect with a tender sort of reverence. Many a man remembers some pretty child who has made a place in his heart and kept her memory alive by the simple magic of her innocence; these little men were just learning to feel this power, and to love it for its gentle influence, not ashamed to let the small hand lead them, nor to own their loyalty to womankind, even in the bud.

14

DAMON AND PYTHIAS

Mrs Bhaer was right; peace was only a temporary lull, a storm was brewing, and two days after Bess left, a moral earthquake shook Plumfield to its centre.

Tommy's hens were at the bottom of the trouble, for if they had not persisted in laying so many eggs, he could not have sold them and made such sums. Money is the root of all evil, and yet it is such a useful root that we cannot get on without it any more than we can without potatoes. Tommy certainly could not, for he spent his income so recklessly, that Mr Bhaer was obliged to insist on a savings-bank, and presented him with a private one – an imposing tin edifice, with the name over the door, and a tall chimney, down which the pennies were to go, there to rattle temptingly till leave was given to open a sort of trap-door in the floor.

The house increased in weight so rapidly, that Tommy soon became satisfied with his investment, and planned to buy unheard-of treasures with his capital. He kept account of the sums deposited, and was promised that he might break the bank as soon as he had five dollars, on condition that he spent the money wisely. Only one dollar was needed, and the day Mrs Jo paid him for four dozen eggs, he was so delighted, that he raced off to the barn to display the bright quarters to Nat, who was also laying by money for the long-desired violin.

'I wish I had 'em to put with my three dollars, then I'd soon get enough to buy my fiddle,' he said, looking wistfully at the money.

'P'raps I'll lend you some. I haven't decided yet what I'll do with mine,' said Tommy, tossing up his quarters, and catching them as they fell.

'Hi! boys! come down to the brook and see what a jolly great snake Dan's got!' called a voice from behind the barn.

'Come on,' said Tommy; and, laying his money inside the old winnowing machine, away he ran, followed by Nat.

The snake was very interesting, and then a long chase after a lame crow, and its capture, so absorbed Tommy's mind and time, that he never thought of his money till he was safely in bed that night.

'Never mind, no one but Nat knows where it is,' said the easy-going lad, and fell asleep untroubled by any anxiety about his property.

Next morning, just as the boys assembled for school, Tommy rushed into the room breathlessly, demanding,

'I say, who has got my dollar?'

'What are you talking about?' asked Franz. Tommy explained, and Nat corroborated his statement.

Everyone else declared they knew nothing about it, and began to look suspiciously at Nat, who got more and more alarmed and confused with each denial.

'Somebody must have taken it,' said Franz, as Tommy shook his fist at the whole party, and wrathfully declared that,

'By thunder-turtles! if I get hold of the thief, I'll give him what he won't forget in a hurry.'

'Keep cool, Tom; we shall find him out; thieves always come to grief,' said Dan, as one who knew something of the matter.

'May be some tramp slept in the barn and took it,' suggested Ned.

'No, Silas don't allow that; besides, a tramp wouldn't go looking in that old machine for money,' said Emil, with scorn.

'Wasn't it Silas himself?' said Jack.

'Well, I like that! Old Si is as honest as daylight. You wouldn't catch him touching a penny of ours,' said Tommy, handsomely defending his chief admirer from suspicion.

'Whoever it was had better tell, and not wait to be found out,' said Demi, looking as if an awful misfortune had befallen the family.

'I know you think it's me,' broke out Nat, red and excited.

'You are the only one who knew where it was,' said Franz.

'I can't help it – I didn't take it. I tell you I didn't – I didn't!' cried Nat, in a desperate sort of way.

'Gently, gently, my son! What is all this noise about?' and Mr Bhaer walked in among them.

Tommy repeated the story of his loss, and, as he listened, Mr Bhaer's face grew graver and graver; for, with all their faults and follies, the lads till now had been honest.

'Take your seats,' he said; and, when all were in their places, he added slowly, as his eye went from face to face with a grieved look, that was harder to bear than a storm of words,

'Now, boys, I shall ask each one of you a single question, and I want an honest answer. I am not going to try to frighten, bribe, or surprise the truth out of you, for every one of you has got a conscience, and knows what it is for. Now is the time to undo the wrong done to Tommy, and to set yourselves right before us all. I can forgive the yielding to a sudden temptation much easier than I can deceit. Don't add a lie to the theft, but confess frankly, and we will all try to help you make us forget and forgive.'

He paused a moment, and one might have heard a pin drop, the room was so still; then slowly and impressively he put the question to each one, receiving the same answer in varying tones from all. Every face was flushed and excited, so that Mr Bhaer could not take colour as a witness, and some of the little boys were so frightened that they stammered over the two short words as if guilty, though it was evident that they could not be. When he came to Nat, his voice softened, for the poor lad looked so wretched, Mr Bhaer felt for him. He believed him to be the culprit, and hoped to save the boy from another lie, by winning him to tell the truth without fear.

'Now, my son, give me an honest answer. Did you take the money?'

'No, sir!' and Nat looked up at him imploringly.

As the words fell from his trembling lips, somebody hissed.

'Stop that!' cried Mr Bhaer, with a sharp rap on his desk, as he looked sternly toward the corner whence the sound came.

Ned, Jack, and Emil sat there, and the first two looked ashamed of themselves, but Emil called out,

'It wasn't me, uncle! I'd be ashamed to hit a fellow when he is down.'

'Good for you!' cried Tommy, who was in a sad state of affliction at the trouble his unlucky dollar had made.

'Silence!' commanded Mr Bhaer; and when it came, he said soberly,

'I am *very* sorry, Nat, but evidences are against you, and your old fault makes us more ready to doubt you than we should be if we could trust you as we do some of the boys, who never fib. But mind, my child, I do not charge you with this theft; I shall not punish you for it till I am *perfectly* sure, nor ask anything more about it. I shall leave it for you to settle with your own conscience. If you are guilty come to me at any hour of the day or night and confess it, and I will forgive and help you to amend. If you are innocent, the truth will appear sooner or later, and the instant it does, I will be the first to beg your pardon for doubting you, and will so gladly do my best to clear your character before us all.'

'I didn't! I didn't!' sobbed Nat, with his head down upon his arms, for he could not bear the look of distrust and dislike which he read in the many eyes fixed on him.

'I hope not.' Mr Bhaer paused a minute, as if to give the culprit, whoever he might be, one more chance. Nobody spoke, however, and only sniffs of sympathy from some of the little fellows broke the silence. Mr Bhaer shook his head, and added, regretfully,

'There is nothing more to be done, then, and I have

but one thing to say: I shall not speak of this again, and I wish you all to follow my example. I cannot expect you to feel as kindly toward anyone whom you suspect as before this happened, but I do expect and desire that you will not torment the suspected person in any way – he will have a hard enough time without that. Now go to your lessons.'

'Father Bhaer let Nat off too easy,' muttered Ned to Emil, as they got out their books.

'Hold your tongue,' growled Emil, who felt that this event was a blot upon the family honour.

Many of the boys agreed with Ned, but Mr Bhaer was right, nevertheless; and Nat would have been wiser to confess on the spot and have the trouble over, for even the hardest whipping he ever received from his father was far easier to bear than the cold looks, the avoidance, and general suspicion that met him on all sides. If ever a boy was sent to Coventry and kept there, it was poor Nat; and he suffered a week of slow torture, though not a hand was raised against him, and hardly a word said.

That was the worst of it; if they would only have talked it out, or even have thrashed him all round, he could have stood it better than the silent distrust that made every face so terrible to meet. Even Mrs Bhaer's showed traces of it, though her manner was nearly as kind as ever; but the sorrowful anxious look in Father Bhaer's eyes cut Nat to the heart, for he loved his teacher dearly, and knew that he had disappointed all his hopes by this double sin.

Only one person in the house entirely believed in him, and stood up for him stoutly against all the rest. This was Daisy. She could not explain why she trusted him against all appearances, she only felt that she could not doubt him, and her warm sympathy made her strong to take his part. She would not hear a word against him from anyone, and actually slapped her beloved Demi when he tried to convince her that it *must* have been Nat, because no one else knew where the money was.

'May be the hens ate it; they are greedy old things,' she said; and when Demi laughed, she lost her temper, slapped the amazed boy, and then burst out crying and ran away, still declaring, 'He didn't! he didn't! he didn't!'

Neither aunt nor uncle tried to shake the child's faith in her friend, but only hoped her innocent instinct might prove sure, and loved her all the better for it. Nat often said, after it was over, that he couldn't have stood it, if it had not been for Daisy. When the others shunned him, she clung to him closer than ever, and turned her back on the rest. She did not sit on the stairs now when he solaced himself with the old fiddle, but went in and sat beside him, listening with a face so full of confidence and affection, that Nat forgot disgrace for a time, and was happy. She asked him to help her with her lessons, she cooked him marvellous messes in her kitchen, which he ate manfully, no matter what they were, for gratitude gave a sweet flavour to the most distasteful. She proposed imposs- ible games of cricket and ball, when she found that he shrank from joining the other boys. She put little nosegays from her garden on his desk, and tried in every way to show that *she* was not a fair-weather friend, but faithful through evil as well as good repute. Nan soon followed her example, in kindness at least;

curbed her sharp tongue, and kept her scornful little nose from any demonstration of doubt or dislike, which was good of Madame Giddy-gaddy, for she firmly believed that Nat took the money.

Most of the boys let him severely alone, but Dan, though he said he despised him for being a coward, watched over him with a grim sort of protection, and promptly cuffed any lad who dared to molest his mate or make him afraid. His idea of friendship was as high as Daisy's, and, in his own rough way, he lived up to it as loyally.

Sitting by the brook one afternoon, absorbed in the study of the domestic habits of water-spiders, he overheard a bit of conversation on the other side of the wall. Ned, who was intensely inquisitive, had been on tenterhooks to know *certainly* who was the culprit; for of late one or two of the boys had begun to think that they were wrong, Nat was so steadfast in his denials, and so meek in his endurance of their neglect. This doubt had teased Ned past bearing, and he had several times privately beset Nat with questions, regardless of Mr Bhaer's express command. Finding Nat reading alone on the shady side of the wall, Ned could not resist stopping for a nibble at the forbidden subject. He had worried Nat for some ten minutes before Dan arrived, and the first word the spider-student heard were these, in Nat's patient, pleading voice,

'Don't, Ned! oh, don't! I can't tell you because I don't know, and it's mean of you to keep nagging at me on the sly, when Father Bhaer told you not to plague me. You wouldn't dare to if Dan was round.'

'I ain't afraid of Dan; he's nothing but an old bully.

Don't believe but what he took Tom's money, and you know it, and won't tell. Come, now!'

'He didn't, but, if he did, I *would* stand up for him, he has always been so good to me,' said Nat, so earnestly, that Dan forgot his spiders, and rose quickly to thank him, but Ned's next words arrested him.

'I *know* Dan did it, and gave the money to you. Shouldn't wonder if he got his living picking pockets before he came here, for nobody knows anything about him but you,' said Ned, not believing his own words, but hoping to get the truth out of Nat by making him angry.

He succeeded in a part of his ungenerous wish, for Nat cried out, fiercely,

'If you say that again I'll go and tell Mr Bhaer all about it. I don't want to tell tales, but, by George! I will, if you don't let Dan alone.'

'Then you'll be a sneak, as well as a liar and a thief,' began Ned, with a jeer, for Nat had borne insult to himself so meekly, the other did not believe he would dare to face the master just to stand up for Dan.

What he might have added I cannot tell, for the words were hardly out of his mouth when a long arm from behind took him by the collar, and, jerking him over the wall in a most promiscuous way, landed him with a splash in the middle of the brook.

'Say that again and I'll duck you till you can't see!' cried Dan, looking like a modern Colossus of Rhodes as he stood, with a foot on either side the narrow stream, glaring down at the discomfited youth in the water.

'I was only in fun,' said Ned.

'You are a sneak yourself to badger Nat round the corner. Let me catch you at it again, and I'll souse you in the river next time. Get up, and clear out!' thundered Dan, in a rage.

Ned fled, dripping, and his impromptu sitz-bath evidently did him good, for he was very respectful to both the boys after that, and seemed to have left his curiosity in the brook. As he vanished Dan jumped over the wall, and found Nat lying as if quite worn out and bowed down with his troubles.

'He won't pester you again, I guess. If he does, just tell me, and I'll see to him,' said Dan, trying to cool down.

'I don't mind what he says about me so much. I've got used to it,' answered Nat, sadly; 'but I hate to have him pitch into you.'

'How do you know he isn't right?' asked Dan, turning his face away.

'What, about the money?' cried Nat, looking up with a startled air.

'Yes.'

'But I don't believe it! *You* don't care for money; all you want is your old bugs and things,' and Nat laughed, incredulously.

'I want a butterfly-net as much as you want a fiddle; why shouldn't I steal the money for it as much as you?' said Dan, still turning away, and busily punching holes in the turf with his stick.

'I don't think you would. You like to fight and knock folks round sometimes, but you don't lie, and I don't believe you'd steal,' and Nat shook his head decidedly.

'I've done both. I used to fib like fury; it's too much

trouble now; and I stole things to eat out of gardens when I ran away from Page, so you see I *am* a bad lot,' said Dan, speaking in the rough, reckless way which he had been learning to drop lately.

'O Dan! don't say it's you! I'd rather have it any of the other boys,' cried Nat, in such a distressed tone that Dan looked pleased, and showed that he did, by turning round with a queer expression in his face, though he only answered,

'I won't say anything about it. But don't you fret, and we'll pull through somehow, see if we don't.'

Something in his face and manner gave Nat a new idea; and he said, pressing his hands together, in the eagerness of his appeal,

'I think you know who did it. If you do, beg him to tell, Dan. It's so hard to have 'em all hate me for nothing. I don't think I *can* bear it much longer. If I had any place to go to, I'd run away, though I love Plumfield dearly; but I'm not brave and big like you, so I must stay and wait till someone shows them that I haven't lied.'

As he spoke, Nat looked so broken and despairing, that Dan could not bear it, and, muttering huskily,

'You won't wait long,' he walked rapidly away, and was seen no more for hours.

'What is the matter with Dan?' asked the boys of one another several times during the Sunday that followed a week which seemed as if it would never end. Dan was often moody, but that day he was so sober and silent that no one could get anything out of him. When they walked he strayed away from the rest, and came home late. He took no part in the evening conversation, but sat in the shadow, so busy with his own thoughts that he scarcely seemed to hear what was going on. When Mrs Jo showed him an unusually good report in the Conscience Book, he looked at it without a smile, and said, wistfully,

'You think I am getting on, don't you?'

'Excellently, Dan! and I am so pleased, because I always thought you only needed a little help to make you a boy to be proud of.'

He looked up at her with a strange expression in his black eyes – an expression of mingled pride and love and sorrow which she could not understand then – but remembered afterward.

'I'm afraid you'll be disappointed, but I do try,' he said, shutting the book without a sign of pleasure in the page that he usually liked so much to read over and talk about.

'Are you sick, dear?' asked Mrs Jo, with her hand on his shoulder.

'My foot aches a little; I guess I'll go to bed. Good night, mother,' he added, and held the hand against his cheek a minute, then went away looking as if he had said goodbye to something very dear.

'Poor Dan! he takes Nat's disgrace to heart sadly. He is a strange boy; I wonder if I ever shall understand him thoroughly?' said Mrs Jo to herself, as she thought over Dan's late improvement with real satisfaction, yet felt that there was more in the lad than she had at first suspected.

One of the things which cut Nat most deeply was an act of Tommy's, for after his loss Tommy had said to him, kindly but firmly,

'I don't wish to hurt you, Nat, but you see I can't afford to lose my money, so I guess we won't be partners any longer'; and with that Tommy rubbed out the sign, T. BANGS & CO.

Nat had been very proud of the 'CO.', and had hunted eggs industriously, kept his accounts all straight, and had added a good sum to his income from the sale of his share of stock in trade.

'O Tom! must you?' he said, feeling that his good name was gone for ever in the business world if this was done.

'I must,' returned Tommy, firmly. 'Emil says that when one man 'bezzles (I believe that's the word – it means to take money and cut away with it) the property of a firm, the other one sues him, or pitches into him somehow, and won't have anything more to do with him. Now you have 'bezzled my property; I shan't sue you, and I shan't pitch into you, but I *must* dissolve the partnership, because I can't trust you, and I don't wish to fail.'

'I can't make you believe me, and you won't take my money, though I'd be thankful to give all my dollars if you'd only say you don't think I took your money. Do let me hunt for you, I won't ask any wages, but do it for nothing. I know all the places, and I like it,' pleaded Nat.

But Tommy shook his head, and his jolly round face looked suspicious and hard as he said, shortly, 'Can't do it; wish you didn't know the places. Mind you don't go hunting on the sly, and speculate in my eggs.'

Poor Nat was so hurt that he could not get over it. He felt that he had lost not only his partner and patron, but that he was bankrupt in honour, and an outlaw from the business community. No one trusted his word, written or spoken, in spite of his efforts to redeem the past falsehood; the sign was down, the firm broken up, and he a ruined man. The barn, which was the boys' Wall Street, knew him no more. Cockletop and her sisters cackled for him in vain, and really seemed to take his misfortune to heart, for eggs were fewer, and some of the biddies retired in disgust to new nests, which Tommy could not find.

'*They* trust me,' said Nat, when he heard of it; and though the boys shouted at the idea, Nat found comfort in it, for when one is down in the world, the confidence of even a speckled hen is most consoling.

Tommy took no new partner, however, for distrust had entered in, and poisoned the peace of his once confiding soul. Ned offered to join him, but he declined, saying, with a sense of justice that did him honour,

'It might turn out that Nat didn't take my money, and then we could be partners again. I don't think it will happen, but I will give him a chance, and keep the place open a little longer.'

Billy was the only person whom Bangs felt he could trust in his shop, and Billy was trained to hunt eggs, and hand them over unbroken, being quite satisfied with an apple or a sugar-plum for wages. The morning after Dan's gloomy Sunday, Billy said to his employer, as he displayed the results of a long hunt,

'Only two.'

'It gets worse and worse; I never saw such provoking old hens,' growled Tommy, thinking of the days when he often had six to rejoice over. 'Well, put 'em in my hat and give me a new bit of chalk; I must mark 'em up, anyway.'

Billy mounted a peck-measure, and looked into the

top of the machine, where Tommy kept his writing materials.

'There's lots of money in here,' said Billy.

'No there isn't. Catch me leaving my cash round again,' returned Tommy.

'I see 'em – one, four, eight, two dollars,' persisted Billy, who had not yet mastered the figures correctly.

'What a jack you are!' and Tommy hopped up to get the chalk for himself but nearly tumbled down again, for there actually were four bright quarters in a row, with a bit of paper on them directed to 'Tom Bangs', that there might be no mistake.

'Thunder-turtles!' cried Tommy, and seizing them he dashed into the house, bawling wildly, 'It's all right! Got my money! Where's Nat?'

He was soon found, and his surprise and pleasure were so genuine that few doubted his word when he now denied all knowledge of the money.

'How could I put it back when I didn't take it? Do believe me now, and be good to me again,' he said, so imploringly, that Emil slapped him on the back, and declared *he* would for one.

'So will I, and I'm jolly glad it's not you. But who the dickens is it?' said Tommy, after shaking hands heartily with Nat.

'Never mind, as long as it's found,' said Dan with his eyes fixed on Nat's happy face.

'Well, I like that! I'm not going to have my things hooked, and then brought back like the juggling man's tricks,' cried Tommy, looking at his money as if he suspected witchcraft.

'We'll find him out somehow, though he was sly

enough to print this so his writing wouldn't be known,' said Franz, examining the paper.

'Demi prints tip-top,' put in Rob, who had not a very clear idea what the fuss was all about.

'You can't make me believe it's him, not if you talk till you are blue,' said Tommy, and the others hooted at the mere idea; for the little deacon, as they called him, was above suspicion.

Nat felt the difference in the way they spoke of Demi and himself, and would have given all he had or ever hoped to have to be so trusted; for he had learned how easy it is to lose the confidence of others, how very, very hard to win it back, and truth became to him a precious thing since he had suffered from neglecting it.

Mr Bhaer was very glad one step had been taken in the right direction, and waited hopefully for yet further revelations. They came sooner than he expected, and in a way that surprised and grieved him very much. As they sat at supper that night, a square parcel was handed to Mr Bhaer from Mrs Bates, a neighbour. A note accompanied the parcel, and, while Mr Bhaer read it, Demi pulled off the wrapper, exclaiming, as he saw its contents,

'Why, it's the book Uncle Teddy gave Dan!'

'The devil!' broke from Dan, for he had not yet quite cured himself of swearing, though he tried hard.

Mr Bhaer looked up quickly at the sound. Dan tried to meet his eyes, but could not; his own fell, and he sat biting his lips, getting redder and redder till he was the picture of shame.

'What is it?' asked Mrs Bhaer, anxiously.

'I should have preferred to talk about this in private,

but Demi has spoilt that plan, so I may as well have it out now,' said Mr Bhaer, looking a little stern, as he always did when any meanness or deceit came up for judgement.

'The note is from Mrs Bates, and she says that her boy Jimmy told her he bought this book of Dan last Saturday. She saw that it was worth much more than a dollar, and thinking there was some mistake, has sent it to me. Did you sell it, Dan?'

'Yes, sir,' was the slow answer.

'Why?'

'Wanted money.'

'For what?'

'To pay somebody.'

'To whom did you owe it?'

'Tommy.'

'Never borrowed a cent of me in his life,' cried Tommy, looking scared, for he guessed what was coming now, and felt that on the whole he would have preferred witchcraft, for he admired Dan immensely.

'Perhaps he took it,' cried Ned, who owed Dan a grudge for the ducking, and, being a mortal boy, liked to pay it off.

'O Dan!' cried Nat, clasping his hands, regardless of the bread and butter in them.

'It is a hard thing to do, but I must have this settled for I cannot have you watching each other like detectives, and the whole school disturbed in this way. Did you put that dollar in the barn this morning?' asked Mr Bhaer.

Dan looked him straight in the face, and answered steadily, 'Yes, I did.'

A murmur went round the table, Tommy dropped

his mug with a crash; Daisy cried out, 'I knew it wasn't Nat'; Nan began to cry, and Mrs Jo left the room, looking so disappointed, sorry, and ashamed that Dan could not bear it. He hid his face in his hands a moment, then threw up his head, squared his shoulders as if settling some load upon them, and said, with the dogged look, and half-resolute, half-reckless tone he had used when he first came,

'I did it; now you may do what you like to me, but I won't say another word about it.'

'Not even that you are sorry?' asked Mr Bhaer, troubled by the change in him.

'I ain't sorry.'

'I'll forgive him without asking,' said Tommy, feeling that it was harder somehow to see brave Dan disgraced than timid Nat.

'Don't want to be forgiven,' returned Dan, gruffly.

'Perhaps you will when you have thought about it quietly by yourself. I won't tell you now how surprised and disappointed I am, but by and by I will come up and talk to you in your room.'

'Won't make any difference,' said Dan, trying to speak defiantly, but failing as he looked at Mr Bhaer's sorrowful face; and, taking his words for a dismissal, Dan left the room as if he found it impossible to stay.

It would have done him good if he had stayed; for the boys talked the matter over with such sincere regret, and pity, and wonder, it might have touched and won him to ask pardon. No one was glad to find that it was he, not even Nat; for, spite of all his faults, and they were many, everyone liked Dan now, because under his rough exterior lay some of the manly virtues which we most admire and love. Mrs Jo had been the chief prop, as well as cultivator, of Dan; and she took it sadly to heart that her last and most interesting boy had turned out so ill. The theft was bad, but the lying about it, and allowing another to suffer so much from an unjust suspicion, was worse; and most discouraging of all was the attempt to restore the money in an underhand way, for it showed not only a want of courage, but a power of deceit that boded ill for the future. Still more trying was his steady refusal to talk of the matter, to ask pardon, or express any remorse. Days passed; and he went about his lessons and his work, silent, grim, and unrepentant. As if taking warning by their treatment of Nat, he asked no sympathy of anyone, rejected the advances of the boys, and spent his leisure hours roaming about the fields and woods, trying to find playmates in the birds and beasts, and succeeding better than most boys would have done, because he knew and loved them so well.

'If this goes on much longer, I'm afraid he will run away again, for he is too young to stand a life like this,' said Mr Bhaer, quite dejected at the failure of all his efforts.

'A little while ago I should have been quite sure that nothing would tempt him away, but now I am ready for anything, he is so changed,' answered poor Mrs Jo, who mourned over her boy and could not be comforted, because he shunned her more than anyone else, and only looked at her with the half-fierce, half-imploring eyes of a wild animal caught in a trap, when she tried to talk to him alone.

Nat followed him about like a shadow, and Dan did not repulse him as rudely as he did others, but said, in his blunt way, 'You are all right; don't worry about me. I can stand it better than you did.'

'But I don't like to have you all alone,' Nat would say, sorrowfully.

'I like it'; and Dan would tramp away, stifling a sigh sometimes, for he *was* lonely.

Passing through the birch grove one day, he came upon several of the boys, who were amusing themselves by climbing up the trees and swinging down again, as the slender elastic stems bent till their tops touched the ground. Dan paused a minute to watch the fun, without offering to join in it, and as he stood there Jack took his turn. He had unfortunately chosen too large a tree; for when he swung off, it only bent a little way, and left him hanging at a dangerous height.

'Go back; you can't do it!' called Ned from below.

Jack tried, but the twigs slipped from his hands, and he could not get his legs round the trunk. He kicked, and squirmed, and clutched in vain, then gave it up, and hung breathless, saying helplessly,

'Catch me! help me! I must drop!'

'You'll be killed if you do,' cried Ned, frightened out of his wits.

'Hold on!' shouted Dan; and up the tree he went, crashing his way along till he nearly reached Jack, whose face looked up at him, full of fear and hope.

'You'll both come down,' said Ned, dancing with excitement on the slope underneath, while Nat held out his arms, in the wild hope of breaking the fall.

'That's what I want; stand from under,' answered Dan, coolly; and, as he spoke, his added weight bent the tree many feet nearer the earth.

Jack dropped safely; but the birch, lightened of half

its load, flew up again so suddenly, that Dan, in the act of swinging round to drop feet foremost, lost his hold and fell heavily.

'I'm not hurt, all right in a minute,' he said, sitting up, a little pale and dizzy, as the boys gathered round him, full of admiration and alarm.

'You're a trump, Dan, and I'm ever so much obliged to you,' cried Jack, gratefully.

'It wasn't anything,' muttered Dan, rising slowly.

'I say it was, and I'll shake hands with you, though you are –' Ned checked the unlucky word on his tongue, and held out his hand, feeling that it was a handsome thing on his part.

'But I won't shake hands with a sneak'; and Dan turned his back with a look of scorn, that caused Ned to remember the brook, and retire with undignified haste.

'Come home, old chap; I'll give you a lift'; and Nat walked away with him leaving the others to talk over the feat together, to wonder when Dan would 'come round'; and to wish one and all that Tommy's 'confounded money had been in Jericho before it made such a fuss'.

When Mr Bhaer came into school next morning, he looked so happy, that the boys wondered what had happened to him, and really thought he had lost his mind when they saw him go straight to Dan, and, taking him by both hands, say all in one breath, as he shook them heartily,

'I know all about it, and I beg your pardon. It was like you to do it, and I love you for it, though it's never right to tell lies, even for a friend.'

'What is it?' cried Nat, for Dan said not a word,

only lifted up his head, as if a weight of some sort had fallen off his back.

'Dan did *not* take Tommy's money'; and Mr Bhaer quite shouted it, he was so glad.

'Who did?' cried the boys in a chorus.

Mr Bhaer pointed to one empty seat, and every eye followed his finger, yet no one spoke for a minute, they were so surprised.

'Jack went home early this morning, but he left this behind him'; and in the silence Mr Bhaer read the note which he had found tied to his door-handle when he rose.

'I took Tommy's dollar. I was peering in through a crack, and saw him put it there. I was afraid to tell before, though I wanted to. I didn't care so much about Nat, but Dan is a trump, and I can't stand it any longer. I never spent the money; it's under the carpet in my room, right behind the washstand. I'm awful sorry. I am going home, and don't think I shall ever come back, so Dan may have my things.

'JACK'

It was not an elegant confession, being badly written, much blotted, and very short; but it was a precious paper to Dan; and, when Mr Bhaer paused, the boy went to him, saying, in rather a broken voice, but with clear eyes, and the frank, respectful manner they had tried to teach him,

'I'll say I'm sorry now, and ask you to forgive me, sir.'

'It was a kind lie, Dan, and I can't help forgiving it;

but you see it did no good,' said Mr Bhaer, with a hand on either shoulder, and a face full of relief and affection.

'It kept the boys from plaguing Nat. That's what I did it for. It made him right down miserable. I didn't care so much,' explained Dan, as if glad to speak out after his hard silence.

'How could you do it? You are always *so* kind to me,' faltered Nat, feeling a strong desire to hug his friend and cry. Two girlish performances, which would have scandalized Dan to the last degree.

'It's all right now, old fellow, so don't be a fool,' he said, swallowing the lump in his throat, and laughing out as he had not done for weeks. 'Does Mrs Bhaer know?' he asked, eagerly.

'Yes; and she is so happy I don't know what she will do to you,' began Mr Bhaer, but got no farther, for here the boys came crowding about Dan in a tumult of pleasure and curiosity; but before he had answered more than a dozen questions, a voice cried out,

'Three cheers for Dan!' and there was Mrs Jo in the doorway waving her dish-towel, and looking as if she wanted to dance a jig for joy, as she used to do when a girl.

'Now then,' cried Mr Bhaer, and led off a rousing hurrah, which startled Asia in the kitchen, and made old Mr Roberts shake his head as he drove by, saying,

'Schools are not what they were when I was young!'

Dan stood it pretty well for a minute, but the sight of Mrs Jo's delight upset him, and he suddenly bolted across the hall into the parlour, whither she instantly followed, and neither were seen for half an hour.

Mr Bhaer found it very difficult to calm his excited

flock; and, seeing that lessons were an impossibility for a time, he caught their attention by telling them the fine old story of the friends whose fidelity to one another has made their names immortal. The lads listened and remembered, for just then their hearts were touched by the loyalty of a humbler pair of friends. The lie was wrong, but the love that prompted it and the courage that bore in silence the disgrace which belonged to another, made Dan a hero in their eyes. Honesty and honour had a new meaning now; a good name was more precious than gold; for once lost money could not buy it back; and faith in one another made life smooth and happy as nothing else could do.

Tommy proudly restored the name of the firm; Nat was devoted to Dan; and all the boys tried to atone to both for former suspicion and neglect. Mrs Jo rejoiced over her flock, and Mr Bhaer was never tired of telling the story of his young Damon and Pythias.

15

IN THE WILLOW

The old tree saw and heard a good many little scenes and confidences that summer, because it became the favourite retreat of all the children, and the willow seemed to enjoy it, for a pleasant welcome always met them, and the quiet hours spent in its arms did them all good. It had a great deal of company one Saturday afternoon, and some little bird reported what went on there.

First came Nan and Daisy with their small tubs and bits of soap, for now and then they were seized with a tidy fit, and washed up all their dolls' clothes in the brook. Asia would not have them 'slopping round' in her kitchen, and the bathroom was forbidden since Nan forgot to turn off the water till it overflowed and came gently dripping down through the ceiling. Daisy went systematically to work, washing first the white and then the coloured things, rinsing them nicely, and hanging them to dry on a cord fastened from one barberry-bush to another, and pinning them up with a set of tiny clothes-pins Ned had turned for her. But Nan put all her little things to soak in the same tub, and then forgot them while she collected thistledown to stuff a pillow for Semiramis, Queen of Babylon, as one doll was named. This took some time, and when

Mrs Giddy-gaddy came to take out her clothes, deep green stains appeared on everything, for she had forgotten the green silk lining of a certain cape, and its colour had soaked nicely into the pink and blue gowns, the little chemises, and even the best ruffled petticoat.

'Oh me! what a mess!' sighed Nan.

'Lay them on the grass to bleach,' said Daisy, with an air of experience.

'So I will, and we can sit up in the nest and watch that they don't blow away.'

The Queen of Babylon's wardrobe was spread forth upon the bank, and, turning up their tubs to dry, the little washerwomen climbed into the nest, and fell to talking, as ladies are apt to do in the pauses of domestic labour.

'I'm going to have a feather-bed to go with my new pillow,' said Mrs Giddy-gaddy, as she transferred the thistledown from her pocket to her handkerchief, losing about half in the process.

'I wouldn't; Aunt Jo says feather-beds aren't healthy. I never let my children sleep on anything but a mattress,' returned Mrs Shakespeare Smith, decidedly.

'I don't care; my children are so strong they often sleep on the floor, and don't mind it' (which was quite true). 'I can't afford nine mattresses, and I like to make beds myself.'

'Won't Tommy charge for the feathers?'

'May be he will, but I shan't pay him, and he won't care,' returned Mrs G., taking a base advantage of the well-known good-nature of T. Bangs.

'I think the pink will fade out of that dress sooner than the green mark will,' observed Mrs S., looking down from her perch, and changing the subject, for she and her gossip differed on many points, and Mrs Smith was a discreet lady.

'Never mind; I'm tired of dolls, and I guess I shall put them all away and attend to my farm; I like it rather better than playing house,' said Mrs G., unconsciously expressing the desire of many older ladies, who cannot dispose of their families so easily however.

'But you mustn't leave them; they will die without their mother,' cried tender Mrs Smith.

'Let 'em die then; I'm tired of fussing over babies, and I'm going to play with the boys; they need me to see to 'em,' returned the strong-minded lady.

Daisy knew nothing about woman's rights; she quietly took all she wanted, and no one denied her claim, because she did not undertake what she could not carry out, but unconsciously used the all-powerful right of her own influence to win from others any privilege for which she had proved her fitness. Nan attempted all sorts of things, undaunted by direful failures, and clamoured fiercely to be allowed to do everything that the boys did. They laughed at her, hustled her out of the way, and protested against her meddling with their affairs. But she would not be quenched and she would be heard, for her will was strong, and she had the spirit of a rampant reformer. Mrs Bhaer sympathized with her, but tried to curb her frantic desire for entire liberty, showing her that she must wait a little, learn self-control, and be ready to use her freedom before she asked for it. Nan had meek moments when she agreed to this, and the influences at work upon her were gradually taking effect. She no longer declared that she would be an engine-driver or a blacksmith, but turned her mind to farming, and found in it a vent for the energy bottled up in her active little body. It did not quite satisfy her, however; for her sage and sweet marjoram were dumb things, and could not thank her for her care. She wanted something human to love, work for, and protect, and was never happier than when the little boys brought their cut fingers, bumped heads, or bruised joints for her to 'mend up'. Seeing this, Mrs Jo proposed that she should learn how to do it nicely, and Nursey had an apt pupil in bandaging, plastering, and fomenting. The boys began to call her 'Dr Giddy-gaddy', and she liked it so well that Mrs Jo one day said to the Professor,

'Fritz, I see what we can do for that child. She wants something to live for even now, and will be one of the sharp, strong, discontented women if she does not have it. Don't let us snub her restless little nature, but do our best to give her the work she likes, and by and by persuade her father to let her study medicine. She will make a capital doctor, for she has courage, strong nerves, a tender heart, and an intense love and pity for the weak and suffering.'

Mr Bhaer smiled at first, but agreed to try, and gave Nan an herb-garden, teaching her the various healing properties of the plants she tended, and letting her try their virtues on the children in the little illnesses they had from time to time. She learned fast, remembered well, and showed a sense and interest most encouraging to her Professor, who did not shut his door in her face because she was a little woman.

She was thinking of this, as she sat in the willow that day, and when Daisy said in her gentle way,

'I love to keep house, and mean to have a nice one for Demi when we grow up and live together.'

Nan replied with decision,

'Well, I haven't got any brother, and I don't want any house to fuss over. I shall have an office, with lots of bottles and drawers and pestle things in it, and I shall drive round in a horse and chaise and cure sick people. That will be such fun.'

'Ugh! how can you bear the bad-smelling stuff and the nasty little powders and castor-oil and senna and hive syrup?' cried Daisy, with a shudder.

'I shan't have to take any, so I don't care. Besides, they make people well, and I like to cure folks. Didn't my sage-tea make Mother Bhaer's headache go away, and my hops stop Ned's toothache in five hours? So now!'

'Shall you put leeches on people, and cut off legs and pull out teeth?' asked Daisy, quaking at the thought.

'Yes, I shall do everything; I don't care if the people are all smashed up, I shall mend them. My Grandpa was a doctor, and I saw him sew a great cut in a man's cheek, and I held the sponge, and wasn't frightened a bit, and Grandpa said I was a brave girl.'

'How could you? I'm sorry for sick people, and I like to nurse them, but it makes my legs shake, so I have to run away. I'm not a brave girl,' sighed Daisy.

'Well, you can be my nurse, and cuddle my patients when I have given them the physic and cut off their legs,' said Nan, whose practice was evidently to be of the heroic kind.

'Ship ahoy! Where are you, Nan?' called a voice from below.

'Here we are.'

'Ay, ay!' said the voice, and Emil appeared holding one hand in the other, with his face puckered up as if in pain.

'Oh, what's the matter?' cried Daisy, anxiously.

'A confounded splinter in my thumb. Can't get it out. Take a pick at it, will you, Nanny?'

'It's in very deep, and I haven't any needle,' said Nan, examining a tarry thumb with interest.

'Take a pin,' said Emil, in a hurry.

'No, it's too big and hasn't got a sharp point.'

Here Daisy, who had dived into her pocket, presented a neat little housewife with four needles in it.

'You are the Posy who always has what we want,' said Emil; and Nan resolved to have a needle-book in her own pocket henceforth, for just such cases as this were always occurring in her practice.

Daisy covered her eyes, but Nan probed and picked with a steady hand, while Emil gave directions not down in any medical work or record.

'Starboard now! Steady, boys, steady! Try another tack. Heave ho! there she is!'

'Suck it,' ordered the Doctor, surveying the splinter with an experienced eye.

'Too dirty,' responded the patient, shaking his bleeding hand.

'Wait; I'll tie it up if you have got a handkerchief.'

'Haven't; take one of those rags down there.'

'Gracious! no, indeed; they are dolls' clothes,' cried Daisy, indignantly.

'Take one of mine; I'd like to help you,' said Nan; and swinging himself down, Emil caught up the first 'rag' he saw. It happened to be the frilled skirt; but

Nan tore it up without a murmur; and when the royal petticoat was turned into a neat little bandage, she dismissed her patient with the command,

'Keep it wet, and let it alone; then it will heal right up, and not be sore.'

'What do you charge?' asked the Commodore, laughing.

'Nothing; I keep a 'spensary; that is a place where poor people are doctored free gratis for nothing,' explained Nan, with an air.

'Thank you, Doctor Giddy-gaddy. I'll always call you in when I come to grief'; and Emil departed, but looked back to say – for one good turn deserved another – 'Your duds are blowing away, Doctor.'

Forgiving the disrespectful word, 'duds', the ladies hastily descended, and, gathering up their wash, retired to the house to fire up the little stove, and go to ironing.

A passing breath of air shook the old willow, as if it laughed softly at the childish chatter which went on in the nest, and it had hardly composed itself when another pair of birds alighted for a confidential twitter.

'Now, I'll tell you the secret,' began Tommy, who was 'swellin' wisibly' with the importance of his news.

'Tell away,' answered Nat, wishing he had brought his fiddle, it was so shady and quiet here.

'Well, we fellows were talking over the late interesting case of circumstantial evidence,' said Tommy, quoting at random from a speech Franz had made at the club, 'and I proposed giving Dan something to make up for our suspecting him, to show our respect, and so on, you know – something handsome and useful, that he could keep always, and be proud of. What do you think we chose?'

'A butterfly-net; he wants one ever so much,' said Nat, looking a little disappointed, for he meant to get it himself.

'No, sir; it's to be a microscope, a real swell one, that we see what-do-you-call-'ems in water with, and stars, and ant-eggs, and all sorts of games, you know. Won't it be a jolly good present?' said Tommy, rather confusing microscopes and telescopes in his remarks.

'Tip-top! I'm so glad! Won't it cost a heap, though?' cried Nat, feeling that his friend was beginning to be appreciated.

'Of course it will; but we are all going to give something. I headed the paper with my five dollars; for if it is done at all, it must be done handsome.'

'What! all of it? I never did see such a generous chap as you are'; and Nat beamed upon him with sincere admiration.

'Well, you see, I've been so bothered with my property, that I'm tired of it, and don't mean to save up any more, but give it away as I go along, and then nobody will envy me, or want to steal it, and I shan't be suspecting folks, and worrying about my old cash,' replied Tommy, on whom the cares and anxieties of a millionaire weighed heavily.

'Will Mr Bhaer let you do it?'

'He thought it was a first-rate plan, and said that some of the best men he knew preferred to do good with their money, instead of laying it up to be squabbled over when they died.'

'Your father is rich; does he do that way?'

'I'm not sure; he gives me all I want; I know that

much. I'm going to talk to him about it when I go
home. Anyhow, I shall set him a good example'; and
Tommy was so serious, that Nat did not dare to laugh,
but said, respectfully,

'You will be able to do ever so much with your
money, won't you?'

'So Mr Bhaer said, and he promised to advise me
about useful ways of spending it. I'm going to begin
with Dan; and next time I get a dollar or so, I shall do
something for Dick, he's such a good little chap, and
only has a cent a week for pocket-money. He can't
earn much, you know; so I'm going to kind of see to
him'; and good-hearted Tommy quite longed to
begin.

'I think that's a beautiful plan, and I'm not going to
try to buy a fiddle any more; I'm going to get Dan his
net all myself, and if there is any money left, I'll do
something to please poor Billy. He's fond of me, and
though he isn't poor, he'd like some little thing from
me, because I can make out what he wants better than
the rest of you.' And Nat fell to wondering how much
happiness could be got out of his precious three
dollars.

'So I would. Now come and ask Mr Bhaer if you
can't go in town with me on Monday afternoon, so
you can get the net, while I get the microscope. Franz
and Emil are going too, and we'll have a jolly time
larking around among the shops.'

The lads walked away arm-in-arm, discussing the
new plans with droll importance, yet beginning already
to feel the sweet satisfaction which comes to those who
try, no matter how humbly, to be earthly providences
to the poor and helpless, and gild their mite with the

gold of charity before it is laid up where thieves cannot break through and steal.

'Come up and rest while we sort the leaves; it's so cool and pleasant here,' said Demi, as he and Dan came sauntering home from a long walk in the woods.

'All right!' answered Dan, who was a boy of few words, and up they went.

'What makes the birch leaves shake so much more than the others?' asked inquiring Demi, who was always sure of an answer from Dan.

'They are hung differently. Don't you see the stem where it joins the leaf is sort of pinched one way, and where it joins the twig, it is pinched another. That makes it waggle with the least bit of wind, but the elm leaves hang straight, and keep stiller.'

'How curious! will this do so?' and Demi held up a sprig of acacia, which he had broken from a little tree on the lawn, because it was so pretty.

'No; that belongs to the sort that shuts up when you touch it. Draw your finger down the middle of the stem, and see if the leaves don't curl up,' said Dan, who was examining a bit of mica.

Demi tried it, and presently the little leaves did fold together, till the spray showed a single instead of a double line of leaves.

'I like that; tell me about the others. What do these do?' asked Demi, taking up a new branch.

'Feed silk-worms; they live on mulberry leaves, till they begin to spin themselves up. I was in a silk-factory once, and there were rooms full of shelves all covered with leaves, and worms eating them so fast that it made a rustle. Sometimes they eat so much they die. Tell that to Stuffy,' and Dan laughed, as he took up another bit of rock with a lichen on it.

'I know one thing about this mullein leaf: the fairies use them for blankets,' said Demi, who had not quite given up his faith in the existence of the little folk in green.

'If I had a microscope, I'd show you something prettier than fairies,' said Dan, wondering if he should ever own that coveted treasure. 'I knew an old woman who used mullein leaves for a night-cap because she had face-ache. She sewed them together, and wore it all the time.'

'How funny! was she your grandmother?'

'Never had any. She was a queer old woman, and lived alone in a little tumble-down house with nineteen cats. Folks called her a witch, but she wasn't, though she looked like an old rag-bag. She was real kind to me when I lived in that place, and used to let me get warm at her fire when the folks at the poorhouse were hard on me.'

'Did you live in a poorhouse?'

'A little while. Never mind that – I didn't mean to speak of it'; and Dan stopped short in his unusual fit of communicativeness.

'Tell about the cats, please,' said Demi, feeling that he had asked an unpleasant question, and sorry for it.

'Nothing to tell; only she had a lot of 'em, and kept 'em in a barrel nights; and I used to go and tip over the barrel sometimes, and let 'em out all over the house, and then she'd scold, and chase 'em and put 'em in again, spitting and yowling like fury.'

'Was she good to them?' asked Demi, with a hearty child's laugh, pleasant to hear.

'Guess she was. Poor old soul! she took in all the lost and sick cats in the town; and when anybody wanted one they went to Marm Webber, and she let 'em pick any kind and colour they wanted, and only asked ninepence – she was so glad to have her pussies get a good home.'

'I should like to see Marm Webber. Could I, if I went to that place?'

'She's dead. All my folks are,' said Dan, briefly.

'I'm sorry'; and Demi sat silent a minute, wondering what subject would be safe to try next. He felt delicate about speaking of the departed lady, but was very curious about the cats, and could not resist asking softly,

'Did she cure the sick ones?'

'Sometimes. One had a broken leg, and she tied it up to a stick, and it got well; and another had fits, and she doctored it with *yarbs* till it was cured. But some of 'em died, and she buried 'em; and when they couldn't get well, she killed 'em easy.'

'How?' asked Demi, feeling that there was a peculiar charm about this old woman, and some sort of joke about the cats, because Dan was smiling to himself.

'A kind lady, who was fond of cats, told her how, and gave her some stuff, and sent all her own pussies to be killed that way. Marm used to put a sponge, wet with ether, in the bottom of an old boot, then poke puss in head downwards. The ether put her to sleep in a jiffy, and she was drowned in warm water before she woke up.'

'I hope the cats didn't feel it. I shall tell Daisy about that. You have known a great many interesting things, haven't you?' asked Demi, and fell to meditating on the vast experience of a boy who had run away more than once, and taken care of himself in a big city.

'Wish I hadn't sometimes.'

'Why? Don't remembering them feel good?'

'No.'

'It's very singular how hard it is to manage your mind,' said Demi, clasping his hands round his knees, and looking up at the sky as if for information upon his favourite topic.

'Devilish hard – no, I don't mean that'; and Dan bit his lips, for the forbidden word slipped out in spite of him, and he wanted to be more careful with Demi than with any of the other boys.

'I'll play I didn't hear it,' said Demi; 'and you won't do it again, I'm sure.'

'Not if I can help it. That's one of the things I don't want to remember. I keep pegging away, but it don't seem to do much good'; and Dan looked discouraged.

'Yes, it does. You don't say half so many bad words as you used to; and Aunt Jo is pleased, because she said it was a hard habit to break up.'

'Did she?' and Dan cheered up a bit.

'You must put swearing away in your fault-drawer, and lock it up; that's the way I do with my badness.'

'What do you mean?' asked Dan, looking as if he found Demi almost as amusing as a new sort of cock-chafer or beetle.

'Well, it's one of my private plays, and I'll tell you, but I think you'll laugh at it,' began Demi, glad to hold forth on this congenial subject. 'I play that my mind is a round room, and my soul is a little sort of creature with wings that lives in it. The walls are full of shelves and drawers, and in them I keep my thoughts, and my goodness, and badness, and all sorts of things. The goods I keep where I can see them, and the bads I lock up tight, but they get out, and I have to keep putting them in and squeezing them down, they are so strong. The thoughts I play with when I am alone or in bed, and I make up and do what I like with them. Every Sunday I put my room in order, and talk with the little spirit that lives there, and tell him what to do. He is very bad sometimes, and won't mind me, and I have to scold him, and take him to Grandpa. He always makes him behave, and be sorry for his faults, because Grandpa likes this play, and gives me nice things to put in the drawers, and tells me how to shut up the naughties. Hadn't you better try that way? it's a very good one'; and Demi looked so earnest and full of faith, that Dan did not laugh at his quaint fancy, but said, soberly,

'I don't think there is a lock strong enough to keep my badness shut up. Anyway my room is in such a clutter I don't know how to clear it up.'

'You keep your drawers in the cabinet all spandy nice; why can't you do the others?'

'I ain't used to it. Will you show me how?' and Dan looked as if inclined to try Demi's childish way of keeping a soul in order.

'I'd love to, but I don't know how, except to talk as Grandpa does. I can't do it good like him, but I'll try.'

'Don't tell anyone; only now and then we'll come here and talk things over, and I'll pay you for it by telling all I know about my sort of things. Will that do?' and Dan held out his big, rough hand.

Demi gave his smooth, little hand readily, and the league was made; for in the happy, peaceful world where the younger boy lived, lions and lambs played together, and little children innocently taught their elders.

'Hush!' said Dan, pointing toward the house, as Demi was about to indulge in another discourse on the best way of getting badness down, and keeping it down; and peeping from their perch, they saw Mrs Jo strolling slowly along, reading as she went, while Teddy trotted behind her, dragging a little cart upside down.

'Wait till they see us,' whispered Demi, and both sat still as the pair came nearer, Mrs Jo so absorbed in her book that she would have walked into the brook if Teddy had not stopped her by saying,

'Marmar, I wanter fis.'

Mrs Jo put down the charming book which she had been trying to read for a week, and looked about her for a fishing-pole, being used to making toys out of nothing. Before she had broken one from the hedge, a slender willow bough fell at her feet; and, looking up, she saw the boys laughing in the nest.

'Up! up!' cried Teddy, stretching his arms and flapping his skirts as if about to fly.

'I'll come down and you come up. I must go to Daisy now'; and Demi departed to rehearse the tale of the nineteen cats, with the exciting boot-and-barrel episodes.

Teddy was speedily whisked up; and then Dan said, laughing, 'Come, too; there's plenty of room. I'll lend you a hand.'

Mrs Jo glanced over her shoulder, but no one was in sight, and, rather liking the joke of the thing, she laughed back, saying, 'Well, if you won't mention it, I think I will'; and with two nimble steps was in the willow.

'I haven't climbed a tree since I was married. I used to be very fond of it when I was a girl,' she said, looking well-pleased with her shady perch.

'Now, you read if you want to, and I'll take care of Teddy,' proposed Dan, beginning to make a fishing-rod for impatient Baby.

'I don't think I care about it now. What were you and Demi at up here?' asked Mrs Jo, thinking, from the sober look in Dan's face, that he had something on his mind.

'Oh, we were talking. I'd been telling him about leaves and things, and he was telling me some of his queer plays. Now, then, Major, fish away'; and Dan finished off his work by putting a big blue fly on the bent pin which hung at the end of the cord he had tied to the willow-rod.

Teddy leaned down from the tree, and was soon wrapt up in watching for the fish which he felt sure would come. Dan held him by his little petticoats, lest he should take a 'header' into the brook, and Mrs Jo soon won him to talk by doing so herself.

'I am so glad you told Demi about "leaves and things"; it is just what he needs; and I wish you would teach him, and take him to walk with you.'

'I'd like to, he is so bright; but –'

'But what?'

'I didn't think you'd trust me.'

'Why not?'

'Well, Demi is so kind of precious, and so good, and I'm such a bad lot, 1 thought you'd keep him away from me.'

'But you are *not* a "bad lot", as you say; and I do trust you, Dan, entirely, because you honestly try to improve, and do better and better every week.'

'Really?' and Dan looked up at her with the cloud of despondency lifting from his face.

'Yes; don't you feel it?'

'I hoped so, but I didn't know.'

'I have been waiting and watching quietly, for I thought I'd give you a good trial first, and if you stood it, I would give you the best reward I had. You *have* stood it well; and now I'm going to trust not only Demi, but my own boy, to you, because you can teach them some things better than any of us.'

'Can I?' and Dan looked amazed at the idea.

'Demi has lived among older people so much that he needs just what you have – knowledge of common things, strength and courage. He thinks you are the bravest boy he ever saw, and admires your strong way of doing things. Then you know a great deal about natural objects, and can tell him more wonderful tales of birds, and bees, and leaves, and animals, than his story-books give him; and, being true, these stories will teach and do him good. Don't you see now how much you can help him, and why I like to have him with you?'

'But I swear sometimes, and might tell him something wrong. I wouldn't mean to, but it might slip out, just as "devil" did a few minutes ago,' said Dan, anxious to do his duty, and let her know his shortcomings.

'I know you try not to say or do anything to harm the little fellow, and here is where I think Demi will help *you*, because he is so innocent and wise in his small way, and has what I am trying to give you, dear

– good principles. It is never too early to try and plant them in a child, and never too late to cultivate them in the most neglected person. You are only boys yet; you can teach one another. Demi will unconsciously strengthen your moral sense, you will strengthen his common sense, and I shall feel as if I had helped you both.'

Words could not express how pleased and touched Dan was by this confidence and praise. No one had ever trusted him before, no one had cared to find out and foster the good in him, and no one had suspected how much there was hidden away in the breast of the neglected boy, going fast to ruin, yet quick to feel and value sympathy and help. No honour that he might earn hereafter would ever be half so precious as the right to teach his few virtues and his small store of learning to the child whom he most respected; and no more powerful restraint could have been imposed upon him than the innocent companion confided to his care. He found courage now to tell Mrs Jo of the plan already made with Demi, and she was glad that the first step had been so naturally taken. Everything seemed working well for Dan, and she rejoiced over him, because it had seemed a hard task, yet, working on with a firm belief in the possibility of reformation in far older and worse subjects than he, there had come this quick and hopeful change to encourage her. He felt that he had friends now and a place in the world, something to live and work for, and though he said little, all that was best and bravest in a character made old by a hard experience responded to the love and faith bestowed on him, and Dan's salvation was assured.

Their quiet talk was interrupted by a shout of delight from Teddy, who, to the surprise of everyone, did actually catch a trout where no trout had been seen for years. He was so enchanted with his splendid success that he insisted on showing his prize to the family before Asia cooked it for supper; so the three descended and went happily away together, all satisfied with the work of that half hour.

Ned was the next visitor to the tree, but he only made a short stay, sitting there at his ease while Dick and Dolly caught a pailful of grasshoppers and crickets for him. He wanted to play a joke on Tommy, and intended to tuck up a few dozen of the lively creatures in his bed, so that when Bangs got in he would speedily tumble out again, and pass a portion of the night in chasing 'hoppergrasses' round the room. The hunt was soon over, and having paid the hunters with a few peppermints apiece Ned retired to make Tommy's bed.

For an hour the old willow sighed and sung to itself, talked with the brook, and watched the lengthening shadows as the sun went down. The first rosy colour was touching its graceful branches when a boy came stealing up the avenue, across the lawn, and, spying Billy by the brook-side, went to him, saying, in a mysterious tone,

'Go and tell Mr Bhaer I want to see him down here, please. Don't let anyone hear.'

Billy nodded and ran off, while the boy swung himself up into the tree, and sat there looking anxious, yet evidently feeling the charm of the place and hour. In five minutes Mr Bhaer appeared, and, stepping up on the fence, leaned into the nest, saying, kindly,

'I am glad to see you, Jack; but why not come in and meet us all at once?'

'I wanted to see you first, please, sir. Uncle made me come back. I know I don't deserve anything, but I hope the fellows won't be hard upon me.'

Poor Jack did not get on very well, but it was evident that he was sorry and ashamed, and wanted to be received as easily as possible; for his Uncle had thrashed him well and scolded him soundly for following the example he himself set. Jack had begged not to be sent back, but the school was cheap, and Mr Ford insisted, so the boy returned as quietly as possible, and took refuge behind Mr Bhaer.

'I hope not, but I can't answer for them, though I will see that they are not unjust. I think as Dan and Nat have suffered so much, being innocent, you should suffer something, being guilty. Don't you?' asked Mr Bhaer, pitying Jack, yet feeling that he deserved punishment for a fault which had so little excuse.

'I suppose so, but I sent Tommy's money back, and I said I was sorry, isn't that enough?' said Jack, rather sullenly; for the boy who could do so mean a thing was not brave enough to bear the consequences well.

'No; I think you should ask pardon of all three boys, openly and honestly. You cannot expect them to respect and trust you for a time, but you *can* live down this disgrace if you try, and I will help you. Stealing and lying are detestable sins, and I hope this will be a lesson to you. I am glad you are ashamed, it is a good sign; bear it patiently, and do your best to earn a better reputation.'

'I'll have an auction, and sell off all my goods dirt

cheap,' said Jack, showing his repentance in the most characteristic way.

'I think it would be better to *give* them away, and begin on a new foundation. Take "Honesty is the best policy" for your motto, and live up to it in act, and word, and thought, and though you don't make a cent of money this summer, you will be a rich boy in the autumn,' said Mr Bhaer, earnestly.

It was hard, but Jack consented, for he really felt that cheating didn't pay, and wanted to win back the friendship of the boys. His heart clung to his possessions, and he groaned inwardly at the thought of actually giving away certain precious things. Asking pardon publicly was easy compared to this; but then he began to discover that certain other things, invisible, but most valuable, were better property than knives, fish-hooks, or even money itself. So he decided to buy up a little integrity, even at a high price, and secure the respect of his playmates, though it was not a saleable article.

'Well, I'll do it,' he said, with a sudden air of resolution, which pleased Mr Bhaer.

'Good! and I'll stand by you. Now come and begin at once.'

And Father Bhaer led the bankrupt boy back into the little world, which received him coldly at first, but slowly warmed to him, when he showed that he had profited by the lesson, and was sincerely anxious to go into a better business with a new stock in trade.

16

Taming the Colt

'What in the world is that boy doing?' said Mrs Jo to herself, as she watched Dan running round the half-mile triangle as if for a wager. He was all alone, and seemed possessed by some strange desire to run himself into a fever, or break his neck; for, after several rounds, he tried leaping walls, and turning somersaults up the avenue, and finally dropped down on the grass before the door as if exhausted.

'Are you training for a race, Dan?' asked Mrs Jo, from the window where she sat.

He looked up quickly, and stopped panting to answer, with a laugh,

'No; I'm only working off my steam.'

'Can't you find a cooler way of doing it? You will be ill if you tear about so in such warm weather,' said Mrs Jo, laughing also, as she threw him out a great palm-leaf fan.

'Can't help it. I *must* run somewhere,' answered Dan, with such an odd expression in his restless eyes, that Mrs Jo was troubled, and asked, quickly,

'Is Plumfield getting too narrow for you?'

'I wouldn't mind if it was a little bigger. I like it though; only the fact is the devil gets into me sometimes, and then I do want to bolt.'

The words seemed to come against his will, for he looked sorry the minute they were spoken, and seemed to think he deserved a reproof for his ingratitude. But Mrs Jo understood the feeling, and though sorry to see it, she could not blame the boy for confessing it. She looked at him anxiously, seeing how tall and strong he had grown, how full of energy his face was, with its eager eyes and resolute mouth; and remembering the utter freedom he had known for years before, she felt how even the gentle restraint of his home would weigh upon him at times when the old lawless spirit stirred in him. 'Yes,' she said to herself, 'my wild hawk needs a larger cage; and yet, if I let him go, I am afraid he will be lost. I must try and find some lure strong enough to keep him safe.'

'I know all about it,' she added, aloud. 'It is not "the devil", as you call it, but the very natural desire of all young people for liberty. I used to feel just so, and once I really did think for a minute that I would bolt.'

'Why didn't you?' said Dan, coming to lean on the low window-ledge, with an evident desire to continue the subject.

'I knew it was foolish, and love for my mother kept me at home.'

'I haven't got any mother,' began Dan.

'I thought you had now,' said Mrs Jo, gently stroking the rough hair off his hot forehead.

'You are no end good to me, and I can't ever thank you enough, but it isn't just the same, is it?' and Dan looked up at her with a wistful, hungry look that went to her heart.

'No, dear, it is not the same, and never can be. I think my own mother would have been a great deal to

you. But as that cannot be, you must try to let me fill
her place. I fear I have not done all I ought, or you
would not want to leave me,' she added, sorrowfully.

'Yes, you have!' cried Dan, eagerly. 'I don't want to
go, and I won't go, if I can help it; but every now and
then I feel as if I must burst out somehow. I want to
run straight ahead somewhere, to smash something, or
pitch into somebody. Don't know why, but I do, and
that's all about it.'

Dan laughed as he spoke, but he meant what he
said, for he knit his black brows, and brought down
his fist on the ledge with such force, that Mrs Jo's
thimble flew off into the grass. He brought it back,
and as she took it she held the big, brown hand a
minute, saying, with a look that showed the words cost
her something,

'Well, Dan, run if you must, but don't run far;
and come back to me soon, for I want you very
much.'

He was rather taken aback by this unexpected permission to play truant, and somehow it seemed to
lessen his desire to go. He did not understand why,
but Mrs Jo did, and, knowing the natural perversity of
the human mind, counted on it to help her now. She
felt instinctively that the more the boy was restrained
the more he would fret against it; but leave him free,
and the mere sense of liberty would content him,
joined to the knowledge that his presence was dear to
those whom he loved best. It was a little experiment,
but it succeeded, for Dan stood silent a moment,
unconsciously picking the fan to pieces and turning the
matter over in his mind. He felt that she appealed
to his heart and his honour, and owned that he

understood it by saying presently, with a mixture of regret and resolution in his face,

'I won't go yet awhile, and I'll give you warning before I bolt. That's fair, isn't it?'

'Yes, we will let it stand so. Now, I want to see if I can't find some way for you to work off your steam better than running about the place like a mad dog, spoiling my fans, or fighting with the boys. What can we invent?' and while Dan tried to repair the mischief he had done, Mrs Jo racked her brain for some new device to keep her truant safe until he had learned to love his lessons better.

'How would you like to be my express-man?' she said, as a sudden thought popped into her head.

'Go into town, and do the errands?' asked Dan, looking interested at once.

'Yes; Franz is tired of it, Silas cannot be spared just now, and Mr Bhaer has no time. Old Andy is a safe horse, you are a good driver, and know your way about the city as well as a postman. Suppose you try it, and see if it won't do 'most as well to drive away two or three times a week as to run away once a month.'

'I'd like it ever so much, only I must go alone and do it all myself. I don't want any of the other fellows bothering round,' said Dan, taking to the new idea so kindly that he began to put on business airs already.

'If Mr Bhaer does not object you shall have it all your own way. I suppose Emil will growl, but he cannot be trusted with horses, and you can. By the way, tomorrow is market-day, and I must make out my list. You had better see that the wagon is in order, and tell Silas to have the fruit and vegetables ready for mother. You will have to be up early and get back in time for school, can you do that?'

'I'm always an early bird, so I don't mind,' and Dan slung on his jacket with despatch.

'The early bird got the worm this time, I'm sure,' said Mrs Jo, merrily.

'And a jolly good worm it is,' answered Dan, as he went laughing away to put a new lash to the whip, wash the wagon, and order Silas about with all the importance of a young express-man.

'Before he is tired of this I will find something else and have it ready when the next restless fit comes on,' said Mrs Jo to herself, as she wrote her list with a deep sense of gratitude that all her boys were not Dans.

Mr Bhaer did not entirely approve of the new plan, but agreed to give it a trial, which put Dan on his mettle, and caused him to give up certain wild plans of his own, in which the new lash and the long hill were to have borne a part. He was up and away very early the next morning, heroically resisting the temptation to race with the milkmen going into town. Once there, he did his errands carefully, and came jogging home again in time for school, to Mr Bhaer's surprise and Mrs Jo's great satisfaction. The Commodore did growl at Dan's promotion, but was pacified by a superior padlock to his new boathouse, and the thought that seamen were meant for higher honours than driving market-wagons and doing family errands. So Dan filled his new office well and contentedly for weeks, and said no more about bolting. But one day Mr Bhaer found him pummelling Jack, who was roaring for mercy under his knee.

'Why, Dan, I thought you had given up fighting,' he said, as he went to the rescue.

'We ain't fighting, we are only wrestling,' answered Dan, leaving off reluctantly.

'It looks very much like it, and feels like it, hey, Jack?' said Mr Bhaer, as the defeated gentleman got upon his legs with difficulty.

'Catch me wrestling with him again. He's 'most knocked my head off,' snarled Jack, holding on to that portion of his frame as if it really was loose upon his shoulders.

'The fact is, we began in fun, but when I got him down I couldn't help pounding him. Sorry I hurt you, old fellow,' explained Dan, looking rather ashamed of himself.

'I understand. The longing to pitch into somebody was so strong you couldn't resist. You are a sort of Berserker, Dan, and something to tussle with is as necessary to you as music is to Nat,' said Mr Bhaer, who knew all about the conversation between the boy and Mrs Jo.

'Can't help it. So if you don't want to be pounded you'd better keep out of the way,' answered Dan, with a warning look in his black eyes that made Jack sheer off in haste.

'If you want something to wrestle with, I will give you a tougher specimen than Jack,' said Mr Bhaer and, leading the way to the wood-yard, he pointed out certain roots of trees that had been grubbed up in the spring, and had been lying there waiting to be split.

'There, when you feel inclined to maltreat the boys, just come and work off your energies here, and I'll thank you for it.'

'So I will'; and, seizing the axe that lay near, Dan hauled out a tough root, and went at it so vigorously, that the chips flew far and wide, and Mr Bhaer fled for his life.

To his great amusement, Dan took him at his word, and was often seen wrestling with the ungainly knots, hat and jacket off, red face, and wrathful eyes; for he got into royal rages over some of his adversaries, and swore at them under his breath till he had conquered them, when he exulted, and marched off to the shed with an armful of gnarled oak-wood in triumph. He blistered his hands, tired his back, and dulled the axe, but it did him good, and he got more comfort out of the ugly roots than anyone dreamed, for with each blow he worked off some of the pent-up power that would otherwise have been expended in some less harmless way.

'When this is gone I really don't know what I *shall* do,' said Mrs Jo to herself, for no inspiration came, and she was at the end of her resources.

But Dan found a new occupation for himself, and enjoyed it some time before anyone discovered the cause of his contentment. A fine young horse of Mr Laurie's was kept at Plumfield that summer, running loose in a large pasture across the brook. The boys were all interested in the handsome, spirited creature, and for a time were fond of watching him gallop and frisk with his plumey tail flying, and his handsome head in the air. But they soon got tired of it, and left Prince Charlie to himself. All but Dan, *he* never tired of looking at the horse, and seldom failed to visit him each day with a lump of sugar, a bit of bread, or an apple to make him welcome. Charlie was grateful, accepted his friendship, and the two loved one another as if they felt some tie between them, inexplicable but strong. In whatever part of the wide field he might be, Charlie always came at full speed when Dan whistled at the bars, and the boy was never happier than when the beautiful, fleet creature put its head on his shoulder, looking up at him with fine eyes full of intelligent affection.

'We understand one another without any palaver, don't we, old fellow?' Dan would say, proud of the horse's confidence, and so jealous of his regard, that he told no one how well the friendship prospered, and never asked anybody but Teddy to accompany him on these daily visits.

Mr Laurie came now and then to see how Charlie got on, and spoke of having him broken to harness in the autumn.

'He won't need much taming, he is such a gentle, fine-tempered brute. I shall come out and try him with a saddle myself some day,' he said, on one of these visits.

'He lets me put a halter on him, but I don't believe he will bear a saddle even if *you* put it on,' answered Dan, who never failed to be present when Charlie and his master met.

'I shall coax him to bear it, and not mind a few tumbles at first. He has never been harshly treated so, though he will be surprised at the new performances, I think he won't be frightened, and his antics will do no harm.'

'I wonder what he would do,' said Dan to himself, as Mr Laurie went away with the Professor, and Charlie returned to the bars, from which he had retired when the gentlemen came up.

A daring fancy to try the experiment took possession of the boy as he sat on the topmost rail with the glossy back temptingly near him. Never thinking of danger, he obeyed the impulse, and while Charlie suspectingly nibbled at the apple he held, Dan quickly and quietly took his seat. He did not keep it long, however, for with an astonished snort, Charlie reared straight up, and deposited Dan on the ground. The fall did not hurt him, for the turf was soft, and he jumped up, saying, with a laugh,

'I did it anyway! Come here, you rascal, and I'll try it again.'

But Charlie declined to approach, and Dan left him resolving to succeed in the end; for a struggle like this suited him exactly. Next time he took a halter, and having got it on, he played with the horse for a while, leading him to and fro, and putting him through various antics till he was a little tired; then Dan sat on the wall and gave him bread, but watched his chance, and getting a good grip of the halter, slipped on to his back. Charlie tried the old trick, but Dan held on, having had practice with Toby, who occasionally had an obstinate fit, and tried to shake off his rider. Charlie was both amazed and indignant; and after prancing for a minute, set off at a gallop, and away went Dan heels over head. If he had not belonged to the class of boys who go through all sorts of dangers unscathed, he would have broken his neck; as it was, he got a heavy fall, and lay still collecting his wits, while Charlie tore round the field tossing his head with every sign of satisfaction at the discomfiture of his rider. Presently it seemed to occur to him that something was wrong with Dan, and, being of a magnanimous nature, he went to see what the matter was. Dan let him sniff about and perplex himself for a few minutes; then he looked up at him, saying, decidedly as if the horse could understand,

'You think you have beaten, but you are mistaken, old boy; and I'll ride you yet – see if I don't.'

He tried no more that day, but soon after attempted a new method of introducing Charlie to a burden. He strapped a folded blanket on his back, and then let him race, and rear, and roll, and fume as much as he liked. After a few fits of rebellion Charlie submitted, and in a few days permitted Dan to mount him, often stopping short to look round, as if he said, half patiently, half reproachfully, 'I don't understand it, but I suppose you mean no harm, so I permit the liberty.'

Dan patted and praised him, and took a short turn every day, getting frequent falls, but persisting in spite of them, and longing to try a saddle and bridle, but not daring to confess what he had done. He had his wish, however, for there had been a witness of his pranks who said a good word for him.

'Do you know what that chap has ben doin' lately?' asked Silas of his master, one evening, as he received his orders for the next day.

'Which boy?' said Mr Bhaer, with an air of resignation, expecting some sad revelation.

'Dan, he's ben a breaking the colt, sir, and I wish I may die if he ain't done it,' answered Silas, chuckling.

'How do you know?'

'Wal, I kinder keep an eye on the little fellers, and most gen'lly know what they're up to; so when Dan kep going off to the paster, and coming home black and blue, I mistrusted that *suthing* was goin' on. I didn't say nothin', but I crep up into the barn chamber, and from there I see him goin' through all manner of games with Charlie. Blest if he warn't throwed time and agin, and knocked round like a bag o' meal. But the pluck of the boy did beat all, and he 'peared to like it, and kep on as ef bound to beat.'

'But, Silas, you should have stopped it – the boy might have been killed,' said Mr Bhaer, wondering what freak his irrepressibles would take into their heads next.

'S'pose I oughter; but there warn't no real danger, for Charlie ain't no tricks, and is as pretty a tempered horse as ever I see. Fact was, I couldn't bear to spile sport, for ef there's anything I do admire it's grit, and Dan is chock full on't. But now I know he's hankerin' after a saddle, and yet won't take even the old one on the sly; so I just thought I'd up and tell, and maybe you'd let him try what he can do. Mr Laurie won't mind, and Charlie's all the better for't.'

'We shall see'; and off went Mr Bhaer to inquire into the matter.

Dan owned up at once, and proudly proved that Silas was right by showing off his power over Charlie; for by dint of much coaxing, many carrots, and infinite perseverance, he really had succeeded in riding the colt with a halter and blanket. Mr Laurie was much amused, and well pleased with Dan's courage and skill, and let him have a hand in all future performances; for he set about Charlie's education at once, saying that he was not going to be outdone by a slip of a boy. Thanks to Dan, Charlie took kindly to the saddle and bridle when he had once reconciled himself to the indignity of the bit; and after Mr Laurie had trained him a little, Dan was permitted to ride him, to the great envy and admiration of the other boys.

'Isn't he handsome? and don't he mind me like a lamb?' said Dan one day as he dismounted and stood with his arm round Charlie's neck.

'Yes, and isn't he a much more useful and agreeable animal than the wild colt who spent his days racing about the field, jumping fences, and running away now and then?' asked Mrs Bhaer from the steps where she always appeared when Dan performed with Charlie.

'Of course he is. See he won't run away now, even if I don't hold him, and he comes to me the minute I whistle; I have tamed him well, haven't I?' and Dan looked both proud and pleased, as well he might, for, in spite of their struggles together, Charlie loved him better than his master.

'I am taming a colt too, and I think I shall succeed as well as you if I am as patient and persevering,' said Mrs Jo, smiling so significantly at him, that Dan understood and answered, laughing, yet in earnest,

'We won't jump over the fence and run away, but stay and let them make a handsome, useful span of us, hey, Charlie?'

17

COMPOSITION DAY

'Hurry up, boys, it's three o'clock, and Uncle Fritz likes us to be punctual, you know,' said Franz one Wednesday afternoon as a bell rang, and a stream of literary-looking young gentlemen with books and paper in their hands were seen going toward the museum.

Tommy was in the schoolroom, bending over his desk, much bedaubed with ink, flushed with the ardour of inspiration, and in a great hurry as usual, for easy-going Bangs never was ready till the very last minute. As Franz passed the door looking up laggards, Tommy gave one last blot and flourish, and departed out of the window waving his paper to dry it as he went. Nan followed, looking very important, with a large roll in her hand, and Demi escorted Daisy, both evidently brimful of some delightful secret.

The museum was all in order, and the sunshine among the hop-vines made pretty shadows on the floor as it peeped through the great window. On one side sat Mr and Mrs Bhaer, on the other was a little table on which the compositions were laid as soon as read, and in a large semicircle sat the children on camp-stools which occasionally shut up and let the sitter-down thus preventing any stiffness in the assembly.

As it took too much time to have all read, they took turns, and on this Wednesday the younger pupils were the chief performers, while the elder ones listened with condescension and criticized freely.

'Ladies first; so Nan may begin,' said Mr Bhaer, when the settling of stools and rustling of papers had subsided.

Nan took her place beside the little table, and with a preliminary giggle, read the following interesting essay on 'The Sponge':

'The sponge, my friends, is a most useful and interesting plant. It grows on rocks under the water, and is a kind of sea-weed, I believe. People go and pick it and dry it and wash it, because little fish and insects live in the holes of the sponge; I found shells in my new one, and sand. Some are very fine and soft; babies are washed with them. The sponge has many uses. I will relate some of them, and I hope my friends will remember what I say. One use is to wash the face; I don't like it myself, but I do it because I wish to be clean. Some people *don't*, and they are dirty.' Here the eye of the reader rested sternly upon Dick and Dolly, who quailed under it, and instantly resolved to scrub themselves virtuously on all occasions. 'Another use is to wake people up; I allude to *boys* par-*tic*-u-lar-ly.' Another pause after the long word to enjoy the smothered laugh that went round the room. 'Some boys do not get up when called, and Mary Ann squeezes the water out of a wet sponge on their faces, and it makes them so mad they wake up.' Here the laugh broke out, and Emil said, as if he had been hit,

'Seems to me you are wandering from the subject.'

'No, I ain't; we are to write about vegetables or

animals, and I'm doing both: for boys are animals, aren't they?' cried Nan; and, undaunted by the indignant 'No!' shouted at her, she calmly proceeded,

'One more interesting thing is done with sponges, and this is when doctors put ether on it, and hold it to people's noses when they have teeth out. *I* shall do this when I am bigger, and give ether to the sick, so they will go to sleep and not feel me cut off their legs and arms.'

'I know somebody who killed cats with it,' called out Demi, but was promptly crushed by Dan, who upset his camp-stool and put a hat over his face.

'I will *not* be interruckted,' said Nan, frowning upon the unseemly scrimmagers. Order was instantly restored, and the young lady closed her remarks as follows:

'My composition has three morals, my friends.' Some body groaned, but no notice was taken of the insult. 'First, is keep your faces clean – second, get up early – third, when the ether sponge is put over your nose, breathe hard and don't kick, and your teeth will come out easy. I have no more to say.' And Miss Nan sat down amid tumultuous applause.

'That is a very remarkable composition; its tone is high, and there is a good deal of humour in it. Very well done, Nan. Now, Daisy,' and Mr Bhaer smiled at one young lady as he beckoned to the other.

Daisy coloured prettily as she took her place, and said, in her modest little voice,

'I'm afraid you won't like mine; it isn't nice and funny like Nan's. But I couldn't do any better.'

'We always like yours, Posy,' said Uncle Fritz, and a gentle murmur from the boys seemed to confirm the remark. Thus encouraged, Daisy read her little paper, which was listened to with respectful attention.

'"The Cat": The cat is a sweet animal. I love them very much. They are clean and pretty, and catch rats and mice, and let you pet them, and are fond of you if you are kind. They are very wise, and can find their way anywhere. Little cats are called kittens, and are dear things. I have two, named Huz and Buz, and their mother is Topaz, because she has yellow eyes. Uncle told me a pretty story about a man named Ma-ho-met. He had a nice cat, and when she was asleep on his sleeve, and he wanted to go away, he cut off the sleeve so as not to wake her up. I think he was a kind man. Some cats catch fish.'

'So do I!' cried Teddy, jumping up eager to tell about his trout.

'Hush!' said his mother, setting him down again as quickly as possible, for orderly Daisy hated to be 'interruckted', as Nan expressed it.

'I read about one who used to do it very slyly. I tried to make Topaz, but she did not like the water, and scratched me. She does like tea, and when I play in my kitchen she pats the teapot with her paw, till I give her some. She is a fine cat, she eats apple-pudding and molasses. Most cats do not.'

'That's a first-rater,' called out Nat, and Daisy retired, pleased with the praise of her friend.

'Demi looks so impatient we must have him up at once or he won't hold out,' said Uncle Fritz, and Demi skipped up with alacrity.

'Mine is a poem!' he announced in a tone of triumph, and read his first effort in a loud and solemn voice:

'I write about the butterfly
It is a pretty thing;
And flies about like the birds,
But it does not sing.

'First it is a little grub,
And then it is a nice yellow cocoon,
And then the butterfly
Eats its way out soon.

'They live on dew and honey,
They do not have any hive,
They do not sting like wasps, and bees, and hornets,
And to be as good as they are we should strive.

'I should like to be a beautiful butterfly,
All yellow, and blue, and green, and red;
But I should not like
To have Dan put camphor on my poor little head.'

This unusual burst of genius brought down the
house, and Demi was obliged to read it again, a somewhat difficult task, as there was no punctuation whatever, and the little poet's breath gave out before he got
to the end of some of the long lines.

'He will be a Shakespeare yet,' said Aunt Jo, laughing as if she would die, for this poetic gem reminded
her of one of her own, written at the age of ten, and
beginning gloomily,

'I wish I had a quiet tomb,
Beside a little rill;
Where birds, and bees, and butterflies,
Would sing upon the hill.'

'Come on, Tommy. If there is as much ink inside your paper as there is outside, it will be a long composition,' said Mr Bhaer, when Demi had been induced to tear himself from his poem and sit down.

'It isn't a composition, it's a letter. You see, I forgot all about its being my turn till after school, and then I didn't know what to have, and there wasn't time to read up; so I thought you wouldn't mind my taking a letter that I wrote to my Grandma. It's got something about birds in it, so I thought it would do.'

With this long excuse, Tommy plunged into a sea of ink and floundered through, pausing now and then to decipher one of his own flourishes.

'MY DEAR GRANDMA, I hope you are well. Uncle James sent me a pocket rifle. It is a beautiful little instrument of killing, shaped like this – [Here Tommy displayed a remarkable sketch of what looked like an intricate pump, or the inside of a small steam-engine] – 44 are the sights; 6 is a false stock that fits in at A; 3 is the trigger, and 2 is the cock. It loads at the breech, and fires with great force and straightness. I am going out shooting squirrels soon. I shot several fine birds for the museum. They had speckled breasts, and Dan liked them very much. He stuffed them tip-top, and they sit on the tree quite natural, only one looks a little tipsy. We had a Frenchman working here the other day, and Asia called his name so funnily that I will tell you about it. His name was Germain: first she called him Jerry, but we laughed at her, and she changed it to Jeremiah; but ridicule was the result, so it became Mr

Germany; but ridicule having been again resumed, it became Garrymon, which it has remained ever since. I do not write often, I am so busy; but I think of you often, and sympathize with you, and sincerely hope you get on as well as can be expected without me. Your affectionate grandson,

'THOMAS BUCKMASTER BANGS

'P.S. If you come across any postage-stamps, remember me.

'N.B. Love to all, and a great deal to Aunt Almira. Does she make any nice plum-cakes now?

'P.S. Mrs Bhaer sends her respects.

'P.S. And so would Mr B. if he knew I was in act to write.

'N.B. Father is going to give me a watch on my birthday. I am glad, as at present I have no means of telling time, and am often late at school.

'P.S. I hope to see you soon. Don't you wish to send for me?

T.B.B.'

As each postcript was received with a fresh laugh from the boys, by the time he came to the sixth and last, Tommy was so exhausted that he was glad to sit down and wipe his ruddy face.

'I hope the dear old lady will live through it,' said Mr Bhaer, under cover of the noise.

'We won't take any notice of the broad hint given in that last P.S. The letter will be quite as much as she can bear without a visit from Tommy,' answered Mrs

Jo, remembering that the old lady usually took to her bed after a visitation from her irrepressible grandson.

'Now, me,' said Teddy, who had learned a bit of poetry, and was so eager to say it that he had been bobbing up and down during the reading, and could no longer be restrained.

'I'm afraid he will forget it if he waits; and I have had a deal of trouble in teaching him,' said his mother.

Teddy trotted to the rostrum, dropped a curtsey and nodded his head at the same time, as if anxious to suit everyone; then, in his baby voice, and putting the emphasis on the wrong words, he said his verse all in one breath:

> '*Little drops* of *water*,
>   *Little drains of sand*,
> *Mate a mighty okum* [*ocean*],
>   And *a peasant land*.
> *Little worts* of *kindness*,
>   *Pokin evvy day*,
> *Make* a *home a hebbin*,
>   *And hep us* on *a way*.'

Clapping his hands at the end, he made another double salutation, and then ran to hide his head in his mother's lap, quite overcome by the success of his 'piece', for the applause was tremendous.

Dick and Dolly did not write, but were encouraged to observe the habits of animals and insects, and report what they saw. Dick liked this, and always had a great deal to say; so, when his name was called, he marched up, and, looking at the audience with his bright confiding eyes, told his little story so earnestly that no one smiled at his crooked body because the 'straight soul' shone through it beautifully.

'I've been watching dragonflies, and I read about them in Dan's book, and I'll try and tell you what I remember. There's lots of them flying around on the pond, all blue, with big eyes, and sort of lace wings, very pretty. I caught one, and looked at him, and I think he was the handsomest insect I ever saw. They catch littler creatures than they are to eat, and have a queer kind of hook thing that folds up when they ain't hunting. It likes the sunshine, and dances round all day. Let me see! what else was there to tell about? Oh, I know! The eggs are laid in the water, and go down to the bottom, and are hatched in the mud. Little ugly things come out of 'em; I can't say the name, but they are brown, and keep having new skins, and getting bigger and bigger. Only think! it takes them two years to be a dragonfly! Now *this* is the curiousest part of it, so you listen tight, for I don't believe you know it. When it is ready it knows somehow, and the ugly, grubby thing climbs up out of the water on a flag or a bulrush, and bursts open its back.'

'Come, I don't believe that,' said Tommy, who was not an observing boy, and really thought Dick was 'making up'.

'It does burst open its back, don't it?' and Dick appealed to Mr Bhaer, who nodded a very decided affirmative, to the little speaker's great satisfaction.

'Well, out comes the dragonfly, all whole, and he sits in the sun – sort of coming alive, you know; and he gets strong, and then he spreads his pretty wings, and flies away up in the air, and never is a grub any more. That's all I know; but I shall watch and try and see him do it, for I think it's splendid to turn into a beautiful dragonfly, don't you?'

Dick had told his story well, and, when he described the flight of the new-born insect, had waved his hands, and looked up as if he saw, and wanted to follow it. Something in his face suggested to the minds of the elder listeners the thought that some day little Dick would have his wish, and after years of helplessness and pain would climb up into the sun some happy day, and, leaving his poor little body behind him, find a new and lovely shape in a fairer world than this. Mrs Jo drew him to her side, and said, with a kiss on his thin cheek,

'That is a sweet little story, dear, and you remembered wonderfully well. I shall write and tell your mother all about it'; and Dick sat on her knee, contentedly smiling at the praise, and resolving to watch well, and catch the dragonfly in the act of leaving its old body for the new, and see how he did it. Dolly had a few remarks to make upon the 'Duck', and made them in a sing-song tune, for he had learned it by heart, and thought it a great plague to do it at all.

'Wild ducks are hard to kill; men hide and shoot at them, and have tame ducks to quack and make the wild ones come where the men can fire at them. They have wooden ducks made too, and they sail round, and the wild ones come to see them; they are stupid, I think. Our ducks are very tame. They eat a great deal, and go poking round in the mud and water. They don't take good care of their eggs, but let them spoil, and –'

'Mine don't!' cried Tommy.

'Well, some people's do; Silas said so. Hens take

good care of little ducks, only they don't like to have them go in the water, and make a great fuss. But the little ones don't care a bit. I like to eat ducks with stuffing in them, and lots of apple-sauce.'

'I have something to say about owls,' began Nat, who had carefully prepared a paper upon this subject with some help from Dan.

'Owls have big heads, round eyes, hooked bills, and strong claws. Some are grey, some white, some black and yellowish. Their feathers are very soft, and stick out a great deal. They fly very quietly, and hunt bats, mice, little birds, and such things. They build nests in barns, hollow trees, and some take the nests of other birds. The great horned owl has two eggs bigger than a hen's, and reddish brown. The tawny owl has five eggs, white and smooth; and this is the kind that hoots at night. Another kind sounds like a bird crying. They eat mice and bats whole, and the parts that they cannot digest they make into little balls and spit out.'

'My gracious! how funny!' Nan was heard to observe.

'They cannot see by day; and if they get out into the light, they go flapping round half blind, and the other birds chase and peck at them as if they were making fun. The horned owl is very big, 'most as big as the eagle. It eats rabbits, rats, snakes, and birds; and lives in rocks and old tumble-down houses. They have a good many cries, and scream like a person being choked, and say, "Waugh O! waugh O!" and it scares people at night in the woods. The white owl lives by the sea, and in cold places, and looks something like a hawk. There is a kind of owl that makes holes to live in like moles. It is called the burrowing owl, and is very small. The barn-owl is the commonest kind; and I have watched one sitting in a hole in a tree, looking like a little grey cat, with one eye shut and the other open. He comes out at dusk, and sits round waiting for the bats. I caught one, and here he is.'

With that Nat suddenly produced from inside his jacket a little downy bird, who blinked and ruffled up his feathers, looking very plump and sleepy and scared.

'Don't touch him! He is going to show off,' said Nat, displaying his new pet with great pride. First he put a cocked hat on the bird's head, and the boys laughed at the funny effect; then he added a pair of paper spectacles, and that gave the owl such a wise look that they shouted with merriment. The performance closed with making the bird angry, and seeing him cling to a handkerchief upside down, pecking and 'clucking', as Rob called it. He was allowed to fly after that, and settled himself on the bunch of pine-cones over the door, where he sat staring down at the company with an air of sleepy dignity that amused them very much.

'Have you anything for us, George?' asked Mr Bhaer, when the room was still again.

'Well, I read and learned ever so much about moles, but I declare I've forgotten every bit of it, except that they dig holes to live in, that you catch them by pouring water down, and that they can't possibly live without eating very often'; and Stuffy sat down, wishing he had not been too lazy to write out his valuable observations, for a general smile went round when he mentioned the last of the three facts which lingered in his memory.

'Then we are done for today,' began Mr Bhaer, but Tommy called out in a great hurry,

'No, we ain't. Don't you know? We must give the thing'; and he winked violently as he made an eye-glass of his fingers.

'Bless my heart, I forgot! Now is your time, Tom'; and Mr Bhaer dropped into his seat again, while all the boys but Dan looked mightily tickled at something.

Nat, Tommy and Demi left the room, and speedily returned with a little red morocco box set forth in state on Mrs Jo's best silver salver. Tommy bore it, and, still escorted by Nat and Demi, marched up to unsuspecting Dan, who stared at them as if he thought they were going to make fun of him. Tommy had prepared an elegant and impressive speech for the occasion, but when the minute came, it all went out of his head, and he just said, straight from his kindly boyish heart,

'Here, old fellow, we all wanted to give you something to kind of pay for what happened a while ago, and to show how much we liked you for being such a trump. Please take it, and have a jolly good time with it.'

Dan was so surprised he could only get as red as the little box, and mutter 'Thanky, boys!' as he fumbled to open it. But when he saw what was inside, his face lighted up, and he seized the long-desired treasure, saying, so enthusiastically that everyone was satisfied, though his language was anything but polished,

'What a stunner! I say, you fellows are regular bricks to give me this; it's just what I wanted. Give us your paw, Tommy.'

Many paws were given, and heartily shaken, for the

boys were charmed with Dan's pleasure, and crowded round him to shake hands and expatiate on the beauties of their gift. In the midst of this pleasant chatter, Dan's eye went to Mrs Jo, who stood outside the group enjoying the scene with all her heart.

'No, I had nothing to do with it. The boys got it up all themselves,' she said, answering the grateful look that seemed to thank her for that happy moment. Dan smiled, and said, in a tone that only she could understand,

'It's you all the same'; and making his way through the boys, he held out his hand first to her and then to the good Professor, who was beaming benevolently on his flock.

He thanked them both with the silent, hearty squeeze he gave the kind hands that had held him up and led him into the safe refuge of a happy home. Not a word was spoken, but they felt all he would say, and little Teddy expressed their pleasure for them as he leaned from his father's arm to hug the boy, and say, in his baby way,

'My dood Danny! everybody loves him now.'

'Come here, show off your spy-glass, Dan, and let us see some of your magnified pollywogs and annymal-cumisms as you call 'em,' said Jack, who felt so uncomfortable during this scene that he would have slipped away if Emil had not kept him.

'So I will, take a squint at that and see what you think of it,' said Dan, glad to show off his precious microscope.

He held it over a beetle that happened to be lying on the table, and Jack bent down to take his squint, but looked up with an amazed face, saying,

'My eye! what nippers the old thing has got! I see now why it hurts so confoundedly when you grab a dorbug and he grabs back again.'

'He winked at me,' cried Nan, who had poked her head under Jack's elbow and got the second peep.

Everyone took a look, and then Dan showed them the lovely plumage on a moth's wing, the four feathery corners to a hair, the veins on a leaf, hardly visible to the naked eye, but like a thick net through the wonderful little glass; the skin on their own fingers, looking like queer hills and valleys; a cobweb like a bit of coarse sewing silk, and the sting of a bee.

'It's like the fairy spectacles in my story-book, only more curious,' said Demi, enchanted with the wonders he saw.

'Dan is a magician now, and he can show you many miracles going on all round you; for he has two things needful – patience and a love of nature. We live in a beautiful and wonderful world, Demi, and the more you know about it the wiser and the better you will be. This little glass will give you a new set of teachers, and you may learn fine lessons from them if you will,' said Mr Bhaer, glad to see how interested the boys were in the matter.

'Could I see anybody's soul with this microscope if I looked hard?' asked Demi, who was much impressed with the power of the bit of glass.

'No, dear; it's not powerful enough for that, and never can be made so. You must wait a long while before your eyes are clear enough to see the most invisible of God's wonders. But looking at the lovely things you can see will help you to understand the lovelier things you can *not* see,' answered Uncle Fritz, with his hand on the boy's head.

'Well, Daisy and I both think that if there *are* any angels, their wings look like that butterfly's as we see it through the glass, only more soft and gold.'

'Believe it if you like, and keep your own little wings as bright and beautiful, only don't fly away for a long time yet.'

'No, I won't,' and Demi kept his word.

'Good-bye, my boys; I must go now, but I leave you with our new Professor of Natural History'; and Mrs Jo went away well pleased with that composition day.

18

CROPS

The gardens did well that summer, and in September the little crops were gathered in with much rejoicing. Jack and Ned joined their farms and raised potatoes, those being a good saleable article. They got twelve bushels, counting little ones and all, and sold them to Mr Bhaer at a fair price, for potatoes went fast in that house. Emil and Franz devoted themselves to corn, and had a jolly little husking in the barn, after which they took their corn to the mill, and came proudly home with meal enough to supply the family with hasty-pudding and Johnny-cake for a long time. They would not take money for their crop; because, as Franz said, 'We never can pay Uncle for all he has done for us if we raised corn for the rest of our days.'

Nat had beans in such abundance that he despaired of ever shelling them, till Mrs Jo proposed a new way, which succeeded admirably. The dry pods were spread upon the barn-floor. Nat fiddled, and the boys danced quadrilles on them, till they were thrashed out with much merriment and very little labour.

Tommy's six weeks' beans were a failure; for a dry spell early in the season hurt them, because he gave them no water; and after that he was so sure that they could take care of themselves, he let the poor things struggle with bugs and weeds till they were exhausted, and died a lingering death. So Tommy had to dig his farm over again, and plant peas. But they were late; the birds ate many; the bushes, not being firmly planted, blew down, and when the poor peas came at last, no one cared for them, as their day was over, and spring-lamb had grown into mutton. Tommy consoled himself with a charitable effort; for he transplanted all the thistles he could find, and tended them carefully for Toby, who was fond of the prickly delicacy, and had eaten all he could find on the place. The boys had great fun over Tom's thistle bed; but he insisted that it was better to care for poor Toby than for himself, and declared that he would devote his entire farm next year to thistles, worms, and snails, that Demi's turtles and Nat's pet owl might have the food they loved, as well as the donkey. So like shiftless, kind-hearted, happy-go-lucky Tommy!

Demi had supplied his grandmother with lettuce all summer, and in the autumn sent his grandfather a basket of turnips, each one scrubbed up till it looked like a great white egg. His Grandma was fond of salad, and one of his Grandpa's favourite quotations was:

> *Lucullus, whom frugality could charm,*
> *Ate roasted turnips at the Sabine farm.*

Therefore these vegetable offerings to the dear domestic god and goddess were affectionate, appropriate, and classical.

Daisy had nothing but flowers in her little plot, and it bloomed all summer long with a succession of gay or fragrant posies. She was very fond of her garden, and delved away in it at all hours, watching over her roses, and pansies, sweet-peas, and mignonette, as faithfully and tenderly as she did over her dolls or her friends. Little nosegays were sent into town on all occasions, and certain vases about the house were her especial care. She had all sorts of pretty fancies about her flowers, and loved to tell the children the story of the pansy, and show them how the step-mother-leaf sat up in her green chair in purple and gold; how the two own children in gay yellow had each its little seat, while the step children, in dull colours, both sat on one small stool, and the poor little father, in his red nightcap, was kept out of sight in the middle of the flower; that a monk's dark face looked out of the monk's-hood larkspur; that the flowers of the canary-vine were so like dainty birds fluttering their yellow wings, that one almost expected to see them fly away, and the snapdragons that went off like little pistol-shots when you cracked them. Splendid dollies did she make out of scarlet and white poppies, with ruffled robes tied round the waist with grass blade sashes, and astonishing hats of coreopsis on their green heads. Pea-pod boats, with rose-leaf sails, received these flower-people, and floated them about a placid pool in the most charming style; for finding that there were no elves, Daisy made her own, and loved the fanciful little friends who played their parts in her summer-life.

Nan went in for herbs, and had a fine display of useful plants, which she tended with steadily increasing interest and care. Very busy was she in September cutting, drying, and tying up her sweet harvest, and writing down in a little book how the different herbs are to be used. She had tried several experiments, and made several mistakes; so she wished to be particular lest she should give little Huz another fit by administering wormwood instead of catnip.

Dick, Dolly, and Rob each grubbed away on his small farm, and made more stir about it than all the rest put together. Parsnips and carrots were the crops of the two Ds; and they longed for it to be late enough to pull up the precious vegetables. Dick did privately examine his carrots, and plant them again, feeling that Silas was right in saying it was too soon for them yet.

Rob's crop was four small squashes and one immense pumpkin. It really was a 'bouncer', as everyone said; and I assure you that two small persons could sit on it side by side. It seemed to have absorbed all the goodness of the little garden, and all the sunshine that shone down on it, and lay there a great round, golden ball, full of rich suggestions of pumpkin-pies for weeks to come. Robby was so proud of his mammoth vegetable that he took everyone to see it, and, when frosts began to nip, covered it up each night with an old bedquilt, tucking it round as if the pumpkin was a well-beloved baby. The day it was gathered he would let no one touch it but himself, and nearly broke his back tugging it to the barn in his little wheelbarrow, with Dick and Dolly harnessed in front to give a heave up the path. His mother promised him that the Thanksgiving-pies should be made from it, and hinted vaguely that she had a plan in her head which would cover the prize pumpkin and its owner with glory.

Poor Billy had planted cucumbers, but unfortunately hoed them up and left the pig-weed. This mistake grieved him very much for ten minutes, then he forgot all about it, and sowed a handful of bright buttons which he had collected, evidently thinking in his feeble mind that they were money, and would come up and multiply, so that he might make many quarters, as Tommy did. No one disturbed him, and he did what he liked with his plot, which soon looked as if a series of small earthquakes had stirred it up. When the general harvest-day came, he would have had nothing but stones and weeds to show, if kind old Asia had not hung half a dozen oranges on the dead tree he had stuck up in the middle. Billy was delighted with his crop; and no one spoiled his pleasure in the little miracle which pity wrought for him, by making withered branches bear strange fruit.

Stuffy had various trials with his melons; for, being impatient to taste them, he had a solitary revel before they were ripe, and made himself so ill, that for a day or two it seemed doubtful if he would ever eat any more. But he pulled through it, and served up his first cantelope without tasting a mouthful himself. They were excellent melons, for he had a warm slope for them, and they ripened fast. The last and best were lingering on the vines, and Stuffy had announced that he should sell them to a neighbour. This disappointed the boys, who had hoped to eat the melons themselves, and they expressed their displeasure in a new and striking manner. Going one morning to gaze upon the three fine watermelons which he had kept for the market, Stuffy was horrified to find the word PIG cut in white letters on the green rind, staring at him from every one. He was in a great rage, and flew to Mrs Jo for redress. She listened, condoled with him, and then said,

'If you want to turn the laugh, I'll tell you how, but you must give up the melons.'

'Well, I will; for I can't thrash all the boys, but I'd like to give them something to remember, the mean sneaks,' growled Stuffy, still in a fume.

Now Mrs Jo was pretty sure who had done the trick, for she had seen three heads suspiciously near to one another in the sofa-corner the evening before; and when these heads had nodded with chuckles and whispers, this experienced woman knew that mischief was afoot. A moonlight night, a rustling in the old cherry-tree near Emil's window, a cut on Tommy's finger, all helped to confirm her suspicions; and having cooled Stuffy's wrath a little, she bade him bring his mal-treated melons to her room, and say not a word to anyone of what had happened. He did so, and the three wags were amazed to find their joke so quietly taken. It spoilt the fun, and the entire disappearance of the melons made them uneasy. So did Stuffy's good-nature, for he looked more placid and plump than ever, and surveyed them with an air of calm pity that perplexed them much.

At dinner-time they discovered why; for then Stuffy's vengeance fell upon them, and the laugh *was* turned against them. When the pudding was eaten, and the fruit was put on, Mary Ann reappeared in a high state of giggle, bearing a large watermelon; Silas followed with another; and Dan brought up the rear with a third. One was placed before each of the three guilty lads; and they read on the smooth green skin this addition to their own work, WITH THE COMPLI-MENTS OF THE PIG. Everyone else read it also, and the whole table was in a roar, for the trick had been whispered about; so everyone understood the sequel. Emil, Ned, and Tommy did not know where to look, and had not a word to say for themselves; so they wisely joined in the laugh, cut up the melons, and handed them round, saying, what all the rest agreed to, that Stuffy had taken a wise and merry way to return good for evil.

Dan had no garden, for he was away or lame the greater part of the summer; so he had helped Silas wherever he could, chopped wood for Asia, and taken care of the lawn so well, that Mrs Jo always had smooth paths and nicely shaven turf before her door.

When the others got in their crops, he looked sorry that he had so little to show; but as autumn went on, he bethought him of a woodland harvest which no one would dispute with him, and which was peculiarly his own. Every Saturday he was away alone to forests, fields, and hills, and always came back loaded with spoils; for he seemed to know the meadows where the best flag-root grew, the thicket where the sassafras was spiciest, the haunts where the squirrels went for nuts, the white oak whose bark was most valuable, and the little gold-thread vine that Nursey liked to cure the canker with. All sorts of splendid red and yellow leaves did Dan bring home for Mrs Jo to dress her parlour with – graceful-seeded grasses, clematis tassels, downy, soft, yellow waxwork berries, and mosses, red-brimmed, white, or emerald green.

'I need not sigh for the woods now, because Dan brings the woods to me,' Mrs Jo used to say, as she glorified the walls with yellow maple boughs and scarlet woodbine wreaths, or filled her vases with russet ferns, hemlock sprays full of delicate cones, and hardy autumn flowers; for Dan's crop suited her well.

The great garret was full of the children's little stores, and for a time was one of the sights of the house. Daisy's flower seeds in neat little paper bags, all labelled, lay in the drawer of a three-legged table. Nan's herbs hung in bunches against the wall, filling the air with their aromatic breath. Tommy had a basket of thistledown with the tiny seeds attached, for he meant to plant them next year, if they did not all fly away before that time. Emil had bunches of pop-corn hanging there to dry, and Demi laid up acorns and different sorts of grain for the pets. But Dan's crop made the best show, for fully one half of the floor was covered with the nuts he brought. All kinds were there, for he ranged the woods for miles round, climbed the tallest trees, and forced his way into the thickest hedges for his plunder. Walnuts, chestnuts, hazelnuts, and beechnuts lay in separate compartments, getting brown, and dry, and sweet, ready for winter revels.

There was one butternut-tree on the place, and Rob and Teddy called it theirs. It bore well this year, and the great dingy nuts came dropping down to hide among the dead leaves, where the busy squirrels found them better than the lazy Bhaers. Their father had told them (the boys, not the squirrels) they should have the nuts if they would pick them up, but no one was to help. It was easy work, and Teddy liked it, only he soon got tired, and left his little basket half full for another day. But the other day was slow to arrive, and, meantime, the sly squirrels were hard at work scampering up and down the old elm-trees stowing the nuts away till their holes were full, then all about in the crotches of the boughs, to be removed at their leisure. Their funny little ways amused the boys, till one day Silas said,

'Hev you sold them nuts to the squirrels?'

'No,' answered Rob, wondering what Silas meant.

'Wal, then, you'd better fly round, or them spry little fellers won't leave you none.'

'Oh, we can beat them when we begin. There are such lots of nuts we shall have a plenty.'

'There ain't many more to come down, and they have cleared the ground pretty well, see if they hain't.'

Robby ran to look, and was alarmed to find how few remained. He called Teddy, and they worked hard all one afternoon, while the squirrels sat on the fence and scolded.

'Now, Ted, we must keep watch, and pick up just as fast as they fall, or we shan't have more than a bushel, and everyone will laugh at us if we don't.'

'The naughty quillies tarn't have 'em. I'll pick fast and run and put 'em in the barn twick,' said Teddy, frowning at little Frisky, who chattered and whisked his tail indignantly.

That night a high wind blew down hundreds of nuts, and when Mrs Jo came to wake her little sons, she said, briskly,

'Come, my laddies, the squirrels are hard at it, and you will have to work well today, or they will have every nut on the ground.'

'No, they won't,' and Robby tumbled up in a great hurry, gobbled his breakfast, and rushed out to save his property.

Teddy went too, and worked like a little beaver,

trotting to and fro with full and empty baskets. Another bushel was soon put away in the corn-barn, and
they were scrambling among the leaves for more nuts
when the bell rang for school.

'O father! let me stay out and pick. Those horrid
squirrels will have my nuts if you don't. I'll do my
lessons by and by,' cried Rob, running into the schoolroom, flushed and tousled by the fresh cold wind and
his eager work.

'If you had been up early and done a little every
morning there would be no hurry now. I told you that,
Rob, and you never minded. I cannot have the lessons
neglected as the work has been. The squirrels will get
more than their share this year, and they deserve it, for
they have worked best. You may go an hour earlier,
but that is all,' and Mr Bhaer led Rob to his place,
where the little man dashed at his books as if bent on
making sure of the precious hour promised him.

It was almost maddening to sit still and see the wind
shaking down the last nuts, and the lively thieves
flying about, pausing now and then to eat one in his
face, and flirt their tails, as if they said, saucily, 'We'll
have them in spite of you, lazy Rob.' The only thing
that sustained the poor child in this trying moment
was the sight of Teddy working away all alone. It was
really splendid the pluck and perseverance of the little
lad. He picked and picked till his back ached; he
trudged to and fro till his small legs were tired; and he
defied wind, weariness, and wicked 'quillies', till his
mother left her work and did the carrying for him, full
of admiration for the kind little fellow who tried to
help his brother. When Rob was dismissed he found
Teddy reposing in the bushel-basket quite used up,

but unwilling to quit the field; for he flapped his hat at the thieves with one grubby little hand, while he refreshed himself with the big apple held in the other.

Rob fell to work and the ground was cleared before two o'clock, the nuts safely in the corn-barn loft, and the weary workers exulted in their success. But Frisky and his wife were not to be vanquished so easily; and when Rob went up to look at his nuts a few days later he was amazed to see how many had vanished. None of the boys could have stolen them, because the door had been locked; the doves could not have eaten them, and there were no rats about. There was great lamentation among the young Bhaers till Dick said,

'I saw Frisky on the roof of the corn-barn, maybe he took them.'

'I know he did! I'll have a trap, and kill him dead,' cried Rob, disgusted with Frisky's grasping nature.

'Perhaps, if you watch, you can find out where he puts them, and I may be able to get them back for you,' said Dan, who was much amused by the fight between the boys and squirrels.

So Rob watched and saw Mr and Mrs Frisky drop from the drooping elm boughs on to the roof of the corn-barn, dodge in at one of the little doors, much to the disturbance of the doves, and come out with a nut in each mouth. So laden they could not get back the way they came, but ran down the low roof, along the wall, and leaping off at a corner they vanished a minute and reappeared without their plunder. Rob ran to the place, and in a hollow under the leaves found a heap of the stolen property hidden away to be carried off to the holes by and by.

'Oh, you little villains! I'll cheat *you* now, and not

leave one,' said Rob. So he cleared the corner and the
corn-barn, and put the contested nuts in the garret,
making sure that no broken window-pane could anywhere let in the unprincipled squirrels. They seemed
to feel that the contest was over, and retired to their
hole, but now and then could not resist throwing
down nut-shells on Rob's head, and scolding violently
as if they could not forgive him nor forget that he had
the best of the battle.

Father and Mother Bhaer's crop was of a different
sort, and not so easily described; but they were satisfied
with it, felt that their summer work had prospered
well, and by and by had a harvest that made them
very happy.

19

JOHN BROOKE

'Wake up, Demi, dear! I want you.'

'Why, I've just gone to bed; it can't be morning yet'; and Demi blinked like a little owl as he waked from his first sound sleep.

'It's only ten, but your father is ill, and we must go to him. O my little John! my poor little John!' and Aunt Jo laid her head down on the pillow with a sob that scared sleep from Demi's eyes and filled his heart with fear and wonder; for he dimly felt why Aunt Jo called him 'John', and wept over him as if some loss had come that left him poor. He clung to her without a word, and in a minute she was quite steady again, and said, with a tender kiss as she saw his troubled face,

'We are going to say good-bye to him, my darling, and there is no time to lose; so dress quickly and come to me in my room. I must go to Daisy.'

'Yes, I will'; and when Aunt Jo was gone, little Demi got up quietly, dressed as if in a dream, and leaving Tommy fast asleep went away through the silent house, feeling that something new and sorrowful was going to happen – something that set him apart from the other boys for a time, and made the world seem as dark and still and strange as those familiar rooms did in the night. A carriage sent by Mr Laurie stood before the door. Daisy was soon ready, and the brother and sister held each other by the hand all the way into town, as they drove swiftly and silently with aunt and uncle through the shadowy roads to say good-bye to father.

None of the boys but Franz and Emil knew what had happened, and when they came down next morning, great was their wonderment and discomfort, for the house seemed forlorn without its master and mistress. Breakfast was a dismal meal with no cheery Mrs Jo behind the teapots; and when schooltime came, Father Bhaer's place was empty. They wandered about in a disconsolate kind of way for an hour, waiting for news and hoping it would be all right with Demi's father, for good John Brooke was much beloved by the boys. Ten o'clock came, and no one arrived to relieve their anxiety. They did not feel like playing, yet the time dragged heavily, and they sat about listless and sober. All at once, Franz got up, and said, in his persuasive way,

'Look here, boys! let's go into school and do our lessons just as if Uncle was here. It will make the day go faster, and will please him, I know.'

'But who will hear us say them?' asked Jack.

'I will; I don't know much more than you do, but I'm the oldest here, and I'll try to fill Uncle's place till he comes, if you don't mind.'

Something in the modest, serious way Franz said this impressed the boys, for, though the poor lad's eyes were red with quiet crying for Uncle John in that long sad night, there was a new manliness about him, as if he had already begun to feel the cares and troubles of life, and tried to take them bravely.

'I will, for one,' and Emil went to his seat, remembering that obedience to his superior officer is a seaman s first duty.

The others followed; Franz took his uncle's seat, and for an hour order reigned. Lessons were learned and said, and Franz made a patient, pleasant teacher, wisely omitting such lessons as he was not equal to, and keeping order more by the unconscious dignity that sorrow gave him than by any words of his own. The little boys were reading when a step was heard in the hall, and everyone looked up to read the news in Mr Bhaer's face as he came in. The kind face told them instantly that Demi had no father now, for it was worn and pale, and full of tender grief, which left him no words with which to answer Rob, as he ran to him saying, reproachfully,

'What made you go and leave me in the night, papa?'

The memory of the other father who had left his children in the night, never to return, made Mr Bhaer hold his own boy close, and, for a minute, hide his face in Robby's curly hair. Emil laid his head down on his arms, Franz went to put his hand on his uncle's shoulder, his boyish face pale with sympathy and sorrow, and the others sat so still that the soft rustle of the failing leaves outside was distinctly heard.

Rob did not clearly understand what had happened but he hated to see papa unhappy, so he lifted up the bent head, and said, in his chirpy little voice,

'Don't cry, mein Vater! we are all so good, we did our lessons without you, and Franz was the master.'

Mr Bhaer looked up then, tried to smile, and said in a grateful tone that made the lads feel like saints, 'I thank you very much, my boys. It was a beautiful way to help and comfort me. I shall not forget it, I assure you.'

'Franz proposed it, and was a first-rate master, too,' said Nat; and the others gave a murmur of assent most gratifying to the young dominie.

Mr Bhaer put Rob down, and, standing up, put his arm round his tall nephew's shoulder, as he said, with a look of genuine pleasure,

'This makes my hard day easier, and gives me confidence in you all. I am needed there in town, and must leave you for some hours. I thought to give you a holiday, or send some of you home, but if you like to stay and go on as you have begun, I shall be glad and proud of my good boys.'

'We'll stay'; 'We'd rather'; 'Franz can see to us'; cried several, delighted with the confidence shown in them.

'Isn't Marmar coming home?' asked Rob, wistfully; for home without 'Marmar' was the world without the sun to him.

'We shall both come tonight; but dear Aunt Meg needs Mother more than you do now, and I know you like to lend her for a little while.'

'Well, I will; but Teddy's been crying for her, and he slapped Nursey, and was dreadful naughty,' answered Rob, as if the news might bring mother home.

'Where is my little man?' asked Mr Bhaer.

'Dan took him out, to keep him quiet. He's all right now,' said Franz, pointing to the window, through which they could see Dan drawing baby in his little wagon, with the dogs frolicking about him.

'I won't see him, it would only upset him again; but

tell Dan I leave Teddy in his care. You older boys I trust to manage yourselves for a day. Franz will direct you, and Silas is here to oversee matters. So good-bye till tonight.'

'Just tell me a word about Uncle John,' said Emil, detaining Mr Bhaer, as he was about hurrying away again.

'He was only ill a few hours, and died as he has lived, so cheerfully, so peacefully, that it seems a sin to mar the beauty of it with any violent or selfish grief. We were in time to say good-bye: and Daisy and Demi were in his arms as he fell asleep on Aunt Meg's breast. No more now, I cannot bear it,' and Mr Bhaer went hastily away quite bowed with grief, for in John Brooke he had lost both friend and brother, and there was no one left to take his place.

All that day the house was very still; the small boys played quietly in the nursery; the others, feeling as if Sunday had come in the middle of the week, spent it in walking, sitting in the willow, or among their pets, all talking much of 'Uncle John', and feeling that something gentle, just, and strong, had gone out of their little world, leaving a sense of loss that deepened every hour. At dusk, Mr and Mrs Bhaer came home alone, for Demi and Daisy were their mother's best comfort now, and could not leave her. Poor Mrs Jo seemed quite spent, and evidently needed the same sort of comfort, for her first words, as she came up the stairs, were, 'Where is my baby?'

'Here I is,' answered a little voice, as Dan put Teddy into her arms, adding, as she hugged him close, 'My Danny tooked tare of me all day, and I was dood.'

Mrs Jo turned to thank the faithful nurse, but Dan

was waving off the boys, who had gathered in the hall to meet her, and was saying, in a low voice, 'Keep back; she don't want to be bothered with us now.'

'No, don't keep back. I want you all. Come in and see me, my boys. I've neglected you all day,' and Mrs Jo held out her hands to them as they gathered round and escorted her into her own room, saying little, but expressing much by affectionate looks and clumsy little efforts to show their sorrow and sympathy.

'I am so tired, I will lie here and cuddle Teddy, and you shall bring me in some tea,' she said, trying to speak cheerfully for their sakes.

A general stampede into the dining-room followed, and the supper-table would have been ravaged if Mr Bhaer had not interfered. It was agreed that one squad should carry in the mother's tea, and another bring it out. The four nearest and dearest claimed the first honour, so Franz bore the teapot, Emil the bread, Rob the milk, and Teddy insisted on carrying the sugar-basin, which was lighter by several lumps when it arrived than when it started. Some women might have found it annoying at such a time to have boys creaking in and out, upsetting cups and rattling spoons in violent efforts to be quiet and helpful; but it suited Mrs Jo, because just then her heart was very tender; and remembering that many of her boys were fatherless or motherless, she yearned over them, and found comfort in their blundering affection. It was the sort of food that did her more good than the very thick bread-and-butter that they gave her, and the rough Commodore's broken whisper:

'Bear up, Aunty, it's a hard blow; but we'll weather it somehow,' cheered her more than the sloppy cup he brought her, full of tea as bitter as if some salt tear of his own had dropped into it on the way. When supper was over, a second deputation removed the tray; and Dan said, holding out his arms for sleepy little Teddy,

'Let me put him to bed, you're so tired, Mother.'

'Will you go with him, lovely?' asked Mrs Jo of her small lord and master, who lay on her arm among the sofa-pillows.

'Torse I will'; and he was proudly carried off by his faithful bearer.

'I wish I could do something,' said Nat, with a sigh, as Franz leaned over the sofa, and softly stroked Aunt Jo's hot forehead.

'You can, dear. Go and get your violin, and play me the sweet little airs Uncle Teddy sent you last. Music will comfort me better than anything else tonight.'

Nat flew for his fiddle, and, sitting just outside her door, played as he had never done before, for now his heart was in it, and seemed to magnetize his fingers. The other lads sat quietly upon the steps, keeping watch that no newcomer should disturb the house; Franz lingered at his post; and so, soothed, served, and guarded by her boys, poor Mrs Jo slept at last, and forgot her sorrow for an hour.

Two quiet days, and on the third Mr Bhaer came in just after school, with a note in his hand, looking both moved and pleased.

'I want to read you something, boys,' he said; and as they stood round him he read this:

'DEAR BROTHER FRITZ, I hear that you do not mean to bring your flock today, thinking that I may not like it. Please do. The sight of his friends will help Demi through the hard hour, and I want the boys to hear what father says of my John. It will do them good, I know. If they would sing one of the sweet old hymns you have taught them so well, I should like it better than any other music, and feel that it was beautifully suited to the occasion. Please ask them, with my love. MEG.'

'Will you go?' and Mr Bhaer looked at the lads, who were greatly touched by Mrs Brooke's kind words and wishes.

'Yes,' they answered, like one boy; and an hour later they went away with Franz to bear their part in John Brooke's simple funeral.

The little house looked as quiet, sunny, and home-like as when Meg entered it a bride, ten years ago, only then it was early summer, and roses blossomed everywhere; now it was early autumn, and dead leaves rustled softly down, leaving the branches bare. The bride was a widow now; but the same beautiful serenity shone in her face, and the sweet resignation of a truly pious soul made her presence a consolation to those who came to comfort her.

'O Meg! how *can* you bear it so?' whispered Jo, as she met them at the door with a smile of welcome, and no change in her gentle manner, except more gentleness.

'Dear Jo, the love that has blest me for ten happy years supports me still. It could not die, and John is more my own than ever,' whispered Meg; and in her eyes the tender trust was so beautiful and bright, that Jo believed her, and thanked God for the immortality of love like hers.

They were all there – father and mother, Uncle Teddy, and Aunt Amy, old Mr Laurence, white-haired and feeble now, Mr and Mrs Bhaer, with their flock, and many friends, come to do honour to the dead. One would have said that modest John Brooke, in his busy, quiet, humble life, had had little time to make friends; but now they seemed to start up everywhere – old and young, rich and poor, high and low; for all unconsciously his influence had made itself widely felt, his virtues were remembered, and his hidden charities rose up to bless him. The group about his coffin was a far more eloquent eulogy than any Mr March could utter. There were the rich men whom he had served faithfully for years; the poor old women whom he cherished with his little store, in memory of his mother; the wife to whom he had given such happiness that death could not mar it utterly; the brothers and sisters in whose hearts he had made a place for ever; the little son and daughter, who already felt the loss of his strong arm and tender voice; the young children, sobbing for their kindest playmate, and the tall lads, watching with softened faces a scene which they never could forget. A very simple service, and very short; for the fatherly voice that had faltered in the marriage-sacrament now failed entirely as Mr March endeavoured to pay his tribute of reverence and love to the son whom he most honoured. Nothing but the soft coo of Baby Josy's voice upstairs broke the long hush that followed the last Amen, till, at a sign from Mr Bhaer, the well-trained boyish voices broke out in a hymn, so full of lofty cheer, that one by one all joined in it, singing with full hearts, and finding their troubled spirits lifted into peace on the wings of that brave, sweet psalm.

As Meg listened, she felt that she had done well; for not only did the moment comfort her with the assurance that John's last lullaby was sung by the young voices he loved so well, but in the faces of the boys she saw that they had caught a glimpse of the beauty of virtue in its most impressive form, and that the memory of the good man lying dead before them would live long and help fully in their remembrance. Daisy's head lay in her lap, and Demi held her hand, looking often at her, with eyes so like his father's, and a little gesture that seemed to say, 'Don't be troubled, mother; I am here'; and all about her were friends to lean upon and love; so patient, pious Meg put by her heavy grief, feeling that her best help would be to live for others, as her John had done.

That evening, as the Plumfield boys sat on the steps, as usual, in the mild September moonlight, they naturally fell to talking of the event of the day.

Emil began by breaking out, in his impetuous way, 'Uncle Fritz is the wisest, and Uncle Laurie the jolliest, but Uncle John was the *best* and I'd rather be like him than any man I ever saw.'

'So would I. Did you hear what those gentlemen said to Grandpa today? I would like to have that said of me when I was dead'; and Franz felt with regret that he had not appreciated Uncle John enough.

'What did they say?' asked Jack, who had been much impressed by the scenes of the day.

'Why, one of the partners of Mr Laurence, where Uncle John has been ever so long, was saying that he was conscientious almost to a fault as a business man, and above reproach in all things. Another gentleman said no money could repay the fidelity and honesty

with which Uncle John had served him, and then
Grandpa told them the best of all. Uncle John once
had a place in the office of a man who cheated, and
when this man wanted uncle to help him do it, uncle
wouldn't, though he was offered a big salary. The man
was angry and said, "You will never get on in business
with such strict principles"; and uncle answered back,
"I *never* will try to get on *without* them," and left the
place for a much harder and poorer one.'

'Good!' cried several of the boys warmly, for they
were in the mood to understand and value the little
story as never before.

'He wasn't rich, was he?' asked Jack.

'No.'

'He never did anything to make a stir in the world,
did he?'

'No.'

'He was only good?'

'That's all'; and Franz found himself wishing that
Uncle John *had* done something to boast of, for it was
evident that Jack was disappointed by his replies.

'Only good. That is *all* and everything,' said Mr
Bhaer, who had overheard the last few words, and
guessed what was going on in the minds of the lads.

'Let me tell you a little about John Brooke, and you
will see why men honour him, and why he was satisfied
to be good rather than rich or famous. He simply did
his duty in all things, and did it so cheerfully, so
faithfully, that it kept him patient, brave, and happy
through poverty and loneliness and years of hard work.
He was a good son, and gave up his own plans to stay
and live with his mother while she needed him. He
was a good friend, and taught Laurie much beside his

Greek and Latin, did it unconsciously, perhaps, by showing him an example of an upright man. He was a faithful servant, and made himself so valuable to those who employed him that they will find it hard to fill his place. He was a good husband and father, so tender, wise, and thoughtful, that Laurie and I learned much of him, and only knew how well he loved his family, when we discovered all he had done for them, unsuspected and unassisted.'

Mr Bhaer stopped a minute, and the boys sat like statues in the moonlight until he went on again, in a subdued, but earnest voice: 'As he lay dying, I said to him, "Have no care for Meg and the little ones; I will see that they never want." Then he smiled and pressed my hand, and answered, in his cheerful way, "No need for that; I have cared for them." And so he had, for when we looked among his papers, all was in order, not a debt remained; and safely put away was enough to keep Meg comfortable and independent. Then we knew why he had lived so plainly, denied himself so many pleasures, except that of charity, and worked so hard that I fear he shortened his good life. He never asked for help for himself, though often for others, but bore his own burden and worked out his own task bravely and quietly. No one can say a word of complaint against him, so just and generous and kind was he; and now, when he is gone, all find so much love and praise and honour, that I am proud to have been his friend, and would rather leave my children the legacy he leaves his than the largest fortune ever made. Yes! Simple, genuine goodness is the best capital to found the business of this life upon. It lasts when fame and money fail, and is the only riches we can take out

of this world with us. Remember that, my boys; and if
you want to earn respect and confidence and love
follow in the footsteps of John Brooke.'

When Demi returned to school, after some weeks at
home, he seemed to have recovered from his loss with
the blessed elasticity of childhood, and so he had in a
measure; but he did not forget, for his was a nature
into which things sank deeply, to be pondered over,
and absorbed into the soil where the small virtues
were growing fast. He played and studied, worked and
sang, just as before, and few suspected any change; but
there was one – and Aunt Jo saw it – for she watched
over the boy with her whole heart, trying to fill John's
place in her poor way. He seldom spoke of his loss, but
Aunt Jo often heard a stifled sobbing in the little bed
at night; and when she went to comfort him, all his cry
was, 'I want my father! oh, I want my father!' – for the
tie between the two had been a very tender one, and
the child's heart bled when it was broken. But time
was kind to him, and slowly he came to feel that father
was not lost, only invisible for a while, and sure to be
found again, well and strong and fond as ever, even
though his little son should see the purple asters blossom on his grave many, many times before they met.
To this belief Demi held fast, and in it found both
help and comfort, because it led him unconsciously
through a tender longing for the father whom he had
seen to a childlike trust in the Father whom he had not
seen. Both were in heaven, and he prayed to both,
trying to be good for love of them.

The outward change corresponded to the inward,
for in those few weeks Demi seemed to have grown
tall, and began to drop his childish plays, not as if

ashamed of them, as some boys do, but as if he had outgrown them, and wanted something manlier. He took to the hated arithmetic, and held on so steadily that his uncle was charmed, though he could not understand the whim, until Demi said,

'I am going to be a bookkeeper when I grow up, like papa, and I must know about figures and things else I can't have nice, neat ledgers like his.'

At another time he came to his aunt with a very serious face, and said,

'What can a small boy do to earn money?'

'Why do you ask, my deary?'

'My father told me to take care of mother and the little girls, and I want to, but I don't know how to begin.'

'He did not mean now, Demi, but by and by, when you are large.'

'But I wish to begin *now*, if I can, because I think I ought to make some money to buy things for the family. I am ten, and other boys no bigger than I earn pennies sometimes.'

'Well, then, suppose you rake up all the dead leaves and cover the strawberry bed. I'll pay you a dollar for the job,' said Aunt Jo.

'Isn't that a great deal? I could do it in one day. You must be fair, and not pay too much, because I want to truly earn it.'

'My little John, I will be fair, and not pay a penny too much. Don't work too hard; and when that is done I will have something else for you to do,' said Mrs Jo, much touched by his desire to help, and his sense of justice, so like his scrupulous father.

When the leaves were done, many barrowloads of

chips were wheeled from the wood to the shed, and another dollar earned. Then Demi helped cover the school-books, working in the evenings, under Franz's direction, tugging patiently away at each book, letting no one help, and receiving his wages with such satisfaction that the dingy bills became quite glorified in his sight.

'Now, I have a dollar for each of them, and I should like to take my money to mother all myself, so she can see that I have minded my father.'

So Demi made a duteous pilgrimage to his mother, who received his little earnings as a treasure of great worth, and would have kept it untouched, if Demi had not begged her to buy some *useful* thing for herself and the women-children, whom he felt were left to his care.

This made him very happy, and, though he often forgot his responsibilities for a time, the desire to help was still there, strengthening with his years. He always uttered the words 'my father' with an air of gentle pride, and often said, as if he claimed a title full of honour, 'Don't call me Demi any more. I am John Brooke now.' So, strengthened by a purpose and a hope, the little lad of ten bravely began the world, and entered into his inheritance – the memory of a wise and tender father, the legacy of an honest name.

20

ROUND THE FIRE

With the October frosts came the cheery fires in the
great fireplaces; and Demi's dry pine-chips helped
Dan's oak-knots to blaze royally, and go roaring up
the chimney with a jolly sound. All were glad to gather
round the hearth, as the evenings grew longer, to play
games, read, or lay plans for the winter. But the
favourite amusement was story-telling, and Mr and
Mrs Bhaer were expected to have a store of lively tales
always on hand. Their supply occasionally gave out,
and then the boys were thrown upon their own resources, which were not always successful. Ghost-
parties were the rage at one time; for the fun of the
thing consisted in putting out the lights, letting the fire
die down, and then sitting in the dark, and telling
the most awful tales they could invent. As this resulted
in scares of all sorts among the boys, Tommy's walking
in his sleep on the shed roof, and a general state of
nervousness in the little ones, it was forbidden, and
they fell back on more harmless amusements.

One evening, when the small boys were snugly
tucked in bed, and the older lads were lounging about
the schoolroom fire, trying to decide what they should
do, Demi suggested a new way of settling the
question.

Seizing the hearth-brush, he marched up and down the room, saying, 'Row, row, row'; and when the boys, laughing and pushing, had got into line, he said, 'Now, I'll give you two minutes to think of a play.' Franz was writing, and Emil reading the Life of Lord Nelson, and neither joined the party, but the others thought hard, and when the time was up were ready to reply.

'Now, Tom!' and the poker softly rapped him on the head.

'Blind-man's Buff.'

'Jack!'

'Commerce; a good round game, and have cents for the pool.'

'Uncle forbids our playing for money. Dan, what do you want?'

'Let's have a battle between the Greeks and Romans.'

'Stuffy?'

'Roast apples, pop corn, and crack nuts.'

'Good! good!' cried several; and when the vote was taken, Stuffy's proposal carried the day.

Some went to the cellar for apples, some to the garret for nuts, and others looked up the popper and the corn.

'We had better ask the girls to come in, hadn't we?' said Demi, in a sudden fit of politeness.

'Daisy pricks chestnuts beautifully,' put in Nat, who wanted his little friend to share the fun.

'Nan pops corn tip-top, we must have her,' added Tommy.

'Bring in your sweethearts then, we don't mind,' said Jack, who laughed at the innocent regard the little people had for one another.

'You shan't call my sister a sweetheart; it is so silly!' cried Demi, in a way that made Jack laugh.

'She is Nat's darling, isn't she, old chirper?'

'Yes, if Demi don't mind. I can't help being fond of her, she is so good to me,' answered Nat, with bashful earnestness, for Jack's rough ways disturbed him.

'Nan is my sweetheart, and I shall marry her in about a year, so don't you get in the way, any of you,' said Tommy, stoutly; for he and Nan had settled their future, child-fashion, and were to live in the willow, lower down a basket for food, and do other charmingly impossible things.

Demi was quenched by the decision of Bangs, who took him by the arm and walked him off to get the ladies. Nan and Daisy were sewing with Aunt Jo on certain small garments for Mrs Carney's newest baby.

'Please, ma'am, could you lend us the girls for a little while? we'll be very careful of them,' said Tommy, winking one eye to express apples, snapping his fingers to signify pop-corn, and gnashing his teeth to convey the idea of nut-cracking.

The girls understood this pantomime at once, and began to pull off their thimbles before Mrs Jo could decide whether Tommy was going into convulsions or was brewing some unusual piece of mischief. Demi explained with elaboration, permission was readily granted, and the boys departed with their prize.

'Don't you speak to Jack,' whispered Tommy, as he and Nan promenaded down the hall to get a fork to prick the apples.

'Why not?'

'He laughs at me, so I don't wish you to have anything to do with him.'

'Shall if I like,' said Nan, promptly resenting this premature assumption of authority on the part of her lord.

'Then I won't have you for my sweetheart.'

'I don't care.'

'Why, Nan, I thought you were fond of me!' and Tommy's voice was full of tender reproach.

'If you mind Jack's laughing I don't care for you one bit.'

'Then you may take back your old ring; I won't wear it any longer'; and Tommy plucked off a horse-hair pledge of affection which Nan had given him in return for one made of a lobster's feeler.

'I shall give it to Ned,' was her cruel reply; for Ned liked Mrs Giddy-gaddy, and had turned her clothes-pins, boxes, and spools enough to set up housekeeping with.

Tommy said, 'Thunder-turtles!' as the only vent equal to the pent-up anguish of the moment, and, dropping Nan's arm, retired in high dudgeon, leaving her to follow with the fork – a neglect which naughty Nan punished by proceeding to prick his heart with jealousy as if it were another sort of apple.

The hearth was swept, and the rosy Baldwins put down to roast. A shovel was heated, and the chestnuts danced merrily upon it, while the corn popped wildly in its wire prison. Dan cracked his best walnuts, and everyone chattered and laughed, while the rain beat on the window-pane and the wind howled round the house.

'Why is Billy like this nut?' asked Emil, who was frequently inspired with bad conundrums.

'Because he is cracked,' answered Ned.

'That's not fair; you mustn't make fun of Billy, because he can't hit back again. It's mean,' cried Dan, smashing a nut wrathfully.

'To what family of insects does Blake belong?' asked peacemaker Franz, seeing that Emil looked ashamed and Dan lowering.

'Gnats,' answered Jack.

'Why is Daisy like a bee?' cried Nat, who had been wrapt in thought for several minutes.

'Because she is queen of the hive,' said Dan.

'No.'

'Because she is sweet.'

'Bees are not sweet.'

'Give it up.'

'Because she makes sweet things, is always busy and likes flowers,' said Nat, piling up his boyish compliments till Daisy blushed like a rosy clover.

'Why is Nan like a hornet?' demanded Tommy, glowering at her, and adding, without giving anyone time to answer, 'Because she *isn't* sweet, makes a great buzzing about nothing, and stings like fury.'

'Tommy's mad, and I'm glad,' cried Ned, as Nan tossed her head and answered quickly,

'What thing in the china-closet is Tom like?'

'A pepper-pot,' answered Ned, giving Nan a nut meat with a tantalizing laugh that made Tommy feel as if he would like to bounce up like a hot chestnut and hit somebody.

Seeing that ill-humour was getting the better of the small supply of wit in the company, Franz cast himself into the breach again.

'Let's make a law that the first person who comes into the room shall tell us a story. No matter who it is, he must do it, and it will be fun to see who comes first.'

The others agreed, and did not have to wait long, for a heavy step soon came clumping through the hall, and Silas appeared, bearing an armful of wood. He was greeted by a general shout, and stood staring about him with a bewildered grin on his big red face, till Franz explained the joke.

'Sho! I can't tell a story,' he said, putting down his load and preparing to leave the room. But the boys fell upon him, forced him into a seat, and held him there, laughing and clamouring for their story, till the good-natured giant was overpowered.

'I don't know but jest one story, and that's about a horse,' he said, much flattered by the reception he received.

'Tell it! tell it!' cried the boys.

'Wal,' began Silas, tipping his chair back against the wall, and putting his thumbs in the arm-holes of his waistcoat, 'I jined a cavalry regiment durin' the war, and see a consid'able amount of fightin'. My horse, Major, was a fust-rate animal, and I was as fond on him as ef he'd ben a human critter. He warn't harnsome, but he was the best-tempered, stiddyest, lovenest brute I ever see. The fust battle we went into, he gave me a lesson that I didn't forgit in a hurry, and I'll tell you how it was. It ain't no use tryin' to picter the noise and hurry, and general horridness of a battle to you young fellers, for I ain't no words to do it in; but I'm free to confess that I got so sort of confused and upset at the fust on it, that I didn't know what I was about. We was ordered to charge, and went ahead like good ones, never stoppin' to pick up them that went down in the scrimmage. I got a shot in the arm, and was pitched out of the saddle – don't know how, but there I was left behind with two or three others, dead and wounded, for the rest went on, as I say. Wal, I picked myself up and looked round for Major, feeling as ef I'd had about enough for that spell. I didn't see him nowhere, and was kinder walking back to camp, when I heard a whinny that sounded nateral. I looked round, and there was Major stopping for me a long way off, and lookin' as ef he didn't understand why I was loiterin' behind. I whistled, and he trotted up to me as I'd trained him to do. I mounted as well as I could with my left arm bleedin' and was for going on to camp, for I declare I felt as sick and wimbly as a woman; folks often do in their fust battle. But, no, sir! Major was the bravest of the two, and he wouldn't go, not a peg; he jest rared up, and danced, and snorted, and acted as ef the smell of powder and the noise had drove him half wild. I done my best, but he wouldn't give in, so I did; and what do you think that plucky brute done? He wheeled slap round, and galloped back like a hurricane, right into the thickest of the scrimmage!'

'Good for him!' cried Dan excitedly, while the other boys forgot apples and nuts in their interest.

'I wish I may die ef I warn't ashamed of myself,' continued Silas, warming up at the recollection of that day. 'I was as mad as a hornet, and I forgot my waound, and jest pitched in, rampagin' raound like fury till there come a shell into the midst of us, and in bustin' knocked a lot of us flat. I didn't know nothin' for a spell, and when I come-to, the fight was over jest there, and I found myself layin' by a wall with poor

Major long-side wuss wounded than I was. My leg was broke, and I had a ball in my shoulder, but he, poor old feller! was all tore in the side with a piece of that blasted shell.'

'O Silas! what did you do?' cried Nan, pressing close to him with a face full of eager sympathy and interest.

'I dragged myself higher, and tried to stop the bleedin' with sech rags as I could tear off of me with one hand. But it warn't no use, and he lay moanin' with horrid pain, and lookin' at me with them lovin' eyes of his, till I thought I couldn't bear it. I give him all the help I could, and when the sun got hotter and hotter, and he began to lap out his tongue, I tried to get to a brook that was a good piece away, but I couldn't do it, being stiff and faint, so I give it up and fanned him with my hat. Now you listen to this, and when you hear folks comin' down on the rebs, you jest remember what one on 'em did, and give him the credit of it. A poor feller in grey laid not fur off, shot through the lungs, and dying fast. I'd offered him my handkerchief to keep the sun off his face, and he'd thanked me kindly, for in sech times as that men don't stop to think on which side they belong, but jest buckle-to and help one another. When he see me mournin' over Major and tryin' to ease his pain, he looked up with his face all damp and white with sufferin', and sez he, "There's water in my canteen; take it, for it can't help me," and he flung it to me. I couldn't have took it ef I hadn't had a little brandy in a pocket flask, and I made him drink it. It done him good, and I felt as much set up as if I'd drunk it myself. It's surprisin' the good sech little things do folks sometimes'; and Silas paused as if he felt again the comfort of that moment when he and his enemy forgot their feud, and helped one another like brothers.

'Tell about Major,' cried the boys, impatient for the catastrophe.

'I poured the water over his poor pantin' tongue, and ef ever a dumb critter looked grateful, he did then. But it warn't of much use, for the dreadful waound kep on tormentin' him, till I couldn't bear it any longer. It was hard, but I done it in mercy, and I know he forgive me.'

'What did you do?' asked Emil, as Silas stopped abruptly with a loud 'hem', and a look in his rough face that made Daisy go and stand by him with her little hand on his knee.

'I shot him.'

Quite a thrill went through the listeners as Silas said that, for Major seemed a hero in their eyes, and his tragic end roused all their sympathy.

'Yes, I shot him, and put him out of his misery. I patted him fust, and said, "Good-bye"; then I laid his head easy on the grass, give a last look into his lovin' eyes, and sent a bullet through his head. He hardly stirred, I aimed so true, and when I see him quite still, with no more moanin' and pain, I was glad, and yet – wal, I don't know as I need be ashamed on't – I jest put my arms raound his neck and boo-hooed like a great baby. Sho! I didn't know I was such a fool'; and Silas drew his sleeve across his eyes, as much touched by Daisy's sob, as by the memory of faithful Major.

No one spoke for a minute, because the boys were as

quick to feel the pathos of the little story as tender-hearted Daisy, though they did not show it by crying.

'I'd like a horse like that,' said Dan, half-aloud.

'Did the rebel man die too?' asked Nan, anxiously.

'Not then. We laid there all day, and at night some of our fellers came to look after the missing ones. They nat'rally wanted to take me fust, but I knew I could wait, and the rebel had but one chance, maybe, so I made them carry him off right away. He had jest strength enough to hold out his hand to me and say, "Thanky, comrade!" and them was the last words he spoke, for he died an hour after he got to the hospital-tent.'

'How glad you must have been that you were kind to him!' said Demi, who was deeply impressed by this story.

'Wal, I did take comfort thinkin' of it, as I laid there alone for a number of hours with my head on Major's neck, and see the moon come up. I'd like to have buried the poor beast decent, but it warn't possible; so I cut off a bit of his mane, and I've kep it ever sence. Want to see it, sissy?'

'Oh, yes, please,' answered Daisy, wiping away her tears to look.

Silas took out an old 'wallet' as he called his pocket-book, and produced from an inner fold a bit of brown paper, in which was a rough lock of white horse-hair. The children looked at it silently, as it lay in the broad palm, and no one found anything to ridicule in the love Silas bore his good horse Major.

'That is a sweet story, and I like it, though it did make me cry. Thank you very much, Si,' and Daisy helped him fold and put away his little relic; while

Nan stuffed a handful of pop-corn into his pocket, and the boys loudly expressed their flattering opinions of his story, feeling that there had been two heroes in it.

He departed, quite overcome by his honours, and the little conspirators talked the tale over, while they waited for their next victim. It was Mrs Jo, who came in to measure Nan for some new pinafores she was making for her. They let her get well in, and then pounced upon her, telling her the law, and demanding the story. Mrs Jo was very much amused at the new trap, and consented at once, for the sound of the happy voices had been coming across the hall so pleasantly that she quite longed to join them, and forget her own anxious thoughts of Sister Meg.

'Am I the first mouse you have caught, you sly pussies-in-boots?' she asked, as she was conducted to the big chair, supplied with refreshments, and surrounded by a flock of merry-faced listeners.

They told her about Silas and his contribution, and she slapped her forehead in despair, for she was quite at her wits' end, being called upon so unexpectedly for a brand new tale.

'What *shall* I tell about?' she said.

'Boys,' was the general answer.

'Have a party in it,' said Daisy.

'And something good to eat,' added Stuffy.

'That reminds me of a story, written years ago, by a dear old lady. I used to be very fond of it, and I fancy you will like it, for it has both boys, and "something good to eat" in it.'

'What is it called?' asked Demi.

'"The Suspected Boy".'

Nat looked up from the nuts he was picking, and Mrs Jo smiled at him, guessing what was in his mind.

'Miss Crane kept a school for boys in a quiet little town, and a very good school it was, of the old-fashioned sort. Six boys lived in her house, and four or five more came in from the town. Among those who lived with her was one named Lewis White. Lewis was not a bad boy, but rather timid, and now and then he told a lie. One day a neighbour sent Miss Crane a basket of gooseberries. There were not enough to go round, so kind Miss Crane, who liked to please her boys, went to work and made a dozen nice little gooseberry tarts.'

'I'd like to try gooseberry tarts. I wonder if she made them as I do my raspberry ones,' said Daisy, whose interest in cooking had lately revived.

'Hush,' said Nat, tucking a plump pop-corn into her mouth to silence her, for he felt a peculiar interest in this tale, and thought it opened well.

'When the tarts were done, Miss Crane put them away in the best parlour closet, and said not a word about them, for she wanted to surprise the boys at tea-time. When the minute came and all were seated at table, she went to get her tarts, but came back looking much troubled, for what do you think had happened?'

'Somebody had hooked them!' cried Ned.

'No, there they were, but someone had stolen all the fruit out of them by lifting up the upper crust and then putting it down after the gooseberry had been scraped out.'

'What a mean trick!' and Nan looked at Tommy, as if to imply that he would do the same.

'When she told the boys her plan and showed them

the poor little patties all robbed of their sweetness, the boys were much grieved and disappointed, and all declared that they knew nothing about the matter. "Perhaps the rats did it," said Lewis, who was among the loudest to deny any knowledge of the tarts. "No, rats would have nibbled crust and all, and never lifted it up and scooped out the fruit. Hands did that," said Miss Crane, who was more troubled about the lie that someone must have told than about her lost patties. Well, they had supper and went to bed, but in the night Miss Crane heard someone groaning, and going to see who it was she found Lewis in great pain. He had evidently eaten something that disagreed with him, and was so sick that Miss Crane was alarmed, and was going to send for the doctor, when Lewis moaned out, "It's the gooseberries; I ate them, and I *must* tell before I die," for the thought of a doctor frightened him. "If that is all, I'll give you an emetic and you will soon get over it," said Miss Crane. So Lewis had a good dose, and by morning was quite comfortable. "Oh, don't tell the boys; they will laugh at me so," begged the invalid. Kind Miss Crane promised not to, but Sally, the girl, told the story, and poor Lewis had no peace for a long time. His mates called him Old Gooseberry, and were never tired of asking him the price of tarts.'

'Served him right,' said Emil.

'Badness always gets found out,' added Demi, morally.

'No, it don't,' muttered Jack, who was tending the apples with great devotion, so that he might keep his back to the rest and account for his red face.

'Is that all?' asked Dan.

'No, that is only the first part; the second part is more interesting. Some time after this a peddler came by one day and stopped to show his things to the boys, several of whom bought pocket-combs, jew's-harps, and various trifles of that sort. Among the knives was a little white-handled penknife that Lewis wanted very much, but he had spent all his pocket-money, and no one had any to lend him. He held the knife in his hand, admiring and longing for it, till the man packed up his goods to go, then he reluctantly laid it down, and the man went on his way. The next day, however, the peddler returned to say that he could not find that very knife, and thought he must have left it at Miss Crane's. It was a very nice one with a pearl handle, and he could not afford to lose it. Everyone looked, and everyone declared they knew nothing about it. "This young gentleman had it last, and seemed to want it very much. Are you quite sure you put it back?" said the man to Lewis, who was much troubled at the loss, and vowed over and over again that he did return it. His denials seemed to do no good, however, for everyone was sure he had taken it, and after a stormy scene Miss Crane paid for it, and the man went grumbling away.'

'Did Lewis have it?' cried Nat, much excited.

'You will see. Now poor Lewis had another trial to bear, for the boys were constantly saying, "Lend me your pearl-handled knife, Gooseberry," and things of that sort, till Lewis was so unhappy he begged to be sent home. Miss Crane did her best to keep the boys quiet, but it was hard work, for they would tease, and she could not be with them all the time. That is one of the hardest things to teach boys; they won't "hit a fellow when he is down", as they say, but they will torment him in little ways till he would thank them to fight it out all round.'

'I know that,' said Dan.

'So do I,' added Nat, softly.

Jack said nothing, but he quite agreed; for he knew that the elder boys despised him, and let him alone for that very reason.

'Do go on about poor Lewis, Aunt Jo. I don't believe he took the knife, but I want to be sure,' said Daisy, in great anxiety.

'Well, week after week went on and the matter was not cleared up. The boys avoided Lewis, and he, poor fellow, was almost sick with the trouble he had brought upon himself. He resolved never to tell another lie, and tried so hard that Miss Crane pitied and helped him, and really came at last to believe that he did not take the knife. Two months after the peddler's first visit, he came again, and the first thing he said was,

'"Well, ma'am, I found that knife after all. It had slipped behind the lining of my valise, and fell out the other day when I was putting in a new stock of goods. I thought I'd call and let you know, as you paid for it, and maybe would like it, so here it is."

'The boys had all gathered round, and at these words they felt much ashamed, and begged Lewis' pardon so heartily that he could not refuse to give it. Miss Crane presented the knife to him, and he kept it many years to remind him of the fault that had brought him so much trouble.'

'I wonder why it is that things you eat on the sly hurt you, and don't when you eat them at table,' observed Stuffy, thoughtfully.

'Perhaps your conscience affects your stomach,' said Mrs Jo, smiling at his speech.

'He is thinking of the cucumbers,' said Ned, and a gale of merriment followed the words, for Stuffy's last mishap had been a funny one.

He ate two large cucumbers in private, felt very ill, and confided his anguish to Ned, imploring him to do something. Ned good-naturedly recommended a mustard plaster and a hot flat iron to the feet; only in applying these remedies he reversed the order of things, and put the plaster on the feet, the flat iron on the stomach, and poor Stuffy was found in the barn with blistered soles and a scorched jacket.

'Suppose you tell another story, that was such an interesting one,' said Nat, as the laughter subsided.

Before Mrs Jo could refuse these insatiable Oliver Twists, Rob walked into the room trailing his little bed-cover after him, and wearing an expression of great sweetness as he said, steering straight to his mother as a sure haven of refuge,

'I heard a great noise, and I thought sumfin dreffle might have happened, so I came to see.'

'Did you think I would forget you, naughty boy?' asked his mother, trying to look stern.

'No; but I thought you'd feel better to see me right here,' responded the insinuating little party.

'I had much rather see you in bed, so march straight up again, Robin.'

'Everybody that comes in here has to tell a story, and you can't, so you'd better cut and run,' said Emil.

'Yes, I can! I tell Teddy lots of ones, all about bears and moons, and little flies that say things when they buzz,' protested Rob, bound to stay at any price.

'Tell one now, then, right away,' said Dan, preparing to shoulder and bear him off.

'Well, I will; let me fink a minute,' and Rob climbed into his mother's lap, where he was cuddled, with the remark,

'It is a family failing, this getting out of bed at wrong times. Demi used to do it; and as for me, I was hopping in and out all night long. Meg used to think the house was on fire, and send me down to see, and I used to stay and enjoy myself, as you mean to, my bad son.'

'I've finked now,' observed Rob, quite at his ease, and eager to win the *entrée* into this delightful circle.

Everyone looked and listened with faces full of suppressed merriment as Rob, perched on his mother's knee and wrapped in the gay coverlet, told the following brief but tragic tale with an earnestness that made it very funny:

'Once a lady had a million children, and one nice little boy. She went upstairs and said, "You mustn't go in the yard." But he wented, and fell into the pump, and was drowned dead.'

'Is that all?' asked Franz, as Rob paused out of breath with this startling beginning.

'No, there is another piece of it,' and Rob knit his downy eyebrows in the effort to evolve another inspiration.

'What did the lady do when he fell into the pump?' asked his mother, to help him on.

'Oh, she pumped him up, and wrapped him in a newspaper, and put him on a shelf to dry for seed.'

A general explosion of laughter greeted this

surprising conclusion, and Mrs Jo patted the curly head, as she said, solemnly,

'My son, you inherit your mother's gift of story-telling. Go where glory waits thee.'

'Now I can stay, can't I? Wasn't it a good story?' cried Rob, in high feather at his superb success.

'You can stay till you have eaten these twelve pop-corns,' said his mother, expecting to see them vanish at one mouthful.

But Rob was a shrewd little man, and got the better of her by eating them one by one very slowly, and enjoying every minute with all his might.

'Hadn't you better tell the other story, while you wait for him?' said Demi, anxious that no time should be lost.

'I really have nothing but a little tale about a wood-box,' said Mrs Jo, seeing that Rob had still seven corns to eat.

'Is there a boy in it?'

'It is all boy.'

'Is it true?' asked Demi.

'Every bit of it.'

'Goody! tell on, please.'

'James Snow and his mother lived in a little house, up in New Hampshire. They were poor, and James had to work to help his mother, but he loved books so well he hated work, and just wanted to sit and study all day long.'

'How could he! I hate books, and like work,' said Dan, objecting to James at the very outset.

'It takes all sorts of people to make a world; workers and students both are needed, and there is room for all. But I think the workers should study some, and the students should know how to work if necessary,' answered Mrs Jo, looking from Dan to Demi with a significant expression.

'I'm sure I do work,' and Demi showed three small hard spots in his little palm, with pride.

'And I'm sure I study,' added Dan, nodding with a groan toward the blackboard full of neat figures.

'See what James did. He did not mean to be selfish, but his mother was proud of him, and let him do as he liked, working away by herself that he might have books and time to read them. One autumn James wanted to go to school, and went to the minister to see if he would help him, about decent clothes and books. Now the minister had heard the gossip about James's idleness, and was not inclined to do much for him, thinking that a boy who neglected his mother, and let her slave for him, was not likely to do very well even at school. But the good man felt more interested when he found how earnest James was, and being rather an odd man, he made this proposal to the boy, to try how sincere he was.

' "I will give you clothes and books on one condition, James."

' "What is that, sir?" and the boy brightened up at once.

' "You are to keep your mother's wood-box full all winter long, and do it yourself. If you fail, school stops." James laughed at the queer condition and readily agreed to it, thinking it a very easy one.

'He began school, and for a time got on capitally with the wood-box, for it was autumn, and chips and brushwood were plentiful. He ran out morning and evening and got a basket full, or chopped up the cat sticks for the little cooking stove, and as his mother was careful and saving, the task was not hard. But in November the frost came, the days were dull and cold, and wood went fast. His mother bought a load with her own earnings but it seemed to melt away, and was nearly gone, before James remembered that *he* was to get the next. Mrs Snow was feeble and lame with rheumatism, and unable to work as she had done, so James had to put down his books, and see what he could do.

'It was hard, for he was going on well, and so interested in his lessons that he hated to stop except for food and sleep. But he knew the minister would keep his word, and much against his will James set about earning money in his spare hours, lest the wood-box should get empty. He did all sorts of things, ran errands, took care of a neighbour's cow, helped the old sexton dust and warm the church on Sundays, and in these ways got enough to buy fuel in small quantities. But it was hard work; the days were short, the winter was bitterly cold, the precious time went fast, and the dear books were so fascinating, that it was sad to leave them, for dull duties that never seemed done.

'The minister watched him quietly, and seeing that he was in earnest helped him without his knowledge. He met him often driving the wood sleds from the forest, where the men were chopping, and as James plodded beside the slow oxen, he read or studied, anxious to use every minute. "The boy is worth helping, this lesson will do him good, and when he has learned it, I will give him an easier one," said the minister to himself, and on Christmas eve a splendid load of wood was quietly dropped at the door of the little house, with a new saw and a bit of paper, saying only,

' "The Lord helps those who help themselves." '

'Poor James expected nothing, but when he woke on that cold Christmas morning, he found a pair of warm mittens, knit by his mother, with her stiff painful fingers. This gift pleased him very much, but her kiss and tender look as she called him her "good son", was better still. In trying to keep her warm, he had warmed his own heart, you see, and in filling the wood-box he had also filled those months with duties faithfully done. He began to see this, to feel that there was something better than books, and to try to learn the lessons God set him, as well as those his school-master gave.

'When he saw the great pile of oak and pine logs at his door, and read the little paper, he knew who sent it, and understood the minister's plan; thanked him for it, and fell to work with all his might. Other boys frolicked that day, but James sawed wood, and I think of all the lads in the town the happiest was the one in the new mittens, who whistled like a blackbird as he filled his mother's wood-box.'

'That's a first-rater!' cried Dan, who enjoyed a simple matter-of-fact story better than the finest fairy tale; 'I like that fellow after all.'

'I could saw wood for you, Aunt Jo!' said Demi, feeling as if a new means of earning money for his mother was suggested by the story.

'Tell about a bad boy. I like them best,' said Nan.

'You'd better tell about a naughty cross-patch of a girl,' said Tommy, whose evening had been spoilt by Nan's unkindness. It made his apple taste bitter, his pop-corn was insipid, his nuts were hard to crack, and the sight of Ned and Nan on one bench made him feel his life a burden.

But there were no more stories from Mrs Jo, for on looking down at Rob he was discovered to be fast asleep with his last corn firmly clasped in his chubby hand. Bundling him up in his coverlet, his mother carried him away and tucked him up with no fear of his popping out again.

'Now let's see who will come next,' said Emil, setting the door temptingly ajar.

Mary Ann passed first, and he called out to her, but Silas had warned her, and she only laughed and hurried on in spite of their enticements. Presently a door opened, and a strong voice was heard humming in the hall:

> *'Ich Weiss nicht was soil es bedeuten*
> *Dass ich so traurig bin.'*

'It's Uncle Fritz; all laugh loud and he will be sure to come in,' said Emil.

A wild burst of laughter followed, and in came Uncle Fritz, asking, 'What is the joke, my lads?'

'Caught! caught! you can't go out till you've told a story,' cried the boys, slamming the door.

'So! that is the joke then? Well, I have no wish to go, it is so pleasant here, and I pay my forfeit at once,' which he did by sitting down and beginning instantly:

'A long time ago your Grandfather, Demi, went to lecture in a great town, hoping to get some money for a home for little orphans that some good people were getting up. His lecture did well, and he put a considerable sum of money in his pocket, feeling very happy about it. As he was driving in a chaise to another town, he came to a lonely bit of road, late in the afternoon, and was just thinking what a good place it was for robbers when he saw a bad-looking man come out of the woods in front of him and go slowly along as if waiting till he came up. The thought of the money made Grandfather rather anxious, and at first he had a mind to turn round and drive away. But the horse was tired, and then he did not like to suspect the man, so he kept on, and when he got nearer and saw how poor and sick and ragged the stranger looked, his heart reproached him, and stopping, he said in his kind voice,

'"My friend, you look tired; let me give you a lift." The man seemed surprised, hesitated a minute, and then got in. He did not seem inclined to talk, but Grandfather kept on in his wise, cheerful way, speaking of what a hard year it had been, how much the poor had suffered, and how difficult it was to get on sometimes. The man slowly softened a little, and, won by the kind chat, told his story. How he had been sick, could get no work, had a family of children, and was almost in despair. Grandfather was so full of pity that he forgot his fear, and, asking the man his name, said he would try and get him work in the next town, as he had friends there. Wishing to get at pencil and paper, to write down the address, Grandfather took out his plump pocket-book, and the minute he did so, the man's eye was on it. Then Grandfather remembered what was in it and trembled for his money, but said quietly,

'"Yes, I have a little sum here for some poor orphans.

I wish it was my own, I would so gladly give you some of it. I am not rich, but I know many of the trials of the poor; this five dollars is mine, and I want to give it to you for your children."

'The hard, hungry look in the man's eyes changed to a grateful one as he took the small sum, freely given, and left the orphans' money untouched. He rode on with Grandfather till they approached the town, then he asked to be set down. Grandpa shook hands with him, and was about to drive on, when the man said, as if something made him, "I was desperate when we met, and I meant to rob you, but you were so kind I couldn't do it. God bless you, sir, for keeping me from it!"'

'Did Grandpa ever see him again?' asked Daisy, eagerly.

'No; but I believe the man found work, and did not try robbery any more.'

'That was a curious way to treat him; I'd have knocked him down,' said Dan.

'Kindness is always better than force. Try it and see,' answered Mr Bhaer, rising.

'Tell another, please,' cried Daisy.

'You must, Aunt Jo did,' added Demi.

'Then I certainly won't, but keep my others for next time. Too many tales are as bad as too many bonbons. I have paid my forfeit and I go,' and Mr Bhaer ran for his life, with the whole flock in full pursuit. He had the start, however, and escaped safely into his study, leaving the boys to go rioting back again.

They were so stirred up by the race that they could not settle to their former quiet, and a lively game of Blind-man's Buff followed in which Tommy showed that he had taken the moral of the last story to heart, for, when he caught Nan, he whispered in her ear, 'I'm sorry I called you a cross-patch.'

Nan was not to be outdone in kindness, so, when they played 'Button, button, who's got the button?' and it was her turn to go round, she said, 'Hold fast all I give you,' with such a friendly smile at Tommy, that he was not surprised to find the horse-hair ring in his hand instead of the button. He only smiled back at her then, but when they were going to bed, he offered Nan the best bite of his last apple; she saw the ring on his stumpy little finger, accepted the bite, and peace was declared. Both were sorry for the temporary coldness, neither was ashamed to say, 'I was wrong, forgive me,' so the childish friendship remained unbroken, and the home in the willow lasted long, a pleasant little castle in the air.

21

Thanksgiving

This yearly festival was always kept at Plumfield in the good old-fashioned way, and nothing was allowed to interfere with it. For days beforehand, the little girls helped Asia and Mrs Jo in store-room and kitchen, making pies and puddings, sorting fruit, dusting dishes, and being very busy and immensely important. The boys hovered on the outskirts of the forbidden ground, sniffing the savoury odours, peeping in at the mysterious performances, and occasionally being permitted to taste some delicacy in the process of preparation.

Something more than usual seemed to be on foot this year, for the girls were as busy upstairs as down, so were the boys in schoolroom and barn, and a general air of bustle pervaded the house. There was a great hunting up of old ribbons and finery, much cutting and pasting of gold paper, and the most remarkable quantity of straw, grey cotton, flannel, and big black beads, used by Franz and Mrs Jo. Ned hammered at strange machines in the workshop, Demi and Tommy went about murmuring to themselves as if learning something. A fearful racket was heard in Emil's room at intervals, and peals of laughter from the nursery when Rob and Teddy were sent for and hidden from sight whole hours at a time. But the thing that puzzled Mr Bhaer the most was what became of Rob's big pumpkin. It had been borne in triumph to the kitchen, where a dozen golden-tinted pies soon after appeared. It would not have taken more than a quarter of the mammoth vegetable to make them, yet where was the rest? It disappeared, and Rob never seemed to care, only chuckled, when it was mentioned, and told his father, 'To wait and see', for the fun of the whole thing was to surprise Father Bhaer at the end, and not let him know a bit about what was to happen.

He obediently shut eyes, ears, and mouth, and went about trying not to see what was in plain sight, not to hear the tell-tale sounds that filled the air, not to understand any of the perfectly transparent mysteries going on all about him. Being a German he loved these simple domestic festivals, and encouraged them with all his heart, for they made home so pleasant that the boys did not care to go elsewhere for fun.

When at last the day came, the boys went off for a long walk, that they might have good appetites for dinner; as if they ever needed them! The girls remained at home to help set the table, and give last touches to various affairs which filled their busy little souls with anxiety. The schoolroom had been shut up since the night before, and Mr Bhaer was forbidden to enter it on pain of a beating from Teddy, who guarded the door like a small dragon, though he was dying to tell about it, and nothing but his father's heroic self-denial in not listening, kept him from betraying the grand secret.

'It's all done, and it's perfectly splendid,' cried Nan, coming out at last with an air of triumph.

'The – you know – goes beautifully, and Silas knows

just what to do now,' added Daisy, skipping with delight at some unspeakable success.

'I'm blest if it ain't the 'cutest thing I ever see, them critters in particular,' and Silas, who had been let into the secret, went off laughing like a great boy.

'They are coming; I hear Emil roaring "Land lubbers lying down below," so we must run and dress,' cried Nan, and upstairs they scampered in a great hurry.

The boys came trooping home with appetites that would have made the big turkey tremble, if it had not been past all fear. They also retired to dress; and for half an hour there was a washing, brushing, and prinking that would have done any tidy woman's heart good to see. When the bell rang, a troop of fresh-faced lads with shiny hair, clean collars, and Sunday jackets on, filed into the dining-room, where Mrs Jo, in her one black silk, with a knot of her favourite white chrysanthemums in her bosom, sat at the head of the table, 'looking splendid', as the boys said, whenever she got herself up. Daisy and Nan were as gay as a posy bed in their new winter dresses, with bright sashes and hair ribbons. Teddy was gorgeous to behold in a crimson merino blouse, and his best button boots, which absorbed and distracted him as much as Mr Toot's wristbands did on one occasion.

As Mr and Mrs Bhaer glanced at each other down the long table, with those rows of happy faces on either side, they had a little thanksgiving, all to themselves, and without a word, for one heart said to the other, 'Our work has prospered, let us be grateful and go on.'

The clatter of knives and forks prevented much conversation for a few minutes and Mary Ann with an amazing pink bow in her hair 'flew round' briskly, handing plates and ladling out gravy. Nearly everyone had contributed to the feast, so the dinner was a peculiarly interesting one to the eaters of it, who beguiled the pauses by remarks on their own productions.

'If these are not good potatoes I never saw any,' observed Jack, as he received his fourth big mealy one.

'Some of my herbs are in the stuffing of the turkey, that's why it's so nice,' said Nan, taking a mouthful with intense satisfaction.

'My ducks are prime anyway; Asia said she never cooked such fat ones,' added Tommy.

'Well, our carrots are beautiful, ain't they, and our parsnips will be ever so good when we dig them,' put in Dick, and Dolly murmured his assent from behind the bone he was picking.

'I helped make the pies with my pumpkin,' called out Robby, with a laugh which he stopped by retiring into his mug.

'I picked some of the apples that the cider is made of,' said Demi.

'I raked the cranberries for the sauce,' cried Nat.

'I got the nuts,' added Dan, and so it went on all round the table.

'Who made up Thanksgiving?' asked Rob, for being lately promoted to jacket and trousers he felt a new and manly interest in the institutions of his country.

'See who can answer that question,' and Mr Bhaer nodded to one or two of his best history boys.

'I know,' said Demi, 'the Pilgrims made it.'

'What for?' asked Rob, without waiting to learn who the Pilgrims were.

'I forget,' and Demi subsided.

'I believe it was because they were not starved once, and so when they had a good harvest, they said, "We will thank God for it," and they had a day and called it Thanksgiving,' said Dan, who liked the story of the brave men who suffered so nobly for their faith.

'Good! I didn't think you would remember anything but natural history,' and Mr Bhaer tapped gently on the table as applause for his pupil.

Dan looked pleased; and Mrs Jo said to her son, 'Now do you understand about it, Robby?'

'No, I don't. I thought pil-grins were a sort of big bird that lived on rocks and I saw pictures of them in Demi's book.'

'He means penguins. Oh, isn't he a little goosey!' and Demi laid back in his chair and laughed aloud.

'Don't laugh at him, but tell him all about it if you can,' said Mrs Bhaer, consoling Rob with more cranberry sauce for the general smile that went round the table at his mistake.

'Well, I will;' and, after a pause to collect his ideas, Demi delivered the following sketch of the Pilgrim Fathers, which would have made even those grave gentlemen smile if they could have heard it.

'You see, Rob, some of the people in England didn't like the king, or something, so they got into ships and sailed away to this country. It was all full of Indians, and bears, and wild creatures and they lived in forts, and had a dreadful time.'

'The bears?' asked Robby, with interest.

'No; the Pilgrims, because the Indians troubled them. They hadn't enough to eat, and they went to church with guns and ever so many died, and they got

out of the ships on a rock, and it's called Plymouth
Rock, and Aunt Jo saw it and touched it. The Pilgrims
killed all the Indians, and got rich; and hung the
witches, and were very good; and some of my greatest
great-grandpas came in the ships. One was the *May-
flower*; and they made Thanksgiving and we have it
always, and I like it. Some more turkey, please.'

'I think Demi will be an historian, there is such
order and clearness in his account of events'; and
Uncle Fritz's eyes laughed at Aunt Jo, as he helped
the descendant of the Pilgrims to his third bit of
turkey.

'I thought you must eat as much as ever you could
on Thanksgiving. But Franz says you mustn't even
then'; and Stuffy looked as if he had received bad
news.

'Franz is right, so mind your knife and fork, and be
moderate, or else you won't be able to help in the
surprise by and by,' said Mrs Jo.

'I'll be careful; but everybody does eat lots, and
I like it better than being moderate,' said Stuffy,
who leaned to the popular belief that Thanksgiving
must be kept by coming as near apoplexy as possible,
and escaping with merely a fit of indigestion or a
headache.

'Now, my "pilgrims", amuse yourselves quietly till
tea-time, for you will have enough excitement this
evening,' said Mrs Jo, as they rose from the table after
a protracted sitting, finished by drinking everyone's
health in cider.

'I think I will take the whole flock for a drive, it is
so pleasant; then you can rest, my dear, or you will be
worn out this evening,' added Mr Bhaer; and as soon

as coats and hats could be put on, the great omnibus was packed full, and away they went for a long gay drive, leaving Mrs Jo to rest and finish sundry small affairs in peace.

An early and light tea was followed by more brushing of hair and washing of hands; then the flock waited impatiently for the company to come. Only the family was expected; for these small revels were strictly domestic, and such being the case, sorrow was not allowed to sadden the present festival. All came; Mr and Mrs March, with Aunt Meg, so sweet and lovely, in spite of her black dress and the little widow's cap that encircled her tranquil face. Uncle Teddy and Aunt Amy, with the Princess looking more fairy-like than ever, in a sky-blue gown, and a great bouquet of hot-house flowers, which she divided among the boys, sticking one in each button-hole, making them feel peculiarly elegant and festive. One strange face appeared, and Uncle Teddy led the unknown gentleman up to the Bhaers, saying,

'This is Mr Hyde; he has been inquiring about Dan, and I ventured to bring him tonight, that he might see how much the boy has improved.'

The Bhaers received him cordially, for Dan's sake, pleased that the lad had been remembered. But, after a few minutes' chat, they were glad to know Mr Hyde for his own sake, so genial, simple, and interesting was he. It was pleasant to see the boy's face light up when he caught sight of his friend; pleasanter still to see Mr Hyde's surprise and satisfaction in Dan's improved manners and appearance, and pleasantest of all to watch the two sit talking in a corner, forgetting the differences of age, culture, and position, in the one subject which interested both, as man and boy compared notes, and told the story of their summer life.

'The performances must begin soon, or the actors will go to sleep,' said Mrs Jo, when the first greetings were over.

So everyone went into the schoolroom, and took seats before a curtain made of two big bed-covers. The children had already vanished; but stifled laughter, and funny little exclamations from behind the curtain, betrayed their whereabouts. The entertainment began with a spirited exhibition of gymnastics, led by Franz. The six elder lads, in blue trousers and red shirts, made a fine display of muscle with dumb-bells, clubs, and weights, keeping time to the music of the piano, played by Mrs Jo behind the scenes. Dan was so energetic in this exercise, that there was some danger of his knocking down his neighbours, like so many nine-pins, or sending his bean-bags whizzing among the audience; for he was excited by Mr Hyde's presence, and a burning desire to do honour to his teachers.

'A fine, strong lad. If I go on my trip to South America, in a year or two, I shall be tempted to ask you to lend him to me, Mr Bhaer,' said Mr Hyde, whose interest in Dan was much increased by the report he had just heard of him.

'You shall have him, and welcome, though we shall miss our young Hercules very much. It would do him a world of good, and I am sure he would serve his friend faithfully.'

Dan heard both question and answer, and his heart leaped with joy at the thought of travelling in a new country with Mr Hyde, and swelled with gratitude for the kindly commendation which rewarded his efforts to be all these friends desired to see him.

After the gymnastics, Demi and Tommy spoke the old school dialogue, 'Money makes the mare go.' Demi did very well, but Tommy was capital as the old farmer; for he imitated Silas in a way that convulsed the audience, and caused Silas himself to laugh so hard that Asia had to slap him on the back, as they stood in the hall enjoying the fun immensely.

Then Emil, who had got his breath by this time, gave them a sea-song in costume, with a great deal about 'stormy winds', 'lee shores', and a rousing chorus of 'Luff, boys, luff', which made the room ring; after which Ned performed a funny Chinese dance, and hopped about like a large frog in a pagoda hat. As this was the only public exhibition ever had at Plumfield, a few exercises in lightning-arithmetic, spelling, and reading were given. Jack quite amazed the public by his rapid calculations on the blackboard. Tommy won in the spelling match, and Demi read a little French fable so well that Uncle Teddy was charmed.

'Where are the other children?' asked everyone as the curtain fell, and none of the little ones appeared.

'Oh, that is the surprise. It's so lovely, I pity you because you don't know it,' said Demi, who had gone to get his mother's kiss, and stayed by her to explain the mystery when it should be revealed.

Goldilocks had been carried off by Aunt Jo, to the great amazement of her papa, who quite outdid Mr Bhaer in acting wonder, suspense, and wild impatience to know 'what was going to happen'.

At last, after much rustling, hammering, and very audible directions from the stage manager, the curtain rose to soft music, and Bess was discovered sitting on a stool beside a brown paper fire-place. A dearer little Cinderella was never seen; for the gay gown was very ragged, the tiny shoes all worn, the face so pretty under the bright hair, and the attitude so dejected, it brought tears, as well as smiles, to the fond eyes looking at the baby actress. She sat quite still, till a voice whispered,

'Now!' – then she sighed a funny little sigh, and said, 'Oh, I wish I tood go to the ball!' so naturally, that her father clapped frantically, and her mother called out, 'Little darling!' These highly improper expressions of feeling caused Cinderella to forget herself, and shake her head at them, saying, reprovingly, 'You mustn't 'peak to me.'

Silence instantly prevailed, and three taps were heard on the wall. Cinderella looked alarmed, but before she could remember to say, 'What is dat?' the back of the brown paper fire-place opened like a door, and, with some difficulty, the fairy godmother got herself and her pointed hat through. It was Nan, in a red cloak, a cap, and a wand, which she waved as she said decidedly,

'You *shall* go to the ball, my dear.'

'Now you must pull and show my pretty dess,' returned Cinderella, tugging at her brown gown.

'No, no; you must say, "How can I go in my rags?"' said the godmother in her own voice.

'Oh yes, so I mus'; and the Princess said it, quite undisturbed at her forgetfulness.

'I change your rags into a splendid dress, because you are good,' said the godmother in her stage tones; and deliberately unbuttoning the brown pinafore, she displayed a gorgeous sight.

The little Princess really was pretty enough to turn the heads of any number of small princes, for her mamma had dressed her like a tiny court lady, in a rosy silk train with satin under-skirt, and bits of bouquets here and there, quite lovely to behold. The godmother put a crown, with pink and white feathers drooping from it, on her head, and gave her a pair of silver paper slippers, which she put on, and then stood up, lifting her skirts to show them to the audience, saying, with pride, 'My dlass ones, ain't they pitty?'

She was so charmed with them, that she was with difficulty recalled to her part, and made to say,

'But I have no toach, Dodmother.'

'Behold it!' and Nan waved her wand with such a flourish, that she nearly knocked off the crown of the Princess.

Then appeared the grand triumph of the piece. First, a rope was seen to flap on the floor, to tighten with a twitch as Emil's voice was heard to say, 'Heave, ahoy!' and Silas's gruff one to reply 'Stiddy, now, stiddy!' A shout of laughter followed, for four large grey rats appeared, rather shaky as to their legs and queer as to their tails, but quite fine about the head, where black beads shone in the most lifelike manner. They drew, or were intended to appear as if they did, a magnificent coach made of half the mammoth pumpkin, mounted on the wheels of Teddy's wagon, painted yellow to match the gay carriage. Perched on a seat in front sat a jolly little coachman in a white cotton-wool wig, cocked hat, scarlet breeches, and laced coat, who cracked a long whip and jerked the red reins so energetically, that the grey steeds reared finely. It was Teddy, and he beamed upon the company so affably that they gave him a round all to himself; and Uncle Laurie said, 'If I could find as sober a coachman as that one, I would engage him on the spot.' The coach stopped, the godmother lifted in the Princess, and she was trundled away in state, kissing her hand to the public, with her glass shoes sticking up in front, and her pink train sweeping the ground behind, for, elegant as the coach was, I regret to say that her Highness was rather a tight fit.

The next scene was the ball, and here Nan and Daisy appeared as gay as peacocks in all sorts of finery. Nan was especially good as the proud sister, and crushed many imaginary ladies as she swept about the palace-hall. The Prince, in solitary state upon a somewhat unsteady throne, sat gazing about him from under an imposing crown, as he played with his sword and admired the rosettes in his shoes. When Cinderella came in he jumped up, and exclaimed, with more warmth than elegance,

'My gracious! who is that?' and immediately led the lady out to dance, while the sisters scowled and turned up their noses in the corner.

The stately jig executed by the little couple was very pretty, for the childish faces were so earnest, the costumes so gay, and the steps so peculiar, that they looked like the dainty quaint figures painted on a Watteau fan. The Princess's train was very much in her way, and the sword of Prince Rob nearly tripped him up several times. But they overcame these obstacles remarkably well, and finished the dance with much grace and spirit, considering that neither knew what the other was about.

'Drop your shoe,' whispered Mrs Jo's voice as the lady was about to sit down.

'Oh, I fordot!' and, taking off one of the silvery slippers, Cinderella planted it carefully in the middle of the stage, said to Rob, 'Now you must try and tatch me,' and ran away, while the Prince, picking up the shoe, obediently trotted after her.

The third scene, as everybody knows, is where the herald comes to try on the shoe. Teddy, still in coachman's dress, came in blowing a tin fish-horn melodiously, and the proud sisters each tried to put on the slipper. Nan insisted on playing cut off her toe with a carving-knife, and performed that operation so well that the herald was alarmed, and begged her to be 'welly keerful'. Cinderella then was called, and came in with the pinafore half on, slipped her foot into the slipper, and announced, with satisfaction,

'I am the Pinsiss.'

Daisy wept, and begged pardon; but Nan, who liked tragedy, improved upon the story, and fell in a fainting-fit upon the floor, where she remained comfortably enjoying the rest of the play. It was not long, for the Prince ran in, dropped upon his knees, and kissed the hand of Goldilocks with great ardour, while the herald blew a blast that nearly deafened the audience. The curtain had no chance to fall, for the Princess ran off the stage to her father, crying, 'Didn't I do it well?' while the Prince and herald had a fencing-match with the tin horn and wooden sword.

'It was beautiful!' said everyone; and, when the raptures had a little subsided, Nat came out with his violin in his hand.

'Hush! hush!' cried all the children, and silence followed, for something in the boy's bashful manner and appealing eyes made everyone listen kindly.

The Bhaers thought he would play some of the old airs he knew so well, but, to their surprise, they heard a new and lovely melody, so softly, sweetly played, that they could hardly believe it could be Nat. It was one of those songs without words that touch the heart, and sing of all tender home-like hopes and joys, soothing and cheering those who listen to its simple music. Aunt Meg leaned her hand on Demi's shoulder, Grandmother wiped her eyes, and Mrs Jo looked up at Mr Laurie, saying, in a choky whisper,

'You composed that.'

'I wanted your boy to do you honour, and thank you in his own way,' answered Laurie, leaning down to answer her.

When Nat made his bow and was about to go, he was called back by many hands, and had to play again. He did so with such a happy face, that it was good to see him, for he did his best, and gave them the gay old tunes, that set the feet to dancing, and made quietude impossible.

'Clear the floor!' cried Emil; and in a minute the chairs were pushed back, the older people put safely in corners, and the children gathered on the stage.

'Show your manners!' called Emil; and the boys pranced up to the ladies, old and young, with polite invitations to 'tread the mazy', as dear Dick Swiveller has it. The small lads nearly came to blows for the Princess, but she chose Dick, like a kind, little gentlewoman as she was, and let him lead her proudly to her place. Mrs Jo was not allowed to decline; and Aunt

Amy filled Dan with unspeakable delight by refusing Franz and taking him. Of course Nan and Tommy, Nat and Daisy, paired off, while Uncle Teddy went and got Asia, who was longing to 'jig it', and felt much elated by the honour done her. Silas and Mary Ann had a private dance in the hall; and for half an hour Plumfield was at its merriest.

The party wound up with a grand promenade of all the young folks, headed by the pumpkin-coach with the Princess and driver inside, and the rats in a wildly frisky state.

While the children enjoyed this final frolic, the elders sat in the parlour looking on as they talked together of the little people with the interest of parents and friends.

'What are you thinking of, all by yourself, with such a happy face, sister Jo?' asked Laurie, sitting down beside her on the sofa.

'My summer's work, Teddy, and amusing myself by imagining the future of my boys,' she answered, smiling, as she made room for him.

'They are all to be poets, painters, and statesmen, famous soldiers, or at least merchant princes, I suppose.'

'No, I am not as aspiring as I once was, and I shall be satisfied if they are honest men. But I will confess that I do expect a little glory and a career for some of them. Demi is not a common child, and I think he will blossom into something good and great in the best sense of the word. The others will do well, I hope, especially my last two boys, for, after hearing Nat play tonight, I really think he has genius.'

'Too soon to say; talent he certainly has, and there is

no doubt that the boy can soon earn his bread by the work he loves. Build him up for another year or so, and then I will take him off your hands, and launch him properly.'

'That is such a pleasant prospect for poor Nat, who came to me six months ago so friendless and forlorn. Dan's future is already plain to me. Mr Hyde will want him soon, and I mean to give him a brave and faithful little servant. Dan is one who *can* serve well if the wages are love and confidence, and he has the energy to carve out his own future in his own way. Yes, I am very happy over our success with these boys – one so weak, and one so wild; both so much better now, and so full of promise.'

'What magic did you use, Jo?'

'I only loved them, and let them see it. Fritz did the rest.'

'Dear soul! you look as if "only loving" had been rather hard work sometimes,' said Laurie, stroking her thin cheek with a look of more tender admiration than he had ever given her as a girl.

'I'm a faded old woman, but I'm a very happy one; so don't pity me, Teddy'; and she glanced about the room with eyes full of a sincere content.

'Yes, your plan seems to work better and better every year,' he said, with an emphatic nod of approval toward the cheery scene before him.

'How can it fail to work well when I have so much help from you all?' answered Mrs Jo, looking gratefully at her most generous patron.

'It is the best joke of the family, this school of yours and its success. So unlike the future we planned for you, and yet so suited to you after all. It was a regular inspiration, Jo,' said Laurie, dodging her thanks as usual.

'Ah! but you laughed at it in the beginning, and still make all manner of fun of me and my inspirations. Didn't you predict that having girls with the boys would prove a dead failure? Now see how well it works'; and she pointed to the happy group of lads and lassies dancing, singing, and chattering together with every sign of kindly good fellowship.

'I give in, and when my Goldilocks is old enough I'll send her to you. Can I say more than that?'

'I shall be so proud to have your little treasure trusted to me. But really, Teddy, the effect of these girls has been excellent. I know you will laugh at me, but I don't mind, I'm used to it; so I'll tell you that one of my favourite fancies is to look at my family as a small world, to watch the progress of my little men, and, lately, to see how well the influence of my little women works upon them. Daisy is the domestic element, and they all feel the charm of her quiet, womanly ways. Nan is the restless, energetic, strong-minded one; they admire her courage, and give her a fair chance to work out her will, seeing that she has sympathy as well as strength, and the power to do much in their small world. Your Bess is the lady, full of natural refinement, grace, and beauty. She polishes them unconsciously, and fills her place as any lovely woman may, using her gentle influence to lift and hold them above the coarse, rough things of life, and keep them gentlemen in the best sense of the fine old word.'

'It is not always the ladies who do that best, Jo. It is sometimes the strong brave woman who stirs up the boy and makes a man of him'; and Laurie bowed to her with a significant laugh.

'No; I think the graceful woman, whom the boy you allude to married, has done more for him than the wild Nan of his youth; or, better still, the wise, motherly woman who watched over him, as Daisy watches over Demi, did most to make him what he is'; and Jo turned toward her mother, who sat a little apart with Meg, looking so full of the sweet dignity and beauty of old age, that Laurie gave her a glance of filial respect and love as he replied, in serious earnest,

'All three did much for him, and I can understand how well these little girls will help your lads.'

'Not more than the lads help them; it is mutual, I assure you. Nat does much for Daisy with his music; Dan can manage Nan better than any of us; and Demi teaches your Goldilocks so easily and well that Fritz calls them Roger Ascham and Lady Jane Grey. Dear me! if men and women would only trust, understand, and help one another as my children do, what a capital place the world would be!' and Mrs Jo's eyes grew absent, as if she was looking at a new and charming state of society in which people lived as happily and innocently as her flock at Plumfield.

'You are doing your best to help on the good time, my dear. Continue to believe in it, to work for it, and to prove its possibility by the success of your small experiment,' said Mr March, pausing as he passed to say an encouraging word, for the good man never lost his faith in humanity, and still hoped to see peace, good-will, and happiness reign upon the earth.

'I am not so ambitious as that, father. I only want to give these children a home in which they can be taught the few simple things which will help to make life less hard to them when they go out to fight their battles in the world. Honesty, courage, industry, faith in God, their fellow-creatures, and themselves; that is all I try for.'

'That is everything. Give them these helps, then let them go to work out their life as men and women; and whatever their success or failure is, I think they will remember and bless your efforts, my good son and daughter.'

The Professor had joined them, and as Mr March spoke he gave a hand to each, and left them with a look that was a blessing. As Jo and her husband stood together for a moment talking quietly, and feeling that their summer work had been well done if father approved, Mr Laurie slipped into the hall, said a word to the children, and all of a sudden the whole flock pranced into the room, joined hands and danced about Father and Mother Bhaer, singing blithely:

> *'Summer days are over,*
> *Summer work is done;*
> *Harvests have been gathered*
> *Gayly one by one.*
> *Now the feast is eaten,*
> *Finished is the play;*
> *But one rite remains for*
> *Our Thanksgiving-day.*
>
> *'Best of all the harvest*
> *In the dear God's sight,*
> *Are the happy children*

In the home tonight;
And we come to offer
Thanks where thanks are due,
With grateful hearts and voices,
Father, mother, unto you.'

With the last words the circle narrowed till the good
Professor and his wife were taken prisoner by many
arms, and half hidden by the bouquet of laughing
young faces which surrounded them, proving that one
plant had taken root and blossomed beautifully in all
the little gardens. For love is a flower that grows in
any soil, works its sweet miracles undaunted by
autumn frost or winter snow, blooming fair and fragrant all the year, and blessing those who give and
those who receive.

LITTLE WOMEN
Louisa May Alcott

The good-natured March girls – Meg, Jo, Beth and Amy – manage to lead interesting lives despite Father's absence at war and the family's lack of money. Whether they're making plans for putting on a play or forming a secret society, their gaiety is infectious and even Laurie next door is swept up in their enthusiasm. Written from Louisa May Alcott's own experiences, this is a remarkable story.

GOOD WIVES
Louisa May Alcott

Three years on from Little Women, the March girls and their friend Laurie are young adults with their futures to find. Although they all face painful trials along the way – from Meg's sad lesson in housekeeping to Laurie's disappointment in love and the tragedy that touches them all – each of the girls finally finds happiness, if not always the way they expect.

JO'S BOYS
Louisa May Alcott

Ten years after the school at Plumfield was
founded, there is now a college, built with a legacy
from old Mr Lawrence. All Jo's original children
are grown young men scattered around the world,
and graceful young women with high ambitions.
But young men face as many troubles as children
do, and they are still 'Jo's boys'.

AN OLD FASHIONED GIRL
Louisa May Alcott

Polly Milton never questioned the way she was . . .
until she went to visit her city cousins, the wealthy
Shaw family. Fanny Shaw looks too glamorous to
be Polly's age and wouldn't be caught dead
sledging down a hill. Only Tom, Fanny's brother,
stands by and supports Polly as she tries to see
where she fits in. Years later, Polly is living in the
city, supporting herself by giving music lessons.
When she learns that the Shaws are facing sudden
poverty, she is more than eager to help but what
can an 'old fashioned girl' do?

EIGHT COUSINS
Louisa May Alcott

Poor Rose Campbell. Left an orphan after her father's death, she has no choice but to go live at the 'aunt hill' with her six aunts and seven boy cousins. For someone who was used to a girl's boarding school, it all seems pretty overwhelming. Especially since her guardian uncle, Alec, makes her eat healthy things like oatmeal and even tries to get her to give up her pretty dresses for more drab, sensible clothes. Will Rose ever get used to her uncle's crazy notions and all her noisy relatives? Will there come a day when she can't imagine living anywhere else?

ROSE IN BLOOM
Louisa May Alcott

After two years of travelling around the world, Rose Campbell has a lot of strong opinions. Why are all her male admirers so boring, expecting her to marry without being in love? Even her dashing cousin, Charlie, is sure he can win Rose's hand. But before she marries anyone, Rose is determined to establish herself as an independent young woman.

ANNE OF GREEN GABLES
L. M. Montgomery

Anne Shirley is skinny, red-haired, and never stops talking – and she is a girl. The Cuthberts, who had meant to adopt a boy to help on the farm, are both exasperated and entertained by her constant chatter and romantic imaginings, and don't know what to make of Anne. But they soon find it hard to remember what Green Gables was like without her.

ANNE OF AVONLEA
L. M. Montgomery

Five years after coming to Green Gables, Anne is 'half past sixteen' and about to start teaching at her old school, set on inspiring youthful hearts and minds with ideals and ambitions. But some of her pupils only respond to very different methods. Meanwhile the young orphan Davy and the Avonlea Improvement Society bring their own headaches for a harum-scarum girl trying to grow up.

ANNE OF THE ISLAND
L. M. Montgomery

As her childhood friends get married and move away, Anne too leaves Prince Edward Island for Redmond College in Kingsport. Though Priscilla Grant and Gilbert Blythe are fellow-students, she at first feels lonely and provincial. But Anne soon makes new friends wherever she goes, one of whom is rich, handsome Roy Gardner, whose attentions to Anne make Gilbert very jealous ...

ANNE OF WINDY WILLOWS
L. M. Montgomery

Now a young woman and her romance with Gilbery Blythe beginning to flourish, Anne Shirley becomes Principal of Summerside High School. But Summerside is virtually ruled by the Pringle family, who don't want Anne at the school. It takes all Anne's courage and tact, and the comfort she draws from the eccentric household at Windy Willows, to overcome local prejudice and outface the dreaded Pringles.

ANNE'S HOUSE OF DREAMS
L. M. Montgomery

Life seems perfect to Anne Shirley, about to marry
her childhood friend Gilbert Blythe and set up
home with him in her 'house of dreams'. But then
tragedy strikes – and it takes all Gilbert's love,
Anne's own courage, and the honesty of her
enigmatic friend Leslie to help her overcome it.

ANNE OF INGLESIDE
L. M. Montgomery

Anne, now Mrs Doctor Blythe, is still sometimes
as impetuous as when she was the girl from Green
Gables. But with six lively children and hard-
worked Gilbert to look after – not to mention
Gilbert's disapproving aunt, whose visit it seems
will never end – Anne has to be practical too.
Especially when the children get into as many
scrapes as she ever did!

READ MORE IN PUFFIN

For children of all ages, Puffin represents quality and variety – the very best in publishing today around the world.

For complete information about books available from Puffin – and Penguin – and how to order them, contact us at the appropriate address below. Please note that for copyright reasons the selection of books varies from country to country.

On the worldwide web: www.puffin.co.uk

In the United Kingdom: Please write to *Dept. EP, Penguin Books Ltd, Bath Road, Harmondsworth, West Drayton, Middlesex UB7 0DA*

In the United States: Please write to *Consumer Sales, Penguin USA, P.O. Box 999, Dept. 17109, Bergenfield, New Jersey 07621-0120.* VISA and MasterCard holders call 1-800-253-6476 to order Penguin titles

In Canada: Please write to *Penguin Books Canada Ltd, 10 Alcorn Avenue, Suite 300, Toronto, Ontario M4V 3B2*

In Australia: Please write to *Penguin Books Australia Ltd, P.O. Box 257, Ringwood, Victoria 3134*

In New Zealand: Please write to *Penguin Books (NZ) Ltd, Private Bag 102902, North Shore Mail Centre, Auckland 10*

In India: Please write to *Penguin Books India Pvt Ltd, 706 Eros Apartments, 56 Nehru Place, New Delhi 110 019*

In the Netherlands: Please write to *Penguin Books Netherlands bv, Postbus 3507, NL-1001 AH Amsterdam*

In Germany: Please write to *Penguin Books Deutschland GmbH, Metzlerstrasse 26, 60594 Frankfurt am Main*

In Spain: Please write to *Penguin Books S. A., Bravo Murillo 19, 1° B, 28015 Madrid*

In Italy: Please write to *Penguin Italia s.r.l., Via Felice Casati 20, I 20124 Milano.*

In France: Please write to *Penguin France S. A., 17 rue Lejeune, F-31000 Toulouse*

In Japan: Please write to *Penguin Books Japan, Ishikiribashi Building, 2-5-4, Suido, Bunkyo-ku, Tokyo 112*

In South Africa: Please write to *Longman Penguin Southern Africa (Pty) Ltd, Private Bag X08, Bertsham 2013*

RAINBOW VALLEY
L. M. Montgomery

Rainbow Valley is the Blythe children's special place for sharing secrets and planning adventures. It is here they meet Jerry, Faith, Una and Carl Meredith, the family of the new minister, with whom they will share numerous adventures that scandalize the village gossips. And unknown to the children, Rainbow Valley is special for some adults, too . . .

RILLA OF INGLESIDE
L. M. Montgomery

When England declares war on Germany it means little to Rilla, at her first party and on the brink of so much delightful fun! Yet the Great War, taking her brothers and beaux to fight in far-off Flanders, and leaving the women in Canada to bear heavy burdens, both in their work and in their hearts, soon changes Rilla's life and outlook completely.